Deep Wedded Blues

**DEEP LAKES
COZY MYSTERY SERIES**
BOOK 5

Orange Hat Publishing
Ten16 Press

JOY ANN RIBAR

DEEP LAKES COZY MYSTERY SERIES

Deep Dark Secrets
BOOK 1

Deep Bitter Roots
BOOK 2

Deep Green Envy
BOOK 3

Deep Dire Harvest
BOOK 4

Deep Wedded Blues
BOOK 5

Deep Flakes Christmas, A Nisse Visit
PREQUEL

BAY BROWNING MYSTERY SERIES

The Medusa Murders

Shake-speared in the Park
(COMING SOON!)

Please visit *joyribar.com*
to contact the author or sign up for newsletters

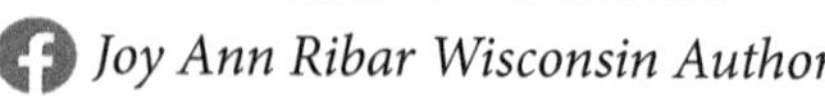 *Joy Ann Ribar Wisconsin Author*

Deep Wedded Blues

DEEP LAKES
COZY MYSTERY SERIES

BOOK 5

JOY ANN RIBAR

Wine Glass Press
U.S.A.

Deep Wedded Blues, Deep Lakes Cozy Mysteries, Book Five
©2024 by Joy Ann Ribar
All rights reserved.

Published in the United States by Wine Glass Press.

GENRES: Cozy Mystery, Amateur Sleuth, Cozy Culinary Mystery, Women's Fiction, Small Town Fiction.

No portion of this book may be reproduced in any form without written permission from the publisher or author, except as permitted by U.S. copyright law.

This book is a work of fiction. Names, characters, places, and incidents are the product of the author's imagination or are used fictitiously. Characters in this book have no relation to anyone bearing the same name and are not based on anyone known or unknown by the author. While some locations and locales are real, the author has added fictional touches to further the story. Any resemblance to actual events, locales, or persons, living or dead, is coincidental.

ISBN (paperback) 978-1-959078-22-7
ISBN (ebook) 978-1-959078-23-4

EDITOR | Kay Rettenmund
COVER | INTERIOR DESIGN: Terry Rydberg, Fine Print Design

First Edition: 2024

NO AI TRAINING: Without in any way limiting the author's [and publisher's] exclusive rights under copyright, any use of this publication to "train" generative artificial intelligence (AI) technologies to generate text is expressly prohibited. The author reserves all rights to license uses of this work for generative AI training and development of machine learning language models.

For the wonder women

who are responsible for my laugh lines

and color my world with unconditional love:

Daughters Erica, Carly, and Jennifer

(in birth order, so they don't feel like I play favorites)

Sisters Kay and Jill

Friends Molly and Bridget

And always, the matriarch of the family:

My mother, Delilas

&

CHAPTER 1

The world's favorite season is the spring.
All things seem possible in May.

⚘

Edwin Way Teale

Alonzo and Frankie packed the last container of boozy cake bombs into Lon's pickup truck, ready to wend its way to Under the Stars Barn outside the town of Deep Lakes. The barn, a posh country venue for weddings and other events, was the perfect locale for a bridal shower, and Frankie couldn't imagine a sweeter spot to celebrate her daughter Sophie's upcoming nuptials.

Barn owners, Hannah and Ashley Turner, were hosting the shower in the name of gratitude and friendship. Bubble & Bake had catered many of the events since Under the Stars opened more than a year ago, and both Frankie and her business partner, Carmen, considered Hannah and Ashley friends.

Alonzo Goodman, county sheriff, volunteered his truck to carry the alcohol-infused cake pops, quiche bites, charcuterie boards, and cases of wine to the venue. Lately, he'd been keeping a watchful eye on his close friend, Frankie.

"Thanks again for letting me use your muscle to haul all this out to Sophie's shower, but you know Carmen and I could have handled it. We do this all the time." Frankie eyed him with suspicion.

The truth is, Frankie was excited for Sophie and Max. The two had been a couple for years now, having met in college. Both were nurses at UW Hospital in Madison, or they had been until last fall when Max was admitted to medical school in Houston, Texas, a change creating a long-distance relationship for the two.

Since Sophie worked a grueling schedule at the hospital, Frankie and her other daughter, Violet, took on many of the wedding plans. The June festivities would be celebrated at Frankie's vineyard, Bountiful Fruits, under an arbor built by Frankie's brother, James. The enchanting arbor featured a roof of wooden flourishes resembling waves on a lake and an inlaid acacia and teak floor in a star pattern. The structure stood in the area Frankie called the "back forty," which was more like twenty acres.

Alonzo frowned and scratched his head. He'd be the first to admit that reading Frankie was like solving a Rubik's Cube. Even though he'd known her over twenty years, she was tough to pin down sometimes. Especially now when life had tossed a storm her way.

"What do you hear from Garrett?" The blurted-out question was poorly timed.

The wine carrier Frankie held teetered precariously on the edge of the truck bed, and she had to thrust her chest into it to right it again. "Ohh, I hate being short!" Frankie exclaimed and shot daggers toward Alonzo.

Today of all days, she wanted to dodge the topic. It had taken a lot of self-talk that morning for Frankie to muster a carefree attitude, remind herself today was all about Sophie, and block out intruding thoughts about Garrett Iverson. Then Alonzo just had to bring him up.

Lon rushed over to the truck bed and shoved the wine deeper inside, then retreated inside Bubble & Bake to carry out another case. He bumped into Frankie's Aunt CeCe, who was rolling the pastry case into the sales area in preparation for opening.

"Good morning, Alonzo. It's so nice of you to help Frankie with the food for Sophie's shower." CeCe paused to peer out the front window and wave to her niece. "It looks like the Universe has donned a display of beautiful sunshine in her honor."

Alonzo rolled his eyes at CeCe's typical world view. She was a remnant of the hippie era and hadn't relinquished her beads, flowered clothing, or zen habits.

"Maybe you should be out there telling Frankie that," he pointed toward the truck.

CeCe sighed and patted Alonzo on the back. "Go easy on her. She's trying to steady her course, but she's in the middle of a tempest." CeCe whispered as if Frankie or the Universe might overhear her.

"Don't I know it." Lon hoisted the wine case on one shoulder and opened the door.

Frankie was leaning against the truck, scrolling through her phone for messages or missed calls. Six days. *Had it been less than a week? Less than a week since life shifted.* Frankie recalled the details, reopening the wound all over again.

Just past Easter, Garrett's old partner from the St. Louis

County morgue in Duluth reached out to ask him for his help. Several unsolved murders had plagued the city for months, prompting officials to reach out to other law enforcement agencies for assistance.

Danny, a medical examiner who had assisted Garrett for five years before taking over his post, had poked, prodded, and cajoled Garrett for days. Garrett's answer remained a resolute "no, thank you."

"I'm not licensed in Minnesota," he'd reminded Danny. "Besides, my life is here."

Frankie's thoughts turned to the quiet Wisconsin winter before the "Danny season." Garrett and Frankie had spent those cold months tenderly cultivating their romance. The two enjoyed music and theatrical productions at the Overture Center, double-date dinners with Carmen and Ryan, snow-shoeing area parks under a moonlit sky, and romps around Garrett's property with Freya, his Norwegian elkhound.

He learned enough about grape cultivation to be dangerous and discovered new connections to the natural world thanks to Frankie's vineyard and birding know-how. He even learned to make Frankie's signature kringle, sort of. Garrett had become positively gooey when Frankie's fingers worked his hands through the dough, radiating warmth, strength, and tenderness.

The couple basked in the comfort of a promising future. Frankie turned Garrett into a believer again and he did the same for her. When Sophie and Max announced their wedding plans, Garrett and Frankie felt more encouraged to bend in the same direction.

Everything shifted six days ago when Frankie prepared to open the wine lounge for Sunday afternoon tastings. April's ending brought rising temperatures and spring blossoms, both of which made people itchy to be out and about. It was far too early to plant gardens in northern climes, so outings of all sorts ruled the day, especially on Sunday afternoons. Bubble & Bake saw more customers, a precursor to tourist season.

When Frankie opened the door, a few people were already waiting outside. She and Jovie manned the wine lounge, giving Frankie's mother, Peggy, a rare Sunday off to spend with friends.

Frankie dispersed tasting menus while Jovie was preoccupied in the kitchen. She began with the group of four sitting together at one end of the polished walnut bar, made from the slab of a once-giant tree on the property Frankie's parents owned before her father passed away. The tree was Charlie Champagne's favorite and since her father had loved it, Frankie kept a piece of it to remember him by, a good omen for her new business.

At the other end of the bar, Frankie heard someone clear their throat loudly, once, then again. She excused herself from the group and scooted to the customer at the other end, whom she assumed was waiting for the rest of their party to show up.

"I'm sorry. I was just settling in the other group. Can I get you a tasting menu or are you waiting for others to join you?"

"I'm here to meet Garrett Iverson." The woman held out her hand in greeting. "I'm sure you know all about me. I'm Dani Edwards."

Frankie couldn't conceal her astonishment and attempted a clumsy recovery. "Oh, no. I mean, yes. Of course, Garrett told me about you. His former partner at the county morgue." Inside, panic erupted. Why didn't she know Dani was a woman and why didn't she know Dani was coming here?

Frankie handed Dani Edwards a tasting menu. "While

you're waiting, you might as well taste some wines. If you'll just mark your choices, I'll be back shortly." Frankie spoke brightly, masking her inner turmoil.

Dani smiled slightly and perused the tasting sheet with disinterest. "Please take your time over there. I'm fine here." Dani gestured toward the foursome, flicking her fingers in dismissal. Frankie tripped over the taped-down electrical cord behind the bar and flushed in embarrassment. She could feel the steely eyes of Dani Edwards behind her.

Frankie tried on her business persona with the group of four, no longer at ease to enjoy her usual repartee. She introduced them to their first samples, read the next choices on their lists, and pulled bottles from the cooler by rote.

Her head was buzzing with questions. She wanted to study Dani Edwards, size her up, but she needed to focus on her customers. Out of the corner of her eye, she saw Dani remove a compact from her purse to touch up her hair and makeup. Frankie guessed she was older than she looked, since she and Garrett had worked together several years earlier. She remembered Garrett telling a few stories from his past, *their* past. She remembered he had said that Dani tried to persuade him to work closer to the western border in Wisconsin, but he had selected Green Bay, on the eastern side.

Whatever her age, Dani wore it well. Her blond hair, streaked in various shades, hung in gentle waves over her shoulders. Blue-green eyes complimented her face, which was accented by playful cheek apples and a strong chin.

Frankie returned to the four, responded to their comments about their first samples, and proceeded to talk about the next varietals. She was keenly aware she was being studied, like a hawk over a mouse. Frankie stood up straighter, all five feet of her intent upon sending a fierce message: don't mess with me.

After she poured the third sample, the front door swung open, and Garrett walked to the bar. To his credit, he never took his eyes off Frankie. She smiled and mustered a friendly wave. What else was there to do?

Dani jumped off the bar stool like a giddy teenager and embraced Garrett tightly. Frankie noticed Dani was as tall as Garrett and shapely in tight jeans and a slinky V-neck shirt. Her bracelet jangled with her moves as she pulled Garrett down into the seat beside her. Immediately, their heads were together, and they were talking quietly. It was impossible for Frankie to gauge the conversation or Garrett's reaction to her presence.

Frankie continued the tasting on the other end of the bar, feeling like she was in a foreign country instead of her beloved Bubble & Bake. As much as she enjoyed her customers, she wished the four would make quick decisions, order wines, and move along.

Soon, she was pouring glasses of their choosing, inviting them to browse and sit in the lounge area to enjoy wine, conversation, and snacks, if they wished.

Frankie whisked herself out of the lounge, holding up a finger to Garrett on the way to the kitchen, to let him know she'd be a minute.

On the other side of the kitchen door, Frankie collapsed against the wall and let out a long gasping breath ending with a hiccup that could easily be the beginning of a sob. She swallowed hard while Jovie stared strangely at her.

"What's wrong, Frankie?"

Frankie looked at her feet as if they might grow roots.

"Garrett is out there with a woman. His ex-partner from Duluth." She spoke in a stage whisper, unsure her words reached Jovie at all. To her, they sounded like an echo chamber.

Jovie looked confused. "His ex-partner is a woman? But I thought…"

"Yeah. Me too. And she's pretty, and I'm not sure what to think right now. I don't want to go out there, Jovie." Frankie wondered if she could trade places with Jovie, let her talk to Garrett and Dani.

Jovie faced Frankie and grabbed both shoulders. "You have to go out there. Be yourself. You don't owe this woman anything. Remember, you're Garrett's partner in crime. She isn't." Jovie's pep talk was remarkably convincing.

Frankie stood up straight, pulled herself away from the wall, and stuck out her chin. "You're right. I'm being silly anyway. There has to be a good explanation for this. For her."

Jovie followed Frankie out to the wine lounge to see if the foursome wanted to place an order. Of course, Jovie was curious about the woman sitting next to Garrett, looking cozy.

"Sorry about that. I asked Jovie to tend the customers so I could introduce myself." Frankie's voice lost its lilt, but she did her best to sound amiable. She figured Garrett would pick up on her tone.

He did, and immediately reached across the bar to clasp Frankie's hand in his. "Sorry I didn't have a chance to call you Miss Francine. Dani decided to surprise both of us. I only found out she was in town a few minutes ago."

Frankie squeezed Garrett's hand to reassure him. At least he was partly off the hook, but there was still the matter of Dani being a woman—quite the shocker. *What was she doing here anyway,* Frankie wondered. She felt an instant dislike for the woman Garrett had praised in so many stories.

Dani reached over to take Garrett's hand away from Frankie's. "Now, now, you two. No need to be upset. You see, Francine, I couldn't think of any way to convince Garrett just how much he's needed in Duluth right now except to show up here in person." Dani squeezed Garrett's hand and gave him a smoldering look.

Her full lips produced a pout. "We make a great team. Remember? The mayor is asking for you, Garrett. We're getting desperate for answers."

"The mayor? Ben Hanson can't still be mayor. He'd be, what? Eighty something?"

Dani laughed at the memory of the mayor the two of them used to work with. "No, not Ben. Believe it or not, Ben's nephew, Curt, is the mayor now. Of course, your stellar reputation is legendary in Duluth, and Ben brought your name up to Curt right away."

"I can't leave Whitman County without a coroner, Dani. It wouldn't be fair." Garrett hoped his practical tone would help her see reason.

Dani looked out the window and snorted. "In this little town? Come on, how much action do you see in a month? I'm sure they could soldier on without you for a few weeks." Dani scrunched her nose as if something smelled bad.

"A few weeks?" Frankie couldn't believe what she was hearing. The thought of Garrett working with Dani for a few days was more than she could stomach.

The two on the opposite side of the bar gave her hard stares, and she realized she spoke too sharply and too loudly considering their surroundings.

Garrett recovered first. "Frankie's right. I couldn't possibly leave for a few weeks, Dani."

"Okay. Just come to Duluth. Look at the autopsy files and evidence. Look at the bodies, Garrett. For God's sakes, these are young women. Losing their lives. We need a fresh pair of eyes on this. And we need your experience." Dani spoke in earnest and commanded Garrett's attention.

Frankie decided Dani would have made an excellent attorney. She was a superb closer. Even Frankie was convinced that Garrett should go and offer his opinion. She snapped back to reality when Garrett responded.

"Okay. You win. I'll come to Duluth and review the cases. But I can't stay weeks, Dani. I have obligations here." Garrett looked over at Frankie to gauge her reaction and noticed the color had drained from her face, but her neck was flushed, and her breath escaped in sputters.

Was Garrett calling her an obligation?

CHAPTER 2

The busy bee has no time for sorrow.

William Blake

Dani was determined not to leave Deep Lakes without Garrett in tow. She handed him a Post-it with her hotel name and room number on it. "Call me when you're packed and ready to leave. You can follow me up." She pecked him on the cheek, offered him a satisfied thanks, and left Bubble & Bake without a word to Frankie.

No matter how many times Frankie reviewed the encounter, she couldn't imagine a different ending. She felt selfish for wanting to demand that Garrett stay. How could she? This was professional, nothing more. Garrett had said as much multiple times before leaving.

"Frankie, I'm sorry I didn't point blank tell you that Dani's a woman. I didn't think it mattered. Our time together was in the past."

"Except now it isn't. She has a thing for you, Garrett. Or does

17

she make a habit of flirting with men to get what she wants?" Frankie knew she was being spiteful, maybe even acting like a teenager. Still, she couldn't quite help but wonder: *How many times in the past two weeks had Garrett had the opportunity to tell her more about Dani?*

Garrett heaved a sigh that darkened his brow. He sat down heavily in the Bubble & Bake kitchen next to Frankie, who was staring vacantly into her lap.

"I guess you deserve to know that Dani and I had a brief romance. We'd been working together about a year, and it just sort of happened. Afterwards, we came to our senses, knowing a relationship would be a bad idea for our careers. That was it. We worked together another three years, and I was ready to get out of the rat race. I never looked back, and we didn't stay in touch."

He pulled Frankie off the stool into his arms. "Dani's not my type. You are, Miss Francine." He planted a few wispy kisses along her neckline. "Just think of her as my coworker for the next few weeks. You know, like Shirley Lazaar."

Frankie raised her head to stare into Garrett's caramel eyes. "Right. Except Officer Shirley is sixty-five and married. And what do you mean by a few weeks? I thought you told Ms. Needy you couldn't be gone that long."

Garrett laughed and kissed her. "I'll be back before Sophie's wedding, and I'll call you as soon as I get settled. You've got your hands full here anyway. You won't even have time to miss me

～

Six days later, Frankie still hadn't heard from Garrett, unless she counted the text message she received upon his arrival with his hotel information and a red heart emoji.

Enroute to Under the Stars Barn beside Alonzo, Frankie let loose a torrent of anxiety.

"I haven't heard from Garrett except for a text message saying that he arrived in Duluth. Do you know he referred to me, to our life here, as an obligation? An obligation, Alonzo. You know, like cleaning up after your dog, or going to your neighbor kid's graduation party." Frankie absently knitted her hands in her lap.

"Calm down, Frankie. I'm sure that's not what Garrett meant. You know how us men are—always saying the wrong thing. I know if I was working on a multiple murder case, I wouldn't have time for a personal life. Give him a break."

Alonzo wasn't sure he'd ever understand the fairer sex. He and his latest girlfriend, Jovie, had parted ways less than a month ago after Jovie said being the life partner of a cop wasn't her cup of tea. They were still friends, which seemed to be Alonzo's curse. Every relationship turned platonic, and the sheriff believed true romance wasn't in the cards for him.

Frankie turned sideways in the seat where the roadside showed off a display of tulips, daffodils, and hyacinths. Still, she wasn't able to enjoy the sunny drive out to the Turners'.

"Hey, look at the asparagus. One more good rain and it'll be ready to pick." Alonzo pointed out the window, thankful to change the subject.

"Yep, and the morels should be popping up, too." Frankie knew fresh-picked seasonal produce made the best quiches and flatbread pizzas, both of which were on the Bubble & Bake menu. She didn't think Lon was interested in lending a sympathetic ear. Besides, she needed to get her emotions under control before arriving at the Turners'.

"I know I'm going to take advantage of the weekend weather

to go trout fishing. It's supposed to be cloudy tomorrow with a little rain, perfect fishing weather." Lon smiled just thinking about it.

Frankie turned. "Are you going alone?" A twinge of guilt ran through her as she'd stupidly forgotten about Lon's recent breakup with Frankie's crew member. Lon had seen Frankie through her divorce and always looked out for her, Sophie, and Violet. She needed to be more sensitive.

Lon laughed. "You make that sound like a bad thing. I don't mind being alone, Frankie. But Russ Green's coming with me tomorrow."

Green was a Whitman County officer, one of the newest permanent members on the force.

Ashley and Hannah were waiting for them to arrive and bounded for the truck to unload it. Frankie noticed that Lon handed one of the lighter boxes to Ashley with a beaming smile and trailed directly behind her with one of the heavy containers.

Hannah and Frankie exchanged curious looks.

"I wonder if the sheriff is sweet on Ashley. What do you think, Frankie?"

Frankie shrugged. "You never can tell with Lon. But he's free as a bird. How's Ashley?"

Frankie knew Ashley had gone through a tough divorce a year or so ago and almost left Deep Lakes with her two children for a fresh start. Hannah had persuaded her sister-in-law to run Under the Stars as partners, and Ashley decided to stay.

Hannah smiled. "She's doing well. She loves running the barn and thanks to the Agri-Stars, she's made some good friends, including you and Carmen."

The Agri-Stars were a group of women, all of whom owned

agricultural related businesses in Whitman County. Carmen's woolen goods online business was well established, and she recently became an officer in the organization. Frankie barely found time for the meetings, but her Bountiful Fruits vineyard provided refreshments when the group gathered.

"That's not what I meant. Is Ashley dating anyone?" Frankie elbowed Hannah playfully.

"Nah. She's not looking, but that doesn't mean she'd turn down a good man. If Alonzo's as good a man as Garrett, well, she might be interested."

Frankie inhaled sharply but let the comment slide.

"It's going to be a textbook perfect afternoon today. I'm excited for Sophie." Frankie's own bridal shower was anything but. Pregnant with Sophie, she'd married quickly. A few months later, her mother and Carmen hosted a baby shower for her. Peggy Champagne was socially embarrassed that her daughter left college, pregnant before marriage. It was persistent coaxing from Frankie's father, Charlie, and Carmen that won Peggy over, and she hosted a baby shower through gritted teeth.

Frankie wouldn't let that unsettling memory cloud the day. Water under the bridge and over the dam, as her Aunt CeCe would say.

Frankie inhaled the heady scent of lavender blooms when she entered the barn's main room.

The area was decorated in a bee and lavender theme, two of Sophie's favorite things. Coral Anders, owner of Lovely Lavender Farm, had been growing lavender in her greenhouse so she'd have enough to supply the shower decorations. The sweet purple-blue stems occupied mason jars, miniature milk cans, and bright white pottery pitchers. Beeswax candles surrounded the blooms with fuzzy bees attached to the tops. Eggshell speckled picket fences adorned the tables decorated with mini lavender wreaths.

Nearly thirty people attended the nontraditional shower, where wine tasting and crafts replaced typical games, followed by eating and karaoke. The barn resounded in laughter with a few tears from Peggy and Aunt CeCe, who still imagined the little girl Sophie had once been. Each guest left with a lavender-themed craft and fond memories of toasting Sophie's future.

Instead of shower gifts, a large money tree decorated with small envelopes and a variety of honeybee ornaments made Sophie gasp with pleasure when it was presented to her. The money tree was a real potted tree that would find its new home with Sophie in Houston.

When Sophie's friends departed, she also said she needed to return home. "I'm working the early shift tomorrow and for the next week." Her heavy sigh and slumping shoulders were abnormal.

Frankie grabbed her in a tight hug. "Is everything okay, Honey?"

Another heavy sigh. "It's just hard to plan the wedding with the distance between Max and me. Besides, he's neck deep in studying. Most of our conversations are five minutes or less." A tear slipped down her cheek.

Frankie's anxiety rose a notch, but she offered encouragement. "Medical school must be tough. I can't imagine how hard Max is working. It will be good for you two to regroup on your honeymoon. Have you found a job in Houston?"

Sophie's bottom lip began to quiver. "That's another thing on the to-do list. Max has to move out of his apartment by the end of July, so we need to find a place to live. He hasn't even had time to start looking. I might not be moving to Houston for a while."

Sophie hugged Frankie tighter and cried on her shoulder. "What a mess, Mom."

Frankie reassured her. "It's going to work out. You'll see. Let me know what I can do to help with wedding plans or moving or anything. I'm here for you, and you have a lot of family here, happy to help." Frankie's sweeping gesture indicated Violet, Peggy, Aunt CeCe, Carmen, and the Bubble & Bake crew who were all waiting their turn to say goodbye to Sophie.

On cue, the women gathered Sophie into a protective group hug and offered their help and encouragement. In the Midwest tradition of the unending party, the group reconvened at Bubble & Bake to help Frankie unload food, wine, and decorations.

Hannah and Ashley Turner suggested the lavender and bee doodads would be charming on the café tables. Peggy and Aunt CeCe, the gifted decorators, set the tables with beeswax candles and containers of lavender, then scattered the picket fence centerpieces around the wine lounge.

With everything spruced up, Carmen called out from behind the wine bar where she held up a bottle in each hand.

"We need to finish up these open wine bottles, ladies. Come and help yourself."

Frankie placed the remaining charcuterie boards on the bar, too. "And leftover food. Remember, the party's not over until the food's gone." She giggled.

The sun hung low in the sky when the rest of the wedding shower group said their goodnights. Violet and Libby, Frankie's sister-in-law, had come from Stevens Point together. Violet faced final exams in the upcoming weeks and would be a senior next fall in the microbiology program at Point. She wanted to specialize in agricultural microbiology focusing on soil fertility and plant diseases. Frankie was happy that Violet had found her passion.

"I'll be home the week of the wedding, Mom, so you can count on my help." Violet smiled brightly, but a small frown immediately replaced the smile.

"What is it?" Frankie wondered why a negative vibe suddenly surrounded her family.

Violet faltered. "I'm worried about Sophie. She doesn't seem like herself."

Frankie decided to be honest. "I'm worried about her, too, Vi. She's not the same Sophie she was before Max left for Houston." Frankie could relate. She felt off-kilter herself and Garrett had only been gone a week.

~

Frankie allowed an audible groan to escape as she sank into one of the lounge chairs in a dark corner of Bubble & Bake. She was relieved to find herself at the end of the day, a day filled with celebration and heartache. She needed time alone to sort herself out. She started with a few cleansing breaths. Her phone sang out a merry tune. It was Garrett. She hesitated.

"Hi." It was the least she could do and the most she could do.

"Hello, Miss Francine. Sorry to call so late."

"No, no. I'm up, still in the wine lounge. How are you?" Did she really want to know? Still, she had to ask.

"I'm alright. Tired. There's a lot here. A lot." Garrett paused, unable to convey to Frankie the gruesome stories of the murder cases. "How was Sophie's shower?"

"It was wonderful. Lots of well-wishers. A good time was had by all." Frankie resorted to the old cliché, unwilling to dive into her worries about Sophie.

"Glad to hear it. What's on your agenda next week?"

Frankie secretly hoped Garrett would ask her to visit him in Duluth, or maybe he would come home for the weekend. "Next weekend is Mother's Day. I expect the shop will be busy. The out-of-towners are beginning to arrive."

Garrett snickered. "I imagine you have plans with your mother."

Frankie shrugged. She and Peggy hadn't discussed Mother's Day, but the two usually brunched after Sunday Mass. Bubble & Bake would be closed for the holiday, making Saturday extra busy. "I suppose I should make brunch reservations tomorrow, before it's too late."

Last year, Garrett had joined Frankie and Peggy for brunch at Edge of the Forest, the posh country club on the Lake Hope golf course. The food surpassed their brunch expectations, and it was fun to dress up and dine in elegance. Frankie wasn't feeling the Forest this year, more like the city dump.

"I'm sorry I can't be there with you."

Frankie sucked a breath of courage. "It's okay, G. Just do what needs to be done and come home. I miss you."

"I miss you, too. It's not the same here." Garrett was at a loss for words.

That was it. The call ended with no plans for a future conversation. It was like talking to a prisoner. Frankie sank back into the chair again momentarily, then bolted upright.

"No. I'm not doing this. I'm not going to wallow. I need some sleep, so I can make things right for my daughter."

Frankie turned off the remaining front lights, then strode to the kitchen to peek at the shop orders for next week. She was spooked to see Carmen sifting flour over a mound of pastry dough. Several stainless-steel containers lined the countertop, each covered in a colorful wrap that resembled a shower cap.

"Carmie, what are you still doing here?" Frankie thought maybe she'd fallen asleep and had missed her morning alarm, then remembered tomorrow was Sunday.

"I don't feel like going home, so I thought I'd get a head start on next week's Mother's Day orders. I can make sweet roll dough in my sleep." Carmen smiled, one dimple showing.

Frankie jumped on the first subject. "What do you mean you don't feel like going home? Everything's okay with Ryan and the twins, right?" Doubt was rising inside Frankie like baking soda in vinegar. What was going on in her universe?

Carmen formed an oh with her mouth. "Everything is just fine at home. Relax, Frankie. I stayed because I wanted to talk to you alone. Was that Garrett on the phone?"

Leave it to Carmen to be a best friend.

"Yes, it was." Frankie started roaming around the kitchen looking for something useful to do. Carmen escorted her to a nearby stool.

"This is the first time he's called since he left, huh?"

Frankie hadn't talked about Garrett's departure to anyone. She intended to swallow it whole, make it disappear. She nodded at Carmen's question.

"So, talk to me. How are things going? How did he sound?"

Frankie fumbled for words. "I guess he sounded okay. A little lonely maybe." She vaulted off the stool and started pacing, becoming a conveyor belt where words spilled out with nowhere to go.

"We made small talk, Carmie. Like we'd just met for the first time on a speed date. Neither one of us said anything meaningful. I didn't tell him I was worried about Sophie."

Carmen grasped both of Frankie's shoulders and redirected her to the stool. "Take a breath, Frankie. Let's talk about Sophie. What's your worry?"

"I'm afraid she doesn't want to get married," Frankie blurted, and tears began to flow. "It's like my past is coming back to haunt me. I had so many doubts about marrying Rick, but I felt like I had to. I was pregnant and scared, and everyone expected me to do it. I don't want that for Sophie."

Carmen patted Frankie's arm with one floured hand. "I understand. I wouldn't want that for my boys either. But you can't make the decision for Sophie. She's a smart woman. You raised her to be strong. Trust that."

"You're right, but with the wedding a month away, it's all a little much."

Carmen stopped kneading to look sternly at her friend. "You mean, it's all a little much because Garrett's gone, too. Let's talk about trust again. Do you trust Garrett?"

Frankie locked eyes with Carmen, ready for a dustup over the question she didn't want to answer. She gave a pat reply. "Of course, I do. I don't trust Dani Edwards, though."

Carmen shook her head and tossed a little loose flour from her hands toward Frankie. "If you can't be honest with me, at least be honest with yourself. You have to decide if you trust Garrett, with or without Dani Edwards. It's all the same, Frankie Champagne."

CHAPTER 3

All great literature is one of two stories;
a man goes on a journey, or a stranger comes to town.

Leo Tolstoy

In a downtown Duluth hotel suite, an unkempt Garrett Iverson opened the case file of the first Garden Killer victim, again. He'd checked out the six victim files for the weekend and holed up in his hotel suite, papers spread out on the executive desk that overlooked the Canal Park walkway, Aerial Lift Bridge, and Lake Superior beyond.

Outside, dog walkers, cyclists, and scooter riders enjoyed the spring sunshine and unseasonably warm breeze. Families picnicked in the park and boaters glided across the bay, many for the first time since autumn. Outside, everything was right with the world.

Inside, Garrett opened the drapes to take full advantage of the light. How he wished he could enjoy the view and the idyllic spring weather. Portable exam lights circled the desk, casting a stark white glow over every photo and paper. Garrett examined, read, and reviewed the case files on repeat. He hadn't slept or showered, and he ignored social calls from his old boss, the former mayor, and especially from Dani Edwards.

"I'll talk to you when I'm ready. I need my head here so I can focus." Garrett had recited the edict to his former colleagues. He would let them know when it was time to talk.

Calling Frankie had been hard enough. He knew something had slid sideways when he decided to come here. He knew there would be a cost. At the same time, he knew he had to be here. It wasn't that he had a savior complex, but he had skills. He was a damn fine medical examiner for St. Louis County twelve years ago. Meticulous, shrewd, intuitive, Garrett had been nicknamed "Juice" by his associates because he managed to squeeze conclusive findings out of dried-up cases, resulting in successful prosecutions. That's why he was here, inside. Inside where nothing was right with the world.

~

Mother's Day weekend brought wind, rain, and downright chilly temperatures to Deep Lakes. Frankie was happy about the weather, which suited her mood. She knew she shouldn't dwell on Garrett's absence, but she couldn't get past the whole Dani Edwards situation. Somehow, it made her feel foolish.

Peggy must have been attuned to her daughter's mood because she chose a brunch spot at a newly refurbished inn on Lake Loki's wild side. The Gray Haven captured the lighthouse era of the early 1900s dramatically with its stark décor and driftwood tones. The restaurant transported diners to Maine in its vibe and menu— crab cakes, lobster bisque, fiddlehead and ramps salad, and blueberry pie. Frankie made a mental note to return.

Mom and daughter discussed the weather, how the Bountiful grape crop was progressing, Violet's summer plans, and Sophie's wedding. Frankie was thankful her mother never brought up Garrett.

Over blueberry pie with lemon crumble frozen custard, Peggy suggested a new recipe for the bakery.

"If I can home in on their fiddlehead supplier, I think you could come up with a delightful quiche," she whispered conspiratorially across the table.

Frankie giggled for the first time in days. "That's a good idea. I need another culinary project. But not until after Sophie's wedding."

"What's left to be done for the wedding, Dear?" Peggy was ready to offer her help.

Frankie shuddered thinking about filling the gardens with annuals in a couple of weeks, a project she and Garrett were supposed to accomplish together. The bower, ceremony, and reception area needed decorating. Frankie was also tracking travel plans for Max's family and helping them with lodging. Sophie made Frankie promise to enjoy the day without fussing over food and cake, so a caterer and baker were hired from Madison. Frankie was secretly pleased that the pressure was off her to make wedding fare, but she agreed to keep track of RSVPs and report final numbers to the caterer and baker.

"Frankie, come back from wherever it is you went. Wedding tasks?" Peggy pursed her lips.

"Sorry, I was going over the list in my head. Thankfully, Violet will be home soon, and she'll keep me organized. The biggest job is going to be the flower gardens surrounding the bower and ceremony spot. I can't plant the annuals for another two weeks, for fear of frost."

Peggy interjected happily. "I'm very good at choosing flowers. Perhaps we can go to the greenhouse together and place the order."

Frankie looked away from her mother's enthusiastic grin. "I'm sorry, Mom. I ordered the flowers months ago from Meredith Healy. Sophie had specific requests, so I wanted to be sure they'd be available."

"Of course," Peggy understood. "Just the same, if you let me know when you plan to plant, I can help arrange the flowers."

Frankie promised she would let her know. Add that to her list: She needed to make her mother feel important and involved.

~

Garrett splashed water on his face to revive himself. He wasn't sure how long he'd been staring at the same file notes for victim number three, but he was pretty sure it was still Sunday. A rhythmic rapping on his door kicked his pulse up a notch. He waited. It sounded again.

Dani Edwards laughed when Garrett opened the door without hesitation.

"I see you remembered our secret knock." She smiled brightly and waltzed into the hotel room. Seeing the dazzling LED stands, she paused to shade her eyes. "I'm not sure if this is a room or a concert hall."

Garrett shrugged. "My eyes are not what they once were, and I don't want to miss anything."

Dani continued perusing the room, then stood at the picture window to admire the view; her long hair bounced around her shoulders as she moved.

"What are you doing here?" Garrett asked.

She turned and her face came into full view, punctuated by a pouting set of lips. "Well, you didn't answer your phone. I wanted to make sure everything was okay." She drew close enough to brush up against him. "You know, the way partners do."

"I said I'd be in touch when I was ready. There's a lot to digest here." Garrett's first week in Duluth was spent at the downtown office being briefed on the cases, but he'd been holed up alone for the past week.

Dani looked offended. "So, what do you think? You've been at it for days."

Garrett inhaled sharply. He didn't want to be pinned down so quickly. He sure didn't miss working under pressure. "You've studied these cases for months. Give me time."

Dani smiled, her face softening. She hadn't come here to solicit his opinion today. "Right. You need a break though, Garrett. Looking at this stuff over and over again will make you stir crazy. A bunch of us are having drinks and dinner at The Ripple. Come with me?"

Dani's invitation seemed so innocent and enticing. Garrett could use some company, some food, and a change of setting. It might help him find connections in the cases later.

"I don't know. Who's a bunch of us?" Garrett had moved away years ago. It was unlikely he'd know anyone besides Dani. Maybe that's what she wanted.

"The chief detectives on the case. Simms and Olaf. You met them last week. Oh, and Mayor Curt will be there. I know he's anxious to meet you." Dani leaned one hip on the desk beside

Garrett and brushed something off his shirt.

Garrett stared beyond Dani out the window. "I have a meeting with the mayor tomorrow morning." Garrett thought it would be nice to find time to visit with Ben, the former mayor. The two men had worked well together in the past.

Dani emitted a small sigh and absently picked up one of the folders sprawled on the desk. "It makes me sick that this savage is out there free, running up his tab while we try to figure out how to catch up."

She set the folder down and stood behind Garrett. Her fingers rose toward his neckline, and she considered rubbing the muscles there, but her hands fluttered away again.

"I miss working with you, Garrett. I miss the old days. Being a one-woman operation isn't what I thought it would be."

Garrett rose and spun around to face her. "You're not flying solo, Dani. You have two good assistants as far as I can tell. Kara and Leo are young, sharp, and eager. Just what any ME could want."

Dani took a step backward. "Sure. But here we are, without an arrest."

She smiled from somewhere far away. "Remember the Erickson case? The dead guy in the swimming pool?"

"How could I forget? It was the last big case we worked before I resigned."

"We couldn't figure out how the pool boy died, other than by blunt force trauma that caused him to drown. I remember we went back and forth between Mr. and Mrs. Erickson, but they stuck to their story."

"Yeah, but it didn't make sense. The kid worked for all the rich people in the neighborhood and was on the swim team.

How did he end up falling into the pool, hitting his head on the bottom, and dead just like that?"

"Right. He had a clean tox screen. No drugs, no alcohol in his system."

Garrett stopped to consider the case. "There's always someone who knows something. That's what CSI Baily used to say, and man if he wasn't right."

Dani laughed. "All it took was the neighbor woman to get miffed at Mrs. Erickson and tattle to the detective about her affair with the pool boy, and Mr. Erickson finding out."

"Mr. Erickson chases the pool boy. Both slip on the wet tile by the pool, but Erickson falls on the tile, scraping up his knee. The pool boy wasn't so lucky. Bad knees Erickson couldn't get up to help the pool boy even if he wanted to."

Dani laughed, recalling how funny the story was at the time among the department colleagues. "In the end, the Ericksons came out smelling like roses, once word got out the pool boy was supplying drugs all over the city."

Garrett snorted, remembering the Ericksons insisted they knew about the pool boy's drug activities and confronted him, saying they planned to go to the cops. Erickson claimed the pool boy dove into the pool on purpose to end it all. The Ericksons had been presented with good citizen awards at a formal banquet. "Yeah, if I never see those people again, I'll be just fine."

Dani clapped Garrett on the shoulder. "We've had some memorable cases, Garrett. Come on, let me buy you a drink for old time's sake."

Garrett nodded grinning. "Just let me clean up a bit."

~

"Thanks to the awful Mother's Day weekend weather, Bubble & Bake made a killing," Carmen broadcasted to the kitchen crew Monday afternoon. "We logged 306 wine tastings Saturday. That might be a new record."

Feeble cheers projected from Jovie and Tess, who were tired from the weekend customer storm. Jovie had bounced between the kitchen and wine bar, while Tess scurried around the kitchen, cooking up flatbread pizzas and quiches. She lost count of how many reserve quiches she'd pulled from the freezer.

Frankie arrived from the bank, where she'd just deposited the week's take. She waved paychecks in the air enthusiastically and handed them out. "Best Mother's Day week we've had since Bubble & Bake opened," she chirped.

Tess motioned toward the cooler and deep freeze. "I hope we're restocking soon. The reserve quiches are depleted. We need cheese, meats, and produce. I thought you were going to the Madison market this morning." Her hands were on her hips as she faced Carmen, but a smile played across her face.

"The Monday market is on Tuesday this week. It's always on Tuesdays following a Monday holiday." Carmen's reply made Tess shake her head hard enough that her brightly colored bandana slipped over her ears.

"And you," Tess pointed her index finger at Frankie. "We had so many orders to fill last week that our baking supplies are low. I made a list. Here you go, Boss." The elongated ending on "boss" sizzled with Tess's Ethiopian accent.

Bubble & Bake was running like a synergetic beehive. Frankie could count on any one of the crew to notice supply numbers, product conditions, or equipment fixes. She and Carmen believed in the "it takes a village" theory, and their partnership reflected the trust they had in their crew.

Trust. That word set up camp in Frankie's mind a lot lately. It tossed and turned with her body in a twisted dance during the night. She counted leaping question marks like sheep, wondering if she doubted Garrett's faithfulness.

"Hey Frankie, snap out of it!" Carmen clicked her fingers in front of Frankie's face.

"Oh. Huh?" Frankie shut off the running faucet where she'd been washing her hands repeatedly.

Carmen raised her brows. "I asked you a question. What shift are you working at St. Anthony's Saturday?"

Frankie and Carmen belonged to St. Anthony's Catholic Church in Deep Lakes, where the annual Spring Swing Fest was slated for Saturday. Kitchen prep for the southern fried chicken dinner started Friday, but Frankie and Carmen would work Saturday shifts.

"I'll be in the game tent all afternoon, wherever they need me. You?"

Carmen laughed. "I'll see you there. I'm sure bingo will keep us hopping. All the old folks flock to play bingo. Will your mother and Aunt CeCe be there?" Carmen hoped the two women would keep track of Tia Pepita, Carmen's wayward aunt from Texas.

Frankie nodded then shook her head, a mixed message. "Mother will probably work indoors. She's not a fan of the big tent. Too stuffy and too noisy. You won't see my Aunt CeCe anywhere near the church. The Catholic faith and CeCe parted ways a long time ago." Frankie giggled thinking about her free-spirited aunt.

"What about Ryan, the twins, and Tia? Are they helping out?"

Frankie enjoyed the swing part of the event where Mr. Grady and Miss Bea from Step in Style Dance Studio offered free dance lessons before the regional community band played ragtime, Dixieland, and jive tunes on the makeshift dance floor in the parking lot. "I hope the twins are at least going to show off their dance moves!"

Carmen beamed. Kyle and Carlos O'Connor had natural-born talent when it came to dancing, singing, and athletics. She just hoped their driving skills were as good. They had their learning permits and would be taking road tests before summer ended.

"Kyle and Carlos will help in the dining room again. Clearing dishes, refilling coffee, and rolling around the dessert cart. Georgia Harris keeps them on their toes. They can't say no to that woman."

Georgia was the religious education coordinator at St. Anthony's, a highly opinionated ball of fire. Father Donnelly admired her and never wanted her to retire. Once Georgia got a hold of the St. Anthony's youth, she expected two things from them: learning and service. Her track record was formidable. She likely dragged some two thousand kids from First Communion to Confirmation in the past twenty years.

"Tia will be floating around, I'm sure, looking for people to talk to. You know her—social butterfly. I just worry about her. She still stumbles sometimes." Tia Pepita, Carmen's aunt, lived with the O'Connors for almost three years now, initially taking part in an experimental eye medication study before undergoing retinal repair in both eyes. Her eyesight was better, but she wasn't fully healed.

"Maybe we can take turns keeping tabs on her. I'll mention it to mom."

Carmen looked quizzically at the tarts Frankie filled with a mystery concoction. "Working on something new over there?"

Frankie nodded. "Yes. I'm calling them Trust Me Tarts."

"Yeah? What's in the filling?" Carmen took a closer look, sniffing the mixture.

Frankie nudged her away. "Trust me, you'll like it." She laughed.

CHAPTER 4

The morning heat had already soaked through the walls,
rising up from the floor like a ghost of summers past.

Erik Tomblin, Riverside Blues

By Friday afternoon, Frankie and Carmen were up to their ears in cornbread, Texas style and headed to St. Anthony's to drop them off. The chicken dinner was the toast of the town at the Swing Fest the past several years, thanks to Cinda Twilley, a Georgia southern belle who married a winter-loving man. Cinda's family recipes for fried chicken and baked beans were unmatched by anyone in town, one reason the church dinner always sold out.

Frankie and Carmen provided the cornbread every year, thanks to a family recipe from Carmen's mother. Sweet peas, picnic potato salad, baked beans, slaw, and peach cobbler rounded out the menu.

Hot weather arrived unexpectedly on Friday and promised to hang around the area for a few days, stirring up weather conversations all over Deep Lakes.

"This weather isn't good for the lambs," Carmen complained. "Ryan says if it keeps up, we're going to have to make cooling areas for the ewes and their babies."

Frankie nodded sympathetically. "I can't remember when we hit ninety degrees in May. Manny and I are talking about irrigation in the vineyard. It's a big expense, though. First, Sophie's wedding, then I'll worry about irrigation."

The two women unloaded several trays of thick golden cornbread onto serving carts that June, the secretary, had wheeled out to the church parking lot.

June wiped her forehead. "I can't take this hot weather. What happened to spring?" She directed Frankie and Carmen to the kitchen, even though they'd been there a hundred times or more.

The kitchen bustled with activity as men and women peeled potatoes, chopped onions, and shelled fresh peas in one half of the area, while Cinda Twilley led the baked bean brigade next to the commercial stoves.

Frankie spied two giant trays of peach cobbler steaming hot from the oven, now sitting on a stainless-steel counter to cool.

The kitchen was unforgivably hot, and everyone looked like wilted lettuce, except for Cinda, who barely noticed the uptick in the mercury.

"Good afternoon, everybody. Make sure you all are drinking lots of iced water." Carmen noticed that most of the volunteers were north of age sixty-five and might need a reminder to stay hydrated.

"I think we need to remind the church council to upgrade the ventilation system," Frankie remarked to Carmen. "It feels like a hundred degrees in here."

The two bakers located lemonade mix and pitchers. In no time, every volunteer had a glass of iced lemonade in front of them. "There's more in the cooler. Be sure to look after each other," Frankie commented on their way out.

~

Saturday morning began with stifling warm air and barely the whisper of a breeze. The temperature promised to reach ninety degrees again, and the cloudless blue sky offered no respite.

Someone had carted two giant barn fans into the game tent at church, which at best, moved around the sticky, hot air. Little kids didn't notice, happily leap frogging from game to game with their stash of prizes.

The older crowd played round after round of bingo, fanning themselves constantly with the cardboard cards or church bulletins. As Frankie predicted, she and Carmen dashed around tables, checking the cards for those who shouted bingo, handing out new cards, and delivering water to the players.

The announcer encouraged players to take breaks inside the church building where classrooms were transformed to a dance studio, rummage sale room, or crafting zone. Frankie looked forward to the end of her shift when she could enjoy a fried chicken dinner with her mother and Carmen's family.

"We tried to talk Aunt CeCe into coming by for dinner with us, but she started acting weird about it." Frankie confided to Carmen in the game tent.

"You mean weird by our definition, or weird for CeCe?" Carmen asked. Aunt CeCe was eccentric most of the time, so weird was a relative term.

Frankie smiled sleepily. The day's heat was getting to her. "I mean weird period. She told me we all better be careful here. She said she could feel bad juju gathering around St. Anthony's."

Carmen snorted. "Wait a minute. Did she actually use the word juju?"

Frankie nodded but stopped short of ridiculing her aunt. "I hate to say it, Carmie, but Aunt CeCe has her own network she's tuned into. And it has a good track record."

Suddenly, a kerfuffle of some sort arose outside the tent as the door to the church hall loudly banged a few times. Frankie saw three of the men from the concession stand dash through the door into the hall, nearly knocking Peggy Champagne down in the process.

Mother and daughter met halfway between the tent and the door, Peggy out of breath and clutching Frankie in a panic. "Something terrible's happened. Elsa Karlsen's collapsed. I think she might be dead."

Frankie led her mother back into the hall where a large crowd was gathering outside the kitchen doorway. Father Donnelly bolted from the office and ran down the short hallway. The crowd parted like the Red Sea for the priest.

The festive din was replaced by alarmed murmurs and questions.

"Did someone call 911?"

"Yes, they're coming."

Frankie's stature allowed her to creep closer to the action. Father Donnelly was praying over Elsa Karlsen, whose rosy glow had been taken over by a colorless pall. She didn't look like she was breathing, but one of the men was working on that, assisted by another. Thank goodness there were some first responders at the festival.

Elsa looked like a tiny frame of bones surrounded by a heap of loose clothing, her body lying askew like a bowling pin knocked to the gutter.

Frankie spun around to face the onlookers and began shooing them back. "The ambulance will need room and we're all in the way here. Let's give Father and these men some space to help Elsa."

The kitchen workers moved in slow motion, heavy from Elsa's collapse and the oppressive heat in the kitchen. The AC in the dining room hummed full throttle preparing for the onslaught of a full crowd of chicken eaters.

"Mom, it's almost four o'clock. We need people posted at the doors to keep customers out of the hall." Frankie knew nobody could take control of a situation better than her mother.

"Right. I'll get Dennis from the bingo tent and Bob from church. I'm sure Bob is setting up the sanctuary for Mass." Peggy was off.

Frankie went through the kitchen's side entrance to speak to the volunteers. "Why don't you all come this way and take a break. You could use some cool air. Let's go sit down in the dining room." Frankie feared people might start tumbling like dominoes if the hot kitchen had anything to do with Elsa's collapse.

"But people will be coming for dinner any minute," Cinda Twilley balked, hands on her hips.

"It's okay. Dinner is on hold for now. We have people posted at the doors. Meanwhile, you all need a break from the heat." Frankie was surprised by her calm voice and the even way she directed the parish volunteers.

Carmen had entered the church hall to assess the commotion and noticed, too. "Good job, Frankie. Way to think on your feet. It's almost like you've been in a crisis before." She leaned in toward her friend and clapped her on the shoulder, trying to lighten the mood.

Several minutes later, Elsa was loaded into an ambulance and a barrage of hungry patrons were allowed into the church hall. The four o'clock hour brought fresh volunteers for the dinner service, a huge relief for Father Donnelly and those who had logged hot hours in the kitchen for most of the day.

Bingo was still rolling in the tent, now filled with the backlog of dinner customers who must wait for a table. Frankie and Carmen returned to their posts, planning for a late meal, if any. The tent was buzzing with chatter about Elsa, which Frankie and Carmen chose to ignore.

Lenny Jensen, one of the church old-timers, took over calling bingo, albeit very slowly as he squinted to read the numbers on the game balls he held in his shaky hand. Finally, he motioned for Carmen to take his place.

By the final game of blackout, only a smattering of diehard players remained, and Carmen hastily announced it was closing time. "If anyone would like to help with the cleanup, we would appreciate it." That was enough to get the old folks moving out the door.

The twins, Kyle and Carlos, poked their heads into the tent to find Carmen and Frankie sweeping around and under tables and stacking up the plastic chairs on a cart.

"Don't tell me. There's no more food left," Carmen pursed her lips tightly. She was tired and way past hungry.

The boys nodded. "We had loads of people. More than ever,

plus everyone was hanging around to talk about the old lady that passed out in the kitchen."

Kyle elbowed his brother. "That old lady is about the same age as Frankie's mother, Carlos," he said under his breath.

"It would have been nice if a few of the men had come out to help get the tent cleaned up," Frankie said through gritted teeth, and Carmen agreed.

"Where's your dad, anyway?"

"He's helping clean up the kitchen and stuff. He sent us out here to get you before all the food's gone," Carlos informed them.

"Don't worry about us though, Mom. The kitchen ladies shoved food at us every time we came into the kitchen with dirty dishes." Kyle beamed, oblivious to the dirty looks he received from both women.

Together, the twins pushed the cart of chairs toward the storage area, while Carmen and Frankie followed with the brooms and bingo board.

They were surprised to see the number of people still sitting in the dining hall. A few volunteers were eating remnants of the prize southern dinner. Peggy waved at them to sit with her, so they took leftovers from the chow line: broken bits of fried chicken, baked beans, cornbread corners, and applesauce someone had pilfered from the church pantry.

Peggy, looking fresh as the morning dew, patted the chair next to hers.

"I heard the cobbler was delicious, but your cornbread received rave reviews, too." She smiled brightly, as if the day was as ordinary as any other. "One of these days I'm going to ask Cinda Twilley for the fried chicken recipe," Peggy exclaimed over a fork bearing a small piece from a chicken wing.

Frankie picked at her meager portions, too tired and too hot to care much about eating.

"Why are all these people still here?" Frankie peered around the dining hall. "Are they waiting for the cash raffle drawing?" She checked the time. The drawing should have happened more than an hour ago.

Peggy continued enjoying her food, but a shadow crept over her face. "We're waiting for Father Donnelly. He's supposed to give us an update on Elsa."

When the update came, it wasn't from Father, and it wasn't good news. Bob Rasmussen, the head usher, said Elsa couldn't be revived and Father asked the congregation to pray for her family. He said Father was at the hospital and wouldn't be returning that evening.

Peggy dropped her fork, her appetite gone. "I just can't believe this. Elsa was the same age as me. She was in good shape, too."

Frankie leaned in to squeeze her mother's shoulder. "I'm so glad you weren't working in that hot kitchen. Anyone could have passed out from the heat." Frankie's mind went to Aunt CeCe's possible premonition.

Cinda Twilley bounced over to their table, making a beeline for Frankie. Her wide smile had a fresh application of dark pink lipstick.

"Congratulations, Frankie. You sure are lucky!"

"Sorry, I don't know what you mean."

"Oh, you didn't hear. You're the grand prize cash raffle winner! June said you can pick up your check anytime next week." Cinda seemed proud to deliver the happy news.

Before she trotted off, Peggy grabbed her sleeve. "Cinda,

would you be willing to trade family recipes with me? I'd love to have your fried chicken recipe, and I'll give you my mother's recipe for…"

Frankie cut her off. "No, Mother. We're not giving away the kringle recipe." As far as Frankie was concerned, Grandma Sophie's kringle recipe was a national secret, and she made sure Cinda knew it.

Cinda laughed. "I understand completely. That's why I can't give out Maw Maw's fried chicken batter recipe either."

"Now, now, Francine dear. I wasn't going to give out the kringle recipe. She's just as famous for her frikadeller…" Peggy spoke smoothly with the poise of an ambassador.

Cinda sniffed. "Well, I won't pretend to know what a fricka-thing is," she said nervously. "But I'm sorry, Mrs. Champagne. The answer's no. I'm glad you enjoyed the chicken. At least, the little bits that were left. I'm going to make sure we order a lot more chicken next year." Cinda puffed out her chest with authority and walked away.

CHAPTER 5

Bad news isn't wine.
It doesn't improve with age.

Colin Powell

Pom and Cherry, the Parker sisters, arrived at Bubble & Bake around ten-thirty the next morning to set up for opening the wine lounge. Frankie usually changed the Sunday opening time starting Memorial weekend, but the warm weather ushered in the summer crowd early, so she wanted to accommodate them.

The sisters were surprised to see Frankie in the kitchen, taking quiches out of the ovens.

"Hi Frankie. I didn't expect to see you today. Sunday's supposed to be your day off," Pom scolded her boss.

Frankie settled two Springtime quiches onto cooling racks, then paused before opening the next oven. Frankie's Springtime recipe was a popular menu choice, made with fresh asparagus, spring onions, and French herbs.

"Weekends have been busy, so I thought I'd pop in and make

more quiches." Frankie's story was a half-truth. With Garrett away, she wanted to occupy her time, so a Sunday off alone suddenly didn't seem too special. She pulled two quiches from the other oven, a new recipe made from morels and ramps, of which she had a limited supply. The earthy mushrooms and garlicky ramps were excellent companions.

Cherry sidled up next to Frankie and inhaled deeply. "Those smell amazing! Something new?"

"Yes," Frankie's eyes sparkled when she talked about new recipes. "It's made with ramps and morels, but I haven't figured out a name for it."

Pom joined the two and admired the golden quiche topped with melted cheese and herbs. "What's the crust, Frankie? That doesn't look like pie crust."

Frankie's brows danced. "It's made from buttery crackers, actually."

Cherry slapped the counter. "How about Cracking Good Quiche?"

"I love it!" Frankie agreed.

Cherry and Pom left to set up wine tasting lists, glasses, and bottles behind the bar. Frankie surveyed her fresh supplies in the chill of the cooler, wondering what to make next. She had enough ramps and morels for three more quiches and decided to use them up while they were fresh.

"Maybe Carmen can pick up more at the market tomorrow," she mumbled to herself. The beginning of another week brought Sophie's wedding that much closer. She'd set aside Thursday, her normal day off, to pick up her order from Healy's Greenhouse and plant the annual garden at the vineyard.

"Ug. It's going to be a nightmare holiday weekend, too. Maybe

I shouldn't take Thursday off after all." She chewed her bottom lip as the many tasks waiting for her tumbled around her mind.

"Frankie, I didn't expect to see you. I tried calling earlier. Twice." Peggy had walked in the back entrance while Frankie was lost in space.

Frankie looked up from the cutting board heaped with morels and gasped. Her mother didn't look at all like her usual put-together cosmopolitan self. Frankie couldn't remember the last time she saw her mother without makeup and realized just how much that could change a person's appearance. Peggy's eyes were red either from allergies or tears, and her hair hung down, undone, natural. Maybe her mother was planning a boat excursion with Dan Fitzpatrick, the man she'd been dating. But that couldn't be. Peggy always gussied up to go out.

"I'm sorry. I left my phone in the office. Is there anything wrong? Are you feeling sick?"

Peggy set her purse on the counter. "I'm not sick, Frankie. But Father Donnelly is. He didn't say Mass today. Rumor has it, he's in the hospital." She sat on a nearby stool like a deflated balloon.

"Who told you that?" Frankie knew her mother hadn't gone to church this morning either, since they'd both been at the special Saturday Mass at yesterday's festival.

"Marie Stevens called me after Mass. A substitute priest was there from Madison and made the announcement that Father was ill. He announced Elsa's death, too. Marie wondered if I knew what was wrong with Father. Of course, I have no idea." Peggy sank deeper into herself.

"Hmm. I hope Father isn't sick from the heat, too. He's usually so robust." Frankie studied her mother, still wondering why she wasn't her usual self. "You know, the wine lounge will run just fine today with the three of us. Take the day off, Mom."

Peggy sat up straighter. "I'm not finished with the news yet, Dear. Father isn't the only one who's sick. June Thompson, the church secretary, is supposedly in the hospital, too. And Marie said that two or three others who worked in the kitchen yesterday have fallen ill."

Frankie stopped slicing morels and folded both arms skeptically. "Just who is Marie's source for all these rumors? Hmm?"

"Marie said she talked to Cinda Twilley this morning. The Twilleys go to breakfast every Sunday morning at Silver's on Lake Hope. Marie and Ralph bumped into them there, and Cinda told her about June and the other kitchen volunteers. I just don't know what to make of this."

Aunt CeCe's warning to stay away from the festival echoed in Frankie's ears. She remembered her conversation with Carmen about the need for better ventilation in the kitchen. She stared at her mother again. Could it be that Peggy worried she might be the next one to get sick?

"Go home and rest. I'll make some calls and see what I can find out, and I'll talk to you later. Please don't worry about this, Mother."

Peggy agreed to go home without a hint of argument, leaving Frankie more concerned for her mother than ever. She walked to the wine lounge, grabbing her phone from the office on the way. The missed calls from her mother were her only notifications. No news from Garrett, but she forced herself to pick up her chin. She had other fish to fry.

"Pom and Cherry, can you two manage for a bit while I run

across the street to Karlsen's?"

Cherry was about to turn on the open sign and she peered out the large picture window that faced the busy intersection of Granite and Meriwether streets.

"I don't see a crowd lined up out there, so it's safe to say we'll be okay here. Is your mom coming in soon?"

"Shoot. I forgot to tell you. She won't be in today. She's not feeling well. I'll be back shortly." Frankie ducked out before Cherry had the chance to ask questions.

Karlsen's Wisconsin Specialty Store was a go-to shop offering hundreds of Wisconsin products perfect for tourists or locals who wanted to send Wisconsin gifts to others. Because of its combined visitor and local appeal, the store was busy most of the year.

Frankie had two reasons to visit today, and she was glad to see Julia, one of the owners, stocking maple syrup, jams, and honey in the front section.

"Hi Julia. I'm so sorry to hear about Elsa." Elsa was Julia's mother-in-law and frequently helped out at the store during the holiday season.

Julia placed the two jars she was holding onto a shelf and raised her eyes to meet Frankie's. "It's such a shock. Lew's at her house today with his sister. They're trying to make plans…" She trailed off.

Frankie imagined more than half of Deep Lakes would be at Elsa's funeral. She and her husband ran the store for decades before retiring and passing it along to Lew and Julia. Elsa's husband died a short time later, and Elsa resumed many of her civic and church activities to keep busy.

Frankie stood silent, searching for the right words to the

questions she wanted to ask. "Please let me know about the funeral. I know my mother is upset about Elsa and will want to know. Did you hear that other people working in the kitchen yesterday are sick?" Frankie was waltzing around her question about the cause of Elsa's death.

Julia nodded. "I heard Father Donnelly was in the hospital and June Thompson, too. I guess they're all around the same age though, so maybe the heat was too much yesterday?" The doubt in Julia's voice resonated with Frankie. It seemed they both wondered what the culprit was.

Frankie jumped on Julia's doubts. "Do you think something else made them sick? Was Elsa on any medication or having other health problems?" She hoped she didn't sound too eager for information.

Julia had resumed settling jars on shelves but paused to consider. "Elsa was healthy as a horse. She only took allergy medications on occasion."

"Well, it's been a rough allergy season this spring," Frankie offered, "what with all the rain in April and the warmth in May. It brought out all the blossoms at once."

A doorbell chime announced another customer, and both women perked up when Georgia Harris rounded the corner by the jams and honey. Here was the all-knowing guru of St. Anthony's and their best hope for answers.

"Hello Julia. Frankie, isn't your shop open? I was going to head over there next." Georgia didn't wait for a reply as she turned toward Julia. "I'm so sorry for your loss, my dear."

"Thank you, Georgia. I appreciate it and will pass along your sympathy to Lew. Do you know anything about Father or June?" Julia was more likely to get something out of Georgia due to the common nature of the illnesses in question.

Georgia sighed. "Father and June are hospitalized, I'm afraid. Both of them are having breathing problems. Nobody is allowed to visit."

The religious education coordinator looked like she had more to say but cut her words short.

"Georgia, there are rumors circulating that other parishioners are sick, too. Do you know if that's true?" Frankie's voice held concern.

"I was about to say more, but I don't want anyone to know the information came from me. Yes, three people working in the kitchen yesterday are sick with the same thing. Coughing, breathing problems, weakness. Ruth Brandt. Ann Malson. Ken Pearse. I heard Ken and Ruth were in the hospital, too, but I'm waiting to hear more from Bob. He's the trustee in touch with Father Dailey—the priest filling in for Father Donnelly."

Frankie knew both Ruth and Ann were at least in their sixties, but she was surprised about Ken Pearse, a soybean farmer who graduated a couple years ahead of Frankie from the same high school.

"Ken Pearse? He's young and in good shape. Plus, he's used to the heat." Julia read Frankie's mind.

Georgia leaned in conspiratorially. "I don't mind telling you that I don't think this has anything to do with the heat wave." She might have shared her opinion on the matter if she hadn't remembered that Elsa had died in the church kitchen and Julia was family.

"Anyway, please let the church know about funeral plans. I'm going to fill in for June in the office until she's feeling better, and I'll let the funeral lunch coordinator know what to expect."

Georgia, all business now, turned her attention to Frankie.

"I was hoping to order some pastries for our year-end gathering, Frankie." Georgia always treated the catechism teachers and helpers to a brunch at her home on Lake Joy to celebrate another successful year.

"Of course. The shop is open. Pom and Cherry are there now, and I'll be back in a minute after I finish here." Frankie remembered her other reason for going to Karlsen's.

"Julia, when the Carr Valley Cheese truck comes this week, could you please send the driver to Bubble & Bake? We've gone through more than the usual supplies this spring."

"Of course. The truck comes Tuesday. If for some reason I'm not here, I'll leave a note for Zoey. She's offered to work extra hours this week."

"Thank you, Julia. Let me know if your family needs anything."

Frankie crossed Granite Street quickly and took the front steps to Bubble & Bake two at a time. She could see Pom was busy with customers at the wine bar, which meant Cherry was probably manning the kitchen orders until Frankie returned.

Georgia was standing patiently at the register, writing out the bakery order form.

"I hope I gave you enough lead time. I know how busy you must be with Sophie's wedding coming up." Georgia handed the form to Frankie for review.

"Let's see: Three kringles, three dozen butterhorns, four quiches. No problem at all, Georgia, and thank you. Pick up date on June ninth." Frankie sighed in relief, knowing Sophie's wedding would be over by then.

"Oh dear, the wedding plans are going okay, aren't they?" Georgia's bloodhound nose picked up on Frankie's mood.

"Things are fine. It's just a busy time of year." Frankie glossed over her anxiety about Sophie and Garrett's absence.

"I wanted to ask you, Georgia. What did you mean about the heat not being the cause of people getting sick?"

Georgia sniffed and narrowed her eyes. "It's no secret that the church kitchen needs an overhaul. I'm surprised it still passes inspection."

"You think there's a ventilation problem?" Frankie wondered the same thing.

Georgia nodded. "And the ovens. And the cooler. Maybe the ice machine." Georgia was just warming up. "You know, Frankie, I ran for church council last fall, but some people thought it was a conflict of interest. I'm just saying, I would bring these matters up and things would get fixed."

Frankie had no doubt that Georgia would contrive a plan to get her way on most matters. But she agreed that Georgia's religious education position was a conflict of interest. Father Donnelly did his best to encourage a variety of people to serve on the council to keep things fair.

When Frankie didn't encourage Georgia, the woman's shoulders slumped. "Well, I hope nobody else gets sick. It's a good thing you're not using the kitchen for Sophie's reception, I suppose." Georgia's insinuation stung like a needle.

Georgia, along with some other parishioners, weren't keen about Sophie getting married at Bountiful instead of in the church and tried to convince Frankie to change her daughter's mind. Frankie bristled at Georgia's jab.

"Yes, I guess it is a good thing. As I told you, Sophie and Max don't want a church wedding. They're adults and can make up their own minds. Anyway, I certainly hope Father and June feel better soon. Thank you for helping at the church until June comes back." Changing subjects was a good tactic with Georgia.

"It's the least I can do. Since religious ed is done for the year, I have the time. Give my best wishes to Sophie. She's such a sweet girl." The old coddling Georgia was back.

The front door jangled announcing the arrival of three of the Buzzards, a group of retired men who met most Sunday afternoons at Bubble & Bake to play cards or games, do puzzles, drink brews, and share town gossip. Their wives, The Knit Witches, gathered next door at Rachel Engebretsen's Bead Me I'm Yours craft shop to knit, crochet, sew, and drink wine from Bubble & Bake.

Frankie raised an eyebrow at the flirtatious exchange between Byron Corey and Georgia. Byron, a retired civil engineer, was new in town and a fine dancer. He'd caught Georgia's eye at the church Spring Swing Fest with his dance moves, and apparently, she'd caught his eye, too.

Frankie greeted the other men and pulled bottles of beer from the cooler for them. Red Robbins was the unofficial head of their group. His knitted brow and clipped hello indicated something serious was brewing. Red and Wally, another Buzzard, claimed spots in their usual corner of the lounge.

Frankie followed them.

"Red, is there anything wrong? You look bothered about something." Frankie had a forthright relationship with the group, who'd been a Sunday fixture at the lounge almost since it opened. Their arrangement was a win-win: Frankie had year-round customers thanks to them and the Knit Witches, and they had a designated space to enjoy themselves with discounted baked goods, beer, and wine.

Red set up the table with his notebook and pen, rather than the Scrabble game he usually played. "We're having a real meeting today, Frankie. We're going to set up a fundraiser for Donna Graham. Do you know the Grahams? They've been farming between here and Zeeland since before you were born."

Frankie didn't know them, but Zeeland was just over the county line, so the Grahams might have done more business there than in Deep Lakes. "I don't think so. The name's familiar. Is Mrs. Graham sick?"

Red and Wally both shook their heads sadly. "Not Donna. Her husband, Harry, died yesterday. They found him in the barn and couldn't revive him," Wally said.

Red motioned Frankie to move in closer so he could lower his voice. "Harry died just like Elsa Karlsen. In the heat. He couldn't breathe. Rumor has it they both suffocated."

Frankie hadn't heard the rumor, but she understood how information spread like wildfire through their small town. Who needed social media when the Buzzards, Knit Witches, and church ladies were around?

"Well, I'm sorry to hear about Mr. Graham. How old was he?"

Red scratched the back of his head. "Harry must've been about seventy. He took the farm over from his dad right out of school. Well, after he came back from the army."

"Please let me know about the fundraiser plans, so Carmen and I can donate something and help promote it." Frankie patted Red on the shoulder and left the men alone.

In front of the shop, Georgia and Byron were conversing quietly, leaning in toward each other. Georgia smiled easily and laughed at Byron's comments, and Frankie noticed she was blushing. Byron's eyes traveled from Georgia's face to her figure.

Frankie sidled toward the wine bar away from the conversation, and scooted into the alcove behind the lounge she used as an office.

With two people in the county dead the same day, it sure was poor timing for Garrett to be away. She wondered if Alonzo or family members of the deceased would request autopsies. If so, she wondered who might perform them.

"Maybe I'll call Lon and pick his brain," Frankie said to herself.

Another week had passed, and Garrett felt helpless. He was missing something, and he knew it was right in front of him somewhere in the files. The mayor and police chief didn't spare him their frustration. Detectives Simms and Olaf smirked whenever he walked past them at their daily powwows, as if to say, So you're the hotshot we heard about? Then there was Dani, pressuring him personally and professionally. His only reprieve was the ME assistants. At least Leo and Kara respected him and talked to him like a person instead of a miracle worker.

It didn't help that he wasn't sleeping. Photos from the crime scenes bounced back and forth in his mind and sucked all the oxygen from the room. He often showered in the middle of the night, fighting his inclination to grab the phone and wake Frankie just to hear her voice.

The couple agreed to limit their calls to once a week. This would help Garrett concentrate on the victim files while Frankie focused on Sophie's wedding and handling both businesses. It was lonely, but better to staunch their contact time. Their conversations had become mundane, filled with lackluster small talk. Neither one poured their heart out. For his part, Garrett missed Frankie deeply and regretted being sweet-talked into coming to Duluth.

Today was just like the past two Sundays. Garrett's room was a museum of victim exhibits, photos, papers, and crime boards. Candy wrappers testified to his go-to sugar fixes to stave off hunger; they littered the floor and coffee table. He couldn't remember if he ate the day before, but he knew he hadn't eaten today.

The room was a self-imposed detention center. He didn't dare take weekends away from the cases. Surely a new victim was already being hunted. It was only a matter of time, and he seemed to be the timekeeper.

His ringing phone jolted him to the present. He saw Dani's ID on the screen and swore out loud. He didn't want her help, maybe. The truth was he didn't want to be near her. She was a habit he'd broken once, but now it taunted him at every turn. He couldn't afford to be distracted, in more ways than one.

At Garrett's request, the hotel concierge had delivered swimming trunks to his room Saturday. A dip in the pool seemed like a good idea. He changed into his trunks and prayed the water was cold.

Johnny, the hotel manager, waved as Garrett walked past, carrying a towel. Johnny knew why Garrett was in town. The mayor told Johnny to get Garrett anything he asked for, treat him like a VIP.

"Hey, Mr. I, it's good to see you out of your room. It's a quiet day here. Nice time for a swim."

Garrett nodded. "I like it quiet, Johnny."

"Can I send out a waiter? You're looking kinda hungry, Mr. I."

Garrett nodded again. "Give me thirty minutes."

The pool was empty, and the water was cool. Garrett swam laps earnestly, as if training for a rescue mission. The water gliding over his body gave his mind fluidity and eased the tension in his neck and shoulders. He was homesick for Deep Lakes, homesick for Frankie and the life they were building. Maybe he was trying too hard to find evidence that would break open the case because he truly didn't want to be there.

Swimming with closed eyes allowed him to shut out the world, and for the first time since he'd arrived in Duluth, he didn't see the murder victims. He kept swimming, happy for the reprieve. Maybe he could sleep in the pool. The idea made him grin.

Finally, breathing heavily from the effort, he was satiated and hungry. He swam to the shallow end of the pool and pushed his dripping hair out of his eyes. He walked up the steps, his eyes taking in the figure of Dani, clad in a shapely crimson swimsuit trimmed in gold grommets along the sides from breast to thigh. Each pair of grommets was home to a dainty black bow.

Garrett was surprised to see her there, or maybe not. "I heard you wanted to look at a menu." Dani smiled boldly and twirled in a little circle for effect.

Garrett walked past her wordlessly and picked up his towel from a nearby lounge chair. He wondered if Dani knew Johnny, the hotel manager. Maybe they were in cahoots, setting a trap for him. Maybe he was being ridiculous.

"How did you know I'd be at the pool?" Garrett was stone-faced.

"When you didn't answer my third call, I called the front desk. Johnny told me I'd find you here and that you planned to order dinner. I figured we could eat together and talk about the case files." Dani was taken aback at Garrett's coolness, something she hadn't anticipated.

"You don't look dressed for eating or working," Garrett stared a little too long at her, his eyes traveling the length of her figure. Dani noticed.

"I brought other clothes with me. I wasn't sure how long you'd be swimming. It sounded like a nice idea on a warm day like today." Dani abruptly walked past Garrett and stepped into the pool. She took long strokes to the other end before turning back to face him. She mistakenly believed he'd watched her swim, mesmerized. But Garrett sat on the lounge chair, his face in the menu.

Dani pretended his aloof behavior didn't matter. She swam a few laps, then rose from the pool like a model in a commercial and pranced on tiptoe to Garrett's side. He didn't look up, but he absently passed a towel to her while studying the menu with interest.

Dani sat in the next chair like a reprimanded child and admired her newly painted fingernails.

"See anything you like, Garrett?" She spoke flirtatiously, but the tactic fell flat.

"Yep. I'm ready to order. Are you really going to stay to work?" Garrett had developed a tick in his jawline.

Dani pouted, offended. "Yes, I came to work. Why do you think I'm here? We've got to give the chief and detectives something new. I think the key to finding the murderer is in our files. Don't you?"

Garrett passed the menu over. He couldn't disagree with Dani. He was sure the victims spoke volumes, telling their stories through their injuries, their last location, and more. "Okay then. Let's get some food and talk about the reports."

Dani offered up a grudging smile. "Oh boy. Dinner and autopsies. Sounds like the perfect date night."

CHAPTER SIX

Aside from painting and gardening,
I am good for nothing.

☙

Claude Monet

Thursday couldn't come fast enough. All week long, Frankie endured customer speculations about the strange illness going around the county. The more levelheaded patrons decided the afflicted had underlying health conditions, while the conspiracy theorists discussed ideas ranging from secret government germ weapon testing to alien drones dropping viruses from other planets.

Logical or whacky, everyone had something to say about the sick and the deceased. Frankie hoped to gain straight answers from Alonzo, but her questions went unanswered.

"Lon, the customers are driving us all crazy with their gossip. Is there something I can say to get them to stop spreading stupid rumors?" Frankie's desperation was genuine.

Lon's response was a mixture of frustration and fatigue. "I

wish I knew what to say. Without Garrett, we're waiting on autopsies from any available coroner. The body count is rising, too. That's not for public consumption, Frankie."

Frankie gasped in surprise. The heat wave had continued, but there must be more going on than hot weather. "Will you call Garrett back to Whitman County?"

Lon's weighty sigh said it all. "I'm afraid I can't do that. Sorry, Frankie. Meanwhile, just tell customers they're causing more harm than good by spreading rumors. Which is exactly why you can't say anything about the death count. The last thing we need is a panic."

"You're right, of course, Lon." Frankie kept the rest of her commentary to herself. There was something amiss in Deep Lakes. She could feel a heaviness in the air, like a dark cloud covering the town.

She knew Aunt CeCe felt it too, at an even deeper level than Frankie. CeCe had a knack with customers and could be counted upon to tally the most sales of anyone at the shop. Lately though, she'd been flummoxed around them and couldn't remember the wine descriptions or the names of pastries. On top of that, her signature macarons were turning out bland and flat. Most of them were inedible.

"I don't understand what the matter is, Frankie and Carmen. I'm usually in sync with the universe, but something is wrong in the atmosphere. I'm so sorry." CeCe scratched at her palms and tilted her head sideways as if she could dump out the negative vibes.

Conversely, Tia Pepita was unstoppable. Working with the public wasn't her strong suit, which is why she was largely relegated to the kitchen, but customers gravitated toward her lately. It was as if CeCe and Tia had swapped bodies.

Frankie hoped the winds of change would start blowing over Deep Lakes soon, while still surrounding Tia with a favorable breeze.

On Thursday morning, Frankie rose with the sun and drove to Healy's Greenhouse to meet Meredith, who had set aside enough annuals to frame an aisle leading to the garden arbor at the vineyard. Sophie would glide down that grassy aisle in about a week.

Frankie waved from the driveway where Meredith stood directing her to the back greenhouse. Meredith and Frankie dressed similarly in old cotton shirts and well-worn jeans made for getting dirty.

"Good morning, Meredith. Thanks again for agreeing to meet me early and for finding the flowers Sophie wanted."

Meredith led the way inside the greenhouse and pointed to a section of hothouse frames loaded with varieties typically found in a French cottage garden: delphiniums, marigolds, bachelor buttons, cosmos, dahlias, coreopsis, snapdragons, pansies, and sweet alyssum. All the blooms were blue, yellow, or white, and Meredith had done due diligence to ensure they would bloom abundantly on the wedding day.

Frankie allowed a delightful squeal to escape. "Oh Meredith, this is going to be stunning!" Frankie embraced the much taller woman tightly. The florist didn't realize how much the flowers meant to Frankie when everything else seemed out of sorts in her world.

"I'm so happy you like them. It's a relief to see how well they're thriving because you just never know with annuals," Meredith confessed.

Frankie nodded but the prolific flowers were no surprise to her. She knew Meredith's green thumb.

"There have been so many ups and downs lately, I'm just excited to see these beauties." It was Frankie's turn to confess.

Meredith's smile faded. "Tell me about it. All the people getting knocked down with this weird illness…" she sucked in her breath.

"Anyone you know? Besides Father Donnelly, June Thompson and…" Frankie paused. "Did you know Harry Graham?" She figured the Healys might know him since they both practiced agriculture in the same area.

Meredith shook her head. "I don't think so, but poor Becky Biddle."

Frankie shrugged.

"You know, Biddle's Blooms in Gibson?"

Frankie nodded. She didn't patronize Biddle's, but she'd driven past it many times.

"Becky collapsed in the greenhouse yesterday. Luckily it was near lunch time, so her husband, Dusty, came to check in. She was sent directly to UW Hospital in Madison." Meredith looked alarmed. "I hope the doctors there can get to the bottom of this."

Frankie hoped so, too. "Did Becky have the same breathing issues?"

"Yep, and she's only forty, Frankie. Dusty said she's in the ICU."

"That's terrible news. Do you know if Becky has asthma or any other health issues?"

"Dusty said she doesn't. I mean, greenhouse work is hot, but those of us in this business are used to it. We have swamp coolers and that helps a lot."

"Swamp coolers?" Frankie wasn't familiar with the term.

"They're large wall coolers with wet pads in them. The pads are like sponges. The hot air goes in, evaporates, and comes out as cooler air. So, kind of like an air conditioner but more efficient," Meredith explained.

Frankie returned to the mystery illness and its victims. "I hope Becky recovers quickly. Let me know if you hear about more people though, will you please?"

Meredith placed her hands on her hips and frowned. "And why do you want to know, Frankie Champagne?"

Frankie was found out. "The more people this is happening to, well it's begging to be investigated. There must be something going on here."

Meredith laughed. "I'm sure you can work in an investigation between Sophie's wedding and tourist season at Bubble & Bake."

Frankie grimaced. "You're right. I don't have time. Guess I better get planting. My mother will be waiting for me at the vineyard."

Indeed, Peggy was a welcome sight, sitting on a bench in the fruit orchard, a canvas bucket of garden tools at her feet, and a drink cooler with a spigot next to her on the seat.

Frankie was driving her vineyard manager's truck, and she leaned out the window to shout to Peggy.

"Hop in, Mom. We can drive this all the way down to the planting area."

Peggy was agile for seventy-three and easily hoisted herself into the passenger seat after settling the bucket and cooler behind her in the cab.

"Thanks for getting the tools. I hope you haven't been waiting too long." Frankie's mother prided herself on promptness.

"Not at all. Your timing was perfect. I thought it would be

nice to have some iced tea. I made it yesterday. Raspberry, rose hips, and mint. Very refreshing."

They pulled up on the grass between the sections of Frontenac and La Crescent grapes. The vineyard was thriving with the extra rain it received that spring, and now the sunshine would bring on the fruit.

Frankie dropped the truck's tailgate and stared at all the work ahead of them. Suddenly, planting dozens of flowers seemed daunting. "I'm sorry we don't have more help, Mom. This is going to be a huge undertaking."

"Now, now. Let's not borrow trouble. We'll do the best we can. If we don't finish today, we'll have to keep at it." Peggy smiled brightly. "Meredith outdid herself. These are gorgeous."

The two women slathered on sunscreen and donned wide-brimmed garden hats. Frankie showed Peggy the diagram she and Garrett had designed for the border beds, and each woman took one side of the freshly tilled dirt.

After a couple of hours, they paused for iced tea and admired each other's work. A gator pulling a metal trailer drove up next to the truck. Manny Vega, the vineyard manager, leapt out of the driver's side like a kangaroo.

"I brought reinforcements, Boss." Manny jerked his thumb behind him. Carmen and Cherry jumped out of the gator, big smiles on their faces.

"What's this?" Frankie asked.

"I knew this project would be too big for you and your mom alone, Frankie," Carmen scolded. "Tess and Jovie are handling the shop just fine, and I brought Tia in to help, too. Lately, she's got the Midas touch."

Frankie ran to the newcomers and gave them both squeezes.

"I'm so happy to see you. We can use all the help we can get."

Manny brought a large cooler from the back seat floor and set it between rows of Frontenacs in a shady patch. "Here's lunch when you're ready. Plenty for everyone."

Many hands do make light work as the saying goes, and a couple hours later, Frankie called lunch. Most of the beds were planted and looked good. While the women dined on sandwiches and tangy cucumber salad, Manny dragged a soaker hose into the beds and said he'd turn on the water as soon as they gave the word.

Even the fresh air and beauty of their surroundings couldn't bury the concern they had about the mysterious ailments afflicting people they knew. Conversation died out, and in the quiet, Cherry asked if anyone had news about the sick. Everyone looked at Peggy.

"I don't know why all of you think I know anything consequential," Peggy protested. "All I can tell you is that mum seems to be the word. And I don't mean chrysanthemum either."

"What's that supposed to mean?" Carmen looked annoyed.

"I tried to visit Father Donnelly and June, but I couldn't get past the front registration desk. They have people posted there standing sentry. I asked about their status and was told it was confidential." Peggy huffed and took a long sip of tea.

Frankie folded her arms. "That's nothing new, Mother. Patient conditions are always kept private unless you're family."

But Peggy was a pillar of the community and had connections everywhere, so Frankie was a bit surprised she couldn't get past the gatekeepers.

"There's more. I had my doubts I could see Father or June since they're in the ICU. So, I went up to the next floor to visit

Ruth and Ann. Same thing. No visitors allowed and there were two police officers there to make sure nobody could sneak through."

"I can't believe you didn't call in a favor with someone." Frankie knew she'd inherited her mother's resourcefulness when it came to sniffing out information.

"I did. I tracked down Fitz Barnard." Dr. Barnard and Peggy were officers in the Deep Lakes Historical Society. Her mother's fingers and toes were in most of the pies in town.

"Well…we're waiting." Carmen didn't believe in a dramatic build-up.

Peggy sniffed, and slowly set down her plate and drink to prolong her delivery. "Now, now. No need to be churlish, Carmen." Peggy didn't mean it, though.

"Dr. Barnard couldn't tell me anything about the illnesses. But he did say the State Board of Health was involved. And," Peggy leaned in toward the others. "Apparently there are several dead in the Amish community." Peggy gasped audibly and expected the others to gasp, too.

"I suppose that's not exactly shocking, given that they work in the heat without any air conditioning. Most of them are farmers, craftsmen, and bakers, all very hot professions. But it does add to the mystery." Frankie told the others about Becky Biddle. "It seems like there are more people getting sick all the time."

Sick people made Frankie think of Sophie. She'd told Frankie last week she was pulling extra shifts all week long, in part because she would be taking two weeks off for her honeymoon and because said honeymoon in Paris was expensive. Sophie said she'd have limited time to chat, but Frankie intended to call her anyway to see what she knew about the mystery illness.

The sun was high in the sky, so the women declared enough work was done on the garden project for one day. Frankie walked up to the faucet and turned on the soaker hose. Carmen took the tool bucket from Peggy and told her to sit in the shade while she put the tools away. Frankie, Carmen, and Cherry carried the remaining plants into the shaded area next to the Le Crescent section. The four squeezed into Manny's truck with coolers squatting on Cherry's and Carmen's laps.

"Let's stop in the winery and cool off before we go back to town. Mom, I'll start your vehicle and get the AC running." Carmen and Cherry did the same.

"Honestly, Frankie, you don't need to fuss. I'm not an invalid you know." Peggy pulled her hair away from her face and wiped off her forehead.

"Oh, yes I do." Frankie wasn't about to take the chance her mother would get heatstroke.

CHAPTER SEVEN

Allie Ray

Sacrifices were a must this year to stock Bubble & Bake for the Memorial weekend tourist siege. In this case, sleep fell victim to night baking. Carmen and Frankie, huddling with Tess and Jovie, made a pact to change the baking schedule in favor of the coolest temperatures Friday offered. They convened in the kitchen at midnight and baked until five a.m.

The cooling fans did all they could, but when the four bakers hung up their aprons on the outside clothesline, the women were weary and sticky with sweat.

"Oh, but this weather is like late July," Tess observed. "It makes me wonder what summer will bring. I think this might be hotter than my home village."

Tess, a transplant from Ethiopia, began working at the bakery as an intern, but when she couldn't return home due to a government collapse, Peggy Champagne became her American sponsor. She lived above the craft store next door in a studio apartment constructed by Frankie's brother, James. When or if Tess would return to her home country was uncertain.

Frankie poured lemon-cucumber water in tall glasses and shoved them at her crew. "We have to stay hydrated. I can't afford to lose any of you," she made light of the heat wave and strange illness that seemed to be its counterpart.

"I turned the AC on a couple hours ago, so it should be decent upstairs. Let's all get a couple hours of sleep. I have room for everyone." Frankie motioned them toward the stairs that led to her apartment above the shop.

Carmen nodded, prodding them along. "Tia and CeCe are coming in at six to load the pastry case and open up. They can handle things while we get a little rest."

"The real crowds won't show until Saturday anyway. I'm grateful you decided not to open on Monday, Frankie." Jovie spoke through a yawn.

"Memorial weekend is always a drain. We're already open Sunday, and I thought that was enough." Normally, only the wine lounge was opened on Sundays. "Extra hours open, extra hours laboring in the kitchen. We're going to need Monday to regroup." Frankie did relish the income the visitors brought to the shop, though.

Carmen gave Frankie a little poke with her thumb. "No rest for you though, Miss Wedding Planner." But Carmen's smile was tender. She and Frankie were lifelong friends since grade school, and she considered Sophie one of her own family.

~

At six-thirty a.m., Frankie pattered past a sleeping Carmen and slid open the glass door to her upper deck. The deck overlooked Sterling Creek, where Frankie saw birds gliding by, catching bugs for their first meal of the day. The air, already warm, held moisture, and the sun was blotted by a gray haze.

She called Sophie and left a message after her daughter didn't answer. She doubled up by sending a text too: *"Know anything about a mystery illness? Maybe heat related. Call me."*

Frankie dressed quietly, careful not to disturb Carmen in the living room recliner. Tess and Jovie were still asleep in Violet's bedroom. No sense in waking anybody yet.

Downstairs, Aunt CeCe was muttering in the kitchen, a clear indication she wasn't herself. She stared in disappointment at a pan of smoking macarons fresh from the oven. What should have been a tray of bright daffodil-yellow cookies were blackened mounds with jaundiced blotches. CeCe turned to march out the back door to toss them into the trash and stepped on Frankie's foot.

"Ow, watch out Aunt CeCe," Frankie stepped back, but offered her aunt an encouraging smile. "I see things are still topsy-turvy with you."

CeCe stomped outside and returned with the hot baking sheet, now empty of the offending macarons. "I just can't imagine why this is happening. There's bad energy in Deep Lakes. That's it."

Frankie scanned her aunt's garb of the day. A black apron replaced the flowered one she usually wore. Underneath the apron, a heather gray T-shirt peeked out over denim capris. Aunt CeCe looked dull as dishwater.

"For starters, I think you should go home and change clothes.

Where are your bright colors and florals? You don't look at all like my Aunt CeCe." Frankie chided.

CeCe puckered her lips and brow into a sorrowful scowl. "I'm feeling uninspired. Like a gray cloud."

Frankie encircled the woman in her arms and rocked her to and fro. "Even a gray cloud is inspired to drop rain. You'll find yourself again. Don't worry."

The older woman sighed heavily. "Thank you, sweetie. Meanwhile, it's a good thing Pepita is out there making sales. She's like a sparkling Moscato. Irresistible."

A rap on the back door ended the conversation. Jim, the delivery driver for Carr Valley Cheese, poked his head inside.

"I've got the rest of your order here from Tuesday. Can I just put it in the cooler?"

Frankie nodded and followed Jim to the cooler to point out places to stock the gouda, aged cheddar, and Havarti cheese blocks.

"Thanks for making a special trip back here, Jim." Carr Valley was over an hour's drive, and Frankie figured Deep Lakes wasn't on the Friday route.

"No problem at all. The Karlsens ordered more products, too, planning ahead for Mrs. Karlsen's funeral. Though, now I guess that's in limbo." Jim steadied the dolly with his foot.

"You mean the funeral's in limbo?" Frankie asked.

"Yeah. The body's been shipped from Outagamie County to Madison. I guess the doctors and scientists are studying it. So, the family has no idea when it, er she, will be released for the funeral."

Frankie paused, thinking. "Jim, has anyone around your area been sick or died from the heat?"

Jim shook his head. "Not that I've heard. And I'm sure I'd hear about it."

Frankie suspected Jim was right. Carr Valley delivered cheese all over the state. If anything was newsworthy, the drivers would spread the word.

"What are you hearing about our area? Besides Elsa's death, I mean." Frankie figured if the bird was chirping, she might as well pluck a few more feathers.

Jim leaned on the empty dolly, warming up to the idea of sharing information. "It's terrible really. I've heard people are dropping like flies all over Whitman County. It's been hot everywhere though, so there's something else going on around here. I'd be careful if I were you."

Jim's information wasn't helpful without more specifics. Frankie tossed aside the conversation like the burnt macarons and busied herself with baking and mentally organizing Sophie's wedding tasks.

A sticky note on her desk calendar glared at her. She'd meant to stop by the church office all week to pick up her check from the raffle drawing, but time had evaporated, and the task was still on her list.

The office wouldn't open until after morning Mass, so Frankie busied herself cleaning the rest of her office desk, which mostly consisted of scraps of paper with scribbled lists and reminders. She tacked the market list for Carmen to the bulletin board where it was visible, then counted the remaining RSVPs for Sophie's wedding dinner. She attached the sticky note with the caterer's phone number to her cell phone screen. Today was the day she needed to call in the final guest count, so the phone screen, which claimed her attention frequently, was the perfect spot for the note.

Her phone dinged as if on cue, reminding her of Freya's appointment at the vet next week. Freya was Garrett's intuitive Norwegian elkhound who had a hand, or paw, in the couple's initial meeting. Frankie imagined both the canine and her master were lonesome for one another, something Frankie understood too well. Freya was a guest at Coral Anders's Lovely Lavender Farm, because the dog was used to the countryside and because Coral had an elkhound, too. Lark and Freya were compatible playmates.

Frankie scrolled the phone calendar and chastised herself for not being more organized. If she could just consolidate her lists and tasks on the phone, she'd receive notifications and wouldn't have to rely on sticky notes. But Frankie loved keeping handwritten notes, so the phone became her backup plan.

Now she could hear chatter and music bouncing around the kitchen, so she assumed the other women were downstairs hard at work. She wandered through the swinging doors to announce she'd be running errands, but paused when she spied a perfect baking sheet of macarons.

"Those smell amazing, and they look beautiful, Aunt CeCe," Frankie pointed to the tray of shiny pink cookies, looking like tiny, delicate yo-yos.

Aunt CeCe was piping strawberry cream filling in the last couple of cookies and raised her smiling face to her niece. "You can thank Tess for these. She helped me get back on track. We're working on the lemon ones next."

Frankie mouthed a silent thanks across the counter to Tess, who nodded and bowed her head humbly. Same old Tess.

"I'll be back shortly. I'm off to the bank and St. Anthony's.

Anyone need anything while I'm out?" Frankie never tired of looking at the activity in the kitchen. The scents mingled with the music, and the bakers practiced their own dance moves, immersed in their tasks.

Jovie iced trays of Bismarck sweet rolls and butterhorns and mixed up more dough to proof overnight for the Sunday crowd. Carmen was out front helping Tia Pepita bag and box customer purchases.

When Frankie parked in the St. Anthony's lot, she noticed the black Amish buggy first and wondered what that was all about. Perhaps Georgia would be able to shed some light. Frankie pulled open the outer office door and found Georgia standing up at the counter, her finger to her lips asking for silence.

Only a large open entryway separated the reception area and inner office area, which didn't allow for any privacy unless people met behind closed doors in the individual offices. That wasn't the case today.

Frankie could hear a loud discussion between Bob, the building trustee, and Mike, the church accounting manager.

"It's not a priority right now. We have other projects already in the budget." Mike was speaking in a raised voice, as if he'd already made this point and now reiterated it.

"You've seen how disruptive they can be, Mike. The women and kids start to panic and the whole Mass is ruined." Bob was equally emphatic.

Frankie raised her brows and poked Georgia on the shoulder. "What are they talking about?" Frankie mouthed the words, but Georgia shushed her.

Now another man joined the discussion. "Your man here is right. They need to be relocated. Pretty soon, you're going to have more trouble on your hands. They're already having babies. It's going to be a mess up there and damage your building." The man spoke with a German accent.

Mike interrupted, a little louder. "I understand what both of you are saying, but I'm telling you that we can't do anything right now. We have to wait for a council meeting to authorize your work, and that's not happening until Father Donnelly is well again."

Georgia abruptly sat down when she heard footsteps coming. An Amish man stood behind Frankie, trying to worm his way past her to the counter.

"Excuse me, Madam." He cleared his throat loudly, and Frankie moved aside a few inches.

"I was told you have a check for me, Mrs." The Amish man was slightly built and wore wire-rimmed glasses. Frankie guessed he was in his thirties. He tapped the counter impatiently with a rugged hand. From past encounters with some men in the Amish community, Frankie remembered many didn't care to interact with women.

Georgia barely smiled and didn't make eye contact when she handed the man an envelope. "Yes, here you are." The usually gregarious Georgia was curt at best.

The man didn't respond, just opened the door, and left.

Frankie waited to say anything until she heard Bob and Mike go into an office and shut the door.

"What was that about?" she asked Georgia.

The secretary stood up again and leaned over the counter, ready to release the information she knew.

"That was Ian Yoder. We have a bat problem in the steeple. A whole colony of bats. With babies." Georgia sucked air through her teeth. Her animated head looked like it might topple during her delivery.

"Oh, I get it. The bats are ruining Mass because people are scared of them." Frankie reconstructed the conversation between the men. She remembered occasions when a stray bat hung out in church, causing a ruckus.

Georgia nodded. "And I agree with Bob. We need to do something before they ruin the steeple. It's just one more thing this church needs to handle." Georgia's breath came out in huffy spurts between sentences. Frankie remembered Georgia's concern about the kitchen ventilation.

"Well, Mike has a point though. The church council needs to decide what projects are a priority. There's only so much money to go around." She meant to be the voice of reason.

"Oh, but I guess we have money to treat the lawn. What a waste if you ask me." Georgia stepped back, hands on hips.

Frankie blinked and shrugged. "Treat the lawn?"

"Yesss," Georgia hissed. "That's what we just paid Ian Yoder to do. He sprayed the church grounds right before the festival."

Frankie comprehended. Many places were spraying this spring due to a huge influx of mosquitoes. "You mean for ticks and mosquitoes? The Swing Fest is a big moneymaker for the church, and a lot of it is outdoors. You can't expect people to put up with bugs, Georgia."

Georgia sat down with a thud and slumped in her chair. "I suppose that's true. But wouldn't you think a giant colony of bats could solve the mosquito problem?" She laughed a little, and Frankie joined in.

"How are Father and June? And the others?"

Changing the subject riled up Georgia all over again. "There's another thing. We get very little information from the hospital. It seems the families don't know anything either. They've all been quarantined in some way—the sick, I mean. The only person who really knows anything is Father Dailey, and he keeps everything under wraps."

"Quarantine? Has anyone explained why that is?" Frankie wondered if the mystery illness was contagious, and the heat was merely a contributing factor.

Georgia looked helpless. "I get so many phone calls every day asking about Father and June, and I don't have any answers to give out." She leaned over the counter again and whispered covertly, "I've heard there are a lot of sick people in our area, just our area, Frankie. Something's not right."

Frankie didn't know what to believe, but in her experience, she knew the rumors would continue to fly until real information came out. She decided to call Abe Arnold. The newspaper editor might be privy to information the rest of the county didn't have.

"I don't envy your position here, Georgia, so I hope things settle down soon for everyone's sake." Frankie turned to leave.

"Wait a minute, Frankie. Didn't you stop by to pick up your prize money? I have it right here." Georgia handed an envelope across the counter, smiling like an expectant feline.

Frankie held the envelope for a moment, then handed it back to Georgia. "I think the church needs this more than I do."

Georgia snatched the envelope back with a garish grin. "Your generosity will be noted, Frankie."

Frankie paused in the parking lot to tap Abe Arnold's contact information.

"Hey Champagne. I wondered when I'd be hearing from you. So, what do you know about this mystery illness and quarantine?" Abe wasn't pulling any punches.

"Funny, I called to ask you the same question. All I have are rumors. Pretty useless." Frankie confessed.

"Looks like we're going to have to ferret out the facts the hard way. Everyone in charge is tight- lipped as a kid waiting for the dentist to pull his tooth." Abe blew out a whistling breath. "I don't have a thing to go on, Champagne. I'm not even sure if our hospital is housing these patients."

Frankie sighed. "I promise to keep you in the loop, but Abe, Sophie's wedding is next Saturday, so don't expect me to do any snooping soon."

~

At three o'clock, Frankie peeled off her apron and chucked it in the laundry bin, then checked on Pom and Cherry in the wine lounge. Tess and CeCe were finishing the last of the macarons, more than enough to fill orders and last the weekend. Carmen had vacated at three with Tia Pepita. Frankie was torn between staying or finishing the border gardens at the vineyard.

"Go on and finish your flowers, Frankie. Everything will be fine here." Tess waved her arms to shoo Frankie away as if she were a large insect. "If we need you, we'll call. You're only a few miles away."

The sun had broken through the haze after lunch, bringing every land feature into sharp focus with its heat. In the vineyard, clusters of tiny green drops were becoming a new grape crop. Everything looked healthy, and Frankie hoped it would stay that way. Grapes demanded a balance of sunshine, heat, and rain to thrive, a trio growers called the magic triangle. Early rains could keep fruit from setting however, so timing was everything.

Frankie couldn't help but wonder about the triangle that bordered her relationship with Garrett. Did she have the power to keep Dani Edwards from raining on her romance? Frankie shoved a pansy plant a little too forcefully into the ground. Its golden blossom broke off, a perfect little flower face stared up at her from the dirt. How delicate this beautiful thing is, Frankie thought. She needed to be more careful.

Manny stepped out of the Frontenacs with his usual broad smile and upbeat mood. "I'm going to help you finish this project before you cook yourself, Frankie." He grabbed a flat of mixed plants and a trowel from the canvas tool bucket.

"Thank you, Manny. But it's Friday. You should be done for the week. Don't you have plans?" She couldn't imagine managing the vineyard without Manny Vega at the helm. He was the grape whisperer, dedicated to cultivating the vines, at home in the natural world.

"Not to worry, Boss. The party starts at nine. Plenty of time for me to help you." Manny turned and started digging holes, inhaling the rich scent of earth as he dug.

Frankie wondered if Manny had someone special in his life. He kept quiet about all things personal except for his love of music and gathering with friends to sing and play country and Spanish tunes.

The last few honey-sweet alyssum were settled into the borders on both sides, and Frankie pronounced the project complete with a simple, "There. Now grow." She fist-bumped Manny and turned on the soaker hose to bathe the soil in a good drink.

Manny picked up the tool bucket. "I'm going that way," he said, indicating the pole building near his office. "We're supposed to get rain on Sunday. If you like, I'll stop by tomorrow and water though."

Frankie was grateful. "That would be nice. Thank you. I'll stay here awhile and let them get a good soaking. Enjoy your party, Manny." Frankie was a little envious, imagining Manny and his friends enjoying the happy escape that comes from music.

She instantly felt guilty. She wasn't one to wallow in self-pity. Since she had an hour to kill while the water soaked the flowers, she might as well call Garrett. Hearing his voice would lift her droopy spirits.

Garrett's call went to voicemail. She left a chirpy message, then rang the hotel where he stayed to leave a message with the concierge, too.

"Superior Lofts. Johnny speaking. How may I help you?"

"Hello, this is Frankie Champagne. I'm a friend of one of your long-term guests, Garrett Iverson. Could I leave a message for him, please?"

"Of course. I can see him right now. He's at the pool. This time of day, you can pretty much count on him taking a swim break. It's his unwinding time. What message can I leave for him?"

Frankie paused. The call was spontaneous, and she hadn't planned out her message. "I'm sorry. Give me a minute to think."

"Take your time. I'm here." But Johnny was almost immediately distracted when Dani Edwards walked over to his desk.

"Just a moment please, I have a customer," he said to Frankie, then set the phone down.

"Well good afternoon, Ms. Edwards. It's good to see you. I assume you'd like a pool towel?" The good-natured Johnny was accommodating.

Frankie could hear the smooth cadence of Dani Edwards's

voice. "Thank you, Johnny, and the room service menu too, please."

Sweat mixed with garden soil trickled down Frankie's angry cheeks, followed by a flood of searing tears. She hung up the phone and sat down on the bench by the Frontenacs. She swallowed hard, bit back a second wave of tears, and began ranting.

"How dare you, Garrett Iverson! Hanging out at the pool with Dani Edwards when you're supposed to be working!" Her voice became shrill. A blue jay darted through the vineyard, cawing sharply.

"In fact, you're supposed to be here. Right here, planting flowers with me. With me. This is our project." She swore under her breath and kicked a loose stone near the walkway. "Room service…" Frankie kicked the air and stomped up the walkway toward the water spigot.

The spigot had two faucets, so she turned a lever and cold water flowed immediately from one side. She let it stream into her hands, where the grime ran in dark rivulets. When she could see clear water, she scooped handfuls of it, wet her face and poured it over her head. She didn't stop until she couldn't feel anymore, couldn't feel sad or angry or afraid of what might happen.

When she turned off the faucet, Manny was standing behind her.

"Frankie, how would you like to go to a party?" Manny grabbed her hand and twirled her around on the spot.

She laughed and couldn't stop. The soaking did her spirit a world of good, and a night of music with Manny and his friends might do the same.

CHAPTER EIGHT

Lead us not into temptation.
Just tell us where it is; we'll find it.

Sam Levenson

Saturday morning's alarm clanged like a fire engine siren next to Frankie's ears. She bolted out of bed before reality hit her like a sledgehammer. Thunder raged in her head, and she closed her eyes against it. She navigated to the bathroom by memory, fumbled through the medicine cabinet, and fought back a wave of nausea. She forced down the aspirin and ibuprofen chaser, then snatched a facecloth from the linen closet and ran cold water over it.

Frankie leaned heavily against the sink cabinet as the water poured loudly over the cloth and down the drain. She squeezed out the excess and headed to the living room to sit up in the recliner, the cold cloth pressed against her whole face. She was thankful for all the yoga hours she'd logged because the meditative breathing kept her from succumbing to her lurching stomach.

She couldn't remember the last time she'd had enough alcohol to feel hungover, but she knew it was BC, before children. Manny had called Carmen and Ryan to join the party and blessedly, they'd come and prevented her from drinking more.

There had been rollicking music, dancing, and so much delicious food, not to mention sangria that packed a wallop, made by Manny's cousin, Pancho. Pancho graciously delivered a few rounds of the stuff to Frankie, garnished with a wide grin and a contagious chuckle. Ryan had driven her home in her SUV with Carmen trailing behind.

Now Frankie opened one eye to check the time. It wasn't quite five a.m. Her body begged for another thirty minutes to ease into the day. If she could make it past a shower and be downstairs by six-thirty, she might survive. Cherry and Pom were running the shop, but Frankie needed to be ready to socialize during wine tastings by eleven, and she couldn't recall if there were baked goods waiting to be prepared or finished.

A second alarm sounded, a distant old-fashioned phone jangle. Her head jerked upward from her chest. Where was she? Oh yes, the living room. Carmen must have set two alarms in her honor. Good thing, too. She shuffled to the bedroom, shut off the alarm, and saw it was quarter after six. At least the storm in her head had subsided. She showered, dressed, and stumbled into the shop kitchen before seven.

Cherry smiled secretly when Frankie robotically donned a purple shop apron. Before she could crawl to the coffee maker, Cherry handed her a thermal mug with a cheeky grin.

"It's your favorite, an oat milk latte, two shots of espresso, honey, cinnamon, and a titch of lavender." Cherry pulled out a stool. "Why don't you sit a bit and absorb that coffee."

"Carmen called you, right?" Frankie asked, enjoying the first enticing sip of latte.

Cherry giggled. "She sure did. I'm glad you had a night out. It was good for you."

Frankie looked around the kitchen. The dough from the cooler was rolled out and cut into donuts, which were now resting on the far counter. A bowl of lemon icing sat waiting nearby and a delightful aroma was drifting from the oven.

"Cherry, did you make the donuts?" Cherry was a baking apprentice. She'd been learning to make simple recipes under the tutelage of Tess, Carmen, and Frankie, but hadn't gone solo yet.

Cherry beamed. "I did. These," she pointed to the ones resting on the counter, "are blueberry and there are lemon ones in the oven. I made the lemon icing with lemon juice and zest and plan to use it for both flavors."

Frankie clapped. "Well done and thank you."

The timer chimed, Cherry crossed her fingers for luck, and in a moment of truth, pulled the donuts from the oven. They were perfect, and Cherry let out the breath she didn't know she was holding.

"They're beautiful. Just right, Cherry. I can't wait to try one later." But Frankie's stomach tumbled a little at the thought of food, no matter how tempting it smelled.

Butterhorns were Frankie's signature sweet roll; she could almost make them in her sleep, so they were a good choice to ease into the day. Cherry encouraged her to go back to bed for a while, but Frankie said vertical was a better position for her queasy stomach.

Three trays of butterhorns later, Frankie tucked the sugary delights into the proofing drawer to rise, and she browsed the cooler for something safe to test her stomach. A sliced apple was just the candidate, and she ate it with peanut butter thinned with a little oat milk. A piece of whole grain toast rounded out the meal.

As she ate, she checked her phone for texts and calls, something she'd been putting off since last night. Now, however, she reminded herself that Sophie might have reached out. Nothing showed up from Sophie, but she had three missed calls from Garrett. Just the thought of talking to Garrett made her stomach do backflips.

Frankie hated conflict and avoided confrontations when they were too personal. Now, she needed to arm herself, but choose her words carefully. She ducked out the back door and sat on the bench near Sterling Creek.

"Miss Francine. I was beginning to worry about you," Garrett's cheerful voice held relief.

Frankie's chest thudded as a flood of emotions swept upward. All she wanted to do was tell this man how much she loved and missed him, but a damning doubt had cast a shadow over her.

"I guess you got my message," she spoke stiffly, careful to keep her tone even.

"I did. What's the matter, Frankie? I can hear it in your voice."

Might as well get it over with. "I called your hotel yesterday. The manager said you were at the pool. I heard him talking to Dani Edwards. She was there to get a towel and room service menu." The words came out in one long breath. She stopped to swallow a hard accusatory lump before continuing.

"What's going on up there, G? Are you involved with her?"

Garrett swore on the other end of the line.

"I'm not involved with Dani. I know it's hard for you to believe, but we are working. I don't take a day off because I want the detectives to make an arrest so I can come home. The pool is a respite. Swimming helps me clear my head."

Frankie could understand Garrett giving his all to the cases. She could understand that being stuck in a hotel wasn't easy, and that a pool would be a welcome distraction. What she couldn't understand was why the alluring Dani Edwards needed to visit him at his hotel, swim with him, eat room service. Tears slipped into the corners of her eyes, but she sucked in air to keep them at bay.

"I get it that you have to work with Dani, but spending time together at the hotel is dangerous, Garrett. You're lonely. She's beautiful. You have history. Don't expect me to be a fool." There, she'd said exactly what she'd wanted to say, direct and to the point.

Garrett felt his blood pressure rising and a knot of pure regret gnawed inside of him. What was he doing up here, and what price would he pay for it?

"Miss Francine. I'm so sorry. I don't intend to hurt you. And I'd never make a fool out of you. I don't know what to say. I thought we trusted each other."

Frankie's ire was ignited now. "Let's start with some honesty. Is Dani trying to make a play for you?"

Garrett swore again. "Yes, she is. Before you ask, I'm not encouraging it, and I'm not welcoming it. She knows better."

Frankie fumed but kept her temper in check. "I wonder. If she knows better, Garrett, why is she bothering? I don't want to talk about this anymore. How is the case going?"

Frankie's distrust was a disappointment, but Garrett buried it. "There haven't been any more victims, so that's good news. There's no definitive suspect though to make an arrest. Each one has an alibi for at least one or more of the murders."

Frankie could hear his frustration and imagined his face, tight and frowning. He truly cared about his work in forensic medicine and how it could make or break a criminal case. "Can you tell me about the victims?"

Garrett spent the next several minutes explaining the case to Frankie, sharing information about the victims, how they'd died from strangulation and were marked with the same object, which was thought to be a thick metal clip.

"We're calling him the Garden Killer because all the victims were found in different gardens or green areas around the city. Based on that, the police are looking at delivery people: mail, furniture, appliance truck drivers, and the like. Anyone who habitually uses straps and clips. It's the common denominator. The victims don't know each other and don't seem to have a connection, except they're all female, all about the same size and age, all physically fit."

"Maybe the detectives need to think outside the box. A lot of different people use straps and clips. Could be someone with a small business or even a hobby." She switched topics. "Anyway, we have our own mystery happening here." Frankie figured it was time to share the news being batted around the county.

"Has Alonzo called you about any of the victims?"

"No, I haven't heard from him. Are autopsies being ordered, Frankie?"

"Yes," she hesitated, wondering if it was a good idea for Garrett to be caught between two fronts. "Lon said they're using the Outagamie and Vandenberg coroners. Rumor has it at least one of the dead was shipped to Madison to the ME."

"I promise I'll keep you posted if I hear more," she quickly added. "G, just focus on the cases in front of you. Then get your butt home."

An honest phone call, Frankie surmised, but the tension had softened. Still, every time Dani's face materialized in Frankie's mind, she wanted to slap it.

CHAPTER NINE

*Live in the sunshine,
swim in the sea, drink the wild air.*

⚬

Ralph Waldo Emerson

The Memorial weekend zeal dwindled to lethargy by Sunday afternoon. Swarms of tourists, many with cranky children, had taxed the Bubble & Bake crew. The Memorial parade, held on Sunday at noon rather than the typical Monday celebration, ushered in even more customers downtown.

"I know we should be grateful to the chamber of commerce for capitalizing on the holiday, but Sunday afternoon tourists can be a handful," Frankie grumbled, after serving a third pitcher of wine slushies to a clan of eight on the deck.

Carmen stood at the wine lounge bar, mixing a pitcher of berry slushies for Pom to take to a table of six in the lounge. Between the deck and the lounge, the place was standing room only. Indeed, Peggy and Jovie teamed up to maneuver tastings for half the bar, while several more customers waited behind the tasters for their turns.

"Tell me about it. I lost count of how many slushies I've mixed up." Carmen winced from shoulder pain brought on by the constant stirring motion. "Next year, we're getting a machine."

Pom cut between the two women to retrieve unopened bottles of Dark Deeds and Spring Fever Riesling. "Tips are really good today," her voice was a happy singsong lilt. "And sales are amazing." She pulled corks from the two bottles and scampered back to the tasters.

Carmen and Frankie exchanged weary smiles. "I guess we shouldn't complain," Frankie said.

Carmen nodded, but her expression turned sour when she saw a large group of customers near the front window. They had pushed two tables together to accommodate the four adults and four children. While the adults enjoyed wine and conversation, the kids were playing with the wooden figures carved by Frankie's father. The nisses and animals were meant to be living unscathed in the woodland scenes Frankie concocted throughout the shop. Unfortunately, the children were thumping them against the picture window, their hands grubby with pastry icing.

Frankie noticed Carmen was stirring furiously and followed her glare to the table. Carmen was a no-holds-barred woman, having grown up in a supersized family where any auntie or uncle might correct an unruly child.

"I've got this." Frankie retrieved colors and coloring pages from a cupboard under the bar, which she kept on the rare occasion children visited the lounge with inattentive parents. She grabbed a few wet wipes and scooted over to the table.

"Hello there. I'm Frankie Champagne, one of the owners

here." She had to wave and talk loudly to get the adults to notice. She wondered how much wine they'd already consumed.

A perky blonde smiled with little interest. "Oh, hi. We're enjoying your wines." She didn't appear to notice what Frankie carried, even when she held them out to the woman.

"I couldn't help but notice your children. They must have liked the donuts." She pointed at the smeared window. "I brought some wet wipes to make clean up easier. And colors and coloring pages to give them something to do." While Frankie spoke, she gathered the loose wooden carvings and slipped them in her apron pocket.

"If I could just have the carvings, please, I'll take them to the kitchen for a bath."

The perky blonde looked at her husband. "Ew, get those dirty things away from the kids, would you? I can't imagine how many germs are on those." The man obliged, handing the figurines to Frankie with a grimace.

"Thank you. I'll get some more wipes for your table. Would you like to order any food? We have a small menu, but it goes nicely with wine and might counter the sugary treats." Frankie handed the man a menu from the stand near the window.

The blonde made a face, either insulted by Frankie's attempt to correct her children or to coerce her to spend more money in Frankie's establishment.

Frankie left them to peruse the menu, then returned with more wet wipes. The man thanked her but said they needed to be somewhere else. He handed the menu back to Frankie without looking her in the eye.

As the day wore on, many more customers came and went. The deck was never empty thanks to a gentle breeze from

Sterling Creek and moderate temperatures. The cloudy skies indicated rain might arrive later, but the clouds went unnoticed. Even on a holiday weekend, the small town had few activities for tourists who didn't want to hike, bike, boat, or fish. The winery crowd didn't hesitate to bring their kids with them and expected them to occupy themselves while they imbibed. Some brought along grandparents to entertain their charges. As many of them as possible squatted on the deck, which dispersed the noise and made cleaning up easier.

When five o'clock arrived, the deck was still half occupied, but the loungers were checking out with their merchandise thanks to Carmen's encouragement.

"Who's going out to the deck to announce closing? Or do you want me to do it?" Carmen's announcement would be a bull horn.

"I already told each table a half hour ago, and again ten minutes ago," Frankie said.

"Yeah, well, you're too nice about it. Follow me." Carmen dramatically pointed toward the deck door.

She walked directly to the small stage where musicians played on Friday nights, stomped loudly up the wooden steps, and wolf whistled like a cowgirl rounding up cattle. The din of chatting customers stopped abruptly.

"Sorry people, but you have to go. Vamanos. It's past closing time. The cops will be here to check people." Carmen smiled wickedly. Frankie shuddered. It was a good ploy to make people leave by thinking they might get breathalyzers, but she didn't want it to backfire.

Frankie funneled the parade of customers back into the shop by thanking them for coming and supporting a small business.

She hoped a few would buy a bottle or two of wine before leaving, but her face drained of color when she spotted Alonzo, in uniform, sitting at the wine bar. The customers noticed, too, and quickly evacuated the shop as if a plague had been released.

Frankie slugged the sheriff on the arm. "Good timing."

Alonzo laughed. "Was it something I said?" It wasn't the first time his presence cleared a venue. "

Not you. It was Carmen." Frankie explained Carmen's performance on the deck.

Alonzo high-fived Carmen. "Nice work. I know you're closing, but I wondered if we could talk."

Pom locked the shop doors behind the last customer and went to grab cleaning supplies. Peggy was right behind her to retrieve a broom and dustpan. The crew knew the closing routine well and shared the chores that came after heavy traffic in the shop.

Frankie and Carmen wiped down the bar and met in the middle. Carmen paused in front of Alonzo, arching one eyebrow. "Should I leave?" She asked.

Lon pushed two dirty tasting glasses toward her. "Nope. Matter of fact, I have a proposal for both of you."

Frankie turned away from the chiller where she'd lifted out bottles of uncorked wine usually consumed by the crew after hours. "Are you off duty?"

When Lon nodded, she tossed him a Spotted Cow, his favorite beer.

"Here, occupy yourself while we clean up."

Cleaning was made easier with a full staff, but it still took an hour mopping and sanitizing. Finally, Carmen took on the sticky frosting smeared on the picture window, muttering in

Spanish as she made the window shine again. Frankie gently scrubbed her father's carved figures in the bar sink, giggling at Carmen's annoyance. Without looking up, she said quietly to Lon, "It's hard to believe Carmen ever had children of her own. She has a special intolerance for the little boogers."

"I heard that, Frankie. Not funny. I can't believe that some parents think it's okay to bring their kids to public places to make messes." Carmen finished her speech with more Spanish curses.

Peggy set a platter and small plates on the bar by Alonzo before joining Jovie, Pom, and Cherry gathered in an alcove in the lounge with leftover quiche.

"Thanks, Mom. Pick your poison." Frankie pointed to the half-empty wines standing on the bar.

Peggy scrutinized her options. "The Spring Fever, Midsummer Picnic, and Summer Sundown."

Spring Fever was a stock favorite and one of the first vintages from Bountiful Fruits Vineyard. Made with Le Crescent grapes, which mimic German Riesling grapes, the wine finishes crisp with notes of vanilla, lemon, and lavender. Midsummer Picnic, a new white vintage bottled in March, combined a blend of St. Pepin and Edelweiss grapes with strawberries, watermelon, and rosewater for a unique drinking experience. Customers either raved about it or despised its robust flavors. Summer Sundown was Frankie's new favorite red blend, an easy wine to drink with almost everything.

Peggy grabbed the bottles and a chiller container. "I'll be back for glasses." She stage-whispered to Frankie: "We'll just be busy talking over there, loud enough not to hear you."

Frankie snickered, picked up four glasses and followed her

mother to the corner alcove.

"Can we turn the music back on, Frankie?" Pom asked, elbowing her sister.

"Oh, by all means, please do." She rolled her eyes and returned to the bar.

Alonzo had already finished his first beer and piece of quiche and was tucking into a second slice. He tilted the empty bottle toward Carmen. "I'll have another one of these if you got one."

Carmen set the beer in front of him, then settled slices of quiche on two plates for herself and Frankie.

"Here's to a profitable weekend." Carmen clinked her glass of Persephone's Temptation, a pomegranate zinfandel, with Frankie's.

"What's up, Alonzo?" Frankie was intrigued since the sheriff, albeit a longtime friend, hadn't asked Frankie for a favor in ages. The fact this favor involved her and Carmen made her wonder. Did the sheriff need some matchmaking help pursuing Ashley Turner?

Unexpectedly, Lon handed Frankie a piece of paper and a pen. "You're going to want to write down some of this."

"This sounds like business. Official business?" Frankie looked skeptical.

"It is," he said quietly. "Harry Graham's farm shares a property line with an Amish family on the south side. That family lost the mother and two other members from whatever illness is going around. There's more." He paused to take a drink. "The next property over—also owned by the Amish. Two dead adults in the family, the older grandparents. Same symptoms of the crud. Based on the timeline, they might be the first victims."

Carmen shook her head and tsked. Frankie outlined the

information in blurbs. "Seems like older people are the ones more often affected," she commented.

Lon shook his head. "These Amish grandparents are in their fifties. Of course, they won't allow autopsies or even medical treatment as far as we know. Makes it hard to get to the bottom of it." He wrinkled his nose in disgust.

"Do you have the Amish families' names?" Frankie relied on personal details as a matter of routine.

"The Shumakers are on the south end, behind the Graham farm, on Tenth Road. The Yoder farm is next to the Graham place on HH."

Frankie inhaled sharply at the Yoder name, wondering if these Yoders were related to the Yoder she'd just seen at St. Anthony's.

"Do you have any autopsy information on Elsa Karlsen or Harry Graham?" Frankie had easily slipped into journalist mode.

Alonzo noticed. "I do. This is not for publication, Frankie. Both died from asphyxiation complicated by blood poisoning."

Frankie gasped. "That doesn't sound like natural causes or heat related. What does the medical examiner make of that?" Then she gasped again. "What about Father Donnelly, June Thompson, and the others? Do they have signs of blood poisoning?"

Lon downed the rest of the bottle and waved away the offer of a third. He spoke low in a tone indicating bad news. "Yes, and they're not responding to treatment so far. Some of the worst are in medically induced comas to slow down the trauma."

Carmen was growing impatient. "What does this have to do with us?"

Alonzo took a deep breath and leaned forward. "I'd like you to quietly investigate. Go out to the Amish properties and make friends. They're suspicious of cops, but you two know how to talk to people. Make nice with the women and see what you can find out."

Carmen narrowed her eyes at Lon, then looked at her business partner to gauge her reaction. Frankie looked thoughtful and a small smile played across her face.

"I'm willing to try if you are, Carmie."

---

CHAPTER TEN

*A little simplification would be the
first step toward rational living, I think.*

Eleanor Roosevelt

Monday arrived with a chilly drizzle and low-lying fog along the river and lakes. Frankie and Carmen agreed to convene early at the shop, visit the Amish families, and use the rest of the day to relax and recover.

"Honestly, I don't see why you couldn't put this off until after Sophie's wedding, Frankie. You don't have the time to sleuth this week." Carmen scolded.

"And miss the chance to investigate with Alonzo's blessing? You've got to be kidding. It would be the last time he ever asked me for help. No, it's our civic duty, Carmen." Frankie raised her right hand as if a Bible had materialized for her to swear an oath.

Carmen blinked twice. "Okay friend, what's your plan?"

"The plan is to go next door and talk to Rachel. She often deals with the Amish community, so she'll have some pointers."

The two slipped on rain jackets and scooted next door. Rachel saw them pass the window and was ready to let them in.

"What brings you two out today? I thought you were closed." Rachel resumed restocking skeins of yarn by weight and color.

"Carmen and I have decided to start getting eggs from the Amish. We're going out there this morning to talk to them and see if there's anything else we might want from them. Honey, maybe." Frankie gave Carmen the nod and knowing eye, as if this were the plan all along.

Rachel paused, tucked some soft gray alpaca yarn into a special display rack and looked over her shoulder at Frankie. "Have you done business with the Amish before?" She smiled widely and shook her head of dark curls to answer her own question. "You haven't, and that's why you want to pick my brain."

She stepped away from the display case and motioned them to the back wall of the shop. "The Amish like to barter. They want to see if you can be trusted. If you haven't done business with them before, that's the starting point."

Carmen balked. "We don't have anything to barter. They make their own pastries, and I don't think they drink wine."

Rachel held up one hand. "That's why you need what I have. Just a minute." She dashed into the back room and came out with a large box filled with scrap fabric.

"Here. Now you have something to barter. I save all the usable fabric scraps when I fill orders, or the ladies leave them behind from their sewing projects. The Amish love getting scraps for quilts and doll clothes."

Carmen and Frankie drove down County HH, with their newfound knowledge and box of scraps, toward the Graham property and neighboring Amish farms.

En route, they almost passed the Graham farm, but Frankie hit the brakes at the last second.

"Ay, what's the problem?" Carmen gave the seatbelt a yank after it locked up at the sudden stop.

"Look over there. That's the Graham farm. There's an Amish buggy in the driveway. I think we should stop here first."

Carmen rolled her eyes and turned to point at Frankie's head. "I don't know what's cooking up there, but I guess we're about to find out."

Besides the Amish buggy, a pickup truck and SUV were parked in the driveway near the house. Frankie and Carmen walked toward the front door when someone called out to them from the driveway that led to the barn.

"Hello, can I help you ladies?" A middle-sized man dressed in jeans and a denim shirt walked toward them.

Carmen froze, but Frankie proceeded to the man and held out her hand in introduction. "Yes, I'm Frankie Champagne. I own the bakery in town."

"Alex Graham. Sorry, I'm not familiar with you or your business, Ms. Champagne." Frankie guessed Alex was about her age but hadn't gone to school in Deep Lakes.

"This is my business partner, Carmen Martinez. Are you related to Harry Graham?" She planned to delay her reason for stopping there until she could come up with something.

"Yes. Harry was my father. I'm going through the barn and equipment shed to get things ready to sell." He looked at the women quizzically.

"My condolences about your father, Mr. Graham. I'm guessing you didn't go to school in Deep Lakes?"

"Thank you. We're still trying to adjust to Dad not being here. And no, I went to school in Zeeland. We're just over the district line. Is there something I can do for you two?" Alex Graham shrugged his shoulders upward to his ears in the dismal drizzle. "Why don't we get out of the rain. Follow me."

The three entered the barn, which was much warmer and blessedly dry. "That's better. Now…"

"I'm sorry to intrude, but we're looking for the Yoder and Shumaker farms. We saw the buggy in the driveway and stopped to see if they might be here." Frankie wore a genuine smile.

Alex shrugged. "Some of the neighbors have come by on and off to check on my mother and bring her food, so maybe they're from the families you're looking for."

Frankie nodded. "Thanks. Is it okay if we go up to the house?" The drizzle turned into a sudden rain shower. "Or when the rain stops, that is."

Alex nodded. "Sure. Do you know my mother? I'm trying to look out for her. She's very fragile right now."

Carmen inched next to Frankie and pinched her elbow from behind, making her jump.

"We're sorry to intrude, Mr. Graham. And I know firsthand how busy you must be trying to run the farm without your father." Carmen's last few words were a stinging reprimand toward Frankie.

"Oh, are you a farmer Ms. Martinez?"

"Please. It's Carmen. And yes, my husband and I run a sheep farm. Thankfully, our sons help out, and we have hired hands. But it looks like you're on your own here." Carmen noticed no other farm trucks or people working nearby.

Alex took off his ball cap, ran fingers through his receding hairline, and pushed the hat back on. "You said it. I'm no farmer. My dad was slowing down. He's been getting ready to sell this place for a couple of years. He only has two fields planted this year, and I doubt they'll bring in enough cash to make it worthwhile."

"Do you mind me asking what you do for a living, Mr. Graham?" Frankie asked.

"Call me Alex. Dad wanted me to be a farmer, but the best I could do was go into the business side of agriculture. I'm a marketing analyst. I like numbers better than dirt." He snickered.

Frankie better understood Alex Graham's comment about the crops not yielding much profit.

"I'm guessing you don't live around here. What are you going to do about this year's crop?" Frankie nosed into the subject.

Alex's shoulders slumped. "I live in Chicago, downtown. I'm going to talk to the Amish neighbors and see if one of them will tend the crops for half the profit. I want my mother to get something out of the deal."

Frankie brightened. "There's no shortage of Amish farmers around, and I hear they like to barter." Carmen nodded enthusiastically.

Alex appeared hopeful. "Maybe I should have you two around when I go talk to them."

The rain shower wound down to a spitting drizzle again. "Looks like the rain's mostly stopped. You two go ahead to the house. My sister, Lindsay, will probably answer the door. She's trying to sort through the household stuff with our mom."

Frankie wanted to explore the barn and ask a million questions about where Harry was found and if any of them had ideas about why and how he died, but every time she opened her mouth, Carmen nudged her closer to the house with a few shoves.

A tall woman dressed in business casual opened the door. Her dark hair was beauty salon polished, and she wore subtle makeup for a finished look. "Hello. May I help you?"

Frankie and Carmen introduced themselves and said they hoped to speak with their Amish visitors.

"Please come in. I'll see if these are the women you're looking for. They're talking with my mother on the back deck. I'm Lindsay James. Donna's daughter."

Lindsay must have been about the same age as Alex. She was poised, with a refined accent that made Frankie wonder if she'd moved much further afield from Wisconsin.

"We're both sorry about the loss of your father, Ms. James. I know it was sudden."

Lindsay's expression was troubled. "Yes, it certainly was. I worry about my mother. She doesn't have a lot of friends or family around. Alex's career keeps him in Chicago and my home is in North Carolina. I'm trying to convince her to move by me. The winters would be much easier for her."

An older woman came into the kitchen with two Amish women trailing behind her in everyday black dresses, their hair in tight buns under bonnets.

Donna Graham looked tired but healthy. Her tanned arms and neck and pink cheeks pointed to a woman who spent a lot of time outdoors, and it looked good on her. She wore her dark silver hair in a cute pixie that moved slightly when she held out both of her hands in greeting.

"I'm Donna Graham. I see you've met both of my children. And now I have the pleasure."

Frankie and Carmen each reached out a warm hand to Donna and said hello.

"Mom, these women want to speak with our visitors." Lindsay nodded toward the Amish women, who looked down at the linoleum.

"Oh, I see. Well, here they are. Joanna Yoder and Emma Dunkel." She politely indicated each woman as she said their names.

Frankie and Carmen exchanged awkward looks, wondering what to say next.

"May we wait for you outside?" Frankie suggested. "Mrs. Graham, we're so sorry to hear about your husband, and I apologize for showing up empty-handed. Next time I drive out this way, I'll bring something for you from Bubble & Bake."

Donna smiled sweetly. "And I'm sorry I've never been to your shop. I get to Zeeland more often than Deep Lakes, I'm afraid. Most of my baked goods come from my Amish neighbors. I'd love it if you stopped by again. It gets lonely out here." She sniffled, fighting tears.

Frankie and Carmen promised to return. Inwardly, both women were plotting ways to involve Donna in the community.

Joanna and Emma followed Frankie and Carmen out the door and gathered around the blue SUV. They looked more curious than puzzled.

"Do we know each other?" Joanna, who looked older by a few years, took the lead.

"No. We've never met, but as you heard me say to Mrs. Graham, we have a bakery in Deep Lakes. We're looking for an egg supplier, and we're hoping you know someone who could provide us with ten dozen eggs a week?" It wasn't an outright lie.

In fact, the Bubble & Bake crew had discussed switching to farm fresh eggs for the past year or so but hadn't taken the time to do it.

Joanna smiled. "I think my cousin and his family could. It's the Gabriel Shumaker farm. They live just over that way from our farm." Joanna pointed backward, beyond the Graham barn. "I can give you the address."

"That would be wonderful, thank you, Mrs. Yoder. Are you two related, may I ask?"

Joanna giggled. "People think that, but we're not. Emma and I are neighbors and friends. We help each other out when we can."

Carmen opened the back of the SUV and pulled out the box of fabric scraps. "Can you use these fabric pieces? Neither one of us make quilts, so we were hoping to find a home for them."

Joanna and Emma feasted upon the fabrics, picking up pieces to examine them and exclaiming over colors and patterns they admired. Emma stepped back from her fawning and came to attention.

"We can't just take them from you without giving you something in exchange. We have just butchered chickens and made maple syrup. Would that do?"

"Sounds perfect," Frankie and Carmen echoed.

"If you follow the buggy to our homes, we will get them for you." Joanna headed to the driver's side of the buggy, and Frankie and Carmen puttered along behind them in the SUV.

The Yoder farm was just down the road, easily recognizable by its large white wooden two-story house and children dressed in blue, brown, or black playing in the yard. Two tots were chasing chickens around, giggling loudly after the clucking birds.

Joanna stepped quickly out of the buggy and called out to a girl of around twelve who was playing with or supervising the children, perhaps both.

"Alice, take Thaddeus and go to the icehouse. Bring back two of the dressed chickens. Be sure they're large ones."

Joanna turned toward Frankie and Carmen. "Please wait here while I go inside. Emma, come help me, please."

Frankie and Carmen amused themselves watching the little kids chase each other around the grass. There were four in all, and they looked to be like stair steps in age.

"How old do you think Joanna is? She doesn't look thirty," Frankie guessed.

"A lot of the Amish girls are married before they turn sixteen. I bet she's only in her twenties."

Joanna and Emma were back and walking toward the SUV with their goodies.

Frankie opened the back hatch and removed the box of fabric pieces. In its place, Joanna set two jugs of maple syrup. Emma carried a carton of four dozen eggs and set them on the back seat floor.

"You have to try the eggs before you decide you want to buy them," Emma explained.

Carmen and Frankie protested. "This is too much in trade. Let us pay for the eggs," Carmen insisted.

Before they could answer, Alice and Thaddeus were back with two large, butchered chickens in plastic bags with ice pieces stuck to them. The children carried them by the knotted bag tops, each bragging they had the heaviest bird.

Frankie and Carmen thanked the two and set the chickens on the floor next to the eggs.

"Are all these children yours, Joanna?" Frankie didn't mind overstepping.

Joanna smiled. "No. Alice and Thaddeus are my cousins. They come over to help in the summer when there's a lot of gardening to do. Those four are mine." She nodded toward the smaller children playing in the grass.

"I'm sorry I couldn't let you in the house, but my oldest is sick." Joanna studied the other children, as if looking for signs of illness. "Well, I should be going inside now. Please come again."

Frankie and Carmen thanked Joanna as Emma turned and began walking toward the road.

Frankie caught up to Emma to see if they could drive her home.

Emma blushed. "No, thank you. I live just there." She pointed across the road toward the left. Then her voice dropped to a whisper. "But please meet me at my house. I have something for you."

Frankie wrinkled her nose, wondering why Emma was being secretive. She walked back up the driveway where Carmen and Joanna were deep in conversation about tending sheep.

"When I come to pick up eggs, I'll bring you some raw wool or yarn, or both," Carmen promised. Joanna clapped in delight.

The SUV backed down the driveway and Frankie turned left.

"Emma wants us to stop at her house. She was acting cagey." Frankie raised her brows rapidly toward Carmen.

"Oh yeah. I'm sure the young Amish lady is a spy, or maybe an FBI agent, Frankie."

Frankie saw the Dunkel farm and turned in, leaving her snappy comeback unspoken. Emma stood on the front porch of the white house, a near twin to the Yoder farmhouse. She waved them over.

Frankie spied a wicker basket sitting on the floor next to Emma. Inside, a fluffy gray and white cat was trying to catch a nap while several kittens squirmed around her. Frankie hoped Emma wasn't offering the basket of cats to them, although she'd probably take one to be a guest at the shop.

"I wanted to give you some of our asparagus. It's a bumper crop this year," Emma smiled, pleased with herself.

The women noticed how quiet the Dunkel yard was, and both wondered if Emma was a newlywed.

"Do you have children, Emma?" Frankie wasn't afraid to find out.

Emma blushed and lowered her eyes. "I've just gotten married in April," she said, "but…" she bit off the rest of the sentence, making Frankie think Emma might be newly pregnant.

Emma went inside and motioned the other women to follow. The house smelled of fresh polished wood, new and welcoming. The plank floors gleamed in the great room where six large windows allowed sunbeams to pour in. A long trestle table covered in a white cloth sat near a modern black woodstove and gas-powered refrigerator. An abundance of cupboards stood in line against one wall, top and bottom, with a wooden counter between them, and a deep farmhouse sink sat in the middle with a water pump at the ready.

Emma motioned the women toward the massive porcelain sink where a bright green pile of asparagus spears was assembled. There must have been twenty pounds or more. Frankie and Carmen gasped appreciatively.

"I was in the middle of cleaning these when Joanna came by. They're tasty, too. Let me get you some." Emma stooped to grab a plastic pail from below the sink and began filling it with plump green spears.

"Really, this is so kind of you. We didn't come here expecting all this." Frankie gushed.

Without looking up from her work, Emma quietly asked, "Why did you come out here? I get the feeling there's more to your visit."

Frankie inhaled sharply and glanced at Carmen to gauge her reaction. Carmen smirked, impressed that the young woman was a sharp cookie.

Frankie smiled. "We are interested in buying eggs for our bakery, Emma, but you're right. There's more to it than that. We're worried about people getting sick and dying, like Harry Graham, and Elsa Karlsen, one of our church friends." She didn't want to give away too much.

Emma's eyes widened. She gazed out the window briefly, maybe to make sure there wasn't anyone else in earshot.

"I know about the illnesses. Mr. Graham isn't the only person around here who died. Some of our people died, too. The Yoder grandparents, on Joanna's husband's side, for starters. We're not supposed to share that information with outsiders." Emma looked out the window again.

"My husband will be in soon from the fields," she spoke rapidly. "Joanna's son has the illness. He's having trouble breathing and is lethargic."

Carmen frowned. "How long has he been sick?"

Emma held up three fingers. "Three days. We have a doctor here, so he's being cared for."

"Has your doctor found out what's going on? Has he been able to treat the illness successfully?" Frankie didn't hold the opinion that western medicine had all the right answers. She knew many home remedies worked well for certain ailments.

Emma shrugged. "The men talk about it. We're not involved in those conversations." She hurriedly scribbled something on a piece of paper and handed it to Frankie.

"If you want to know more, you should talk to her." She pointed to the paper. "Sarah Van Cleef is my sister-in-law. That's her address and telephone number. She left our community to marry an outsider."

Emma handed the pail of asparagus to Frankie. "You should probably go now. I hope to see you both again."

Carmen and Frankie loaded the asparagus in the back, but not before a young Amish man, wearing dark blue, approached them from behind the house.

"What do you want here, may I ask?" The young man had a pleasant enough face trimmed with a broom-like brown beard, but his beady eyes penetrated the two women.

Frankie smiled pleasantly and looked down demurely at the man's work boots, covered in soil. "We just met your wife at the Grahams' house. We came to pay our respects and hope to become egg customers of the Shumakers."

"Huh. Well, I see. I hope my Emma was helpful then." Without waiting for a response, Mr. Dunkel walked to the house.

"Nicely played, Frankie," Carmen commented. "So much for our afternoon of relaxation, though. I guess we're going to visit Sarah Van Cleef."

CHAPTER ELEVEN

There is a way that nature speaks, that land speaks.
Most of the time we are simply not patient enough,
quiet enough, to pay attention to the story.

Linda Hogan

The drive to Zeeland on the back roads was only a few miles past a series of Amish farms and businesses.

"I didn't realize how much property the Amish owned over here," Carmen exclaimed. "It seems like their community has exploded."

Frankie pointed at a few empty acres along the way in contrast. "Yes, but a lot of these fields are empty, which makes me wonder if there's vacant land for sale out here. The Amish have a resourceful network. Once property is on the market, they contact relatives and friends to purchase it and extend their community."

The speed limit sign announced twenty-five miles per hour ahead and soon the SUV rolled into the small town of Zeeland, a quiet community settled mostly by Dutch immigrants. Two Dutch Reformed churches occupied prominence on the main street, along with a few shops, a diner, and convenience store. Zeeland was mainly an agricultural town where two canning factories from competing companies offered the most employment, that is, until the ethanol plant was erected on the outskirts. Many area farmers now sold their corn to the plant, making bigger profits than before.

Sarah Van Cleef's home was on the hilly end of town on Vermeer Drive which curved upward toward the town's water tower. Sarah was expecting them and waved from the open front porch of a Dutch colonial house, gray with a red shingled gambrel roof.

Frankie guessed Sarah was in her forties but there were no remnants of Amish style present in her appearance. Her dark hair was cut in an uneven textured shag with tawny streaks throughout, and she wore denim capris with a brightly striped smock shirt and open-toed sandals.

"Hello, I'm glad Emma sent you to talk with me." Sarah's greeting indicated a woman eager to spill the beans. "Follow me out to the backyard, and we'll talk on the patio."

The rain had stopped but the sky was layered in thick gray clouds, threatening to shower them. The stone patio overlooked a huge vegetable garden bordered on all sides by a willow fence with a gate. Flowers surrounded the outer fence in a riot of colors and sizes.

Fresh picked zinnias and lilies adorned the patio table where Sarah placed a pitcher of lemonade and a plate heaping with sugar cookies.

"Please sit here. Are you two with a newspaper or TV station?"

Sarah looked from Carmen to Frankie, who stared back in surprise.

"We own Bubble & Bake bakery and wine lounge in Deep Lakes, actually, but I work as a part- time reporter for *Point Press* in Stevens Point," Frankie leveled with Sarah.

"Have you spoken with other reporters?" Carmen wondered if Sarah was more gossip than reliable source, anxious to speak with the press for fifteen minutes of fame.

Sarah smiled thinly. "Oh no, I've avoided them. Madison sent a TV reporter here right after my husband died, but I wouldn't talk to him."

Frankie and Carmen exchanged puzzled looks. "Let's back up a minute, please," Frankie said. "Did you say your husband died?" Emma Dunkel hadn't mentioned that.

"Yes. My husband John passed away last weekend. I'm still waiting to bury the poor man." Sarah's blue eyes were downcast.

"We're sorry. We didn't mean to intrude. Emma didn't tell us that your husband died when she suggested we talk with you. I believe she meant for us to ask you about the deaths in the Amish community." Frankie tried to right the course of the conversation.

Sarah brightened a little. "Emma is a sweetheart, and I'm fortunate that her husband, my brother Simon, allows me to visit her. I suppose she told you that I married an outsider. I'm no longer part of the Amish way of life."

"How long have you been away from the community, if you don't mind my asking?" It was Carmen's turn for a bold inquiry.

Sarah poured lemonade and passed the cookie plate around. "I was married to an Amish man, but it turned out I couldn't have children, so he wanted to replace me. At that time, our bishop demanded I ask him for a divorce. I knew a divorce meant I would have to leave the community, which was okay with me. I'd seen too much hypocrisy by that time. I guess I'm a rebel at heart. I moved to Zeeland and worked in the canning factory. That's where I met John, who was the manager there. He was much older than me, but kind and open-minded. He saw my craving for education and offered to pay for college classes. I dabbled in lots of areas and finally got a horticulture degree. We married twelve years ago."

Sarah paused and swept her hands toward the garden and backyard landscaping. "My life's work."

"You're certainly an accomplished gardener. Everything is lush and lovely," Frankie declared. "We're both so sorry about your husband. Do you want to tell us what happened?"

Sarah nodded. "It goes back to the Amish community. The Yoders are cousins to the Shumakers, who are shirttail relatives of the Dunkels. All of them live on or near County HH. The Yoders have the biggest family in the area, and they were the first to lose people. One set of grandparents came down with breathing problems and collapsed while they were working outside. They couldn't be revived."

"Did anyone let the county know? Or call for an autopsy?" Frankie had to ask.

Sarah snorted and threw her head back. "Of course not. Amish people are rarely autopsied. If someone dies, it's God's will and families must bear the suffering as best they can. Most Amish doctors do not work with English doctors."

The women knew the term English was commonly used by the Amish to mean outsiders.

"When Lydia Shumaker became afflicted, I went to see her.

Lydia and I grew up together and she used to take care of me because she was a few years older. I followed her around everywhere. Anyway, Lydia struggled to breathe and was bedridden. Her skin was ashen. The Amish doctor prescribed tea and natural remedies. I watched her die."

Sarah choked on the last sentence. Instinctively, Carmen and Frankie reached out to comfort the woman.

"How sad for you and her family," Frankie murmured.

"Yes. Lydia had nine children. I was allowed to attend the funeral as long as I stayed in the background and dressed appropriately. Two of her littlest were nowhere to be seen that day, so I asked Eliza, the oldest, where they were. She confided they were sick in bed."

Frankie and Carmen gasped at the sad story.

Sarah nodded. "I know. I felt the same way. I sneaked into the house and found them, nearly lifeless. With Eliza's help, I carried one and she carried the other to my car. I came home, picked up John, and we drove them to the hospital in Madison before anyone else found out."

Her brows shot upward defiantly when Frankie and Carmen gasped again. "What could the community do to me? I was already shunned."

"Did the children survive?" Carmen asked.

Sarah shrugged. "I wish I knew. Once they were in the hospital, they were quarantined. I can't get any information, and nobody in the Amish community is about to talk to me. I know for certain they are either dead or still in the hospital."

Sarah's face darkened in sudden despair mixed with bitterness. She pulled one of the zinnias from the flower vase and began nervously picking single petals from the large bloom.

"I learned my lesson though. Never mess with the Amish. My John collapsed the next day in church, right in the middle of the service, and couldn't be revived."

"What are you saying?" Carmen narrowed her eyes and crossed her arms.

"I think they did something to John. That's why he died."

"Has anyone else in your church become sick? Frankie thought of her own St. Anthony's and all the people who were ill.

Sarah looked puzzled for a moment. "Well, I don't know. I haven't heard that anyone else is ill though, and it's a small church."

"Do you think Lydia's children were contagious?" Frankie was trying to reason with Sarah.

Sarah shook her head. "No, I don't. I think they were poisoned. So was Lydia. And the Yoders. And probably your people, too. I'll be finding out very soon if my John was. The Madison ME has him, and the autopsy is scheduled for tomorrow."

"Poisoned?" Frankie and Carmen exclaimed together. "How? With what? And who did it?" They spoke over each other in disbelief.

Sarah was calm, her face devoid of any emotion now. "I can't explain it, but I know it just the same. Something's rotten in Whitman County. Promise me you'll find out what it is."

Frankie shuddered outside and in. Sarah Van Cleef's proclamation echoed Aunt CeCe's. She glanced at Carmen who still sat with her arms crossed and her lips puckered.

Distant thunder sounded in the absence of conversation. Finally, Frankie broke the eerie silence. "I promise I'll try to find out." She spoke so quietly she wasn't sure if her words were real, but Sarah patted her hand in reply.

"I'll call you if I learn anything that might help," Sarah said.

Before the business partners left Zeeland, they stopped at the church where Sarah's husband collapsed. Unlike St. Anthony's, a brick structure, the Dutch Reformed church was a two-story white clapboard design with a tall upper tower, cupola, and finally, a steeple. The height from the second story to the top made the church appear off-balance. Due to its age, Frankie wondered if the church had ventilation issues of its own. She'd learned from Sarah that the fellowship hall and kitchen were in the basement, and a funeral luncheon was the last event held there on the day before John Van Cleef died; both John and Sarah had attended.

Unfortunately, nobody was around on Memorial Day to find out if others were ill or dead, so the two wound their way back to Deep Lakes, once more traversing Amish country roads. They didn't encounter any buggies or wagons on the road, just horse apples, proving people were about. They saw many men and boys working in the fields or tending livestock and passed by some of the same empty fields they'd seen earlier.

Rounding a curve, Frankie saw a familiar white Escalade splashed with a large advertisement for Callahan Realty parked just off the roadway. Bram Callahan stood in the driveway, deep in discussion with two older Amish men. The famous Deep Lakes realtor might have come right from the links, dressed in white golf slacks and sage green polo shirt.

Frankie slowed, poked Carmen's leg, and pointed out the driver's side window so Carmen would notice.

"Looks like Deep Lakes's millionaire realtor is striking another land deal, eh?" Frankie remarked. Bram Callahan was the wealthiest realtor in the county and perhaps beyond. He was a shark, who always seemed to smell blood in the water when it came to acquiring land on the cheap.

Carmen wrinkled her nose. "He might have met his match with the Amish. They're no slouches when it comes to business deals."

CHAPTER TWELVE

Like it or not, we humans are bound up with our fellows,
and with the other plants and animals all over the world.
Our lives are intertwined.

Carl Sagan

Tess whistled a perky Ethiopian folk tune coming into the Bubble & Bake kitchen but stopped abruptly when she saw Frankie at one long counter, assembling quiches from a lineup of containers loaded with onions, crispy bacon pieces, shredded cheeses, and a heaping pile of asparagus. Tess's whistle became a sliding chirrup.

"Have we become a quiche factory?" she asked with a giggle.

"Good morning, Tess. You know how it goes when the produce starts coming in fast and furious! A nice Amish woman gave us almost ten pounds of fresh asparagus, so Springtime Quiche will be on the menu for a while."

Tess stepped along Frankie's station to look at the ingredients, nodding her approval. "Looks like you have this under control, so I'll start icing pastries." Tess scuttled to the next workstation where trays of bare butterhorns, cinnamon knots, rhubarb Bismarcks, lemon cream cheese Danishes, and date tarts waited for their final dollops and swirls.

Frankie paused her rote movements along the counter to admire the baked goods and Tess's cute camisole dress with its cheerful print of tiny flowers on a magenta background, perfect for the hot kitchen.

"It looks like the crew accomplished a lot yesterday with the bosses out of the way," Frankie quipped.

Tess nodded and her collective of tiny braids bobbed pleasantly. "You'll be happy to hear that Cherry is picking up recipes and techniques rapidly. And Auntie CeCe seems to have found her groove again, at least in the macaron department." Tess's contralto chuckle reverberated around the room.

Frankie noticed how happy it made Tess to teach others baking techniques and wondered if the young woman had found her calling. "Thanks to you, Tess, for working with Cherry and Aunt CeCe. You have a gift."

Tess bowed her head, but Frankie still saw her beaming smile. "It's wedding week, yes? You must be getting excited, Boss."

Frankie had nearly forgotten about the upcoming wedding, between her task list, missing Garrett, and investigating the strange illness going around. She blushed, embarrassed. "It will seem more real tomorrow when Violet arrives and Max flies in. I'm not in a panic—yet." She laughed.

Carmen walked through the back door with Tia Pepita trailing behind her. Tia had stopped to throw some seeds to the tiny chipping sparrows and gold finches pecking around the back.

"Whoa Frankie, did you stay up all night sautéing asparagus?" Carmen's black hair barely peeked out from the red bandana covering her head. She was ready to stay cool in the kitchen, too, dressed in a summer cotton smock dress and breathable clogs.

Tia zipped into the room, wearing makeup and a bright yellow tunic over a white skirt, ready to serve customers at the front counter. "Those little chicky birds are so cute outside, but when are we getting a new kitty, Frankie?" Her voice had traveled from sweet to demanding in the same breath.

"Good morning, Tia. I miss the shop kitties, too. As soon as Sophie's wedding is over, I'm picking one up from Dr. Sadie." Frankie's eyes twinkled. "Carmen could have brought you a whole basket of kittens from the Amish farm we visited yesterday."

Carmen shot Frankie a warning look. "No, thank you. We have plenty of barn cats at home. Do you need help with those quiches? You're taking Freya to the vet this morning, right?"

Leave it to Carmen to have everyone's schedule memorized. Frankie nodded. "The appointment's not until eleven, and these are just about ready to go to the ovens." She checked the wall clock. "It's not even six yet, Carmen. Aren't you early?"

"I'm making Tia's empanadas this morning. Fresh for customers. We're going to tag team. The dough's in the cooler." Carmen tied on a clean white apron from the drawer and turned on the fryer under the range hood, after filling it with fresh oil.

"Have you heard from Sophie or Garrett lately?" Carmen remained on high alert for changes in Frankie's mood that might be brought on by stress, especially after yesterday's Amish escapade and visit to Sarah Van Cleef.

Carmen knew Frankie would return to the Amish community to nose around as soon as the last of the wedding confetti was swept up. Carmen also wondered about the Amish families and if Callahan Realty was buying properties from any of the recently deceased.

Since Carmen was lost in thought, she didn't notice Frankie standing right beside her until Frankie handed her a container of chopped chorizo and crumbled Cotija cheese.

"Did you even hear me? No word from Sophie or Garrett yesterday, and I'm getting worried about Sophie. I asked her to call me a couple of days ago. It's not like her to blow off my messages. She's working double shifts, but still…"

"You'll see her tomorrow when she brings Max here from the airport, right? That's still the plan?"

"Right. Sophie works the overnight shift and will pick up Max in the morning to bring him here. He's staying at the Divine, but they'll both pop in to say hello." Frankie worried about Max's family coming in on Friday. She'd never met his parents and hoped they would be happy staying at The Divine, a restored Victorian B & B operated by Mike and Lorie Hansen. The Hansens were delightful hosts, so she was obviously borrowing trouble.

Frankie carried the steaming quiches from the oven to settle them on cooling racks, then she excused herself for the drive out to Lovely Lavender Farm to pick up Freya for her annual checkup with Dr. Sadie.

Coral Anders met Frankie on the expansive front porch of her log home with a friendly smile. She patted the cushion next to her on the wicker love seat, inviting Frankie to sit a minute, and handed her a small paper sack she pulled out of her work apron.

"What's this?"

"I've been making sachet pillows ahead of my next workshop

offering. I made one for each of the Bubble & Bake crew. I already gave CeCe hers."

Frankie's aunt had been living above the workshop at Coral's farm for almost two years after she decided to stay in Deep Lakes. CeCe's artistry was on full display in the workshops at the farm, and she was the perfect assistant to Coral at the retreats held there six times a year. The two women had similar personalities and worked well together.

Frankie opened the sack and pulled out the dainty sachets, made from cotton sackcloth, trimmed in eyelet with a different colored ribbon running through each one. She lifted one miniature pillow to her nose to inhale the calming lavender scent.

"These are so nice. Thank you, Coral. I love how you personalized each one with our first initial." Frankie's letter F was bright violet, embroidered in a fancy script. "This is the perfect pick-me-up for the busy tourist season ahead. You must have a lot going on here, too."

Coral smiled serenely, her face awash in a natural sun-kissed glow showcasing her eternal youth. "As a matter of fact, I'm working pretty hard right now on wedding bouquets." Both dimples showed around her mouth when she spoke.

Frankie puckered her lips, then broke into a giggle. "I keep forgetting that's happening this week. Honestly, there's just so much going on. I think my head's going to explode." She giggled again and patted Coral's weathered hand.

"Thank you for agreeing to make the bouquets. Sophie loves lavender and I can only imagine what your creativity will dream up."

Coral tucked a lock of long silver-gray hair behind one ear.

"Well, I'm glad I have CeCe's help. We make a good team. But I suppose you need to get going. I'll just grab Freya's leash."

Freya and Lark, Coral's Norwegian elkhound, were lying side by side on the front porch under one of the plant tables. Freya stood up when she heard her name, loped over to Frankie, and nuzzled her hand while laying her head in Frankie's lap.

"I miss him, too, Freya. Hopefully, Garrett will be home soon." She gave Freya a cuddle and scratched her neck and ears.

"I imagine it's not the same for you without Garrett around, hmm?" Coral, who moved like dandelion fluff, spoke over Frankie's shoulder, giving her a start. Coral placed one hand tenderly on Frankie's arm. "Well, I'm happy to report that Freya and Lark are good company for each other."

Frankie took the leash and attached it to the elkhound, walked her to the SUV, and waved goodbye to Coral. "See you Friday. Just let me know when the bouquets are ready."

Dr. Sadie's assistant, Gail, greeted Freya and Frankie at the clinic door. Freya showed how well behaved she could be, sitting pretty while Gail signed them in.

Dr. Sadie emerged from the exam area behind a tiny woman holding a large cat carrier with an enormous cat inside, who did its best to look unimpressed with the situation.

"Poor Pumpkin. It's so hard to be a kitty, isn't it? Shots are no fun. Poor sweety." The tiny woman cooed at the long-haired orange cat as she walked to the front desk.

Sadie smiled at Frankie and told her to bring Freya to the second exam room. She waited until the woman and Pumpkin exited before saying to Gail, "Clean up in exam room one, please." Apparently, Pumpkin had found a way to show her displeasure.

Sadie sat down hard on the wheeled exam chair, blinked a few times, then smiled at Frankie. "I hope it's okay with you, but I just need to get some ointment and a bandage on this." She pointed to her left wrist, which was gouged and bleeding.

Frankie gasped. "Pumpkin, I take it?"

Sadie sighed. "Let's just say there's no making friends with that one. I'm happy to see you and Freya." Sadie reached over to rub the elkie's neck, then pulled out a tub of ointment, rubbed some onto the wound and applied a bandage. "There we go. Problem solved."

Sadie patted the exam table and Freya obediently jumped onto it and made herself comfortable. The vet listened to the dog's vitals, looked in her ears and mouth, and proclaimed her in good health. "She needs a dental cleaning, so we should get that on the books for an upcoming visit. What do you hear from her master?"

It was Frankie's turn to sigh, and she looked away at some invisible spot on the wall. "He's working hard in Duluth on multiple murder cases, all related. I hope to see him Saturday at Sophie's wedding."

Sadie frowned and scrunched her eyebrows together. "You don't sound too sure about that. Is it possible he won't be there?"

Frankie shrugged. "I'm changing the subject now," she announced to make it obvious. "What have you heard about the mystery illnesses and deaths around the county?"

Sadie brushed some animal hairs from her lab coat, sat down, and crossed one leg over the other. "If you mean, am I seeing animals getting sick, the answer is yes. The mosquitoes are abundant this year. A few farmers have lost cows due to mosquito swarms."

"Cows?" Frankie was shocked. "I had no idea that could happen. Do you think the mosquitoes are related to the illness people are getting?"

Sadie leaned back in her chair, closed her eyes to think, and carefully chose her words. "I'm not sure. I'm a vet and I'm not about to diagnose humans." She cleared her throat. "However, I'm concerned about whether there's a relationship between the mosquitoes and the deaths. Mosquitoes are excellent carriers of blood-borne diseases."

Frankie looked thoughtful. "Maybe this is a strange question, but are the dead animals autopsied to confirm the cause of death?"

Sadie nodded. "Not a strange question at all. In an outbreak, even a small one, it's my job to contact the USDA or Veterinary Diagnostic Lab to transport a dead animal. The nearest one is in Madison where diseased animals undergo a necropsy. That's the animal version of an autopsy."

"Oh, I see. Will the lab report its findings to you? And how long does that take?" Frankie wondered.

"Yes, the treating vet and the animal's owner receive the lab report. But it can take some time, especially if there is an outbreak." Sadie rose from her seat.

"Sorry to cut this short, Frankie, but I've got to prepare to snip a Great Pyrenees, if you know what I mean." She made a cutting gesture with two fingers. "I'll see you Saturday at Sophie's wedding. And hopefully, Garrett, too."

Before returning to Lovely Lavender Farm, Frankie treated Freya to a walk at Bountiful Fruits. The two headed through the orchard and walked along the grassy path between the border gardens where Sophie would walk Saturday.

Manny Vega waved to Frankie and greeted Freya with a hand to paw shake and an allover back rub. Freya practically purred, laid down in the grass, and offered her belly up to the vineyard manager.

"How are you doing, Frankie?" Manny asked, squinting in the sunlight. "The flowers are looking beautiful, right?"

Frankie nodded. "I thought it would be nice to get a walk in with Freya. I've been too busy to spend much time with her, and we're on our way back to Coral's farm from the vet, so…" Lovely Lavendar was just a stone's throw away from the vineyard.

"Things are looking very good here, Boss Lady. The flower clusters are coming on strong, which makes me hopeful for a good harvest." That was Manny, the eternal optimist, something Frankie admired about the man.

"I've been wondering. How are we handling the insect population out here?" She'd always trusted Manny to contend with pest control, but now she decided she needed more information.

Manny produced a lopsided grin. "You noticed we don't have many mosquitoes or ticks. For starters, we keep the grass cut short. We keep the area trimmed around the vineyard and orchard, and we don't have any standing water around." He raised an instructive finger and shook it. "Those are the best ways to keep pesty bugs away."

Frankie smiled in appreciation. "So, we don't spray at all?"

Manny waved his hand. "I didn't say that. Sometimes, we have to spray. But the Healys have good organic sprays when we need to use them. We make our own soapy water spray for beetles that show up and a baking soda mixture for fungus. If any of the vines show disease, we often cut the vine down. It's better for the whole vineyard that way."

Frankie nodded. "I guess you're not telling me anything new. Thanks for the reminder, though." Frankie was part of every bug and fungus discovery Manny found as the seasons passed at Bountiful, but she trusted and relied on him to handle whatever might come their way.

~

At the downtown Duluth morgue, Garrett studied his notes once more before Detectives Simms and Olaf arrived. He'd called a meeting with the two detectives after a long weekend of thinking, reviewing case files, and thinking some more.

Leo and Kara were already in the morgue office where Garrett briefed them about his ideas from the autopsy reports. Dani was surprisingly absent, having called in sick with a migraine.

Simms and Olaf opened the morgue office door and swooped into the room, skeptical expressions firmly in place.

"I hope you've got something good for us, Juice," Simms, the elder detective said with a smirk, as he placed "Juice" in air quotes.

Olaf gave Simms a friendly elbow and a wink. Kara and Leo sneered.

"That's enough, gang," Garrett said, his voice tired. He'd had all the jabs he planned to take. The last thing the city needed was division in its ranks. Simms and Olaf were pitting the ME office against the police unnecessarily.

"Look, I'll be leaving soon, but you all have to learn to work together or you're doing your community a huge disservice. So, figure out how to play nice. It's a big sandbox." Garrett's hands gestured around the foursome then landed in a resolute crossing of his arms across his chest.

Leo and Kara stood up straighter, their eyes widened in surprise. Simms and Olaf stuffed their hands in their pants pockets, their eyes scanning the floor for specks.

"Here's a few facts." Garrett went to the whiteboard, picked up a marker, and began writing. "One. All the victims were killed in the morning before seven a.m. or in the early evening after four p.m. Two. All of them were killed with the same kind of strap. Three. All of them had impressions from a carabiner clip. Four. All of them were dumped in parks or green spaces sometime in the middle of the night."

Simms jumped in. "Yeah, and we have a map showing where the vics were found. We drew a perimeter, tried to connect the locations, but nothing's standing out. We're dealing with a clever killer who's got us on a long leash."

Garrett nodded. "I know and it's frustrating. I'm not telling you how to do your jobs, but I wonder if focusing on delivery drivers is the wrong answer. Most delivery drivers don't deliver that early in the morning. It looks like the killer is encountering victims either before or after work."

"So, we need to brainstorm what other kinds of people are likely to be around at those times. Other kinds of people who use straps and clips?" Olaf offered.

"You haven't made any headway in finding any one delivery person that had contact with every victim, so maybe it's time to get more creative. That's all I'm saying." Garrett tried to sound encouraging.

"I think talking about the case helps a lot. We need to do this more often." Kara gave her best cheerleader pep talk. "Look at the victims. They're all about the same age with similar body types. All of them were dressed in gym clothes."

"That's right, so they couldn't have been going to or coming from work. But only one of the vics had a gym membership, and she hadn't signed into the gym on the day she was killed." Simms, for better or worse, had decided to join the conversation.

"But she'd been to the gym two days earlier," Olaf reminded the detective. "Maybe our killer kidnapped her and held her a couple of days first."

"I still think our guy's a trucker that comes and goes in the area. It fits that a semi driver might have encountered all the vics at their workplaces, then left the area on a long haul, ready to kill again when he's back in town." Simms cracked his knuckles and stared down the three medical examiners.

Garrett cocked his head to the side and scrutinized Simms. "Could be true. Have you checked to see if there are similar victims in other places? A killer with an appetite might not wait to be in Duluth for the next kill."

"Yeah, we've checked that out. And no, we haven't found any similar vics." Simms swore and kicked the table leg. "Have you got anything else, Iverson?"

Garrett shook his head. "It isn't often the dead have a lot of new things to say. I'm just making sure they get to tell their whole story, which is why I keep going over the same information again and again. Believe me, I'd like to have more answers for you."

Olaf thanked Garrett. "Sorry about earlier. It's hard for us when an outsider is called in. Makes us feel like we're not good enough."

"I get it. But let's remember that we're not enemies. The killer is." Garrett looked at Simms, who had stuffed both hands back in his pockets and turned toward the door to leave.

"Thanks for bringing all of us together," Kara said. "That's what's been missing from the start on these cases. Leo and I haven't been privy to any of this information."

A startled Garrett looked at Leo, who confirmed what Kara said. *Just what kind of operation was Dani Edwards running here?*

CHAPTER THIRTEEN

There's such a difference between us.
And a million miles. Hello from the other side.

Adele

Frankie was up before the birds began to sing Wednesday, her mind busily running up, down, and around her to-do list, until she finally gave up on sleep. She took advantage of the early hour to have coffee on her balcony overlooking Sterling Creek. Cliff swallows and purple martins skimmed the creek for breakfast bugs while Frankie allowed the rich brown Guatemalan blend to trickle through her system. She smiled at a pair of bluebirds, taking turns flying back and forth to their nesting house across the creek. The pair were busily bringing takeout food to hungry babies. How grateful she was for all the insect eaters out there.

A leisurely shower beckoned Frankie and she obliged, figuring it would be the last long shower she'd enjoy until post wedding. Violet would be home sometime that day, and Sophie would be picking up Max from the airport before noon and making a short visit to Deep Lakes later. She was anxious to see Sophie and Max together, hoping for some reassurance that all was right in their world.

She toweled off her hair, worked in a big puff of mousse, and gave her bob a quick blow dry. She picked lightweight capris off the floor and grabbed a fresh Bubble & Bake T-shirt from the closet, this one a tie-dyed swirl of blues on white. She saw her forgotten cell phone flashing a notification on the nightstand.

She'd missed a call from Sophie more than an hour earlier. Darn. She quickly entered her voicemail password and waited. A garbled message from Sophie came out amid distressed spurts, static, and dead air.

Frankie listened to the message several more times. As best as she could decipher, Sophie might be quarantined at the hospital. The whimpering and sniffling seemed to suggest there might not be a wedding Saturday.

Fuming she'd missed her daughter's call, she quickly tapped Sophie's name. After one ring, an automated voice droned: "Message MD. This number is temporarily out of service." Frankie made a face, ended the call, and tried again. Same robotic voice, same message. She restarted her phone and tried a third time with the same result.

"What the…? Oof. Now what?" Pacing around the apartment, Frankie muttered to herself, thinking. "Does Max know what's going on? Yikes! Who's going to pick up Max?"

Frankie brought up her contact list and tried Max's number, which went straight to voicemail.

"Hi Max. It's Frankie. Have you heard from Sophie? I got a strange message from her this morning. You're probably at the airport already. Call me when you get a chance."

She looked at the contacts again and decided to call Nora, Sophie's best friend and maid of honor. To her surprise, the same robotic automated message droned in her ears as before. Nora worked with Sophie at the hospital. She wondered if Nora was in quarantine, too. "Perfect. Guess I'll call Violet."

"Mom. What's wrong? It's six a.m.," Violet mumbled into the phone.

Frankie explained the situation as she understood it. "Have you heard from your sister?"

Silence on the line probably meant Violet was looking for messages on her phone, chat, and voicemail. "Nope. I don't see anything. Let me get dressed. I can pick up Max at the airport while you're working. We'll see you this afternoon and figure this out."

Without a bride, Frankie decided there wasn't much the three of them could figure out.

~

Pacing around the apartment wasn't doing Frankie, or her floors, a bit of good and after ten minutes of that, she wasn't any closer to deciding if her next call would go to her mother, Garrett, or Carmen. Maybe she should go downstairs and bake in her sanctuary instead.

In stark opposition to the chaos Frankie was feeling, the world downstairs was humming along in harmony. Tess said a cheerful good morning over her shoulder as she pushed the full pastry case down the hallway, turning on shop lights along the way.

Frankie heard Aunt CeCe's chipper greeting to Tess, so Frankie assumed everything was ready to open for customers.

Frankie ducked into the kitchen and found Jovie and Cherry making tart pastry. Jovie stood beside Cherry as she flew solo making tarts from start to finish.

Frankie momentarily forgot her dilemma and bade the women a good morning. "How's the tart pastry treating you, Cherry?"

Cherry's brows were knit in concentration as she labored to roll out dough to a precise thickness, then cut and shape it into the tart molds. She kept her eyes on her project when she spoke. "I always thought making fillings and finishing pastries was difficult, but this is whole lot harder."

"Since the dough is the foundation for all delicious pastries, that's where the real proof lies. Not 'in the pudding' as they say. Don't worry though. You'll get the hang of it." Frankie was impressed with Cherry's ability to pick up on dough handling skills.

Cherry allowed a small smile to play on her face. "Thanks. That means a lot coming from you. I'm surrounded by good teachers, so that's a huge help."

Jovie smiled. "I learned from the boss so I'm just paying it forward. We're making raspberry chocolate tarts and lemon-lime tarts today. There isn't a lot on the task list, Frankie. We tried to keep a light schedule this week knowing you'd be swamped with wedding arrangements."

Frankie bit her lower lip when tears started forming. The short lapse from reality was over, and she had to face facts. Jovie noticed the change immediately, but before she could ask her anything, Frankie's cell phone rang.

It was Max. "I've got to take this." Frankie darted out the back door onto the sunny deck.

"Max, thank God. Do you know what's going on?" Frankie's high-pitched tone indicated anxiety.

"Sophie called late last night from the hospital. It was a poor connection, so I wouldn't call it a conversation. Some mystery illness has the hospital in a spin. Sophie and Nora and a few other nurses and docs are being quarantined in a separate area of the hospital."

Frankie gasped again, even though Max's news confirmed what she was already thinking. "Has Sophie been exposed to the illness? Is she okay?"

Max's sharp inhalation contained worry. "Wish I could tell you. She didn't sound sick, but if she's part of the team treating these patients, I'd say the hospital is following protocol, taking precautions to be sure anyone in the exposure area is staying put."

Frankie was grasping at straws. "Did Sophie say how long the quarantine would last?"

"There's no way to determine that. I'm flying into Madison and hope to find out more, but it's safe to say we're going to have to reschedule the wedding."

Hearing Max say the words made Frankie's heart hit bottom, adding another layer of stress to her fears about Sophie's safety. "I know," she whispered. "Violet will pick you up at the airport. I suppose the three of us will manage the fallout together. Safe travels, Max. I'm so sorry."

Frankie had the morning to formulate an agenda of phone calls and plans for managing the wedding details that couldn't be undone at this stage. But first she needed to call her mother and Garrett, calls that were certain to temporarily unravel her. She tapped Carmen's number.

"Is everything okay at the shop?" Carmen's first thought surfaced. Wednesday was her traditional day off when she caught up around the farm, helped Ryan with the sheep, or worked on processing wool. She was elbow deep in sudsy hot water, soaking wool, when Frankie's call came.

Frankie spilled the story of Sophie's irregular messages to her and Max, ending with the inevitable proclamation. "There isn't going to be a wedding this week, Carmen." Frankie's voice caught on the words.

Carmen walked out of the workshop and stared out into the green pastures beyond. She took a deep breath of fresh country air before speaking. "I can't believe this. What do you need me to do?" She and Frankie had been through plenty of sticky situations that seemed impossible, and the two had always managed to come out unscathed, but this time the odds against them were stacked even higher.

Frankie let the tears flow now. Counting on Carmen was a sure thing, and sometimes that certainty overwhelmed her. "I need to call Garrett and my mother," she said tearfully.

"I'm glad you called me first. I'll switch gears here and…," Carmen trailed off. Meeting at the bakery didn't seem like the best idea. Too public, too many coworkers, too much discussion. "Why don't we meet at Bountiful, Frankie? The winery office is quieter than the shop, and we can make all the calls from there."

Carmen's task now was to fortify her friend so she could steel herself for the onslaught of calls and revelations she'd be making the rest of the week. She knew the best way to keep Frankie intact was to make a plan and help her execute it.

"How about if you call Garrett and I'll call your mother?" Carmen offered.

"That's sweet of you, Carmie, but those are two calls I have to make myself. Your idea to handle cancellations and details from the winery is great. I'll meet you there at noon. I need to involve Violet and Max, so I'll tell them to come there from the airport."

Carmen confirmed and the two disconnected, so Frankie tapped the M key on her phone index to bring up Peggy's number. She closed her eyes and allowed her brain to gather the necessary words but was interrupted when Jovie cleared her throat. The woman stood by the iron table, bearing a wide-mouthed mug filled with creamy espresso and oat milk. The surface bore a pretty heart surrounded by more creamy hearts. She held the mug out to Frankie.

"I'm not sure what's up, but it looks like you might be out here a while, and it appeared reinforcements were in order." Jovie grinned as Frankie took the mug and smiled weakly in response.

"Thanks, Jovie. This won't hurt, that's for sure." She indicated the latte. "I have to make a couple of calls, but then I'll be in to talk to all of you."

Jovie nodded and left.

Frankie wasted no more time and tapped on Peggy's name.

"Frankie, is anything the matter? You don't usually call this early." Peggy answered within seconds.

"Mother, I'm afraid I have bad news. The wedding's being postponed. Sophie has been quarantined at the hospital and nobody knows how long the quarantine will last."

Peggy blew out air and sat down at her breakfast nook. "Oh my. Is Sophie okay? What's the quarantine for?"

Frankie hesitated. "I wish I knew, Mom. Sophie's message was disjointed and when I try to reach her, I can't get through. I get a weird recording that her phone isn't in service. Both

Max and I heard the quarantine is due to a mysterious illness. I can't help but think it's the same illness Father Donnelly, June Thompson, and others have."

Peggy bolted out of her seat. "You're right. It must be. I've heard many rumors the sick were all transferred to Madison. I bet the hospital has them together in a closed area, so they can limit exposure to others. How did Sophie get into this mess?"

Frankie sighed. "Let's not jump to conclusions yet, Mom. Sophie's been working double shifts ahead of the wedding. I'm sure she was placed wherever she was needed most. She'll be leaving them short-staffed to go to Houston with Max you know. Maybe not now, though. Oh, I have no idea what's going to happen now." Frankie was on the verge of a wail and reeled her thoughts back in.

"Never mind, Dear. What can I do to help? You must have a million details to tend to." The resourceful Peggy Champagne was back.

Frankie explained the plan to meet at Bountiful that afternoon. "Sweet Violet is retrieving Max from the airport at noon, so they should be at the winery around one o'clock. By the time everyone gets there, I'll have a checklist and phone numbers ready." Frankie sat up straighter knowing she had a plan of action.

"Right now, I need to call Garrett, Mom. I'll see you later at the winery."

Frankie didn't have a plan when she tapped on Garrett's name, but the call with her mother had been easier than imagined so she was hopeful.

"Is this my favorite baker and wedding planner?" Frankie could feel the sugar in Garrett's voice all the way from Duluth, which made tears pool in her eyes.

"Hi G." Frankie couldn't disguise her stress and disappointment when she told Garrett the wedding was off for Saturday.

"I'm so sorry Frankie. I hope Sophie's all right. Would you like me to make some phone calls? I'm sure I can tap the Madison ME for information." In the wake of the couple's recent conversations, Garrett was desperate to win her favor.

Frankie swallowed hard, once, twice. "If you have time, that would be nice. I've got more than enough to do right now to connect with wedding guests, the caterer, baker, florist, and more." She didn't mean to sound crisp, but her words were coated in something sour.

"At least you won't have to rush to be back by Saturday." Frankie instantly regretted letting the sentence escape. "I'm sorry, G. How are the cases going there?"

Garrett felt like a spanked puppy. "No new bodies. No new suspects. So, I'd call it a tie right now. Damn frustrating. You'll be happy to know that I'm working out of the downtown office, and included Dani's assistants, Leo and Kara, in all the reviews and meetings."

Frankie felt a shameful heat rising within, mixed with relief, and garnished with guilt. "That's good. I hope the assistants can help. I mean, that's part of their job, too, right?"

"Right. Dani's kept them out of the loop, and I can't understand why. She's lucky to have assistants funded by the city. Small county offices can't afford that kind of luxury." Garrett was still trying to wrap his head around Dani's operation, but he couldn't ignore the worry and sadness in Frankie's voice and decided to let her off the hook.

"You know I planned to come for the weekend no matter

what was happening up here. You matter more to me than this job, Frankie."

Frankie's emotions were barely in check, but she was happy to have some reassurance from the man she loved. "Thanks, G. I know that. Things are just topsy-turvy here, and you..." she bit off the rest of her comment.

"And me being gone adds to the muddled mess. It's okay if you tell me how you feel. Just know that I'm a little lost, too. It doesn't feel right to be here, but it wouldn't be right to walk away either."

Frankie's heart was refueling. "G, you have something to offer, or you wouldn't be there. And I know you're a man of commitment." Frankie let her own words sink into her being.

For the first time in weeks, the conversation ended in warm affection.

As promised, Frankie gathered Aunt CeCe, Tess, Jovie, and Cherry into the wine lounge as soon as the shop closed to bakery customers and before the wine lounge opened. Their worried faces warmed her heart.

A communal gasp sounded when Frankie announced the wedding cancellation because Sophie was placed in quarantine at the hospital. The women murmured questions and concerns, all of which were met with shrugs and head shakes from Frankie.

"There's nothing to do but wait things out." Frankie checked herself. "Actually, there's a lot to do today, so I'm going to meet my mother, Carmen, Violet, and Max at Bountiful and we're going to organize calling everyone."

"What can we do to help out here?" Tess's rich voice showed she was ready to lead the charge.

Frankie smiled and clutched her hand warmly. "Business as

usual. You can look ahead at orders if there's anything that can be prepped for next week. Be nice to customers as usual, and don't act like the world is ending. We'll get through this together." Frankie's words belied the stress swimming in her gut.

"What about the locals? What should we tell them if they ask? You know it's going to happen." Cherry pursed her lips while her hands flew about in exasperation.

"I think we should tell them the truth as we know it," Frankie said, calmly. "But no more than that. Don't speculate, because some people will run with it, and rumors will fly. Of course, people will say they heard it from you first, even if they didn't. Offer them the bare-bones facts and thank them for their concern." Frankie sounded like the president preparing for a press conference. She stood tall and nodded firmly to seal the deal.

Aunt CeCe followed her niece to the back door and pulled her into a tight embrace. "What should I do about the flowers? I'm going to help Coral clean them later today after wine tastings."

Frankie nodded in understanding. "I'm going to repurpose the bouquets and centerpieces. Some will go to the nursing home and senior center; some will decorate the shop. Just keep working on them. I'll call Coral this afternoon and explain."

"But my darling, that's a lot of flowers and a huge expense." CeCe's face sagged in sadness.

"Right. It's a huge expense for Coral. She can't return the flowers." Frankie hugged her aunt and grinned. "Hold on, because the Champagne family is about to get creative with wedding commodities. Food, drinks, decorations, and more. I can't wait to see your artistry on display."

The afternoon passed all too quickly with the number of

necessary calls and rearrangements. Frankie gave Max a lot of credit for staying cool and focused, despite a seismic shift in plans. Carmen and Peggy were forces of reason and efficiency and came to the rescue every time Frankie or Violet felt an onslaught of tears coming on.

When Frankie tossed out an idea to host an impromptu dinner Saturday night with the catered wedding feast, questions and comments flew around the lab.

"With a full kitchen crew, I think we can pull it off," Frankie began. "The caterer can drop off the food in bulk, and we can plate as we go in the kitchen. We have the means to keep the hot food hot and the cold food cold. We'll use study paper plates and the plastic wear we always have on hand, so nothing fancy."

Peggy smiled. "That's good PR for the shop. What happens when we run out of food and there's a line out the door?"

Violet picked up on her mother's plan. "That's the beauty of a pop-up dinner. Nobody signs up because they don't know it's happening. And the dinner's free, right Mom?"

Frankie's brows creased together in contemplation. "I was thinking we could accept donations? Is that tacky?" She looked at Peggy, the Miss Manners of Deep Lakes.

"I'm afraid so, Dear. It looks like you're trying to capitalize on Sophie's misfortune." Peggy held up her index finger. "But you might be able to garner extra wine sales from the diners as a side effect."

Carmen weighed in. "Giving the food away is the smart thing to do. A little good will goes a long way. Are we going to look for volunteers to help at the shop on Saturday night? It could get crazy."

"I'll call some of my friends who are still in town," Violet volunteered, while the others agreed to round up anyone they knew who could help.

The winery office provided enough space for each of the calling crew to set up their phones, papers, and checklists. Zane Casey, the Bountiful intern wine maker, relocated to the lab when Frankie and company showed up.

Zane was there to measure the progress of the vintages currently fermenting in the stainless- steel tanks, along with taking delivery of frozen zinfandel grape must from the Sonoma Mountain region, Petite Sirah must from Paso Robles, and a field blend from vines in the Columbia Gorge. Frankie and her lab crew were excited to expand their wine offerings to include some west coast grapes from renowned vineyards for the first time.

Zane wasn't well versed in expressing condolences and opted to change the subject instead. "Frankie, I'm stoked about the must delivery today. Are we still meeting Monday to slay the recipes for these new mashes?" Zane's black hair stuck up every which way as usual, but Frankie noticed he was wearing neon green Crocs, which managed to make her smile despite the circumstances.

"Yes, Zane, the meeting's still on for Monday. Violet will be there, and I assume you'll be bringing Jade with you?" Zane confirmed and blushed. Jade was the newest intern from the UW-Stevens Point microbiology department and Zane had a little crush on her, of which Jade was completely unaware.

"All right, then. I'm just going to get out of your way then." Zane nearly tripped over his neon Crocs, snatching his laptop, mouse, cord, phone, and energy drink in his rush to go. They didn't see hide nor hair of him until after their last calls.

As the group finished up about the same time, Frankie noticed the cooler of food she'd brought with her was still parked on the floor next to the entrance.

"Boy, am I a terrible host. I brought sandwiches and salads from the bistro and completely forgot about them. Come on everyone and get something to eat. I know I'm hungry." Frankie opened the cooler and made a pile of sandwiches on the longest of the office tables, then arranged salads next to them. She found a sack with plates, plastic wear, and napkins and set them out.

"There's water and pop in the fridge. Help yourself." She pointed to the corner where a fridge, microwave, and toaster oven formed a kitchenette next to a sink and small set of cupboards.

Max grabbed an Italian sub in one hand and turned toward the door. "I'm calling my friend, Dre, at the hospital. He's head of security. I talked to him after my plane landed, and he texted me a phone number that isn't being blocked by the state board of health. He said I should call after four."

Frankie was surprised and impressed. "So, the state is blocking cell calls. That's why I couldn't reach Sophie or Nora. Huh." She made a shooing motion at Max. "Go make your phone call so you can tell us what's going on."

Violet, Peggy, Carmen, and Frankie lined up to fill plates with salads and took wrapped sandwiches to the table. Frankie ducked momentarily into the lab with a plate for Zane, who was bebopping along to whatever played through his earbuds.

Zane smiled gratefully and pulled the earbuds out where they dangled around his neck on their plastic cords. "Hamilton," he noted, pointing to the buds. "I love the soundtrack."

Frankie agreed. "No delivery yet? If you need to get going, I can stay and check in the order."

Zane shook his mad scientist hairdo, which moved in one large swoop. "No, I wouldn't miss it. Besides, I was hoping Violet would hang around so we could swap ideas on the new vintages."

"I'll send her back to chat after we've had something to eat. Thank you, Zane."

Frankie noticed the group looked a little bedraggled from the marathon afternoon of calls, and nobody said anything during the much-needed food break.

"Everyone I talked to was understanding and sympathetic," Peggy broke the ice. "Did any of you have issues with anyone?"

Carmen sniffed in displeasure. "Just one guest. I don't know where she fits into the mix, but she actually asked if we would reimburse her hotel fees if she isn't able to get her deposit back. I mean, seriously?"

Frankie shrugged. "I think Max called the hotel where the block of rooms was reserved, so I'll find out what was said there. He took care of most of his side of the guest list, along with the tux rental store and the photographer."

Carmen winced. "Dios mío. When I think of all the expenses that are part of a wedding, it makes me shudder. I suppose they won't get any of their deposits back."

"No, only if they had insurance. Can you believe people insure their wedding plans and vendors these days?" Peggy, an avid news reader, was knowledgeable about an abundance of topics.

Frankie smiled. She understood the business point of view all too well regarding profits and losses. "You can't expect a business to return your money in a case like this. The photographer isn't going to get another gig in three days' notice. That's true for most of these vendors. The best deal I got was through A to Z Rentals. The manager there agreed to hold our deposit on the pavilion, chairs, dance floor, etcetera for nine months. We can use the credit for a future date." She held up both hands, fingers crossed.

Max walked back into the office area and retrieved a second sub sandwich. He sat down across from Frankie and leaned over the table in anticipation.

"Well, go ahead. What's the news?" Frankie bent toward Max while the rest of the group turned their chairs in his direction.

"Dre said the quarantine went down late Monday night. They have twenty or so patients with a blood-borne illness, same symptoms. Shortness of breath or even more severe breathing problems, and sometimes, dehydration. Many of them are systemic and are in a medical coma. The ME in Madison has performed a few autopsies and has several more waiting, but the cause hasn't been identified."

"And Sophie?" Frankie held her breath.

Max looked at the table. "Sophie and Nora were pulled from their regular duties to assist. Since Sophie was working extra shifts, she ended up being the primary nurse assigned to the patients who presented with the same symptoms. The quarantine is precautionary. This illness doesn't appear to be contagious, but it's too soon to tell. Many of the patients were in the same places or are related to one another."

"Sophie feels fine then?" Frankie pushed.

"Yes, according to Dre. He was able to talk to her briefly with a glass window between them. She sends her love and apologies to all of you," Max grinned sweetly.

"One more thing." Max stared directly into Frankie's eyes.

"Sophie wanted to make sure you know that all the patients are from Whitman County."

Peggy raised an eyebrow toward her daughter, who remained stone-faced. Frankie wasn't the least surprised to hear what Sophie said. She and Carmen exchanged knowing glances. Peggy noted the exchange. Violet just looked bewildered.

"What's the deal with the state and Sophie's phone?"

Max, who would soon be a medical resident, knew the protocol. "Most state boards of health operate like any other government agency. If there's an emergency, the agency needs to control and monitor communications and other resources. Likely, the state sees this illness as a potential health crisis and wants to get ahead of it. The last thing the hospital needs is to have jammed phone lines that interfere with their ability to do their job."

"That makes sense. I thought maybe officials wouldn't want unverified information to leak out of the quarantined area. I mean, it looks like the media have been left in the dark."

Max affirmed Frankie's perspective. "Yes, that's another piece of managing a health crisis."

"I want to know how your parents took the news, Max. Especially, your grandfather. He was flying here from Arizona, wasn't he?" Peggy had heard enough about quarantine policies for the moment.

Max frowned and looked at his hands, which were balled-up fists rubbing the tabletop. "They're disappointed, obviously. My mom said she's going to help my grandpa change his flight destination to Minneapolis. That way, he can fly up to see my parents. I guess it's better than nothing. But I'm sad I won't get to see him."

"You could go up to Minneapolis from here and see your family, Max. Maybe that's just what the doctor ordered," Frankie suggested.

Max shook his head. "I've already changed my flight. I'm going back to Houston tomorrow."

The women exchanged astonished looks that couldn't be disguised.

"There's no reason for me to stay, and I can spend time preparing for my next set of medical exams. Besides, I still haven't found a new place to live, so I need to get on it."

Frankie remembered that Sophie had mentioned she would be looking for an apartment in Houston right after the wedding for the two of them. Sophie was upset with the uncertainty of not having an apartment, nor a starting date for a new job. And now, there were even more loose ends.

Frankie swallowed her next question when Max rose from his seat and turned toward Violet.

"Violet, do you think you can take me back to Madison? I'm going to stay with Dre tonight. It's close to the airport."

Violet nodded, still bewildered, and Max addressed the women. "I'm really sorry to just leave like this. I'll see you all again soon."

Max waved and abruptly walked out the front door.

"Vi, are you okay with driving Max back to Madison? I mean, someone else could if you're tired." Frankie needed time to process the afternoon and didn't think a knee-jerk reaction toward Max's decision to leave now would help matters.

"No, I'm fine to drive. I'll see you back home, Mom. I'm going to stay through Monday just as we planned."

Violet had always been the more fragile of Frankie's two

daughters, and Frankie was certain she was reeling from her sister's derailed wedding. Maybe a change in topic would lighten her mood. "By the way, Zane would like to chat with you about the new vintages we're making with the west coast grapes. Maybe you can slip in for a minute now to chat."

Violet nodded and looked relieved to have something else to occupy her mind. She exchanged texts with Zane, typical of the modern mode of communication, even though there was merely a wall between the two of them.

Frankie's phone buzzed, reminding her she had several missed calls, all from the same number, the sheriff's. It was time to play catch up with Alonzo.

"Frankie, I talked to your mother, so I know about Sophie. But I called to see if you have time to stop by my office today." Alonzo's muffled chewing came through.

"Lon, today is practically over. It's after five. What are you still doing at work, besides eating at your desk?"

A little cough followed by crinkling paper could be heard. "I see your wits are still intact, Frankie. I was hoping you and Carmen could debrief me on your Amish excursion. And it's time I showed you something in my office."

"I'll have to check with Carmen to see if she can come. It's her day to work on the farm and I've already monopolized most of it," Frankie spoke loudly enough for Carmen to overhear her side of the call.

Carmen nodded, shrugged, and mouthed the word "sure."

"See you in about fifteen minutes, Sherriff."

Carmen and Frankie gathered their belongings but noticed Peggy hadn't moved. She sat at the office table, her chin resting in her hand, wearing a downtrodden expression.

"Mom, thank you for your help today. Honestly, you're the best at handling situations like this. Wish I'd inherited that." Frankie put one arm around her mother's shoulder and tilted her head to meet hers.

Peggy leaned her head closer to Frankie's and patted her hand affectionately. "I'm glad I could be here for you, and I hope Saturday's free meal turns out. But there's something going on with you two." She raised her head, darted her eyes, and pointed one finger alternately at Carmen and Frankie. "What are you two up to?"

Frankie set down the pile she was carrying. "Carmen and I are trying to gather information about the mystery illness. We went to see Mrs. Graham yesterday. Her husband died from the same illness; we think. The Graham farm is in Amish country near the county line. We'd heard about some sick and dead Amish, all seemed to have the same illness. So, we talked to a couple of them."

"I see. Apparently, Alonzo knows about your little investigation, too. That's why he wants to see you?" Not much got past Peggy.

"Yes, that's right. Why do you look so down, Mom?" Frankie suspected she knew. Her mother hadn't been the same person since Elsa Karlsen's death and since Father Donnelly and June got sick. She wondered if her mother was facing her own mortality.

Peggy huffed. "I wonder. There doesn't seem to be any rhyme or reason for this strange illness. My daughter is keeping secrets from me. First about Garrett, then about investigating an illness that's killing people. My granddaughter's wedding has been canceled, and don't tell me you didn't notice how weird Max is behaving? It's almost as if he doesn't care." The last brick in

Peggy Champagne's wall gave way in a burst of tears.

Frankie gathered her into her arms and held on for dear life. "I'm worried about Sophie and all the sick people, too, Mom. Alonzo told Carmen and me we absolutely couldn't tell anyone we were talking to the Amish. We were instructed to be discreet. And I don't know what to say about Max. I have to think about it." Had she covered Peggy's litany of woes?

Peggy sniffled and wiped her face with a tissue Carmen offered her. "What about Garrett? Is everything okay with you two? He's been away an awfully long time." Fresh tears were forming in the woman's icy blue eyes.

Frankie offered her mother a genuine smile. "I think everything is going to be fine between me and Garrett."

CHAPTER FOURTEEN

Charles R. Swindoll

The concrete and block Whitman County building sat like a brooding beige monster next to the historical cream brick courthouse on Kilbourn Avenue. Maybe because it housed the sheriff's department, jail, and morgue, the county executives decided it should look as foreboding as possible. The Whitman Historical Society had petitioned the county board to construct the building in the flavor of its counterpart, the 1905 Romanesque style courthouse with its rounded arches, decorative chevrons, and two rectangular wings separated by its centerpiece, the turret clock tower facing four directions.

Modern thinking prevailed from a slim majority on the county board, bent on saving taxpayer dollars with the bland modern style, and that majority was forced to defend the end product, which was deemed an eyesore by the bulk of county residents and visitors.

Frankie and Carmen wearily drifted through the entrance, laid their handbags on the x-ray conveyor belt, and ambled through the metal detector. The night security officer, Maggie Margolis, greeted them cordially. Maggie and her friends sometimes perched in the Bubble & Bake lounge on a quiet weekend afternoon during the off-season.

"It's a little late for business, isn't it?" Maggie asked, half suspiciously.

"Tell that to Sheriff Goodman. We were summoned here," Carmen retorted. "Good to see you, Maggie. We've expanded the back deck, so there's more room to hang out. You and your friends should check it out."

Maggie nodded as she handed the women their bags and buzzed them through the entry doors. "I might just do that. Maybe an afternoon like today. Wednesdays are usually slow. Too bad you're not open Mondays."

Frankie grinned in apology. "Yep, Wednesday afternoons are nice and quiet at the wine lounge. Now that it's tourist season, we're open late on Wednesdays and Thursdays, too. Are you always on the p.m. shift?"

"No. I'm on a flex schedule. Some days, some evenings, some overnights. It varies, as do my days off. I heard you have new wines, too. Going to have to get in there soon." She smiled.

The women trotted up the stairs to the second floor, past the empty coroner's office, to the end of the first hallway where they spied Alonzo sitting at the reception desk, a clear indication everyone else had gone home for the day.

He waved as they approached the glass office door. "It's about time you two got here." His stern frown was ameliorated with a chuckle. "Sorry to hear about the wedding, Frankie. How's everyone holding up?"

Frankie sat heavily on the chair opposite the sheriff while Carmen remained standing, even though there was another chair beside Frankie.

"Everyone's doing okay. Some better than others." Frankie was thinking of Max, who wasn't playing the part of the upset groom to her liking. Then she remembered Alonzo might have inside information about the quarantine.

"Hey, what do you know about this quarantine? We heard the patients are all from this county." She cocked one eyebrow and wore a shrewd expression.

Alonzo didn't deny it. "I'm talking now to my friends, Frankie and Carmen, not members of the press or apprentice sleuth club, got it?"

Frankie nodded. Carmen planted her hands on her hips and tapped one foot impatiently.

"I've been talking with the ME in Madison and an officer at the State Board of Health. Anyone with symptoms mimicking the mystery illness has been quarantined at UW Hospital. They don't think this illness is contagious, but they don't know its origin either. That makes it difficult to treat." Alonzo stood up and motioned the women to follow him to his office.

"You know Sophie is smack in the middle of this business. She's in quarantine because she's working with these patients, so I hope there's a way to get some answers soon." Frankie walked briskly beside Carmen.

Alonzo stopped and turned to face them. "By the way, the professionals have named the illness Robli24. It's short for something to do with the blood and respiratory system along with the year of its origin."

"Here," he opened the office door and pointed at the far wall behind his desk. "I made an official map showing every case in the county. The red circles represent where the patients or victims live in the county. The black triangles mark the location of each victim when they presented ill or died."

Frankie pulled her phone out of her bag. "Mind if I take a picture of the map? It would help Carmen and me to help you." She tried to keep a straight face.

Alonzo folded his arms. "I suppose so. I don't know if I need the two of you to do any more investigating, though. There haven't been any new cases of the illness in four days."

"If you're still looking for the cause, and there's something rotten in Whitman County, I'd say you could use all the help you can get." Carmen folded her arms to mimic Alonzo and puffed out her chest.

Frankie scrutinized the map, which showed the neighboring counties. "Lon, why isn't there a circle or triangle here, in Zeeland?" She pointed to the town in Vandenberg County.

Alonzo gave her a pointed look and waited.

"Carmen and I spoke with Sarah Van Cleef at her home in Zeeland. Her husband, John, collapsed at church and died about two weeks ago. She told us she's waiting on an autopsy from the Madison ME. She believes he had the mystery illness, ah Robli24, that is."

Alonzo unfolded his arms and faced the map. "Enlighten me about how you came to be in Zeeland."

"One of the Amish women you sent us to see told us to talk to Sarah. You should probably write this down, Alonzo," Carmen instructed. "You can take it from here, Frankie. You have all the details."

Frankie sat at the desk and pulled the folded notes out of her bag. "It's a good thing I forgot I even had these stuffed in here." She flattened the paper onto the desk. "Let's see. We started at the Graham farm." She stood up again, papers in hand, and walked over to the map.

"Here. This circle with the number two. Is that Harry Graham? It looks like the right location."

Alonzo cross-checked his list of contacts. "Yes. What made you stop there?"

"We saw two Amish buggies in the driveway and thought we'd make the most of the opportunity," Frankie said, proud of being clever.

"We met the whole Graham family. Harry's wife, Donna, and their son and daughter. Two of the Amish neighbors were there, so we talked to them; Joanna Yoder and Emma Dunkel. Emma Dunkel was talkative. She told us about the Yoder grandparents who died. Joanna's husband is their grandson. She gave us Sarah Van Cleef's phone number and said we should talk to her about the mystery illnesses."

Alonzo's knitted brow confirmed he wasn't exactly following. "How did this Amish woman know Sarah and have her phone number?"

Frankie half-frowned. "Sorry. Sarah used to be part of the Amish community until she left to marry an outsider. She's Emma's sister-in-law."

Frankie went on to share Sarah's story about her Amish friend Lydia and the two Shumaker children, who might be quarantined at UW Hospital. "Obviously, Sarah and her husband were both exposed to the illness. John died at their church service the next morning."

Alonzo scratched at his chin where a thick stubble of whiskers was visible. "Maybe Van Cleef hasn't been included among the victims yet pending the autopsy. I'll call the ME and check. And yes, I'll see if I can find out if the Shumaker children are at the hospital."

"If Van Cleef had the same illness, it either means the cases aren't confined to Whitman County or the illness is contagious. But you said Van Cleef wasn't at the Shumaker home?"

Frankie nodded. "Sarah said she was allowed to come to Lydia's funeral because she'd been part of the Amish community, but no outsiders were allowed to attend."

She viewed the map again. "The numbers in this area here: are these Amish people?" Frankie pointed to the circles and triangles spread around County HH, the area she and Carmen had cruised around Monday.

"Yes. Number three and four are the Yoder grandparents. Let's see, I have them listed as Joseph and Martha Yoder, age seventy and fifty-two." He paused to process the age difference then continued looking at his list.

"And numbers five and six are Amish, too. Unidentified is what I have written here." Lon swallowed hard as Frankie and Carmen sucked in air, fearing the worst for the Shumaker children.

"Do you have Lydia Shumaker on your list?" Frankie asked.

Alonzo ran his finger from the top to the bottom of the paper twice. "No, I don't. These unidentified could be anybody. I only have the information released by the ME. I'm surprised we have any Amish on this list. A family member must have insisted on emergency medical treatment outside of the community. If that happened and the person died, the ME could hold the body for autopsy in certain cases."

"Do you think there are more sick or dead Amish people not on this map?" Carmen asked.

"I know there are, based on the little information you got the other day. It confirms what I've heard. The trouble is, we can't tell how many. We might be hearing about the same people or many different ones." Alonzo huffed in frustration.

Frankie calculated the map included twenty-two circles, more victims than she knew about. "Has anyone tried to speak with the Amish doctor or the bishop to reason with them or ask for their help? It's certainly in their best interest to share information."

Alonzo admitted that nobody had. "We've always kept our dealings, religion, and governments separate. Midwest-mind-your-own-business policy."

Frankie and Carmen laughed out loud with derision. "Oh, come on, Lon. When's the last time you've seen anyone in Deep Lakes minding their own business?" Frankie blew a raspberry, then her face darkened when she remembered the town's number one realtor.

"You should talk to Bram Callahan. Carmen and I saw him at one of the Amish farms on Monday, talking with two elderly Amish men, dressed for business. If Bram has an in with the Amish, maybe he can help the whole county for a change."

"It couldn't hurt. Every time you start snooping around Frankie, you dig up something unexpected. I'll let you know what I find out." Alonzo produced a wicked grin. "If I can, that is."

Carmen and Frankie parted ways with dinner on the horizon.

"I hope Tia Pepita took charge of dinner, since I'm running

late. I texted Ryan to let him know I'm on my way home." Carmen checked her phone for an answer and smiled. "Looks like Tia came through. Ryan says dinner's waiting for me."

Frankie inhaled deeply and stifled a yawn. "I could skip dinner, but I think I'll go grab a bite with Violet, maybe at the Mud Puppy." The Mud Puppy sat a block down Meriwether from the bakery, where owner Kerby Hahn served up ten different varieties of juicy burgers the size of a baseball mitt. Thinking about a bar burger set Frankie's mouth watering.

She returned to an empty Bubble & Bake and found a note from Tess detailing the day's business. For a Wednesday after a holiday weekend, the numbers were decent, and the place was as neat as a pin. Tess jotted down a few varieties of wines low on inventory at the shop, so Frankie could pick them up at Bountiful before the weekend.

Upstairs, Frankie found Violet sitting in her bedroom looking at a scrapbook filled with photos of her and Sophie from a beach trip the two took together right before Vi left for her first semester of college. Violet had a faraway expression.

Frankie sat down beside her on the bed. "Hey there. How did it go with Max?"

Violet shrugged and a tear slipped down one cheek. "Very quiet, Mom. Max barely said a word the whole car ride. I tried to ask him about future plans, and empathize with him about the wedding, but he either mumbled or changed the subject."

Frankie put one arm around her daughter and bit the inside of her cheek, thinking of the right words. "Well, Max might be processing this situation differently than you or me. He's also under a lot of pressure right now. Medical school is grueling." Frankie bit back her last thought that perhaps now wasn't a good time to get married.

Violet cried harder, angry warm tears. She closed the scrapbook and hugged Frankie hard. "I'm infuriated at him. It's like he isn't even thinking of Sophie's feelings at all. It's BS if you ask me."

Frankie smiled over her daughter's shoulder; her mood brightened by Violet's feisty spirit. "You're a good sister, Vi. I'm proud of you. Sophie's probably going to lean on you when she's out of quarantine. Now, how about if we go down to the Mud Puppy and get some fat-bottom burgers?"

After a bacon cheeseburger for Frankie and a California avocado burger for Violet, the two were filled to the brim and ended the day with a chick movie. Neither one could get their minds off of Sophie though, thick in the mire of a health crisis.

CHAPTER FIFTEEN

Rise up this morning, smiled with the rising sun.
Three little birds pitch by my doorstep.
Singing sweet songs of melodies pure and true.
Saying, 'This is my message to you'.

Bob Marley

Frankie tiptoed around the apartment Thursday morning to let Violet sleep in, a challenging feat for the clumsy baker. Noise typically followed her wherever she went. A cool front moved in overnight, so she donned a pair of old jeans but stuck to her habit of wearing loose T-shirts, which provided the most comfort in the hot kitchen.

She arrived downstairs before anyone else and set up her workstation for quiche-making as she routinely did on Thursdays and Fridays. She brought her tablet to life, a new piece of equipment that modernized the bakery. Each workstation included a tablet with recipe files organized into folders for kringles, pastries, cookies, quiches, and other offerings. The computer files gave access to everyone at once, so there was no waiting for the recipe binder, and the digital documents were always legible, never caked in syrup or egg yolk or scribbled in messy script.

What should she make for the weekend? As she scrolled the possibilities, she wondered if Sad Tomato Pie was in order, given the mood surrounding her family. The pie shell, chock full of caramelized onions and blistered tomatoes, was versatile in that spinach, roasted peppers, or spicy sausage could be added to make a unique creation each time.

Frankie usually reserved that pie for later in summer when tomatoes were in abundance, but Carmen had purchased a load of Campari tomatoes, so Frankie set her mind on Sad Tomato Pie, and scampered off to the cooler where she found packages of spicy Italian and Andouille sausages. Both would make yummy versions of the pie.

She loaded the squeaky cart with ingredients and found herself humming the tune, "Here Comes the Rain Again" by the Eurythmics. She stopped abruptly when she came face to face with Carmen, who was holding a supersized travel mug.

"I knew you'd be in early today, Frankie. Here's an oat milk latte with a squirt of brown sugar. I see you're making Sad Tomato Pie. Can we turn on the radio and play some happier music?"

Frankie scooted around the cart to give her friend a hug. "Thank you for this and for everything you helped with yesterday."

Carmen nodded, walked to the next station, and awakened the tablet. "Tia's under the weather, so I told her to take a day off. We're not busy and figured we could get along without her."

"Oh, no. What's wrong with Tia?" Frankie suspected Tia's feelings had something to do with the canceled wedding. Carmen's aunt had an internal barometer that fluctuated when trouble brewed in the lives of others.

Carmen confirmed Frankie's thoughts. "You know Tia. She's upset about Sophie's wedding. She says it brings back memories of her last engagement that ended when she caught her fiancé with his cousin, in his rowboat of all places." Carmen rolled her eyes.

"Oh my. I didn't know Tia had been engaged besides the three husbands she had." Frankie wondered if she would ever know all of Tia's life stories.

Carmen came to Frankie's station to grab the metal cart. "There's more engagements in that woman's life than there are weeds in the garden." She pushed the cart to the cooler to gather empanada ingredients, stopping by the music system to choose something upbeat for the morning.

Carmen searched the music app for their favorite stations. "I'm feeling the fifties or Calypso, Mon. What do you think?" Carmen spoke with a Jamaican accent.

In response, Frankie started swaying her hips, singing, "Baby don't worry about a thing, cause every little thing's gonna be all right."

Calypso music filled the kitchen, greeting Tess, Pom, and Cherry into the Bubble & Bake world. Tess laughed when Frankie grabbed her by the arm and twirled her as she walked by to take an apron from the baker's rack.

Tess laughed in surprise. "I didn't expect to find you in a good mood this morning, Boss."

Frankie looked momentarily sober. "It's all Carmen's fault.

Well, and Bob Marley's." She grinned again. "We took care of all we could yesterday. The rest is up to Sophie, Max, and the state board of health."

Frankie continued. "We have an announcement, everyone. We're going to host a pop-up dinner here after the caterer delivers the wedding food Saturday. We could use everyone's help if you're available." Frankie explained how the surprise free dinner would work.

Tess, Pom, and Cherry were enthused and immediately agreed to be on duty. Originally, the shop was going to close Saturday afternoon and evening so the entire Bubble & Bake staff could enjoy the festivities, but now an about-face was in order.

The morning routine resumed with Tess pulling Cherry to a workstation to make muffins. "We're going to learn to bake with alternative flours today: teff and almond," Tess announced aloud.

Frankie registered Pom's presence for the first time. "Oh hi, Pom. I didn't expect to see you until next week. I thought you would take time off since you just finished the school year."

Pom came over to the baker and jabbed her playfully in the side, laughing out loud. "I'm here for you, Frankie. You're supposed to be off today."

Frankie looked down at the counter and shook her head. "Thursday. Yes, my normal day off. Gee, I forgot I took off the rest of this week to help with wedding plans. My head is not working right. Sorry, Pom. Do you still want to work?"

Pom nodded. "Sure. I can ease my way back into the bakery the next couple of days before things get crazy around here." Pom normally worked in the wine lounge, serving customers on the deck, and conducting tastings, so a refresher in the front of shop wouldn't hurt. She donned a crisp colorful apron in sky blue with the Bubble & Bake logo scattered about the background. Her long blond ponytail swished as she skipped out the swinging doors to the customer area.

Frankie rolled out eight pie crusts and eased them into tins, then popped them into one of the commercial ovens with pie weights to blind bake. She turned back to the stove where a pile of sliced onions was glistening in a skillet on their way to caramelization. Her phone jangled in her apron pocket.

"Hey, Garrett, just let me turn down the burner here." She turned the gas off and walked out the back door for some fresh air. "Okay, all good. How are you?"

"Doing okay. You sound better than expected considering recent events." Garrett was surprised to hear the sunshine in Frankie's voice and hoped it might be because he was calling.

"Well, it's out of my hands. You and Carmen always tell me 'this too shall pass' and I'm trying to put that into practice."

Garrett was impressed. "That's good to hear, but I don't think I've ever heard Carmen use that phrase."

"Oh, she doesn't. She usually whispers 'three little birds' like a tune in my ear, and we both know. It's a Bob Marley reference. In fact, we were listening to that very song this morning." Frankie grinned. "But you must have news for me?"

"I do. I spoke with the Madison chief ME first thing this morning. He says he's just completed five additional autopsies besides what's been reported to Alonzo. All five died from a blood-borne pathogen combined with pulmonary edema or more simply, fluid in the lungs. All five are being connected to Robli24, which is the name assigned to the illness, and all five are from Whitman County, except for one."

"Let me guess. The one is from Zeeland, Vandenberg County."

"I never underestimate you, Miss Frankie. Are you investigating Robli24?" Garrett tried to piece together how Frankie would have time to make wedding preparations and investigate a strange virus.

"I hope you're sitting down because Alonzo asked me and Carmen to talk to some of the Amish women about the illnesses. The Amish have their own doctors and treatments, but rumor has it that many of them are sick or dead from the same thing."

"The sheriff was hoping you could use your friendly feminine charm to get the women to open up, right? Did it work?" Garrett had little doubt when it came to Frankie's ability to procure information.

"It did, at least in part. I think what we discovered just scratched the surface though. I wish someone could figure out the cause. Did the ME share anything else? Frankie asked.

"He said the quarantine would continue until they could get real answers, and I'm afraid they're not even close. The other possibility to ending the lockdown would be if no new cases emerge or they have success treating the current patients. Right now, the patients are in stasis while their lungs are failing to function, and their blood is being cleaned." Garrett's voice carried his sorrow to Frankie.

Frankie lifted her chin in defiance. "Looks like I have plenty to do then, and I'm determined to get to the bottom of this. For starters, I need to visit a widow. No, make that two. I have to go, G. Thank you for this." She made a last second decision not to tell Garrett about the impromptu free dinner at the shop slated for Saturday. She didn't want him to feel like he was missing out, although part of her hoped he would magically be home in two days.

Frankie rescued the crusts from the oven in the nick of time and set them on racks to cool before adding the tomato, onion, and sausage fillings. Tess and Cherry were immersed in making banana sunflower seed teff muffins and pumpkin cardamom almond flour muffins and didn't notice Frankie's departure from the kitchen, but Carmen took a break from folding empanadas onto a baking sheet to check on her friend.

"Any news?"

Frankie briefed her business partner, telling her she'd be gone the rest of the day. "I'm going out to Amish country, Carmen, and this time, I'm going armed." She snagged a large bakery box from the shelf, held it in front of her as an offering, her eyebrows bouncing up and down.

Carmen understood. "Good luck, and I expect a full report when you return."

For the second time in days, Frankie's SUV traversed County HH toward the county line, this time armed with baked goods, including three packaged kringles from the freezer, one each for Donna Graham, Joanna Yoder, and Emma Dunkel. The box included a variety of filled Bismarcks and leftover tarts from yesterday.

She navigated to the Graham farm with no trouble, remembering the fieldstone fronted house that was distinctly different from the white wooden Amish ones. She pulled into the driveway, retrieved the bakery box, and rang the doorbell. Nobody answered the first three rings, so Frankie set the box on the front porch swing and walked to the attached garage. She could see a sedan parked inside, probably belonging to Mrs. Graham. The farm truck was parked by the barn.

She guessed it was time to look around and started with

the garden behind the house, but it was empty. There were a few outbuildings on the property, but Frankie chose to visit the barn first. It was nearby and there was likely a reason for Mrs. Graham to be there.

When she neared the barn, she began calling out Donna's name in order not to startle her but received no answer. Frankie entered the barn anyway and waited for her eyes to adjust from the outside light to the darkness in the barn. The day was warming rapidly with the promise of above-average temperatures, making the barn air stifling.

Hay was stored there from the season before, so there was plenty of empty space for the new crop, if there was a new crop. Frankie wasn't sure if the Grahams kept any livestock beyond a few chickens, so perhaps the hay was a cash crop only. She wrinkled her nose as she walked about, smelling dead mice, a whiff of cat pee, and something musty. She sneezed, disturbing a cat that pounced off the top of a haystack, hissing and complaining.

That's when she saw a pair of black rubber boots peeking out from behind the hay. Dread overtook her, but she moved forward, rounded the haystacks, and came upon Donna Graham sprawled out in a comma shape, her eyes and mouth both open. Before she touched the woman's neck and wrist to find a pulse, she already knew she was dead and had been for hours or longer. There was blood around Donna's mouth and on the collar and yoke of her flannel shirt. Frankie instantly suspected she may have coughed up the blood, and she thought of Elsa Karlsen.

A call to the sheriff's department conveyed that Alonzo would be coming out personally. After disconnecting, Frankie decided she needed fresh air, but noticed a five-gallon pail just a foot away from Donna's head. That's when she discovered the second surprise of the day: a hoard of bats, looking lifeless, filled about half the pail. Frankie began to cough and gag at the same time, so she darted outside and leaned against the barn, gulping fresh air.

She met Alonzo's truck on arrival, looking worse for wear, and rushed to him as he got out.

"Whoa, are you okay, Frankie?" Alonzo grabbed her hands to steady her.

"Donna Graham is dead. For how long, I don't know. There's a bucket of bats in there, too. I think they're dead as well. Is a coroner coming?"

"First things first. I need to check on Mrs. Graham, but yeah, I called the coroner from Vandenberg County. He won't get here for an hour, probably." Lon was walking to the barn as he spoke with Frankie beside him. She stopped outside the door, unwilling to breathe the foul air again.

"Wait a second. Do you have a mask? I'd recommend it," Frankie suggested.

Lon pulled a first aid kit from the truck and donned a face mask. To his credit, he was in the barn a while, administering emergency care to no avail. He emerged from the barn and took off the mask. "I think you're right. She's been dead maybe a few hours. Why were you out here, Frankie?"

"I was bringing her goodies from the bakery, as I promised I would do the next time I came this way. But I had an ulterior motive. I wanted to talk to her about her husband's death and ask her some pointed questions about the Amish, but I'm too late. That means I'm off to my next stop." She started toward the front porch to grab the bakery box.

"Wait a minute, Frankie. I smell something fishy. You're leaving before the coroner gets here? I thought you'd want to stick around to see what he says." Alonzo narrowed his eyes and stuck out his chest.

"There's no point really. By the looks of the dried blood around her mouth and front of her shirt, she coughed up blood, just as Elsa Karlsen did, and just as John Van Cleef did. She died in the barn, the same place her husband died." Frankie turned back toward the porch.

"You think you've got this figured out, eh?" Alonzo taunted.

"Not at all, which is why I'm moving on. I forgot to tell you something that might be important. Dr. Sadie told me about some dead cows from Amish farms out this way. She suspects they died from multiple mosquito bites. The cows were sent to the state lab in Madison for necropsies. If I were you, I'd send those bats to the same lab." Frankie spoke with authority.

Alonzo registered the connection. "Because mosquitoes are the main diet of bats. You think there's a connection between the mosquitoes and the dead people?"

"I don't know what to think, Lon. It doesn't make sense when I think about the people from St. Anthony's who were working in the kitchen. But if they died from a blood-borne pathogen and pulmonary edema, then mosquitoes could be the culprits."

Alonzo wagged a finger at her. "Who have you been talking to, Frankie?"

"Garrett called this morning after a conversation with the Madison ME. I was planning to call you after making my rounds today."

Alonzo wondered if she indeed planned to keep him in the

loop. "What's your plan of action with the Amish women?"

Frankie stared at the roadway. "It starts with baked goods and leads to friendly conversation that I hope will produce names and locations of sick and dead people."

Lon scoffed and kicked at the ground with one boot. "Flying by the seat of your pants."

"I pay attention. That's always my plan. Have you spoken to Bram Callahan?" Frankie doubted Lon would have had the chance yet.

Lon shook his head no. "If you do find a way to get the Amish talking, see if you can find out the names of their doctors. I'm going to pay them a visit."

He opened the truck door to begin paperwork on Donna Graham but called to Frankie's retreating figure. "Frankie! I appreciate you doing this. The Amish clam up as soon as they see anyone in uniform, so I can't send Pflug or Shirley out here."

Frankie nodded, smiled broadly, and pointed the SUV down the road to Joanna Yoder's farm, strategizing along the way. She hit the brakes hard seeing a huge collection of buggies parked in the Yoder driveway, lined up on the lawn, and trailing down to the barn. She pulled over and parked across from the farm where the shoulder was level.

Walking warily toward the farmhouse, she saw a few children sitting on a patch of grass, quietly reading. An old woman and Emma Dunkel sat with them. Emma raised her eyes demurely at Frankie, who wondered if the Amish woman recognized her from their meeting just a couple of days earlier.

"What do you want here?" The old woman raised her eyes upward toward Frankie with puckered lips, her tone a mixture of concern and disapproval.

A sudden realization that she had stepped into a situation made Frankie pause. She swept her eyes downward, folded her hands together humbly, and murmured. "I was hoping to have a word with Mrs. Dunkel, please." Somehow it seemed the old woman controlled the gathering of children and Emma.

Emma lifted her face toward the elder and carefully touched her hand, which was laid against an open prayer book. "Please Aunt Esther. Let me help the English woman. She's a customer."

Aunt Esther produced a nearly imperceptible dip of her head, then picked up the prayer book to continue reading in a whisper to the children.

Frankie walked over toward the front pasture fence line, out of hearing range. "Emma, I'm so sorry. What's going on here, may I ask?"

A shadow passed over Emma's face. "Joanna's sister has died. We are starting the funeral today."

Frankie clasped both of Emma's hands, which were cold and shaking. "How terrible. But I thought Joanna's son was sick on Monday when I last saw you?"

Emma nodded through tears. "Yes. That's true, but Micah is recovering now. Joanna's sister has been visiting for weeks though, and she became sick, too. Joanna is beside herself. You see, she wanted to take her to the hospital. We're all a little scared." Emma patted the front of her stomach, another sign she may be pregnant.

Frankie was distracted by a group of men dressed in church clothes, circled together just outside the front door of the house. "I'm sorry. What's going on over there?" She discreetly gestured toward the men.

"The men will lead prayers now. They will continue until dark.

This is the first day of the funeral where we assemble at the home. Tomorrow we will be here, too, then at the church and cemetery on Saturday."

Emma's eyes darted toward the old aunt who closely watched her conversation with Frankie. "The women are gathered inside the home, praying in the big room. Tomorrow, the Zeeland mortician will bring Judith back home and all of us will assemble in the barn."

Frankie wasn't versed in Amish funeral traditions but was surprised to hear the body was being embalmed and by a commercial mortician. She sensed she had precious little time to ask Emma questions, so it was necessary to be direct. "Emma, I need some information from you to help the doctors get to the bottom of this illness we're all afraid of. Can you give me all the names of the sick and dead in your community?"

Emma appeared frightened and shriveled. "Maybe. With Joanna's help. You must come to my house after the funeral. Not Sunday. Monday morning."

Frankie acknowledged with a brief nod. "Is your doctor here?" She indicated the group of men.

Emma scanned the group. The men were dressed identically, making it difficult to distinguish among them, but they all held their hats in their hands to pray, and she only needed to look at the bald men to locate the doctor. "Dr. Miller is right next to our bishop, who is in the middle of the prayer group. The bald man with the wide bushy white beard."

"Thank you." Frankie was pleased Emma had answered two questions at once. "What is your bishop's name?'

Emma looked puzzled. Surely Frankie didn't intend to speak with either of the men directly? That kind of behavior violated protocol in every sense of the word. "His name is Jacob Yoder. The Yoder family is extensive. But you mustn't speak to him. He won't talk to you."

Emma began to fidget under the scrutiny of Aunt Esther now. Frankie knew she'd overstayed her welcome and would have to leave with unanswered questions for the moment. She clasped both of Emma's hands in gratitude. "I will see you Monday morning. Is eleven a.m. a good time?"

Emma nodded, lifted her dark skirt, and dashed back to the children and Aunt Esther. Frankie noticed a few other young women had joined the group sitting on the grass in prayer. She recognized Alice, Joanna's cousin, among them.

Frankie headed toward the roadway again, but something strange caught her attention. Off to the right, between the farmhouse and a large shed, she saw two women engaged in a pantomimed argument. Staying low and moving quickly, Frankie scooted toward the shed and made her way around the back to the corner. She could see the Yoder house and backyard, but there were no other people around.

Frankie peered around the corner and had to cover her mouth to keep from gasping. Joanna Yoder stood in Frankie's sight line, and she was loudly whispering at another woman who's back was toward Frankie. The bishop and men's group could be heard chanting prayers in unison, which provided enough cover for the two unhappy women to raise their voices.

Joanna spoke through tears. "And if I have any other sick family, Caroline, I will find someone who will take them to the hospital. Or I'll take them myself."

Caroline moved closer and slapped Joanna across the face. "You know you cannot. Now, get a hold of yourself. This display won't help your family."

Joanna laughed, unfazed by the slap. "It's not forbidden to seek medical help outside the community. Don't tell me what I cannot do." Joanna yelled in Caroline's face and started walking toward the shed, Caroline glaring at her backside every step.

Frankie froze in position, exhaled as she watched Caroline stride to the side entrance of the farmhouse, then sidled her way across the back wall of the shed, until she reached the rear window and heard voices coming from within.

What in the world have I uncovered this time? She ducked below the window, and glanced in every direction, relieved to see nobody was in view. The window was partly open, and she could hear low voices but wasn't able to catch the gist of the conversation. She risked raising herself up to investigate. She recognized Joanna but was shocked to see a woman who was certainly an outsider based on her dress alone. She wore a denim skirt, navy blue dotted blouse, and her hair hung loosely about her shoulders.

The two women embraced. The stranger spoke over Joanna's shoulder where Frankie could catch her words. "Come to me if you need anything at all, Joanna. Especially if you need to take your children to the hospital. I'm here for you."

"I don't know what I'm going to do now, but I'm glad I have you. You are a godsend." Joanna's voice was muffled, but Frankie detected a sisterly bond that reminded her of the friendship she had with Carmen.

When they separated, Joanna pulled something from a basket that was sitting on a bench and handed it to her friend. "I can't keep this here. Please make sure nothing happens to it."

The woman nodded in assurance, palmed the small item, and

placed it in the shoulder bag that sat at her feet. Joanna motioned for them both to be quiet, then she exited the shed's front door. Frankie slid back down into a squat and waited. She didn't hear the shed door open or close again, so she rose, peered through the window, and sidled around the side to the front. She tried the door and entered easily into a large space meant for crafting. A quilting frame was set up on one side of the shed with a quilt in progress. Several baskets containing spools of thread, needles, thimbles, and small scissors sat on benches surrounding the quilt frame. An armoire faced outward from one corner, which likely contained fabric. Boxes and chests lined the wall around the back window, probably containing more crafting items. Stools crowded together on the wall opposite the quilting area. The shed smelled pleasantly of fresh cottons and sawed lumber.

Frankie made a beeline for the bench where the woven basket sat from which Joanna had plucked something secret. The basket had two hinged covers on either side of a thick handle. She opened both sides and noticed pieces of soft flannel. She poked around but didn't feel anything solid. She sniffed inside, too, but the supple flannel didn't reveal anything about the secret item.

Frankie was certain she had overstayed her visit, which was sure to be noted since her SUV was parked nearby, so she stealthily exited the shed and skirted the edge of the road. She crossed over to the other shoulder before reaching the front side of the farm and bounded to her vehicle.

Once inside, she glanced to her left and found the tableau of the praying children supervised by Aunt Esther and Emma just as before. The circle of black clad men droned on in prayer, stark against the white farmhouse, resembling figures in a Rembrandt painting. Where was Joanna right now? *Had she rejoined the women in prayer for her sister, or had she slipped away for some private grieving?*

Frankie glanced at the forgotten bakery box on the passenger seat. The SUV was blessedly cool thanks to open windows and a country breeze, but she wanted to home her pastries as quickly as possible. The next driveway belonged to the Dunkels, and Frankie decided to leave two kringles and a few Bismarcks on the screened-in porch of their home with a note explaining the treats were a thank- you for the asparagus and syrup.

The next few miles were a blur, and soon Frankie rolled into Zeeland, and ascended the hilly Vermeer Drive to the Van Cleef home. As she trotted up the front walk, she saw Sarah loading boxes into the back of a pickup truck in the open garage. Frankie called out to her, and Sarah turned in surprise.

"Frankie Champagne! You're back already. Something must be up. Where's Carmen?" Sarah seemed to be jovial, so Frankie suspected she was unaware of the funeral going on just down the road.

"Did I catch you at a bad time? Are you going somewhere?" Frankie noticed the shiny new truck was filled to the brim.

Sarah followed Frankie's eyeline to the truck bed. "Oh, that. No. I'm starting to clean out some of John's things. The man was a pack rat, God love him." She walked to the truck, closed the tailgate, and shut the overhead garage door.

"I brought you one of my signature kringles, a raspberry cream cheese version, and a variety of filled Bismarcks to sample." She held out the white box in offering. "Carmen is working at the bakery."

Sarah exclaimed over the pastries, then looked expectantly at

Frankie. "Something's brewing up there. I can see you're holding back. Is there news about the illness?"

Frankie allowed her gaze to drift to the bright geraniums and impatiens spread around the garden fence. She didn't know where to begin. "I wanted to ask you about your husband's autopsy." It was an abrupt start.

"The ME called this morning. It's inconclusive. The cause of death is a blood-borne illness and fluid in the lungs that rendered him unable to breathe. They can't explain why it was so sudden. Maybe I'll never know. I may get my John back next week though, so I can plan the funeral." Sarah removed her work gloves and gestured toward the patio. "Can I get us some iced tea and plates, and we'll sit a bit and enjoy your lovely baked goods?"

It was well past lunch and Sarah's mention of food registered in Frankie's stomach with a growl. Sarah returned with small pottery plates, painted pine boughs and pinecones decorated the borders. Two metal tumblers balanced on top of the plates and a metal pitcher of iced tea swung to the table from her other hand. "I'll pour and you can plate."

Frankie plated a large wedge of kringle and different Bismarck halves—one lemon custard and one chocolate cream— and presented the treats to Sarah. On her own plate, she nibbled at a small wedge of kringle and ate one of the almond poppyseed muffins.

Sarah made yummy noises after biting into the kringle. "Where has this been all my life?" She examined the buttery layers and licked icing from one finger.

Frankie smiled and gave the briefest of explanations about the Danish kringle and her beloved baking tutor, her grandmother Sophie Petersen.

"What treasured memories you must have, Frankie. My mother was a strict taskmaster in the kitchen, and maybe that's why I can sew, paint, and keep a lovely garden. Just don't ask me to bake anything." Sarah cringed, whether at the memory of her mother or her ineptitude at baking, Frankie couldn't be certain.

"Now, let's get down to brass tacks. What else brings you here? I see how conflicted you look." Sarah could add intuition to her many gifts.

Frankie tried to determine how to walk the fine line between babbling about the Amish community and inquiring about the woman named Caroline and the outsider who befriended Joanna.

"I do have questions for you. You may not know this, but Joanna Yoder lost her sister, probably to the same illness."

Sarah gasped. "No, I didn't know. I'm not on the best of terms with the Yoder clan, and I don't know who would tell me besides Emma. How did you come to find out?"

Frankie inhaled sharply. "I was just there. I had follow-up questions for Donna Graham and the Amish women. I saw a bunch of buggies and wagons parked at the Yoder farm. I spoke briefly with Emma, under the watchful eyes of someone named Aunt Esther. It was the first day of the funeral ceremony. Judith—the sister—was still at the mortician's, being embalmed I gather."

Sarah confirmed. "Some Amish districts don't embalm their dead, but ours does as a matter of routine. The Whitman County community has some modern beliefs when it comes to funerals and medicine. Poor Joanna. Did you hear anything about Lydia's children?"

"I'm working on it. I asked the sheriff to specifically find out. He's in contact with hospital officials and the Madison ME. The sheriff is keeping a map of the victims and their locations. You know, so far, your husband is the only person from outside Whitman County. Any thoughts on that?" Frankie was desperate to find commonalities among victims.

Sarah shook her head. "I don't, but I will think about it. You said that someone died in your church. That seems odd to me, and I wonder what the two churches might have in common."

Frankie wondered the same thing. "Do you know anyone in the community named Caroline? From what I saw, she was rail thin, very tall, and had a sharp nose with nearly no bridge, and tiny wire glasses that barely stayed on."

Sarah narrowed her eyes, picturing the woman in question. "If you saw her at the Yoder farm, I'm sure you're describing Caroline Yoder. She's married to Ian, the brother of Joanna's husband, Ethan. I don't know much about Caroline except that she isn't friendly, but then she'd have no reason to be nice to me, I suppose. Why do you ask?"

Frankie stared into her drink tumbler for answers. "It may not be nice to say, but it might matter, too. I saw Caroline and Joanna having a disagreement outside when I was leaving the farm. I think they were arguing about seeking outside medical help for the sick."

Sarah chewed thoughtfully on a bite of lemon Bismarck. "I don't understand that. It's always been the practice of our district to seek modern medical treatment when illnesses are life threatening, or when the family wishes to do so. This illness seems to have everyone baffled, so maybe the Amish bishop determined the community will deal with it privately. That's how I see it. Is your sheriff going to talk with the bishop or the Amish doctor?"

Frankie shrugged. "I suggested the sheriff talk with both men."

Frankie considered asking Sarah about the outsider seen consoling Joanna Yoder in the shed, but since Sarah had left the community years ago, she thought it was unlikely she knew the woman. Better to wait until she could ask Joanna directly, she decided.

"Now that you'll be able to have your husband's funeral, do you think you'll stay here afterwards?" Frankie wondered if Sarah had friends in Zeeland to comfort her.

"I'm not sure. I'd like to live someplace where I can keep horses again. Kentucky comes to mind. I miss the farm animals," Sarah confessed.

Frankie reiterated her promise to call Sarah as soon as she heard about the Shumaker children and asked Sarah to do the same if she thought of anything that might help. Frankie drove to the bottom of Vermeer Drive and pulled over to park, letting the SUV idle. She pulled out her phone and tapped on Alonzo's contact.

"Sheriff Goodman," the weary voice came across the line, then, "Oh, it's you, Frankie. How's the rest of Amish country? I'm still wrapping up with poor Donna Graham."

"I stumbled upon another death. Down the road from the Graham farm. Joanna Yoder's sister, Judith. Most of the community was gathered there for a prayer service on the first day of the funeral. When I was there on Monday, Emma told me the Yoder boy had the same symptoms that matched Robli24. Emma said the boy was recovering now. Joanna's sister was visiting though, and it appears she died from the same illness."

Alonzo clenched his fists and inhaled heavily. "I'm sure you weren't welcome there. I don't suppose there will be an autopsy."

"Here's what I do know. Judith is being embalmed in Zeeland. The mortician will return the body to the family tomorrow, so you may want to prod the mortician ASAP. While I had the chance, I saw the doctor and the bishop, standing side by side in the prayer group in front of the Yoders' house. Dr. Miller and Bishop Jacob Yoder are your men, and I think you should dress like a civilian and go see them."

"Frankie Champagne, are you telling me how to do my job?" Alonzo's voice was playful. "What do you suggest I say to break the ice with them, Smarty?"

Frankie laughed. "For starters, you all can congratulate yourselves for being men. They might like that from what I've heard."

Lon blew a loud raspberry that vibrated in her ear.

"You're better at small talk than you give yourself credit for, Lon. They're just men. Talk to them the way you talk to any men, but level with them. It's time for everyone to work together to get to the bottom of this illness. You've got this, Alonzo."

CHAPTER SIXTEEN

*The next time you encounter a difficult obstacle or problem,
you should smile and say, "Here's my chance to grow."*

&

Zig Ziglar

Friday arrived without a change in the outdoor temperature. The air felt more like the dog days of summer than early June, and the cool front twenty-four hours ago was a ghost of a memory. Frankie bypassed Bubble & Bake, instead taking the outside stairs from her deck, and ripped the SUV down the alleyway before being noticed.

She wouldn't sacrifice her morning brew though, so she treated herself to a stop at Trickster Coffeehouse near Founders' Square downtown. The salted caramel lavender latte was a rare allowance Frankie intended to savor all the way out to Lovely Lavender Farm.

Today was the day the canceled wedding would begin to feel real now that Frankie was picking up a boatload of flowers from Coral Anders.

She let the SUV crawl down the gravel driveway and imagined herself somewhere else until the log cabin came into view. Coral met Frankie in the driveway, accompanied by an excited Freya, Garrett's elkhound. Seeing Freya conjured happiness and disappointment at the same time. Both females missed Garrett.

Coral glowed with perspiration and contentment—a healthier woman couldn't be found in Deep Lakes. "I thought you might like to see a friendly face this morning, Frankie." Coral handed the dog leash to her, and Freya began turning circles, then lay down in a puppy pose to play.

"There's a good girl." Frankie stroked the elkie's neck and chin while her tail thumped against the ground. "Thanks, Coral. I needed a little extra love."

Coral looped her arm through Frankie's and led her to the greenhouse behind the cabin. "I have everything ready to go. I already filled the first wagon." She opened the door revealing an explosion of colorful arrangements ready for a flower show.

"Oh wow! Everything's just gorgeous. You're so talented." Frankie tamped down her disappointment that Sophie wasn't beside her to witness the spectacle.

Coral lost her glow momentarily. "I'm truly sorry, my dear. I cannot imagine how you must be feeling right now."

Frankie jutted out her chin and donned her brave face. "The nursing home and senior village are going to love these. I'm also dropping flowers off at my church. And Bubble & Bake will never look better dressed for the season. Stop in Saturday for dinner and you'll see." She told Coral about the impromptu dinner with the catered wedding food.

Coral smiled and patted her arm. "I'll leave you to it, Frankie.

I have to get some plants ready for pickup." Coral took Freya's leash and walked her back to the house.

Frankie arranged the first load of flowers in the back of the SUV and was reassured the whole order would fit in one trip. The day was heating up already, so she was glad she'd started early. Finally, she was dragging the last wagon load of bouquets down the path from the greenhouse, feeling fatigued from the radiating sun.

A second vehicle pulled in next to Frankie's and when the driver ascended from the car, Frankie knew she looked familiar. She paused to place the woman when another rose from the passenger side dressed in a plain pine green shift. The passenger's hair was neatly pinned into a bun underneath a clear bonnet. When the woman turned, Frankie gasped in surprise. It was Joanna Yoder and the woman from the shed.

"Hello Joanna. How are you?" Frankie waved her hand in greeting, startling the Amish woman.

"Hello. It's nice to see you again. What beautiful flowers." Joanna's eyes soaked in the colorful display of lavender, yellow irises, blue delphiniums, and daisies. For a moment, her admiration replaced her sorrow.

The other woman gazed from Joanna to Frankie and back again. "Hello. I don't think we've met. I'm Samantha Quade, Joanna's next-door neighbor. And you are?"

Frankie sensed protectiveness. "Nice to meet you, Samantha. I'm Frankie Champagne. I own Bubble & Bake in Deep Lakes." She thought Samantha might have heard of the bakery/wine lounge.

"Oh, I've been meaning to stop by sometime. I get most of my bakery from the Amish community. You know—because I live so close." Samantha looked around awkwardly, ready to resume her business.

"Joanna, I heard about your sister. You have my sympathy." Frankie couldn't find a reason to pretend she didn't know.

Joanna blushed scarlet and looked down at her black buttoned shoes. "Thank you. I asked Samantha to bring me here for some lavender. It was my sister's favorite and ours is still very small."

"Coral grows the best lavender around. It's nice you will have something to remind you of your sister." Frankie wanted to comfort Joanna but wasn't sure if she should touch her.

"That's a lot of flowers you have there." Samantha changed the subject. She peered inside the hatchback for a closer look. "Wow, those are Cape Daisies, right?"

Frankie stared into the back of the SUV, a traveling parade float. "Yes, they are. My daughter picked out all of these. She was supposed to be getting married tomorrow, but the wedding's been postponed."

Both women looked stricken. "I'm so sorry to hear that," Joanna spoke with sincerity while Samantha nodded the sentiment.

"It's because of this illness," Frankie's face darkened. "My daughter is a nurse at UW Hospital in Madison. She was exposed to the illness and is quarantined at the hospital until they can get to the bottom of it all."

"Oh no. Is she sick, too?" Joanna's face was pale with sorrow and panic.

"No, no. She's helping the sick. I just wish we could figure it all out—the cause I mean. It would help if the Amish elders would work with our authorities. I know your community has suffered many losses." Frankie's eyes implored Joanna.

Samantha stood in front of her friend to shield her from Frankie. "There isn't anything Joanna can do. She's a woman. She has nothing to say." Samantha was defensive, and Frankie instantly regretted her suggestion.

"I'm sorry. I know this is hard on you and your community. I didn't mean to imply anything was your fault, Joanna."

Frankie reached into the back of the SUV and pulled out a large mixed bouquet in a glass vase. "Here, please take this in memory of your sister."

Joanna objected. "I wish I could take it. It's so thoughtful of you. I'm already in trouble for coming out here with Samantha. My sister is being returned today, and the funeral will continue. I must get back."

"I understand." Frankie stuffed the vase back into the SUV. "If you have any information you'd like to share with me, I'm happy to listen. Before anyone else gets sick." She spoke quietly without accusation but directed her comment to Samantha. Was Frankie mistaken or did Samantha Quade look guilty?

Samantha's gaze shifted back to the array of flowers, and she smiled in admiration.

"You must like flowers. You seem to know them well," Frankie softened her tone.

Samantha's smile widened. "I teach science at Deep Lakes Middle School. I've had my own flower patch since I was a child."

"Deep Lakes Middle School? One of my Bubble & Bake crew is a teacher there, too. Pom Parker?"

Samantha's face relaxed even more. "I know Pom. She teaches English, and she's been very kind to me. This was my first year there."

Frankie reached back into the SUV and pulled out the same flower bouquet to offer to Samantha. "Happy end of your first year at Deep Lakes." Samantha grinned in appreciation.

A mile down the road, Frankie stopped at Bountiful Fruits to say hello to Violet and check on the grapevines. The hot weather was sure to bring on early fruiting, and Frankie worried there wouldn't be enough rain to ensure a healthy harvest later. She was pleased to see thriving green leaves and tiny grape clusters forming in abundance.

She ducked inside the winery where Zane and Violet were engaged in a lively exchange about the Pacific area award-winning wines, and their equally award-winning winemakers.

"I think we should try to mimic the Prima Donna red from Pondera winery," Zane said. "We have the red blend juice from the region, and I wager we can duplicate it," he boasted.

Violet snickered. "You're only saying that because you have a bromance going with Shane Howard, the vintner. You'd like to see the Shane and Zane show." Violet gave Zane's foot a little kick.

"To be fair, the man did win vintner of the year. Why not try to follow in the footsteps of the great ones?" Zane elevated his head grandly, his voice perfectly haughty.

"Good morning. Listening to you two, I imagine we're going to have a lively debate about how to use our Pacific area grapes on Monday." Frankie grinned.

Violet jumped up to give her a hug. "Mom, can I talk to you for a minute? I want to show you something in the orchard."

She led Frankie into the nearest shady spot and stopped. "I talked to Max this morning."

"Any news on Sophie?" Frankie was anxious.

"No. Max talked to Dre last night. He wanted to let us know the Shumaker children were stable but still getting intensive treatment."

Frankie's bubble burst. She'd hoped to hear from Sophie. "That's good news for the Amish anyway. Anything else?"

"Yes. Dre said UW scientists might have isolated the carrier. They're studying mosquito-borne diseases: West Nile Virus, Yellow Fever, Dengue. But this disease isn't any of those. They worry it's something new."

"Ugh. That's not good news." Frankie wondered about Dre. How did a security guard at the hospital have access to such specific information? "I'm glad Max has a good contact at the hospital though," was all she said.

Violet wore a sullen expression as she kicked at the dirt. "I'm just so mad at Max, I might explode."

Frankie understood. "I'm assuming he hasn't spoken directly to Sophie yet."

Violet shook her head as if it might come off. "I'm not sure he's trying. You'd think a guy like Dre could pull off a quick phone conversation. I don't think Max cares. Poor Sophie."

Frankie gave her a tight hug. "Hey. That kind of talk doesn't help anyone. We don't know how Max feels. But I'm glad you're such a loyal sister. What are you doing tonight, Vi? Should we go out for dinner?"

Violet reddened and looked at the ground. "It's supposed to be rehearsal party night," she stammered.

Frankie remembered. After the rehearsal, everyone was supposed to meet up at The Viking Snug Pub, a hot spot that attracted tourists and locals alike. Live music and specialty drinks were featured in the industrial chic setting. "Well, we could still check out the Viking Pub. Maybe Carmen will want to come with us."

Violet raised her eyes and pouted. "A bunch of us are going to The Snug together tonight." She looked away.

"Oh good." Frankie understood Violet made plans with her friends and was happy to hear it, even if those plans excluded her.

"I hope that's okay, Mom. If I invited you, I'd have to invite Gram and Aunt CeCe..." Violet's tone took on a tinge of disgust at the prospect.

Frankie giggled. "I get it. When I was younger, the last thing I wanted to do was go out with my mother. Sometimes I still feel that way. Go blow off some steam, Kiddo."

Violet squeezed her mom tightly before Frankie retreated to the SUV. "I need to get these flowers delivered before they wilt in this heat."

The first two stops at Sunnyvale Elder Care and Birdsong Senior Village took longer than usual with several residents waylaying Frankie to chat about their current ailments or bygone days. She felt some satisfaction in brightening up the sterile environments with the colorful flowers and offering her listening ear.

When she pulled into St. Anthony's parking lot, she stopped to check the date. Yes, it was still Friday, but where were all the cars? Friday was a big day for visitors and volunteers. The church operated a free food pantry and thrift shop offering clothing and household items at cheap prices. The combination generally drew a lot of customers, but today the lot was unoccupied save for two vehicles.

Frankie retrieved two of the largest flower bouquets from

the rear of the SUV and swiftly paraded through the outer office entrance. She set the arrangements on the hallway floor and opened the office door to find Georgia sorting mail in the common area where the office copier was situated.

She jumped when she saw Frankie, pointed at Mike's open door, and made a shush gesture with her hand. Mike, the accounting and office manager, was talking to someone on the phone, and Georgia was trying to gather facts from one side of the conversation.

Frankie stood still until the call ended, then followed Georgia back to her desk in the reception area. "I brought flower arrangements for the church, part of the Sophie wedding offering." Frankie attempted to make light of the situation.

Georgia threw both hands in the air, remembering the date. "I'm so sorry, Francine. How are you managing all of it?" Georgia was prone to dramatics.

"Well, nobody's died, so it could be much worse." Frankie's offhand remark landed poorly, and she felt silly for saying it. "Yikes. I'm sorry, Georgia. Where is everyone today? Shouldn't the food pantry and thrift shop be open?"

Georgia shushed her again and whispered. "No, they're shut down—indefinitely." She abruptly rose from the office chair. "All right. If you insist, let's get these flowers up to the sanctuary right now, Frankie." She spoke much louder than necessary.

"Mike, please listen for the phone. I need to use the restroom and go up to church."

Georgia is acting strange. Now what's going on?

Georgia's heels clicked down the hallway that led to the sanctuary. Frankie spoke from behind a clump of delphiniums. "What is it, Georgia?"

"Just a minute. Let's set these flowers in the church first." Georgia placed the large bouquet under the altar and pointed to the statue of Mary where some bedraggled roses sat in a vase by Mary's feet. Frankie replaced the dying roses with the fresh bouquet.

Georgia tugged Frankie's arm and led her outside to the grotto where St. Francis of Assisi presided. She flopped down on one of the benches out of the sight line of Mike's office window.

"There's been another death," she began.

Frankie reacted appropriately, with fear and disappointment. Another death at St. Anthony's would most certainly extend the hospital quarantine. "Not Father or June?"

Georgia shook her head. "No, thankfully. But there's nothing new to report about them. They're in Madison, still. Intensive care—still. Father Dailey is the only one in the know, and he's silent as that statue." She stamped her foot and pointed at St. Francis.

Frankie couldn't muster much patience. "Then who? And how?"

"You know Helen Thurston volunteers in the archive room. Once we get several requests for dates of burials, weddings, and the like, Helen gets the recorded information and sends it to the requestor."

Georgia paused to brush away a ladybug. "Helen worked yesterday. Gene, you know the maintenance man…"

Frankie nodded.

"Gene opened the records room in the basement, and we all forgot she was down there. When Gene left for the day, he saw Helen's car was still in the lot. He found her in the records room, slumped over a stack of file boxes, like she'd been knocked out.

She was gone, just like that." Georgia squashed a rose beetle between her thumb and index finger to illustrate.

Helen Thurston had taught first grade to most of Deep Lakes, Frankie included. Just last year, she'd adopted one of the Bubble & Bake shop cats. Frankie felt the blow of another loss. "Can you back up a bit for me? Why are the food pantry and thrift shop closed?"

"The bishop decided to do it right after Helen died until we can have a full inspection of our building. There's something rotten in St. Anthony's and if you ask me, it's the ventilation system." Georgia was back on her soapbox, but Frankie reluctantly agreed. It seemed something in the air was claiming the health of St. Anthony's parishioners.

"What about Masses? What about you and Mike and Father Dailey?" Frankie surmised if the building wasn't safe for a food pantry, it wasn't safe for any reason.

"That's being decided even as we speak. Elsa Karlsen's funeral is going to be at St. Mary's in Portage on Wednesday. Our kitchen is officially off-limits." Georgia blew a curl off her forehead. "It's too hot out here, Frankie, and I don't have anything else to tell you. Oh yes. Nobody knows about Helen, so keep it quiet. Besides, she's been shipped to Madison to determine the cause of death. As if we didn't know."

Frankie walked through the building to the back lot, wishing she'd kept the AC and the engine running for the poor flowers. A few minutes later when she arrived at the shop, Carmen and Jovie met her outside to help her unload.

The flowers crowded the kitchen counters looking like a lavish indoor garden. In no time, Peggy, Carmen, Aunt CeCe, Jovie, and Frankie dispersed the vases around the café tables and lounge alcoves, turning the place into a space Martha Stewart would relish.

Aunt CeCe tended to an older couple requesting a wine tasting, which gave Frankie the chance to pull aside her mother, Carmen, and Jovie. She motioned them to follow her out to the deck.

"What's happened, Dear?" Peggy was as astute as ever.

"I just came from St. Anthony's, and I'm not supposed to tell anyone this, but I can't keep it from the three of you." Frankie blurted out the news. "Helen Thurston passed away yesterday in the archives room at church. Her body is being autopsied in Madison, according to Georgia." She waited for the news to sink in.

Jovie spoke first. "She was my neighbor. A kind lady," Jovie murmured.

Everyone nodded their agreement. "Goodness, she taught almost everyone in Deep Lakes between first grade and catechism," Peggy remarked.

"There's more." Frankie continued. "The bishop has closed the church kitchen, food pantry, and thrift shop. Furthermore, we might not be able to continue having Masses at church until the cause of this illness is determined. At least, according to Georgia Harris."

Peggy was sober. "As difficult as it is, we can't afford to lose any more people. What will be, will be." Peggy spun around and hurried back inside before anyone could see she was about to cry.

CHAPTER SEVENTEEN

You say you love rain, but you use an umbrella to walk under it.
You say you love sun, but you seek shade when it is shining.
You say you love wind, but when it comes, you close your window.
So that's why I'm scared when you say you love me.

Bob Marley

Saturday arrived gray with low clouds spraying a steady mist over Deep Lakes. The bakery was busier than usual as the weather seemed to support indoor pastry consumption. Tia Pepita was back in form, the picture of optimism in a bright green muumuu trimmed in yellow and turquoise pom-poms. For some reason, Tia challenged gloomy weather by creating her own landscape.

Aunt CeCe had also resumed her sorcery with customers. She and Tia made a dynamic duo in the shop.

"It's good to see the two aunts working their magic this morning," Frankie commented while reviewing the to-do list of details for the day.

Carmen giggled. "I think they're excited about the impromptu dinner tonight. You know those women like a party. Speaking of which, do we have enough volunteers on tap?"

Frankie nodded. "I think so. I talked to Julia Karlsen yesterday and gave her a heads-up on dinner. I wanted to invite her and Lew, with everything they've been through lately. Anyway, she popped over this morning to say Kirsten and Dana would volunteer. Violet's friends, Tara and Haley, are on the list, too."

"Don't forget about Kyle and Carlos. They're happy to help." Carmen reminded Frankie, then laughed quietly. "I think Dana Karlsen is sweet on one of the twins, so that could be fun to watch."

Frankie shook her finger at her friend. "You're positively sinister sometimes, Carmie."

"I know, it's good, right?" Carmen grinned. "Did Julia say anything about Elsa's funeral?"

"Shoot. I completely forgot. Yes. Elsa's funeral is Wednesday at St. Mary's in Portage. The bishop decided St. Anthony's will need to have funerals elsewhere until the cause of this illness is determined."

Carmen inhaled sharply. "Is there any new information about having Masses?"

Frankie nodded. "Julia said Father Dailey told the family that the bishop's main concern is with St. Anthony's basement, kitchen, and fellowship rooms. It seems the sanctuary isn't a problem."

Carmen frowned. "Hmm, that makes me wonder about the church in Zeeland where John Van Cleef died. Didn't his wife say the church just had a funeral dinner there?"

Frankie's eyes widened. "Yes, and Sarah said both she and John had been in the church basement. What do basements and kitchens have in common? Poor air quality, maybe." She pulled her phone from her apron pocket, swiped it to life, and tapped a note to herself about the matter.

Jovie, who was preparing butterhorn dough at the next station, joined the conversation. "I wonder about Helen Thurston. What will they decide about her death? She was in the basement at St. Anthony's, right?" Jovie knew Helen didn't have family nearby, and she had a soft spot for the older woman who had been helpful to her. Helen sometimes sat with Jovie's mother, a hypochondriac, before she moved to Florida.

Frankie put her arm around the sorrowful Jovie. "I'm sorry about Helen. I promise I'll let you know as soon as I hear anything about her. You're right though. She was in the basement, and it makes me wonder about these strange deaths. There's a connection we're missing somewhere between barns, kitchens, and basements. I mean, everyone has a basement and a kitchen. The other churches aren't having issues. Plenty of farmers with barns are doing just fine. So, what's the link?"

Jovie heaved a long sigh. "Let's change the subject. We've got a big day today. No point thinking about all this garbage now." She gave Frankie a quick hug. "If I know you, you'll figure things out before the scientists do."

Frankie recalled her average grades in chemistry and biology but smiled her thanks at Jovie anyway.

The morning mist gave way to pleasant rain showers that brought relief from the long streak of hot weather. The crisp air smelled of Wisconsin spring: lilacs, fresh grass, wet earth, and stone. The combination was a mood booster celebrating the moment.

Frankie took a few minutes to drink in the freshness by Sterling Creek before Casey arrived to deliver Sophie's wedding cake. Casey's Cakery had been a unanimous choice to create the three-tiered Sun Velvet cake, a light lemony sponge made decadent with a mascarpone pastry cream filling and an abundance of fresh lemon zest for an explosion of lemon cream flavor.

Casey pulled her silver van into the alley and parked next to Frankie's SUV. Frankie scampered to the van as both front doors opened.

Casey, a short, rounded woman around fifty, pounced on Frankie with a tight squeeze that conveyed how much she wished the day were different. "Frankie, it's good to see you again. I just wish Sophie and Max were here beside you."

"Thank you, Casey. I do, too." Frankie and Casey paused to let the moment pass.

"I'd like you to meet Jamie. She's one of the bakers and a first-rate decorator. Show us where the cakes are going, and we'll follow you."

The bakers and Frankie carried the cake layers to the shop cooler. As Frankie instructed, the cakes were frosted but not decorated except with a simple rope border. Each layer was nestled in its own freezer box for storage until Sophie and Max could decide on a new date.

Casey and Jamie stood in the kitchen and gladly accepted the iced tea and butterhorns Frankie offered them.

"As I explained on the phone, cool the layers for a few hours or overnight, then place them in the deep freeze. They will taste fresh up to four months. Beyond that, I can't guarantee how the cakes will stand up to the freezer. I'm sorry." A deep furrow settled between Casey's eyebrows. She understood how expensive wedding items were, and the thought of repeat spending made her stomach turn.

"Understood. Thank you for keeping your end of the bargain. I hope we're able to cut into that delicious cake sooner than later." Frankie offered a friendly smile, but inside she wondered how Sophie and Max would replicate their event.

Casey brightened. "Have you had a chance to experiment with a Sun Velvet cake recipe yet?" Frankie had melted into her seat at the cake tasting appointment when she sampled the Sun Velvet and was thrilled Sophie and Max had chosen that flavor. Frankie vowed on the spot she would be creating her own version.

"I've played with a few different concoctions, but I haven't settled on any one recipe yet. Yours is simply scrumptious," Frankie said.

Casey raised the last bite of butterhorn in a toast. "Right back at you on these butterhorns. They're extra buttery, flaky, sweet, spicy. They're perfect."

Frankie packed a few more into a box and handed them to Casey as she and Jamie departed.

Less than an hour later, Best Day Ever Catering pulled up in front of Bubble & Bake, flashers on, double doors open, ready to unload. Kyle and Carlos were camped near the front door and sprang into action when the van pulled in.

Frankie dashed down the front steps to greet the couple who were already unloading insulated carriers onto a dolly to cart up the ramp next to the shop entrance. She gave them a business wave.

"Hi. I'm Frankie Champagne, the owner. And you are…"

The petite woman introduced herself as Mitzi Day, the Day of Best Day Ever. "I'm the Jill of all trades, so to speak. I prepare or supervise prep of all our dishes, drive them to the site, and set up everything. This is Geno, one of my best assistants."

Frankie was surprised the most valuable people were dispatched for a simple food delivery. "It's good to meet you both. I spoke with you, Mitzi, on the phone. You remember that you're dropping off the food and won't need to set up anything, correct?"

Mitzi nodded, then pointed to black insulated carriers on one side of the van. "Those will go in next, please." She directed the comment to Kyle. Carlos was already helping Geno find the kitchen.

"Yes, Frankie I remember our phone discussion. Such a shame the wedding has to be rescheduled. Still, I want to make sure our food is properly plated for the ultimate enjoyment, so I'm going to demonstrate that to your kitchen staff."

Mitzi was an unstoppable force. She followed Kyle to the kitchen, with Frankie scampering to keep up. She could barely contain her surprise at seeing her shop crew lined up in military fashion behind the counter, waiting for instructions.

All eyes were on Geno, a tall muscular man with matching bushy mustache and eyebrows, the only hair on his head. With a flourish, Geno produced an elegant white square plate from somewhere behind him and settled it on the counter.

Mitzi, hands behind her back, strutted along the counter, pointing out insulated carriers as she spoke. "The black carriers hold your meat entrées: Bourbon glazed salmon and grilled citrus pork chops. This white carrier has the vegan entrée: Italian stuffed zucchini boat and pasta a la olio with broccolini and pine nuts. The red carriers contain all the garnishes: asparagus bundles, rustic smashed baby gold and rose potatoes, and the extras—celery and carrot curls, radish flowers, curly parsley, and fresh rosemary and dill sprigs. The blue tubs hold the fresh salad mixes, Tuscan and Greek varieties, and the dressings as well.

It was obvious Mitzi and Geno took great pride in their work. As each meal was plated, the two chefs choreographed precise locations of each dish, including the decorative elements. Frankie longed for Sophie and Max to witness the beauty and care taken with every element.

Mitzi smiled brightly, passed her hand across each plate like a game show host, and proclaimed her work was finished. "So, we'll be going now. Someone will come tomorrow to pick up the carriers. All set?"

Frankie abandoned her reverie to snap to attention. "Yes. We're here tomorrow from noon until five o'clock."

The caterers found their own way out while the kitchen workers remained caught up in the spell of the fabulous plating performance. Frankie and Carmen snapped their fingers simultaneously.

"It almost makes me wish Bubble & Bake was a fine dining restaurant," Cherry said, still awestruck.

"I think we learned something that might come in handy when we host the Valentine's Day food and wine pairing event, right? I hope we can remember what they did," Frankie said.

Carlos held up his cell phone. "Never fear, I recorded the whole thing." Carlos planned to go to culinary school and was entranced by the caterers' spiel.

Frankie beamed. "Nice job, Carlos. We'll refer to that in February. Meanwhile, you know we're plating on these very nice, but disposable, plates." Frankie opened a cupboard to pull out stacks of plant- based bamboo plates the shop purchased. "I know they're not elegant, but they are environmentally friendly." She smiled, waving around one of the natural plates with a pretty scalloped edge. Carlos and Cherry groaned, while Tess giggled.

"Hey, a free dinner is a free dinner. It's what's on the plate that counts." Carmen emphasized practically. "Besides, who wants to wash dishes?"

Frankie and Carmen assigned stations to all the regulars and volunteers. Peggy and Aunt CeCe would handle wine tastings while Jovie and Cherry would serve customers, shadowed by Kyle and Violet.

Violet's friends, Tara and Haley, would plate food along with Carlos. Frankie and Carmen would keep an eye on the food to ensure quality and act as floaters wherever they were needed. Kirsten and Dana Karlsen would do whatever Tess told them to do in the kitchen or wine lounge. Pom would serve as hostess, sign up customers for wine tastings, seat them if necessary, and act as cashier along with Tia Pepita.

At five-thirty p.m., Carmen and Frankie set a sandwich board in front of Bubble & Bake inviting people to come in for a free "Dinner Break." For the next two hours the shop looked like A *Family Circus* comic with every volunteer and crew member crisscrossing through the wine lounge and in and out of the kitchen. The din was continuous, but at least there were no clattering dishes to compete with conversation.

Many of the patrons were local wedding guests, so they enjoyed the catered dinner in a celebratory mood, thanks to wine and beer orders. Frankie smiled to see the jovial atmosphere. It made her aware of the importance of celebrating life, even during tough times.

At seven-thirty, Pom pulled Frankie and Carmen aside in the kitchen hallway.

"We've served more than a hundred dinner guests. Do you think it's time to take down the sign?"

The co-owners exchanged nods. "Yes, I think we should. I want to be sure the whole crew here gets to enjoy a meal, too. If someone we know comes in while we're still open, especially if they were a wedding guest, we'll be able to offer dinner to them." Frankie calculated serving around 135 dinners, but plating by her crew was sure to be less precise, so portions might be off.

She and Carmen hoisted the sandwich board up the shop ramp and slid it around the corner by the bakery case. Both women took advantage of the lull to take a breath in the office alcove.

"I'd say by all the racing around our people did, we had a lot of wine sales tonight." Carmen stifled a yawn.

"I feel so much better knowing the wedding food didn't go to waste. People enjoyed the dishes and companionship. They almost forgot they were supposed to be at a wedding." Frankie's half-smile conveyed her own mixed emotions.

Carmen patted her shoulder. "And our customers who didn't know anything about the situation were ecstatic about a surprise free meal. I think a lot of them bought extra wine because of it."

Frankie frowned. "It's not all about the money, Carmen. Having great sales doesn't make up for a canceled wedding." She stamped one foot on the last two words, then instantly regretted losing her temper. "I'm sorry. I know what you mean."

Carmen stood up and took Frankie's hand. "Come on. You need something to eat. Let's each grab a plate while the food's still hot. We can eat on the deck."

Frankie didn't protest, although she made sure to check on her crew first. The women entered the kitchen where a beaming Carlos was preparing a couple of dinner plates with great finesse. Carmen smiled at her son.

"Looks like the kitchen is slowing down. Frankie and I took the front sign down, so it's time for all of you to make plates for yourselves. Tess, when you've finished, will you please relieve the aunties and Peggy, so they can eat? Maybe Tara and Haley can help out front, too. We're going to eat now, and then relieve Pom, Violet, and Kyle."

Tess said she would take care of eating arrangements, and Tara gave a little hand clap.

"I can't wait to taste this food. We've been smelling it all night and my stomach is growling in anticipation," Tara gushed.

Carlos picked up two plates and laid them out by the entrées. "Mom, let me do the honors for you and Frankie. Tell me what you'd like."

As Carlos constructed the two plates like a master, Dana Karlsen looked on with admiration or something beyond that.

Just about closing time, Alonzo stepped through the shop door and inhaled deeply. The place was all but empty of customers now and the whole Bubble & Bake crew were relaxed and walking around to slowly tidy up.

Frankie was behind the tasting bar talking with her mother and Aunt CeCe. She looked at Alonzo, who was patting his stomach.

"Good evening, all. I don't suppose there's any dinner food

left." It was a hopeful statement.

Frankie laughed. "We saved you a plate. You can head into the kitchen and watch the magician at work." Her reference to Carlos was lost on the sheriff, but he didn't care. He was hungry.

"The food was certainly delicious. You never know with a catering service, but I think we could use them again." Peggy weighed in like a critic. "But what will you do about the wedding wine, Dear?"

Frankie and Violet had painstakingly crafted a special vintage for Sophie and Max. The wine, made from Frontenac Gris grapes was a sassy pink color with notes of vanilla, candied almonds, orange blossoms, and peach nectar. The semi-sweet vintage was christened Spinning Dreams, a limited edition of only one hundred bottles.

"Spinning Dreams," Frankie loved saying its name, "is safely tucked away at the winery for now. It's meant to be enjoyed young, so I'm hoping it will be uncorked within the next six months or so." Her inner voice told her not to count on it. Who knew when the wedding would be rescheduled?

Alonzo emerged from the kitchen wearing a wide grin and carrying an extra-large plate of food. He found squatting space next to Carmen's husband, Ryan, in the wine lounge and immediately praised the twins for being hard working volunteers. "I wish all the teenagers around here had as much ambition as Kyle and Carlos," he said. The comment instigated a whole conversation about work ethics in America.

The front doors were locked, and the open sign was off, so Frankie was surprised to see Samantha Quade accompanied by Pom coming in through the back deck entrance.

"Samantha, what brings you here? Would you like a wine

tasting? We still have bottles ready to go." Frankie welcomed the woman she'd just met who was a friend to Joanna Yoder.

"Pom invited me to come tonight, but I'm afraid I was waylaid. Sorry for arriving so late. I don't want you to go to any trouble, but I was hoping to speak with you about Joanna Yoder."

Frankie gestured for Samantha to sit at the bar, and she passed a wine checklist to her for marking her selections. Pom sat next to Samantha, pointing out some of her favorite wines and best sellers.

"I didn't know that you knew Samantha, Frankie, until we bumped into each other yesterday. I told Samantha she should get to know more people, and this was a good place to start. Now that school's out for the summer, we have more time for socializing." Pom nodded as she made her point.

Frankie started pouring wine samples while Pom took on the hostess role of describing each vintage.

"Are you hungry, Samantha? We have a lot of leftover food. Let me get something for you and perhaps you can enjoy a glass of wine after your tasting." Frankie went to the kitchen and returned with a vegan entrée and side dishes. She wasn't sure if Samantha was a meat eater, but she was sure if Joanna's friend wanted to talk, Frankie wanted to make her as comfortable as possible.

"This looks and smells amazing," Samantha exclaimed over the stuffed zucchini boat, pasta with pesto, and Greek salad.

Frankie smiled. "I didn't know whether or not you eat meat, but the pasta and zucchini are delicious."

Samantha took a small bite from the steaming plate, followed by a generous sip of Persephone's Temptation, the pomegranate zinfandel, she'd selected to have with dinner. "I eat pretty much everything! This tastes really good." She dabbed one corner of her mouth with a napkin. "Wait a minute. Today was supposed to be your daughter's wedding. Is this...?" She pointed to her plate.

Frankie smiled appreciatively. "Yes, this is part of the wedding dinner. The catering fees were all but paid and nonrefundable, so I figured our customers might enjoy a good meal."

"You're very kind, Frankie," Samantha murmured.

"Please take your time. I'm going to send my workers home and help with cleaning up. Then we can talk, okay?"

Frankie left Pom to visit with Samantha and wandered to the kitchen. Dana, Kirsten, and Carlos were putting away leftovers, making trips to and from the walk-in cooler, bantering back and forth. Well, Dana and Carlos did the bantering, while Kirsten rolled her eyes at the pair.

Cherry and Tess washed and dried wine glasses and placed them on the cart to go back to the bar where Jovie was putting them away. Kyle wheeled the mop bucket out front to clean floors, Tara and Haley helped Violet clean up the deck, and Peggy closed out the registers. Tia Pepita and Aunt CeCe, ready to call it a day, propped up their feet on a lounge coffee table and made chitchat with Alonzo and Ryan.

Frankie watched the display with satisfaction and a healthy dose of emotions. Carmen sidled up beside her, startling her out of her reverie. "It's been quite the month, hasn't it Frankie?"

Frankie didn't speak, just nodded, and reached over to squeeze Carmen's hand.

"Are you going to introduce me to Pom's friend? She's got the inside scoop on the Amish, right?"

Frankie grinned. "It couldn't hurt for both of us to hear what she has to say. You might even think of something to ask her that I won't," she teased.

"Very funny, Ms. Smarty. By the way, what are you doing tomorrow? Don't you need a day off?"

Frankie sighed heavily. "Boy, do I. What did you have in mind?"

"You'll find out tomorrow. Be at my house no later than five a.m. Dress for the outdoors," said Carmen, her voice heavy with mystery.

"Five a.m.? That doesn't sound like a day off!" Frankie couldn't imagine what Carmen had dreamed up. "All right. Now let's go see what the Amish scuttlebutt is all about." Frankie turned off her mother persona to assume the role of super newshound, notebook in hand. She untied her apron, jammed it in the bin with the other dirty ones, and waltzed out to the bar.

Carmen stood behind the walnut bar top, pouring two glasses of wine from leftover tasting bottles. Pom excused herself to join the aunties in the lounge. Carmen passed a glass of Persephone's Temptation to Frankie and refilled Samantha's glass with the rest.

"Thanks, Carmie. Samantha Quade, please meet my business partner and best friend, Carmen Martinez. Samantha teaches middle school here, that's how she knows Pom."

"Happy to meet you. My twins are in high school now, but I don't believe they had you in middle school." Carmen tried to recall the names of their former teachers.

"No, I just finished my first year at Deep Lakes. It sure went by quickly, and I'm so glad it's summer. This is such a great space, you two." Samantha's complimentary and easygoing nature made her likeable. No wonder Joanna Yoder trusted her.

"I hope it's okay if Carmen joins the conversation. She's met Joanna and her neighbor Emma Dunkel. We're hoping they will supply eggs to the shop, and of course, we're deeply concerned about the illness that's killing people here." Frankie wondered if that disconnected explanation would suffice.

"Sure. I've heard you're good at solving crimes and such, Frankie. Pom said you helped find the person who killed her cousin. And I know you're a reporter, so I talked to Joanna and convinced her it was okay to share information with you."

Frankie was more intrigued than ever. "Okay. What information?"

Samantha pulled her cell phone from her purse and laid it on the bar top but didn't open anything to show them. Instead, she began to narrate details about her friendship with Joanna.

"I just moved into my house after Christmas last year, and you know how tedious winter can be around here. Joanna came to my door one January afternoon with an offering of friendship bread, fresh butter, and homemade strawberry jam. She introduced herself and was very shy at first. But we broke the ice in no time."

Samantha paused to drink some water. "Don't worry, I'm not going to share every visit we've had since then." She laughed.

As much as Frankie enjoyed hearing the quaint cozy details between friends, she was anxious for Samantha to get down to the nitty-gritty.

"Do you know anything about the Yoder family?" Samantha asked.

Both women shook their heads. "Except there seem to be a lot of them," Frankie offered.

"Right." Samantha leaned in and covertly whispered, "Have you ever heard of the Amish Mafia?"

Frankie and Carmen laughed out loud. "You mean like in the TV show? Come on, that's not real." Carmen jumped in.

Samantha's expression sobered as she nodded. "Well, the Yoders are not exactly mafia, but they have a lot of power and control in their community."

"Go on, please," Frankie said.

"The Yoders have a huge clan here and own a lot of the properties around me. The bishop, Jacob Yoder, is an uncle to Joanna's husband, Ethan. The community doctor, Peter Miller, is a Yoder cousin. Most of the bigwigs in the community are related in some way to the Yoders."

"Hmm, the blood lines must be getting thin in the community." Frankie considered how much easier it was to pass on genetic defects with too many closely related families. "Does Joanna think the Yoders are predisposed to getting the illness going around?"

Samantha shook her head no. "That's not the worry. It has to do with the Yoder brothers. Joanna's husband, Ethan, and his brother, Ian, own a pest control business. Joanna said their partnership began after she married Ethan. First, you need to know more about Joanna's background."

Frankie turned to a new page in her notebook, and Carmen took the cart of clean wine glasses from Cherry and wheeled it behind the bar to put them away. Cherry scooted away quickly as she sensed a private conversation.

"Joanna was raised in Ohio with her five sisters. Her parents never had a son, so Joanna's father decided to educate his daughters in agriculture, natural sciences, carpentry, and mechanics," Samantha continued. "Her father had a penchant for science, especially biology and chemistry. He invented a natural mosquito repellent and other pest control products using natural ingredients. When Joanna and Ethan married, he taught Ethan how to make the repellents."

Frankie's brows shot upwards. "I imagine word got around the Amish community, and other farmers wanted to use Ethan's products."

Samantha nodded. "Add to that Ethan's brother. Ian's very ambitious and sought to capitalize on the products. While Ethan was willing to share them with the community, Ian wanted a profit. The two formed a business."

Carmen weighed in. "I don't see a problem with that. In the farming community, things like that happen all the time. Nobody expects to get something for nothing." She understood the business side of farming, after years of running the sheep ranch with her husband.

Samantha nodded. "Right. Except that Ian was greedy. He wanted to do business outside the community."

"Many Amish enterprises do, Samantha. I see Amish roofers and carpenters all over Whitman County working for the English, as they refer to us." Frankie heard people saying they hired the Amish, since handymen were few and far between in the area. The Amish developed a reputation for a solid work ethic at reasonable prices.

"Yes, that's true, but Ian was hard-core. He came on strong to cut out his main competitor, Pate's Pest Eraser. Have you heard of it?"

Frankie and Carmen nodded. "Ray Pate had everyone's business in the county, I think," Carmen said. "We used him a few years ago at the farm for a rat infestation and here, too, when Frankie bought this building, right?" She turned toward Frankie.

"Yes. When I bought this place, it had been empty for a few years, so the vermin made themselves at home. Pate's has been around for as long as I can remember," Frankie added.

"Not anymore. Pate's sold out the business to Ian Yoder." Samantha waited for their reaction.

"Does that mean the Yoders have free reign? No competition whatsoever?" Frankie asked.

"Not unless people want to go a few counties away. The Yoders undercut all the competitors' prices because they can." Samantha informed them.

Frankie looked at Samantha's cell phone, which she covered protectively with one hand. "Why do I get the feeling your cell phone contains something important?" She didn't want Samantha to know she'd overheard her and Joanna in the Yoders' shed the other day.

"Ah, you're sharp, Frankie." Samantha uncovered the phone and began tapping and scrolling. "Here, Joanna took these photos."

Frankie and Carmen gazed at several photos showing an exchange between Ray Pate and Ian Yoder. Frankie recognized both men. "Ian Yoder is doing some kind of business with Ray Pate. You can easily see the wording on Pate's van and the Amish wagon. What's going on?"

Samantha tapped from photo to photo which almost looked like time-lapsed action shots. The two men shook hands. Ian handed a large envelope to Pate. Pate helped Ian load large canisters onto his wagon. A close-up shot of the canisters showed skull and crossbones—clearly poisonous contents were on board.

"What does Joanna think it means?" Frankie avoided speculating.

"Joanna said that Ethan confided some things to her. For starters, he and Ian disagreed about taking over Pate's products. Ethan is firmly rooted in using natural products for safety reasons. When people started getting deathly ill, Ethan told Joanna he believed the illness might be connected to Pate's chemicals."

"Wait a minute. How did Joanna get these photos? Were they taken before people started getting sick?" Frankie was trying to connect the dots.

"Ethan started complaining to Joanna weeks before Pate and Ian sealed the deal. Joanna thought it would be a good idea to protect her husband by spying on Ian, in case their partnership fell apart. She confided in me because she needed to borrow a cell phone for photos. She needed help with her children to pull off her spying, so Emma helped, too. Joanna trusted her to care for her children so she could sneak away."

"But she needed modern technology and a car, I imagine, to pull it off without being away from home too long." Carmen supposed.

"Yes, I was there when she took the photos, just parked out of sight," Samantha confessed.

"Once people started getting sick, Ethan guessed the chemicals were somehow involved? Did Joanna say anything else about Ian?" Frankie inquired.

Samantha nodded. "Ethan and Ian disagreed about using the chemicals. It blew up into an argument between the brothers and their families. Ian said they were under contract by farms that wanted to use proven pesticides and herbicides. The natural products discouraged pests but didn't kill them. I'll send the photos to you, Frankie, even though they don't prove anything."

"It's a trail worth following. Thank you and thank Joanna, please." With Samantha's permission, Frankie clicked on the sequence of photos and sent them to her cell phone.

"How did you end up buying property in Amish country anyway?" Frankie hoped to learn some new information about properties on HH.

"The land belonged to a farmer who lost his wife a few years ago. None of his relatives were interested in continuing the farm, and it was getting to be too much for him. He sold the whole parcel to Callahan Realty and my parents bought one plot for me, so I could live closer to them and the school."

"Who built your house?"

"Another one of the Yoder brothers, Ezra and his business partner, Adam Barr. Mr. Callahan suggested them. He said they'd get the work done faster and cheaper. My house is just a simple one-story bungalow."

"Are there other plots for sale and do you have other non-Amish neighbors?" Frankie kept firing.

"The plots are for sale, but I think they're going to be part of a development. At least that's what I heard. Lucky for me, my parents bought the plot before the development plans were in the works."

Frankie made notes on her cell phone as Samantha talked, but she didn't know if any of it mattered or was remotely connected to the mystery illness.

Samantha and Pom chatted briefly before saying good

night to the remaining crew. Carmen leaned over to whisper to Frankie.

"Are you sharing these photos with Alonzo? Now's your chance. He's sitting right over there shooting the bull with Ryan and the aunties." Carmen had both hands on her hips. Skepticism was written all over her face.

Frankie peered around Carmen as if she could see through the wall where the sheriff was camped out. "We don't know if these photos mean anything, Carmen. It's not a crime to buy or sell pesticides, is it? The Yoders must have a license to…" Frankie stopped cold, mid-thought.

"What is it?" Carmen asked.

"I don't know which Wisconsin business laws apply to the Amish, but I imagine they must need a license or permit to use pesticides. Maybe not for the natural homemade products, but certainly for the chemical ones." Frankie spoke excitedly.

"What's your point?"

"Maybe there is a crime in selling licensed chemicals if the Yoders don't have a use permit for them. And if that's true, maybe Whitman County can get to the bottom of this illness faster."

"Ah, good old leverage, right?" Carmen warmed up to the idea.

"Right, but we're not showing our cards yet, Carmie. We need to investigate this a little deeper first." Frankie rubbed her hands together, scheming.

Carmen smirked. "Let me guess: you think we should disguise ourselves as Amish?"

Frankie giggled. "Very funny. Actually, I probably could shadow one of the bakers there."

"Count me out." Carmen raised her hands in mock surrender.

"Don't worry. I've got a better idea." Frankie tucked her phone into her pocket and said good night.

CHAPTER EIGHTEEN

The antidote to exhaustion isn't rest.
It's nature.

⌛

Shikoba

In the predawn purple of Sunday morning, Carmen drove a clueless Frankie into the secluded Baraboo bluffs. The quartzite outcropping stood high above the Wisconsin River and was home to a must-see state park, Devil's Lake. Both women visited the park throughout their lifetime, first with family and friends, later with their own children. The park was a popular place to hike, climb, picnic, and swim in the cool deep waters. When Carmen's van passed the familiar entrance sign, Frankie was surprised.

"I guess we're not going to Devil's Lake today. Where are we going, Carmen?"

"Relax. We're almost there." Less than a mile down the road, the van turned onto a gravel driveway that followed an expansive grassy field for a half-mile. Fingers of pink light edged the sky's horizon. Frankie squinted into the dawn, seeing nothing but an empty field on either side of the driveway and a tiny wooden shed just coming into view.

Carmen parked at the top of the driveway where it widened into a spread of gravel and sand. She emerged from the van, opened the back, and grabbed binoculars and a hat. Frankie did the same.

"Are we birdwatching?" Frankie wondered if the surprise Carmen concocted was a wildlife excursion. In the past, the two had been on an owl prowl and monarch butterfly tagging expedition guided by pros. She pulled the binoculars to her eyes but there wasn't enough light to catch anything but shadows.

Carmen laughed. "Maybe. We'll have to see." She checked her phone. "We're early but the others should be here anytime."

Minutes later, a Suburban drove in, pulling a utility trailer carrying something oddly shaped, clattering, crunching, and spitting gravel all the way. A sign on the Suburban told the secret. "Baraboo Birdy Balloon Tours," it said.

Frankie turned to Carmen, her mouth wide open, her eyes the size of half-dollars. "Carmen," she barely whispered. Going for a hot-air balloon ride had been high on Frankie's bucket list for years. The two friends always said they would do it together someday. Summers came and went, and they could never fit it into their schedules.

"Today is someday, Frankie Champagne," Carmen said in a singsong voice.

A woman dressed in an official cotton shirt with a Birdy Balloon logo on it, approached the two women.

"I'm Lara Reed, your captain. You must be Frankie and Carmen." Lara, possibly in her mid- thirties, swung out a lean arm and greeted them with a confident handshake. Her face wore the warmth of the sun and her smile rose all the way to her blue eyes.

"Nice to meet you. Are we your only takers today?" Frankie asked.

"As a matter of fact, yes. Sundays are usually low-key. Sometimes I don't have any rides scheduled at all. Of course, that will change as soon as tourist season zooms in."

The bakers understood. The week after Memorial weekend was quiet, but it was simply the calm before the tourist storm.

Lara gestured toward the trailer where four figures unloaded the balloon. "My crew will be flying with us today, too. I need to go help them get set up. Come with me if you want a lesson in the workings of a hot-air balloon."

Frankie and Carmen joined the crew by the trailer and helped unload the heavy basket. The balloon and its ropes were already in the field. Next came the burners and propane tanks needed for power.

The adept crew of four set up in no time and invited Frankie and Carmen to climb into the wicker basket. The basket was divided into four sections surrounding the center space where the captain manned the balloon and propane gas. Frankie and Carmen had their own section. Two crew members climbed into one section on the opposite side and the other two claimed spots in the middle to balance out the weight.

"I brought the small basket today. On Saturdays, we use the large basket which holds around twenty flyers," Lara explained. "This controller lights up the pilot flame into the envelope." She pointed to the multi-colored nylon balloon, then pulled on one of its strings. "These metal cables support the envelope and basket. The basket is made from wicker and steel supports. All these features make our flight safe and enjoyable."

"Today we're going to fly as high as eighteen-hundred feet. If you're feeling at all queasy, you can sit down in the basket and take some deep breaths, or you can keep your eyes on the horizon and breathe deeply. If you have any questions, feel free to ask me or one of the crew. I know you both signed a waiver online, but now's the time to tell me if you have concerns."

Frankie shot Carmen a sly smile and kicked her foot. She knew Carmen had forged her signature on the waiver, but she didn't care one bit. Carmen smiled, her eyes on the skies.

"No questions. We're all in. Let's do this!" she said in excitement.

At first, the balloon ascended slowly, but picked up speed as hot flames inflated the envelope, then leveled off. Both women were amazed at the smooth sensation of floating in the quiet surroundings. The only sound was the soft hiss of flames into the envelope.

Frankie drank in the many green hues of the tree-covered bluffs and fields with newly sprouted corn and soybeans of brilliant lime green. The gray-blue evergreens cast shadows across the earth as the pink and orange sunrise dazzled the balloonists. Carmen and Frankie busily snapped photos of the scenery for a while, pleased when one crew member offered to take photos of them to show off later.

Along the way, Lara pointed out a few highlights visible below: The International Crane Foundation that housed endangered species of cranes from around the world; Ski-Hi orchards, famous for its hilly location and views as well as delicious varieties of apples and home pressed cider; and Devil's Lake State Park.

The balloon descended over the park, and skimmed the bluffs where climbers ascended the dark rock faces, experienced guides beside them. Frankie gasped seeing the climbers from her vantage point. With binoculars, she had a close view of the choreographed dance along the bluff where climbers clipped into anchors, waited in crevices for the next call from the leader, or momentarily hung free from crimps barely large enough for a fingertip hold. She watched the group until it reached the pinnacle; silent and still until every single climber finished, then whooping in loud joyous abandon.

Carmen pointed further down the East Bluff Trail where she spied a few people bouldering, free climbing from one mammoth rock to the next with no safety equipment. Frankie shook her head at their daring moves, awestruck by their audacity.

The balloon ascended again above the bluffs and over the Wisconsin River, a wide band of dark blue surrounded by so much green. Sandbars formed ribbons and swatches between pooling waters, waiting to carry tubers and picnickers to claim their own private river beach.

As the balloon glided again to its starting point, it floated over a quilt of purple, the many acres of lavender fields that inspired Coral Anders to begin farming lavender in Deep Lakes. A bluff rose upward once more when the crew flew over slopes of grapevines laid out in a captivating grid at one of the famous bluff wineries. The spectacle filled Frankie's heart with pure gratitude for all the variety Earth offered. She inhaled deeply to capture the scents of flying: Wisconsin's tree blossom perfume, the heady aroma of soil, the metallic whiff of boulders, and the hot aromatic sulfur from propane flames engraved themselves in her mind and heart. *This is what it means to feel contented.*

A ground crew helped land the balloon as it thudded across the empty field and stopped with a final bump. Carmen and Frankie embraced tightly, giddy in the moment of discovery. Tears trickled down their cheeks amid smiles as wide as canyons.

"What a Sunday," was all Frankie could say.

~

The two women breakfasted at the local Log Cabin restaurant, a rare event for both, then discussed their next plans.

"Honestly, I don't want to think about doing anything else today. I just want to bask in the afterglow of ballooning." Frankie seemed far away as she nibbled on Mediterranean style eggs benedict and sipped regular perked coffee, nothing fancy.

Carmen agreed. "It was magical, and it's not often you'll hear that coming from me."

They stretched out breakfast for nearly two hours before conceding to the almighty clock.

"I hate to say this," Frankie began.

"Ugh. The spell is broken. Tell me what we're in for today. I know you want to investigate." Carmen began eating her orange slice garnish, the only morsel left on her plate.

"Not today. Tomorrow, will you come with me to Ray Pate's? I want to surprise him by dropping by for a business call."

"Sure. It appears we have pests to eradicate?" Carmen enunciated each word in a high nasal tone. "Baking first, right?" With Carmen, Bubble & Bake always took precedence over investigation.

In the O'Connor driveway, both women sighed, unwilling to leave the van. "Once we get out of the van, reality awaits,"

Carmen commented. "I'll be down at the barn helping Ryan with a few straggler lambs." Every spring, a couple of ewes had late babies.

Frankie closed her eyes wondering what reality would offer next. She wasn't sure she was ready. "This was one of the best times I've ever had. I don't know how to thank you."

Carmen patted her hand, smiled, and turned off the engine. "You just did. No better way to thank me than to share the experience together."

Frankie felt tears springing to her eyes again and tried to blink them back. "I'll see you tomorrow morning, right? My mother and Pom are manning the wine lounge today, but I'll check in to see if they need me."

"See you tomorrow. Baking first," Carmen reminded her.

~

Frankie glided along the back roads, reluctant to leave the beauty of the countryside behind. She headed to her vineyard to admire the vines and orchard and to see how the new border gardens were faring. The weather offered a break in the heat wave, if only for a day. Temperatures would warm to seventy degrees before climbing again in the next few days.

Frankie walked the property, enjoying the peaceful setting. After feeling the soil in the border garden, she turned on the faucet to let the soaker hose run while she admired the French-inspired blooms.

She reached in her pocket for her phone and called Garrett.

"Hello G." Frankie's sweet tone reflected her current mood.

"Miss Francine. Music to my ears. How are you doing?" Garrett sounded lonesome.

Frankie chuckled. "Well, I made it past Saturday. I guess there is life after a canceled wedding."

"Oh Frankie. I'm sorry. Any news from Sophie?"

"None. The quarantine continues. Helen Thurston died in St. Anthony's basement toppled over a box of church records, no less. Before you ask, it looks like the same illness."

Garrett groaned on the other end. "Any progress being made?"

"I can't tell for sure. I managed to find out the scientists are looking at mosquito-borne diseases, but this appears to be something they haven't seen before."

Garrett was impressed. "How did you come by this information, Ace?"

Frankie scoffed. "I can't take the credit. Max has a contact in hospital security. He seems to have connections to sensitive information. I'm still chasing around leads in the Amish community, but that's not why I called." Frankie's heart was filled to the brim after sailing around in the balloon, and she wanted to share that feeling with Garrett.

"What's on your mind? I'm ready." Garrett sat down on his hotel room sofa, prepared for the worst.

"Carmen surprised me this morning with a hot-air balloon ride. I wish I could describe the way it made me feel. Alive, grateful, for starters." Frankie felt a breathless exhilaration in relating the experience.

Garrett grinned. "That's great, Frankie. I know you two had ballooning on your wish list a long time. Just the break you needed and deserved." Inside, Frankie's news made Garrett feel more isolated than ever.

"Thanks, G. We flew over the Baraboo bluffs, practically on top of a group of climbers ascending the face of Devil's Doorway.

I wanted to tell you." Frankie wavered, searching for the right words. "I watched the lead guide hold the climbers in check, clip them onto the anchors, reassure them, encourage them. It made me think, G." She stopped, choking back tears.

"Think about what? Go on Miss Francine." Garrett's voice was just above a whisper.

Frankie swallowed a hard lump and gulped in air. "It made me ask myself: If I were dangling by a rope with no foothold, nothing under my feet but air, who would I want holding the other end of that rope? And you know what? Your face, that handsome face with those melted caramel eyes, popped right up in front of me. I guess what I'm trying to tell you is: I trust you, Garrett, with my life. And my heart." Tears slipped down Frankie's cheeks as she waited in silence.

Garrett too, was overcome with emotion and could barely speak. "Well, that's good news. Really good news. I'd climb a bluff ten times higher than the Devil's Doorway if I knew I'd find you waiting at the top."

Frankie exhaled in relief. The act of baring her soul was rare. "Thank you, G. Now tell me how you're doing. Any leads on the cases?"

"Leads, maybe. A lot of dead ends. This city isn't that big. It just seems like this should be easier to figure out. I suppose you're feeling the same way trying to find what's making people sick in little Whitman County."

"Yes. I know there's a line that connects barns, basements, and kitchens, but I don't know what the common denominator is. Not yet at least. I think I have a strong lead to follow thanks to one of the Amish women. I'll know soon if that pans out."

"Hey, thank you, Frankie."

"For what, G?"

"For coming back to earth after your flight. I was afraid you were going to tell me you thought it was time to fly away from me," Garrett confessed.

"Not a chance. And when you get back, we're taking a balloon flight together. I want you to have the thrill I had."

"You're on, Sweetheart. Meanwhile, did you get any pictures you can send me? I'm lonesome for your face, too."

The two said goodbye and Frankie shared the folder of balloon trip photos with Garrett. She'd logged almost a mile during their conversation and wound her way back to the border garden to turn off the water spigot.

Her phone rang and she thought it might be Garrett with a comment or two about the photos, but the caller ID showed it was Shauna, her sister-in-law.

"Hello Shauna. I didn't get the chance to say goodnight to you and James after dinner last night. Did you enjoy it?"

"That's exactly why I'm calling, Frankie. I didn't get much chance to talk to you at all and wondered how you're holding up."

"You know, I'm doing okay. Thanks for asking. It was a relief to host the dinner, you know. I think it gave me a sense of purpose. Something to do with the food that didn't feel wasteful."

"Yes, and you gave people a nice break from their worries about this strange illness going around. Listen, will you stop by my studio one day this week? I'm planning the open house and want to order some items from the shop. Talk about wines to pair with nibbles and such."

Shauna had opened her own home design studio months ago, but she waited to host an open house until she could show off some of her projects, which meant the business came first.

"Are you at the studio now?" Frankie suspected her driven sister-in-law might be working on a Sunday.

Shauna absently bit one fingernail. "You caught me. I'm here. I've been logging a lot of hours to get things running. I'll be here for a while."

"I'm out at the vineyard, but I'm coming your way. I'll see you in a bit." Frankie disconnected.

Frankie sang along with the radio all the way to town, talking to herself between tunes. "I feel light as a feather. If this is the end result of pouring my heart out, I guess it's worth it."

She sailed past the bakery and turned onto Meriwether Street. Shauna's shop, Rooms and Roosts Design Company, was situated about midway on the second block. Formerly a hair salon, the brick front building had just recently been a Napa Valley knockoff wine lounge owned by Frankie's competitor. Business didn't end well, and Shauna was able to lease the building while it went through foreclosure.

Lucky for Shauna she was married to Frankie's brother James, a construction specialist. Together, they transformed the former dimly lit lounge atmosphere. The interior was light and airy, filled with asymmetrical lines in contrasting colors, a clean creative space.

"Knock, knock Shauna," Frankie called out.

Shauna emerged from her office and gently hugged her sister-in-law. "Thanks for coming. Have you had a chance to talk to Garrett or Sophie?"

Frankie had once helped Shauna overcome the shock of finding a dead body, an act that melted Shauna's cool exterior and paved the way for the two to enjoy a more personal relationship.

"As a matter of fact, I just talked to Garrett before your call. The cases he's working on seem to be at a standstill, but he's managing. As for Sophie, no. I wish I could talk to her. It's frustrating."

"I imagine. I'd have a terrible time handling it if something like this happened to Marcus." Shauna's only child, a son from her first marriage, lived in Minnesota where he attended law school.

"How is Marcus doing?" Frankie hadn't heard much about him lately.

Shauna sighed. "He has a girlfriend and I think they may be getting serious." Frown lines appeared on her forehead.

"Would that be bad? Marcus is what: twenty-four?" Frankie guessed he'd be old enough for a serious relationship.

"Yes. Twenty-four, but you see, he has two years left of law school. It wouldn't be good to mess that up," Shauna declared.

Comprehension sunk in. *Is that what's going on with Max? Medical school was making it difficult to navigate his personal life?* Frankie filed away that thought for another time.

"Let's sit down over here. I have a few notes about the open house." Shauna gestured to a space where two purple barrel chairs, with wing arms, rested on gleaming black tile, against a white backdrop covered by a black word collage. The words were all synonyms of "passion" and "creativity." A round glass table separated the chairs, and a large, patterned bauble light hung over the table.

"I love this space," Frankie said. "It's definitely your brand, Shauna."

The two discussed mini quiche varieties for the event as well as which wines should be offered. "I think a couple kinds of macarons will do for sweets. It's not a party after all," Shauna stated.

Frankie giggled and leaned toward her. "Of course, it's a party. This is and should be treated like a celebration, but it's okay to keep it simple and understated. I like your choices. Now, have you decided on a date?"

Shauna looked at her work calendar. "It has to be after I finish the Callahan project. That's a big one, and I want to be able to win their recommendation."

"Frankie's ears pricked. "Callahan project?"

"I'm designing the office for Callahan Title Corporation. Barnaby and Courtney Callahan purchased a new space on Dairyland Way." Seeing Frankie's blank expression, she added, "The new subdivision beyond the old quarry. I guess you wouldn't drive over there unless you had a reason."

"You mean that giant hunk of land the Spurgeon family owned for eons?" Frankie asked. The Spurgeon family ran the nationally famous granite quarry for decades until it was no longer safe or profitable to do so. The wealthy Spurgeons owned all the land surrounding the quarry, much of it wooded, all of it undeveloped.

Shauna pursed her lips, ready to educate her sister-in-law. "That hunk of land was purchased two years ago and has been cleared and plotted for all kinds of residential and commercial enterprises. Geesh Frankie, for someone with a nose for news, you don't seem to know what's going on around town."

Frankie remembered reading the city council article that discussed the possible development, but nothing beyond that. "I guess I'll go out and see it for myself when I leave. But can we back up? I thought the Callahan dynasty operated under one roof, right down the street from my bakery."

The Callahan family began its real estate venture under Bram's grandfather, Sean. The business was passed down to Bram's father, Ronan, who purchased the old Crystal Lake, a hotel and boarding house on Granite Street, and turned it into Callahan Realty. Barnaby, the oldest of Ronan's children, expanded the dynasty with the title corporation, which occupied one-third of the building. When Ronan became gravely ill, he legally transferred the realty to his wife, Estelle, and two remaining children, Bram and Charlotte.

Shauna dropped her voice, despite the empty room. "There's been bad blood between Bram and Barnaby for years now. Rumor has it Barnaby bought the Spurgeon property before it even went public, right under Bram's crooked nose. Barnaby and Courtney planned to build new as soon as they could clear the land."

"Did James get the contract for the title corp building?" Frankie asked.

Shauna clapped. "He did, and that paved the way for the Callahans to hire me to work on the interior. It's been quite an undertaking, but we're finally down to finishing touches. Window coverings, furnishings, wall art, and flourishes." Shauna's hands fluttered happily, like butterflies, when she spoke.

"I'm thrilled for you. This will be an achievement leading to even bigger and better projects. How much longer are you working today? I could bring you a plate of leftover wedding food."

Shauna looked at her fit watch, then vaulted out of the chair. "I lost track of time. I need to go to the realty office and take some measurements. Courtney wants some of the family treasures transferred from the old office to the new one. It's easier for me to work outside of business hours when there's nobody in the way."

Frankie spoke without thinking. "You have a key to the realty office?"

Shauna's eyes narrowed. "Why? What's going on in that head of yours, Frankie?" The cooler Shauna was back.

"Nothing…nothing. I, well…" Frankie couldn't decide how to make her next play. "Shauna, the truth is, I need to look at, I mean I need to look around the real estate office for something."

Shauna blinked repeatedly, arms folded, waiting for more.

"I'm not sure what I'm looking for, but I'll know it when I see it." Frankie raised her voice at the end, turning it into a question.

"Absolutely not. You can't snoop around the realty office. My professional reputation is on the line. I can't afford to blow it because you have a whim." Shauna puffed out her cheeks, annoyed.

"Of course, you're right. Could I tag along? I promise not to poke around. I'm just going to look."

"And by look you mean you won't open any drawers, turn on any computers, listen to voice mails, or rifle through papers?" Shauna didn't like how fishy the situation appeared.

Frankie nodded enthusiastically, putting on her best angelic expression. "Yes." Best not to expand on Shauna's conditions.

CHAPTER NINETEEN

I see my path, but I don't know where it leads.
Not knowing where I'm going is what inspires me to travel it.

Rosalia de Castro

Shauna told Frankie to meet her at the realty office at five o'clock sharp. She had several loose ends to tie up at the studio, which allowed Frankie the chance to check in at Bubble & Bake and catch up with Violet.

Upstairs, Frankie found an empty apartment and a note. Violet was hanging out on Lake Loki with friends, jet skiing. Along with the typical "don't worry" verbiage, she told her mom she hoped the balloon ride was a blast. Frankie should have known Carmen would let Vi in on the secret adventure.

Downstairs, the wine lounge hosted typical mellow Sunday customers. A few couples scattered throughout the comfortable alcoves. The once-a-month reading club, The Wine-Knows, occupied the shady part of the deck.

Because the tourist season determined it was officially

summer, even if the calendar didn't, the Buzzards only met at the shop one Sunday a month until after Labor Day. Frankie waved at her mother who stood behind the bar giving a professional wine tasting to a group of six. Frankie paused in the front part of the shop to admire the sunlight flooding the café tables, highlighting the flower arrangements. She pulled out her phone to capture the scene and waved at Pom as she came in from the deck carrying an empty serving tray.

"Hey Frankie. Just took food out to The Wine-Knows. It's been a relaxing day. Steady stream of customers but nothing hectic." Pom noticed Frankie was snapping photos of the shop. "The flowers are hypnotic, aren't they? They transform the place."

"They sure do. I wish I could afford to keep fresh flowers here all the time," Frankie confessed. "Guess we'll enjoy them while they last.

Pom smiled. "Yep. I made sure I changed their water this morning when I got here. I added some of that mix that's supposed to keep them fresh, too."

"Thanks, Pom. Good thinking." Frankie knew she was blessed to have such a crew. She resisted the urge to check the order board to prepare for tomorrow, and instead started composing a text to her brother, James. She needed to pick his brain and since Shauna was occupied, maybe now would be the time to do it.

Mid-sentence, Frankie saw Ava Andersen come through the front door. Ava, dressed in her Sunday best, was Callahan Realty's main competitor. She owned Deep Lakes Properties, the other original real estate business in town, this one purchased by Ava from her father and uncle, who inherited it from one of the city founders: Hans Andersen.

Ava, all businesslike, acknowledged Frankie while looking

about the shop for someone.

"Hi Ava. Are you meeting someone?" Frankie prided herself on customer service and just maybe capitalizing on a chance conversation.

"Hello Frankie. As a matter of fact, I'm meeting your brother here." Ava was a cool cucumber, stately, well-spoken, and experienced. She'd been managing properties in the area for over thirty years with several state realtor awards to her name.

"Oh, I see. I haven't seen him yet. Is this a business meeting, and can I bring you anything to eat or drink?"

Ava glided to a corner table away from the other patrons and sat down, facing the picture window. She paused to admire the flower centerpiece, gently lifted a cerulean blue delphinium, and sniffed. "Beautiful flowers, Frankie. A lovely touch."

Ava picked up the vase and set it on the nearest table. "I hope you don't mind. I'm allergic." She sat down again, smoothing her navy-blue skirt in place. "I'd like some tea please. Nothing floral. Nothing fruity. Perhaps a suitable Ceylon or Irish Breakfast?"

Frankie had few tea drinkers at the shop. Most preferred coffee with their pastries or came in later in the day for wine or beer. Still, she kept tea on hand to keep her customers satisfied. "Coming right up. Would you like something to eat?"

"Hmm. I'll think on it," Ava said, then waved Frankie away so she could set up business on the café table.

When Frankie returned with Irish Breakfast tea in a glass pot complete with infuser, James was sitting opposite Ava, dressed casually but polished just the same.

"Hello Frankie." James stood and gave her a quick half-hug. He stared at her garb and cocked his head to one side. "Isn't today your day off?"

Frankie remembered she was dressed for an outdoor hike as Carmen suggested. No wonder Ava was put off, at least that's what Frankie decided. "Oh, it is. I just stopped by to see if the shop needed anything. I saw Ava come in and wanted to help."

"Actually James, I was going to text you. I have a few questions I'd like to ask when you finish your business with Ava if you have time. Meanwhile, can I get you something?"

James looked at Ava's tea with momentary disappointment. "I'll have a…," he stopped to think about what Ava might find acceptable. When he indulged, he enjoyed a Spotted Cow beer and brandy old-fashioneds. He looked at the tea again.

"How about iced tea? I have a pitcher of blackberry in the cooler. It's delicious." Frankie to the rescue. Ava didn't mix business with pleasure, and alcoholic beverages were the latter.

"Sounds good. And yes, let's talk after my meeting." James cleared his throat and gave Ava his full attention.

Frankie brought the iced tea and disappeared out the back door to sit by Sterling Creek, resisting the urge to eavesdrop on James and Ava. She wasn't sure how long she sat mesmerized by the continuous surge of birds skimming the creek for insects. Like bats, she knew several varieties of birds dined on mosquitoes, and she hoped she wouldn't find any dead ones littering the shore. She wondered about the bats from the Graham barn. Then she thought back to the conversation she overhead at St. Anthony's. Ian Yoder insisted he could get rid of the bat colony before the problem got worse, but Mike had said it wasn't possible without Father Donnelly's recommendation. And the priest was in the hospital.

Pom tapped her on the shoulder, startling her back to the present. "Sorry, I didn't mean to scare you, Frankie. James told me he can talk to you now."

Frankie stopped in the kitchen to grab a Spotted Cow from the walk-in cooler and a glass of iced blackberry tea. On her way to the table, she glanced around the corner to see if her mother was occupied. Peggy had finished the tasting with the six but was trekking between two other groups of tasters now, so Frankie figured her conversation with James was secure.

"Hey. How's the tea?" Frankie grinned and set the Spotted Cow in front of him.

James laughed. "You know Ava. She's a stickler for straitlaced business meetings. And that's okay. I'm happy to see this, though." He lifted the beer to his lips and took a slug. "What's on your mind?"

"The Amish," she got right to it.

"What about them?"

"Do they compete against your construction company?" Frankie imagined the answer but had a plan.

"Well, yes. Probably now more than ever. People are looking for the cheapest labor these days. Why?" James leaned back a little and took another drink.

"You were just meeting with Ava. Do the realtors work with you when they sell vacant land?"

James pondered the question. "If by working with me, you mean do they bring me business, the answer is sometimes. It's important for construction companies to stay on the good side of realtors. Land and home buyers ask the realtors to recommend contractors, you know. Word of mouth remains one of the best ways to keep business alive."

"Are you on Bram Callahan's good side?" Frankie's poker face gave nothing away.

James was shrewd. "Bram Callahan. It's not easy staying on his good side. Bram takes the side of anyone who will help him make the most money. Why. What's this about?"

"Do you know if Bram is doing a lot of business with the Amish, especially the community out on HH?"

James picked up the beer bottle and began examining it like an artifact. After a minute he set it down and looked into Frankie's eyes. "Bram bought property out there, but not from the Amish. Rumor has it he's buying out large farm parcels from some of the old-timers who don't have anyone to take over their farms. He's cashing in on the new wave of people leaving the city for the country."

"Is Champagne Construction getting any contracts for new or remodeled houses on the lands Bram purchased?"

James tapped one finger against his chin. "I can tell you we used to get more from Callahan than we're getting lately. I think the Amish builders are getting most of the jobs out on HH."

Frankie grimaced at James's statement and added another reason to dislike Bram to her internal list. Bram was a Bubble & Bake customer, albeit a rude and demanding one.

"You don't need to worry about Champagne Builders. We're doing just fine. There's other business to be had out there, Frankie. The way people are buying up lake property, we still have more work than we can manage. Most of the lake people prefer a contractor with modern technology. They don't live here full time, so they can't transport Amish builders back and forth from the job site, for one thing." James reassured Frankie.

Ah yes, lake property. Most of the retired wanted their own lake property after sampling a slice of lake life as tourists; they hoped to buy their own piece of paradise. Buying and selling lake property was how the Callahan family made their fortune, starting with Bram's grandfather. "James, what's Callahan's interest in farm property? I thought he was on the constant hunt for liquid gold—lake lots."

"Well, subdividing the land is easier on long-standing farms. There's less work to clean the property, and there's often no need to dig new wells and go through perk tests because the septic systems are in place. People still want lake property, but it's pricey. Those who can't afford lake life can still live a quiet life in the country."

Frankie was relieved the construction company was doing fine, but that didn't make her less suspicious about Bram's dealings. "What's happening with the old Spurgeon property?"

James was surprised at Frankie's sudden interest in real estate holdings. "You may not know this, but Callahan Title is moving over there. You should check out the area. You wouldn't recognize it. The woods have been carefully cleared, leaving some of the healthy trees for shade. A residential complex is going up there. That's what Ava and I were discussing. If we get that contract, it's going to keep us busy."

Frankie's mouth fell open. "You mean Ava Andersen owns the property? Why would Callahan Title build over there?" Frankie recalled Shauna saying Barnaby Callahan had bought the Spurgeon land.

James grinned like a jackpot winner. "Barnaby Callahan and Ava Andersen are joint owners of the Spurgeon property." He swallowed the rest of the beer.

Frankie smiled in satisfaction. *There really must be some bad blood between the Callahan brothers.*

"Frankie, have you had any serious talks with Cherry Parker

lately?" James asked as he rose to leave.

"Nothing serious. Oh, oh, is this about Cherry and Nick?" Their brother, Nick the charmer, had a relationship of convenience with Cherry. Frankie wondered if something went off the rails.

"No, not at all. I just wondered," James let the comment hang.

At five p.m., Frankie walked up the long set of steps to rap on the back door of Callahan Realty. Shauna's Lexus was parked behind the white brick building, barely visible from the large veranda that overlooked Sterling Creek. The building, once a hotel and boarding house, was restored to resemble its former self. The whitewashed brick two-story structure, trimmed in ornate black metalwork, would have looked more at home in New Orleans, but the Callahans wanted to stand out, and they succeeded. Even the back door was elegant, gleaming black wood with eight glass panels adorned with wrought iron diamonds and curlicues.

Shauna swung the door open to admit Frankie, swiveled her head left and right to be sure nobody was watching, then followed directly on her heels into the back waiting area. Frankie had the decency to wait there for instructions.

"The back third of the building belongs to the title company, so that's where I'll be taking photos and measurements. You can take a quick look around at the rest of the building, but don't touch anything. I mean it, Frankie." Shauna spoke like a police officer.

Frankie mock saluted her sister-in-law but didn't say a word. She wasn't about to be locked into a promise she couldn't keep. Shauna called down the hallway after her. "I mean it. Don't make me regret this."

Frankie passed the title office reception area where Shauna was already writing down heights, lengths, and widths of an antique ebony library desk. Across the hall, a white door opened onto a powder room that could have come from the Moulin Rouge. Frankie laughed at the gaudy flowered wallpaper and upholstery, trimmed in fuchsia brocade. "I thought Bubble & Bake had a lot of flowers. This room takes the cake," she said under her breath.

She passed two black wooden doors opposite each other: one designated to Barnaby, the other designated to Courtney Callahan. She kept moving. The next office had Estelle Callahan's name on it. "Ah, the matriarch herself," Frankie whispered. Opposite Estelle's office, a pair of French glass doors opened into a fully equipped kitchen and dining area, large enough to comfortably seat twenty. Frankie would revisit this room later.

Next to Estelle's office, a room that had once been a salon housed the copy machine, a worktable with office staples, a conference table and chairs, shelves, and a closet. Unlike the powder room, the workroom was understated, painted in muted sagebrush green with gray ceramic floor tile. Still, the space was breathtaking with its central bay window guarded by floor to ceiling windows on either side. An antique wrought iron chandelier lorded over the conference table with six alabaster flared lampshades.

Beyond the workroom, double doors opened onto a conference room simply furnished with a long intimidating table and chairs over which loomed twin chandeliers, replicas of the wrought iron affair in the workroom. "Nothing to see here," Frankie surmised and moved back to the hallway.

She was in the front half of the building now, where the realty offices resided. The doors matched the title company except for the names. One door led to Charlotte Callahan's office and the other belonged to Bram. The door next to Charlotte's office housed a second powder room, a twin to the garish one in the rear. The door next to Bram was locked and might have been a supply closet or a vacant office, maybe even a records room.

The front reception area spread across the expanse of the building. The elegant chandelier might have come from a medieval ballroom or the Addams family mansion. Matching wall sconces demanded attention from visitors coming through the double door entrance. The reception desk made Frankie feel small—she was short anyway—but the high reception counter, a composite of white and black granite with black lattice overlay, conjured images of a high-end New York hotel.

Frankie snooped around the desk, which appeared to be unoccupied by any kind of human she knew. "Who keeps their desk this clean?" She grumbled. Not a sticky note in sight or a speck of dust either. The telephone perched next to a desktop computer. The desk drawers were locked. "You couldn't borrow a pen or paper clip if you wanted to," she complained a bit louder. She turned the name placard around to face her. "Poor Kimberly Nichols, whoever you are. Not a single personal item, knickknack, or even a photo to mark your territory."

Two waiting areas flanked either side of the grand entrance. Both contained French period furnishings upholstered in gold, white, and black fabrics. Photographs of Deep Lakes from the late 1800s to early 1900s occupied the white walls.

Frankie noticed the elegantly framed print of the Crystal Lake hotel, horse drawn carriages parked in the wide brick street leading to its double arched doors, typical of French Colonial style. Two gentlemen stood on the balcony above the double doors, each with one hand inside their waistcoat. One wore a monocle. The foreground featured the Bentsen family, owners of the hotel. Mr. Bentsen honored his wife, Crystal, in naming the hotel, although the word "lake" was certainly an exaggeration. Sterling Creek was wider and deeper in the early days of Deep Lakes, but its waters were diverted during the granite quarry's heyday. Now the creek was robust, but a creek was all it would be.

Frankie remembered why she was there, which was not to view the museum pieces and décor. She retraced her steps and turned the handle of Bram's office door. Of course, it was locked. She tried Charlotte's door, then Estelle's with the same result. Even if Shauna's key worked in the realty offices, which she doubted, how was she supposed to nab it?

Downtrodden, she walked back to the workroom and snooped around. The worktable was empty and polished to a fine shine. She opened the closet and rummaged through office supplies, all of which were unused and therefore, useless for her purposes. Frankie lifted the lid on the copier, triggering it to awaken from its cyber slumber. Electronic buzzes and trills echoed about the room. Frankie peered down the hallway, thinking the noises would alert Shauna, but the copier settled into silence.

She investigated the copy trays just in case any telltale documents had been forgotten, but they were empty. She stared at the computer screen with its options for printing and sorting, and noticed a red flag lit up in the output option. She pressed on the tab and a new window opened on the screen showing a document icon that indicated it was processed and ready to print.

Frankie looked around. "Oh, why not? I didn't promise I wouldn't look at something in plain sight." She pushed the print button. The copier began its electronic song as copies skidded forth into one of the trays. After eight pages, the machine quieted again.

Frankie scooped out the warm papers, straightened them, and walked over to the worktable. The first page got her attention. It was a land survey with marked lot lines entitled Callahan Acres, a line of property running along County HH up to and down Tenth Road, including part of Wagon Trail Road, before crossing over to HH again. Part of the map included properties marked with slashed lines. Frankie saw the key on the map indicated those properties were not yet acquired.

A sense of urgency welled inside of her, and she didn't want to be caught red-handed with the copies. She quickly looked at the other papers, making sure she wouldn't accidentally abscond with a customer's personal information. The other pages detailed the proposed plan for a country condo subdivision and golf course including the Amish picnic park on private Lake Nochber.

The last pages were DNR permits requesting to change the name of Lake Nochber to Lake Serenity and to annex a piece of property adjacent to the lake as a right-of-way. Frankie didn't understand what it all meant, but it smelled fishy. She needed someone versed in land acquisitions to explain it. That someone was her old boss, Attorney Ward Dickens.

She folded the papers, stuffed them in her purse, and pressed the shutdown button on the copier. It was time to find Shauna, thank her for letting her browse the building, and get out with the goods.

"Shauna," Frankie called out as she scooted past Estelle's office again. Courtney's office door stood open, so Frankie peeked inside. "Oh, there you are. I'm leaving. Thanks for letting me look around. Turns out you didn't have anything to worry about. Everything in this place is locked up like Fort Knox. I've never seen a reception desk that clean in my life."

Shauna turned to study Frankie, skepticism written all over her face. "Really. How come it took so long for you to look at nothing?"

Frankie chewed her bottom lip. "The front reception area is really something. I was checking out the framed photos from Deep Lakes's storied past. History never gets old." She cleared her throat as a little nervous tick tapped on her jawline.

"You sound like Barnaby Callahan. I can't believe how many antiques he wants jammed into the new office space. This is going to be a real decorating challenge, Frankie." Shauna blew a few stray hairs away from her face.

"How so?" Frankie was happy to change the subject.

"You see all this French nonsense. What are we here— Southern Creole? I mean, it's beautiful in its place. This furniture doesn't fit the new office space design they planned one iota. Besides, they both wanted their own brand, not a repeat of this." She extended her arms wide around the French colonial décor.

"Yep, I saw the powder rooms. I get what you're saying. So, what will you do?"

"They're my clients. I will advise them, show them alternatives, and…," she swallowed hard, "ultimately do whatever they pay me to do. Ugh."

Frankie patted her sister-in-law's shoulder. "Shauna, you're a pro and your designs are amazing. You can handle the Callahans. You could always suggest a place to rehome their antiques, somewhere they could be showcased, like the historical society?" Frankie was almost purring as Shauna's eyes brightened.

Bubble & Bake was empty, its blinds shutting out the early evening sun, making everything cozy. Frankie's pulse wouldn't settle down as she contemplated the contents of her purse. She couldn't call Ward Dickens on a Sunday. He'd be at the country club or out on his boat and wouldn't pick up anyway. Thankfully, he was an early riser and she planned to connect with him as the first task of a hectic Monday.

Sitting in the quiet, dim wine lounge, Frankie almost drifted off to sleep. She realized she hadn't been alone for the past several days, hadn't taken time to process the complicated mess intertwining her beloved community and personal life. The cell phone in her purse sounded off, another interruption when she needed stillness. She pondered ignoring the blare, then reached in by rote, and answered.

"Hello Magda. I can't say I'm surprised to hear from you." Frankie wondered what had kept the hungry regional editor of *Point Press News* from calling before now.

"Oh yeah. What's going on down there anyway? Some lady…" Magda rifled papers, probably trying to find her notes. "Adele someone. She called me to ask if Frankie Champagne was working undercover to investigate a plague. You want to enlighten me?"

Frankie would have laughed but for the seriousness of the

problem. "Adele Lundgren, the mayor of Deep Lakes?" She couldn't understand why Adele hadn't cornered her somewhere to get the answer from the horse's mouth.

"That's the one. I poked around but I don't see any plague coming over the news wires. Not even obituaries. What's the story?" Magda didn't have time or patience when there was breaking news to consider.

Frankie explained what she knew, downplayed the idea of a plague, and omitted that her own daughter was smack in the middle of it. "The locus of control on this story is in Madison, Magda. I can't just barge into the State Board of Health and demand answers." Frankie hoped she sounded reasonable.

On the other end of the line, Magda drummed her desk with a pen. "So that's it? You have no details. Some dead county citizens along with dead Amish. Some are being autopsied and the sick are at UW Hospital."

"That about sums it up." It was the second time today Frankie lied through her teeth, first to Shauna, now to the news editor who helped her break into the investigation biz. She flushed with guilt.

"What about your buddy, Abe Arnold? He's a bulldog, so don't tell me he's not chasing balls around and digging up bones everywhere." Magda spoke through gritted teeth.

"We've chatted about the deaths and illness, but neither of us has any answers. The hospital and board of health have shut out the press. I haven't even been able to talk to my own daughter." Frankie clapped her hand over her mouth and kicked herself. Magda was worse than a priest for coercing a confession.

"What does that mean? Your daughter, the one from Stevens Point?" Magda had met both Violet and Sophie last fall when

Bountiful Fruits launched Violet's Golden Desire mead at a Halloween bash. Apparently, Magda only remembered one daughter.

Frankie's silence gave Magda time to consider.

"Oh, you mean the nurse? She works at UW Hospital, right?"

There it was. Uh-oh. "Right. Sophie is quarantined with the sick. She's fine, but she's been exposed. Honestly Magda, if I had any way to talk to her, I'd do it in a heartbeat."

"Relax. I believe you. I'm sure you're doing your own investigation, Frankie. I know you won't just sit on your hands. But you better call me as soon as you have something to report. Got it?"

"Got it." Before Magda could say another word, Frankie pressed the red button to end the call.

CHAPTER TWENTY

An observer of men who finds himself steadily repelled by some
apparently trifling thing in a stranger is right to give it great weight.
It may be the clue to the whole mystery.
A hair or two will show where a lion is hidden.
A very little key will open a very heavy door.

Charles Dickens

Frankie rose early Monday, recalled her promise to Carmen about baking first, but placed a call to Ward Dickens before entering the shop kitchen.

"Francine Champagne. Unless you're inquiring about an early tee time, I'm guessing this is a business call." Ward's jovial remark held no animosity. Frankie had been his favorite paralegal at the law firm of Dickens and Probst. Frankie had Ward to thank for settling her fire claim that allowed her to buy the building which was now Bubble & Bake, the craft store next door, and two apartments above.

Frankie blushed. "I know, I should call once in a while just to check in. How are you doing?"

"I can't complain. I think I'm going to retire next year, Frankie. Winters are getting too long here, and Arizona has golfing year-round."

Frankie was skeptical. "I don't believe it for a minute. You're never going to retire. You like the game too much, and you're too good at playing it." She didn't mean his golf game either.

"We'll see what happens. What have you got for me today?"

Frankie admired Ward's finesse and intellect. She read pieces of the Callahan Acres plan, specifically the information about changing the name of the private Amish lake and acquiring an annexation for right-of-way. The wheels turned in Ward's head. He didn't need a visual to understand what Callahan was trying to do.

"It's common to request an annexation or easement to gain access to property that the person owns but can't get to for some reason. In this case, it sounds like the private lake can't be accessed from the property in question, maybe because the land is above the lake with no way down to it, for instance."

Frankie hadn't mentioned the name of the development or that the Callahans, famous in several counties, made the annexation request. "Since the lake seems to be central to this residential development, is there a way the developer could gain control of the private lake, leaving the current owner out in the cold?"

"Ah, smart question. Do you think someone is trying to swindle the Amish out of their lake?" Ward laughed merrily. He loved this kind of stuff. "There are legal ways the developer could gain control to the extent the Amish would sell him the rest of the lake property and walk away."

Frankie grunted. "It's hard for me to picture a resort

community of gentrified folks playing golf and boating among Amish picnickers. I doubt the Amish would enjoy that scenario."

"Right-o, Frankie. You would have made an excellent attorney, I've always said. Anything else?"

Ward probably had a golf date to get to.

"One thing, Ward. Please come this way and have a glass of wine with me sometime. Pastries are on the house," Frankie said sweetly.

Frankie tacked the Callahan Acres plans next to the mystery illness map in her bedroom office. *Could there be a connection between the two, or am I looking at completely different puzzles? Maybe the Amish are the key.*

Downstairs, Frankie dove into baking, starting with kringle dough for this week's orders. Georgia reminded her at church she'd be in Wednesday morning at seven o'clock on the dot to pick up the order for her annual catechism teacher gathering.

"The show must go on, Frankie. Mike's going to have to man the front office without me Wednesday," Georgia had said.

As Frankie ran the rested kringle dough through the sheeter, she wondered what her grandma would say about that. Grandma Sophie had lovingly taught Frankie the art of crafting the buttery pastry by hand, the same way Sophie Petersen's mother had. Layers of cold butter were rolled between layers of pastry repeatedly until the thin crust was laminated and ready for filling, but only after three days of rolling, chilling, re-rolling, and re-chilling. The mechanical sheeter hummed along, cutting three days down to one overnight rest. Its metal arms reached out to deliver up to two hundred sheets in an hour. Grandma Sophie would shake her head in wonder.

"Whad'ya doing there?" Carmen shouted over Frankie's

shoulder, making her jump.

"Sorry, lost in thought. Are you trying to make me wet myself, Carmie?" Frankie recovered. "I'm working on the kringle orders for the week. Are you feeling tarts, scones, or coffee cakes?"

"I'll tackle the chai coffee cake for the library board meeting tonight. You get next choice."

Frankie eyed the kringle filling bubbling away on the stovetop. "I'll just take the cherry, apple, and almond fillings off to cool, then I'll make the rhubarb and pear tarts. I need to make pecan, cream, and raspberry fillings, too. That will complete our kringle orders for this week."

Carmen wore her business smile. "Sounds good. I'll make the chive-cheese, cinnamon-rhubarb, and blueberry-lavender scones. I'll leave the other coffee cakes and yeast donuts for Jovie and Tess to tackle." Carmen scrolled through the tablet showing the week's orders and smiled in satisfaction. "Woo hoo, the orders just keep coming in."

Frankie looked up after pouring cherry filling into a metal bowl to chill. "Are you worried about the business?"

"No. But I figured you'd be happy to make money after all the cash you doled out for wedding stuff."

Frankie swallowed hard. "I'm more worried about the money the kids lost. I didn't have as much invested as they did."

Thinking about the wedding drew her mind once again to Sophie, wondering and worrying about what her days had been like since quarantine. She finished pouring the other fillings into metal bowls and carted them off to the walk-in cooler.

She pushed the cart back to her station loaded with rhubarb stalks, raspberries, and whole milk for her next endeavor. A raft of eggs sat between Frankie and Carmen along with a basket of Anjou pears and Honeycrisp apples. Frankie noticed a large travel mug peeking out from behind the apple basket.

"That your coffee?" Frankie pointed at the mug.

"Aw shoot. No. That's your coffee. I stopped at Trickster this morning and picked it up special. Mine's over here." Carmen leaned back to reveal her travel mug. The shop had a shelf full of travel mugs that did exactly what they should—travel back and forth from a coffee shop to Bubble & Bake.

"Hmm. Perfect." Frankie lifted the lid and inhaled the chocolatey dark roast with a hint of cinnamon. "Thanks, Carmie. I'm going to make a quick call. Be right back."

Frankie ducked onto the deck and swiped Max's phone number. He picked up immediately.

"Is there anything wrong, Frankie?" Max was breathless, and Frankie was sorry to unnerve him.

"Everything's okay. I'm calling to ask you for a favor." She hesitated but Max didn't say anything.

"Can you please ask Dre, your hospital guy, to have Sophie call me. There must be a way I can talk to her, even for just a minute."

"I can ask him, I suppose. I don't know though, Frankie. Hospital protocol probably won't allow it. No phones are allowed in a quarantine area, so Dre would have to sneak her out of there or sneak a phone into her. I mean, I can't ask him to put his job on the line…" The more he talked, the more annoyed he sounded.

"I'm sorry. I'm being selfish, I guess. But I might have useful information about the illness." Frankie grasped at any straw she could.

"I'll call Dre and see if he thinks there's a way. I'll be in touch.

And Frankie? If you have information about the illness, passing it on to Sophie won't help. She's not in charge. She's not a doctor." The annoyance in Max's voice couldn't be mistaken.

Frankie bristled. "I know Sophie's not in charge, but she can pass the information along to someone who is." She bit off the temptation to say something insensitive.

Max managed a clipped goodbye and was gone.

At eight-thirty, Tess, Jovie, and Aunt CeCe traipsed in the back door together, giggling about their in-sync timing.

After wishing them a good morning, Frankie showed Tess where she and Carmen left off on the orders. "So, there's the donuts for the park board meeting tonight, four dozen since they're expecting a lot of people to discuss summer events; one lemon cream and one cherry-rhubarb coffee cake for the conservation club meeting; and a banana-peanut butter coffee cake for Cinda Twilley, a gift to her mother-in-law.

"Carmen and I will be out the rest of the morning," Frankie spoke like a woman with a secret mission.

"Yes, we're going to be investigating," Carmen revealed, emphasizing the "investigating" part.

Tess shook her head while Jovie giggled and shrugged. "I'm glad Carmen is hanging out with you, Frankie. That gives me the chance to go to the Madison market. I can't wait to see all the fun produce and other goodies there." Frankie and Carmen were delegating more duties to their crew, so everyone would learn all aspects of running the shop.

"Well, I hope your investigation is productive. All I know is; somebody has to get to the bottom of this plague," Aunt CeCe called after the them.

Frankie started the SUV, took a swig from her mug, and

checked the time. "I told Emma Dunkel I'd be at her place around eleven o'clock. So, we should have plenty of time at Ray Pate's."

Carmen giggled. "Aye, aye, Captain. Let's practice what we're going to say on the way."

Ray Pate lived in one of the older neighborhoods on the far end of Kilbourn Avenue, past the sheriff's department and county jail. Many of the one-story ranch dwellings had seen better times. The neglect showed in the weed-choked yards, rusty sheds, and mildewed siding.

An old mustard yellow pickup, circa 1980, crouched at the back of the buckled concrete driveway, its body covered in stray sticks and windblown weeds. Frankie wondered the last time it had seen the street. She and Carmen went up the crumbling front steps, which were missing its handrails, and knocked on a door in great need of fresh paint.

After the fourth or fifth knock, the neighbor appeared from his own front door, dressed in a bathrobe, and called over.

"Are ya looking for Ray?" The bald man asked.

When the two nodded, he pointed up the street away from the neighborhood. "You all can usually find him at the Iron Skillet. He goes there about every day. Ya know where I mean?"

"You mean the truck stop restaurant? Out on Highway Five South?" Carmen asked.

The man affirmed and the two women left.

The Iron Skillet was quite low-key at the moment, but generally populated by truckers looking for fuel, showers, and meals. Frankie and Carmen saw Ray sitting in a corner booth with two other men. As the women made a beeline in his direction, he looked up curiously.

"Hello, Ray. You did some work for us a few years ago downtown at the bakery. Frankie and Carmen." Carmen gestured to Frankie and herself to jog his memory.

Ray stared at them with little acknowledgement. He raised his coffee mug and sipped. "Yeah, I remember. What did you need?"

"Just your expert advice, if you don't mind," Frankie added syrup to her voice.

The two other men at the booth got up and offered the women a place to sit. They waved at Ray and wandered up to the cash register.

A server in jeans and Iron Skillet T-shirt asked if they'd like anything. Frankie felt guilty taking up space meant for customers. "Sure, can you bring us one of those giant cinnamon rolls and two forks, please?"

"Anything to drink?"

Already coffee-logged, Carmen asked for lemonade and Frankie ordered iced tea.

Ray continued poking at the fried potatoes on his breakfast platter. "So, you want advice. About what?"

"We have a rodent problem," Frankie began.

"Not at the bakery. It's out at Frankie's vineyard. Squirrels..." Carmen continued.

Frankie shot Carmen an irritated look. "The squirrels are going to be relocated actually. We're setting up live traps for those. But there's a colony of bats living in the barn rafters."

Ray snorted. "You got something against bats? They eat a lot of bugs, probably help more than they hurt."

"We put up bat houses and they're all full, so we've got too many of them. They're making a gunky mess all over the floor.

We can't have guano falling from the ceiling into the grape vats." Carmen shuddered in disgust.

"Right, it's gross, Ray. What can we do to get rid of them?" Frankie asked.

"Guess you ladies didn't know I'm out of the pest control business." Ray gulped his coffee and set it near the table's edge for a refill.

A server hoisting two coffee pots stopped over to pour regular into Ray's mug, looked at the empty space in front of Carmen and Frankie and said she'd check on their order.

"We didn't know that. Can I ask why?" Carmen crossed her fingers under the table.

"No money to be made, what with the Amish doing business all over the countryside. I figured if I can't beat 'em, I might as well sell my stuff off to 'em."

"I guess you didn't keep any of your products then?" Frankie asked.

"Nope, sold it all, lock, stock, and barrel to the Yoder brothers. Sorry I can't help ya out."

"That's okay. We'll get in contact with the Yoders. What are you doing now that you're not in pest control?"

Ray grinned. "I went to trucking school to get my CDL. I just started hauling for Skinner Transfer."

That explained why Ray was hanging around The Iron Skillet with fellow truckers. Frankie and Carmen were about to lay on their pity party when a burly man with neck and arm tattoos approached Frankie.

"Frankie Davidson! I thought that was you. By God, I haven't seen you in years. I still run into your old man once in a while, mostly on my long runs to Nevada and California."

Frankie recognized her ex-husband's trucker friend, Moe. "Hi Moe. Please meet my business partner, Carmen. You know, Rick isn't my old man anymore. We've been divorced for fifteen years or so. Are you still trucking with Rhonda?" Moe and Rhonda were a husband-wife trucking duo, an arrangement Rick had once suggested to Frankie, except Moe and Rhonda didn't have kids. She declined Rick's idea but still enjoyed Rhonda's company when the duo was in town, until she and Rick split. She hadn't seen the pair since.

"Oh yeah. Rhonda's taking care of some family business in Missouri though, so I'll be swinging by that way on my next run to pick her up. I heard about you and Rick, but I wasn't sure, ya know."

"Please tell Rhonda I said hello and wish her the best," Frankie smiled warmly as Moe patted her arm.

The server brought the platter-sized cinnamon roll to Frankie and Carmen along with their drinks. Talking about bat guano didn't whet their appetites and the two just stared at the pastry.

"Ain't you gonna eat it?" Ray asked.

Frankie looked at Ray with her best impression of distress. "I just don't know what we're going to do if the Yoders can't help us with the bats. We've had enough batches of contaminated grape juice that the state is thinking of shutting us down. And we're losing money because we had to throw away the juice. Do you think the stuff the Yoders use will work on bats?" Frankie pleaded for good news from Ray.

Ray looked away, then over his shoulder to see who was around. "Look ladies, I wouldn't use the Yoders if I was you."

"Why not?" Carmen asked, disappointment on her face.

"The Yoders don't have the right products you need. I'd look for someone else from Oshkosh or Madison maybe. If the state's already on your case, you don't want to make things worse. Get a licensed pro." Ray gulped the rest of his coffee, grabbed the check from the table, and rose. "Gotta go now. Good luck to ya." He waggled his finger under their noses. "Remember, don't hire the Amish."

After Ray left, Moe swung back over to the booth and slid into the seat Ray had occupied. "Frankie, I don't know how you know Ray or what your business is with him, but that guy is bad news."

"How so?"

"Word on the street is he's crooked, can't be trusted." Moe leaned his heavy frame across the table. "I heard he made a bad business deal with the Amish, and now he's trucking so the cops won't catch up with him."

Frankie knitted her brows and frowned. "What does that mean—a bad business deal? He used to run a pest control operation. He sold his leftover products to an Amish business. At least, that's what he says."

"Which is illegal. You can't sell licensed chemicals to someone else. You have to dispose of them properly through the Department of Natural Resources. He ripped off the Amish, probably thought they were too dumb to know." Moe spoke with authority, and both women wondered if they were missing anything else important.

"Don't worry. We're not friends with Ray. We just needed information about how to control a pest problem. But I'm not interested in using chemicals, so we'll keep looking," Frankie assured him.

～

Carmen and Frankie slogged across Iron Skillet's parking lot to the SUV, thankful they had parked far enough from the front door to log some extra steps.

"I'm stuffed from that cinnamon roll," Frankie complained, holding her stomach.

"I wonder what kind of junk they use to make those: concrete and glue?" Carmen moaned as she fastened her seat belt.

"I guess I'll be taking Sonny for a long walk today. You feel like coming along?" Frankie asked.

"Maybe. I'll see what else is cooking. What do you make of Ray Pate and that trucker's warning?"

"I have no reason to doubt Moe. Truckers are like hair stylists—they know everything. I guess Ray Pate can't be trusted. Which makes me wonder about the stuff he sold to the Yoders."

Carmen tilted her head and laid it against the vehicle's window. "I was thinking the same thing. He could have sold them garbage. The canisters weren't labeled, so he could have filled them with any old poison. Wait a minute; that's it, isn't it?"

Frankie wagged her head up and down. "It could be. If there's poisonous stuff in those canisters, it might be making everyone sick. We need a customer list from the Yoder brothers."

"Good luck getting your hands on that." Carmen closed her eyes while the cinnamon roll unleashed its tranquilizing properties.

Frankie passed the O'Connor driveway and almost dropped off the sleepy Carmen but thought better of it. The Amish community was another ten miles past the O'Connor farm, enough for a power nap.

She slowed the SUV down as the Graham farm came into view, and Frankie spied familiar vehicles she'd seen before. The

Graham children must be there, preparing for their mother's funeral. She wanted to speak to them but in the name of punctuality, she continued down the road to Emma Dunkel's to check in first.

Carmen stirred when the SUV rolled down the bumpy driveway, hitting most of the ruts along its stretch.

"Ow, thanks a lot, Frankie." Carmen rubbed the side of her head that had knocked on the window. "If I didn't know better, I'd swear you did that on purpose." She looked around and noticed Emma standing in the garden.

"Emma's over there, and it looks like she's alone." Carmen pointed.

Frankie stopped the car but left the engine running. "Be right back."

Less than a minute later, Frankie pulled out of the Dunkel driveway and turned left onto HH. "We're stopping at the Graham farm. I saw two vehicles there, so Alex and Lindsay must be back, this time to prepare for Donna's funeral. Poor things."

At the women's knock, Lindsay opened the front door and ushered them into the kitchen where she and her brother, Alex, were poring over bills and other mail.

"I'm so sorry to hear about your mother," Frankie began.

"It must have been a terrible shock for you both," Carmen added.

The siblings accepted their condolences then asked why they'd stopped by.

"I have a couple of questions, and I don't want to be insensitive, but I don't want to beat around the bush either. I'm trying to help figure out why people are getting sick and dying. I promise not to take up much of your time." Frankie pleaded her case. The siblings nodded.

"Did your parents hire the Yoder Brothers to do any spraying recently? Maybe for bats. Maybe in the barn?" Frankie had her phone in hand, ready to take notes.

"Yeah. Mom mentioned it after Dad died. Last time we were here, one of the Amish came to collect the money for treating the barn and fields," Lindsay said.

"I remember that because I asked her why Dad wanted the empty fields sprayed when he wasn't planning to grow anything in them." Alex turned toward Lindsay to jar her memory.

Frankie and Carmen exchanged questioning looks. "What did your mother say?"

Lindsay shuffled through documents and selected one. "Here we go. Our parents accepted an offer to purchase the farm. One of the conditions was to have the fields sprayed to get rid of noxious weeds and the outbuildings treated for rodent control. That's what the Amish brothers did."

"Wait a minute. When did your parents accept this offer?" Frankie didn't remember any of the Grahams mentioning the farm would be sold, but it wasn't any of Frankie's business, so why would they.

"Before our dad died. He'd already decided to sell, since he'd stopped farming for the most part a few years ago. He and Mom were trying to sort out where they would live," Alex offered.

"Was there a timeline for them to move out?" Carmen asked.

"Yes. They had until the end of the year. They could harvest the hay and have time to get everything in order, but then Dad died, and now Mom. At least we won't have to worry about finding a buyer. We're waiting for updated paperwork. We'll have to sign off on the purchase," Alex said.

Frankie grew quiet. "May I ask who the buyer is, please?"

Lindsay held up the offer. The letterhead was easy to read. "Callahan Realty. I understand this realtor is buying up a lot of old farms in the area. Family farms are becoming scarcer every day, so it's no surprise a realtor would want to buy large parcels and sell off smaller ones."

Lindsay was savvy about the real estate market in rural America to say the least.

Frankie and Carmen sighed together. Neither one wanted to see their county go through such drastic changes. Both longed to keep the farms around as sources of local meats, dairy, and produce.

"I guess we can be thankful there's no corporation coming in to make a commercial dairy or chicken farm in the county, but it's sad to see the landscape change," Frankie said.

"It's hard to imagine this land will eventually look like a city subdivision," Alex said, "but we're not keeping it. That's out of the question."

"I'm surprised none of the Amish families have inquired. The farm is surrounded by their community. Usually, they know family or friends from another community looking for farmland," Carmen explained.

"It's our understanding that the Amish hope to take the land off the farmer's hands at a low price. Mom said one of the families asked about it a couple of years ago, but they didn't want to pay anywhere close to what it was worth." Lindsay shrugged. "We're not opposed to selling it to the Amish, but my parents already accepted this offer."

"Speaking of your parents, have you received any information about them so you can make funeral plans?" Frankie changed topics.

"My father died of that illness they've named Robli24. The autopsy is complete, and the health department will keep his records pending further investigation of the illness. They can't explain it because they don't know the cause. I suspect my mother's autopsy will have the same findings." Lindsay patted her brother's hand sympathetically.

"Wait a minute. You said you were trying to find information about the illness. Do you know something we don't know?" Alex asked.

"I'm afraid not. Only that scientists are studying mosquito-borne diseases for comparison, and that many Amish are ill or have died from it. All of the people are from this county except one. I guess that's good news in that the disease is contained, but bad news for the people living here," Frankie spoke with caution, realizing she wasn't supposed to divulge that much.

The two women wished the siblings well and once again aimed the SUV toward the Dunkel farm. Emma stooped over the garden pulling weeds from around the tomato rows. When she stood up, Frankie and Carmen noticed a small baby bump, barely protruding through her work apron.

"Good morning, Emma. Thank you for taking time to see us." Frankie held out a box of Bubble & Bake butterhorns.

Emma brushed away a few hairs stuck to her perspiring forehead. "The bakery you left last time was delicious. My husband liked them very much. Come inside and we will sit and talk before Simon comes home for lunch."

Frankie and Carmen followed Emma inside where she directed them to sit at the gleaming kitchen table, which still smelled like fresh-cut lumber. She pumped water into the sink, washed her face and hands, then scooped up handfuls to drink. Frankie thought Emma looked more like a child than a woman.

"There. That feels better." Emma's skin glowed from time spent outdoors and maybe pregnancy, too. She went to the icebox, brought out a pitcher of lemonade, grabbed glasses, and poured one for each of them.

"How have you been feeling?" Frankie opened the conversation with everyday pleasantries.

"Tired and a little sick every day. They say the sickness will pass when I'm further along." Emma looked at her stomach with a serene smile.

"Congratulations to you and your husband," Frankie said, and Carmen chimed in, "I hope you will start feeling better soon."

"Thank you both, but let's talk about the reason you're here."

"Do you know Samantha Quade? I believe she is friends with Joanna." Frankie wanted to gauge Emma's feelings toward the outsider.

"Why yes. She lives right across the road. I know her. She has been helpful to Joanna." On the word *helpful*, Emma glanced sideways, her eyes downcast.

"How was Samantha helping Joanna?" Frankie prodded.

"Joanna doesn't trust her brother-in-law, Ian. He is a business partner to Ethan, Joanna's husband, but the brothers disagree on how to run the business." Emma offered a safe answer, maybe out of loyalty to Joanna or the Amish community, Frankie suspected.

"The Yoder Brothers do pest control all over the county, but Ian wanted to use stronger products than Ethan did. Isn't that right?" Frankie proceeded.

Emma peered downward, then raised her face and nodded. "Ethan learned to make natural products from Joanna's father, and that's the Amish way. We don't want chemicals and poisons around our food, livestock, or people. Joanna says Ian is greedy. He loves money. Ian wanted to take a, what do you call it? A shortcut. He bought chemicals from an English going out of business." Emma's voice, filled with emotion, rose with each sentence.

"That's when people began getting sick and dying, isn't it? Does Joanna believe the chemical sprays are to blame?" Frankie persisted.

Emma nodded. "Yes. It seems to make sense. Ian sprayed fields and barns of the Amish and the English. Joanna spied on Ian. She saw him buy cans of chemicals. She took pictures with Samantha's phone."

Frankie couldn't reconcile how the chemical sprays related to mosquito-borne diseases, but then she wasn't a scientist. It was time to pursue another set of questions.

"Your sister-in-law, Sarah, said it's common for this community to seek outside medical help when traditional Amish medicine isn't working. Can you explain why the families here didn't take their sick to the hospital? Especially after people started dying?"

Emma pressed her lips tightly together and closed her eyes, shutting out the question she didn't wish to answer.

"Emma, what is it? Please tell us the reason. We don't want to lose any more of the people we love, do we?" Frankie pleaded.

"The bishop told us to care for our own, told us not to look to outsiders. We were to put our faith in God for protection and healing. That's why Sarah taking the Shumaker children to the hospital caused so much trouble. When Joanna's son and sister were ill, she wanted them to go to the hospital, and she asked Samantha for help." Emma choked back a sob.

"But they never went to the hospital and Judith died. What happened?" Frankie asked.

"Caroline happened. Ian's wife. She told Joanna it was forbidden, and she would be separated from her family if she disobeyed the bishop." Emma spoke with dread about the Amish punishment of being shunned by the community.

Clearly, this was the subject of the argument between Joanna and Caroline that Frankie saw on the day of the funeral. "Is Caroline a powerful woman in the community?" She asked.

"She is one of the midwives, so people listen to her. She is a Yoder, and the Yoders carry a lot of weight here. Bishop Yoder is Ian's uncle," Emma explained.

Carmen poked Frankie on the shoulder and pointed to the time. Frankie had more questions to ask Emma, and time might be running out before her husband stopped back at the house to cool off.

"Emma, do you know anything about the properties for sale around here? For instance, why didn't Amish buy the farmland where Samantha lives?"

"It's all confusing. A lot of people here are whispering about it. Before, any property for sale in this area was bought by Amish. But lately, the English are buying instead. I heard Simon talking to Ethan Yoder about it. When the Millers died, we all thought one of the young men would buy the property. Same thing on the other side of Lake Nochber."

Frankie's sharp gasp made Emma stop talking and Carmen stare at her with a crinkled brow. "Sorry. You mentioned Lake

Nochber." The name was foreign to Frankie, and she stumbled over its pronunciation.

Emma smiled softly. "It means *neighbor*. The lake is like a good neighbor. The whole community came together to build the park, tables, shelters, changing rooms, and piers. We spend a lot of time there."

Frankie redirected the conversation. "Who owned the property on the other side of the lake?"

"Another Amish couple. They were aging and wanted to move near some of their children, so they went back to Pennsylvania. Instead of Amish buying it, it was sold to outsiders, too."

"Did your husband shed any light about why this has been happening with the land around here?" Frankie prodded again.

"He and Ethan said the bishop didn't want our people on those properties. He said the land was tainted and no good for crops or animals, so better to be sold to the English. He said it was ordained by God." Emma's wide-eyed innocence held a twinge of doubt.

Frankie started to see a pattern that started and ended with Bishop Yoder and Bram Callahan. In between the two men she smelled a fishy business deal. How was she supposed to prove it and would it even matter? Fishy business isn't the same as illegal business.

"Emma, how long has Bishop Yoder been the bishop here?"

"Oh, about five years. He moved here from Indiana after his wife died. Once he arrived, most of the other Yoders followed him. I know, because I grew up here. So did Simon."

"So, I guess your sister-in-law, Sarah, grew up here, too. Did she know any of the Yoders?"

"No. Sarah left the community long before that. She was close to the Shumakers, but Sarah was much older than me, and I'm the oldest in my family, so I didn't know her until after Simon started courting me." Emma blushed, a young woman in love.

"Who gave her permission to attend the Shumaker funeral? I'm under the impression only the bishop would have that authority." Frankie wondered at the tiny threads connecting Sarah to the Amish community, despite the fact the woman had left long ago, had a college degree, and attended a different church.

Emma shrugged. "I don't know. It could have been the bishop, I suppose. Maybe Sarah gave herself permission to come to the funeral. That would be like her." Emma's voice faltered, and she abruptly stood up to clear away the glasses.

"I think you should be going. There are chores I need to finish before Simon comes home." A sudden chill crept into Emma's voice momentarily, then was gone. "I hope I was able to help."

CHAPTER TWENTY-ONE

Horse sense is the thing a horse has
which keeps it from betting on people.

W.C. Fields

After all the mileage Frankie logged Monday, she made the grave mistake of falling asleep at eight o'clock. She awoke at midnight with a crick in her neck and low back pain from dozing off in the living room recliner. Worse, she figured it must be almost time to get up for the new day. She cringed when she read the numbers on the clock.

She gingerly clambered out of the recliner after a few attempts at rocking the footrest up and down. Her dry mouth begged for water, so she shuffled to the kitchen where the blazing refrigerator light assaulted her further. After downing a glass of water, she started rummaging through cupboards to retrieve tea, and settled the kettle on the burner.

She didn't need to tiptoe since Violet returned to Stevens Point after the vineyard team huddle yesterday afternoon.

The meeting was a bright spot in Frankie's day. The team batted around ideas for the new vintages, and now tingled in anticipation to craft three different wine varieties from the frozen Pacific coast grape juices. Frankie was grateful for the two constants in her life: Bountiful Fruits and Bubble & Bake.

She sipped chocolate mint tea perched on a stool at the counter and rewound the events of the day. She was haunted by the ghosts of days past too, namely the plan for Callahan Acres and the photos Joanna Yoder took showing her brother-in-law with Ray Pate. Naturally, those ghosts wound their way to the graveyard of dead people in the county, the sick at UW Hospital, and her daughter.

"I just don't get it. How do pesticides cause mosquitoes to kill people? Can mosquitoes carry pesticides in their little bodies, then infect people when they bite them? If that's true, why aren't there more sick people? Maybe some people have immunity? If the pesticides are toxic, why are mosquitoes the only carriers?" Frankie directed her queries to the faucet, refrigerator, and walk-in pantry as she paced.

After an hour of reciting the same facts and spinning circuits around the apartment, Frankie surrendered her thoughts and donned pajamas before climbing into bed. Instead of counting sheep, she chased phantoms still flying around her brain.

At two a.m. her cell phone sounded off loudly on her nightstand. The unknown number didn't stop her from picking up. "Nobody calls at two in the morning without a good reason," she mumbled.

"Is this Frankie Champagne?" The deep male voice rattled her.

"Yes." She held her breath.

"Hold please for Sophie."

Sophie?

A few seconds later, the phone made a shush noise, then clicked. Frankie's face fell.

"Mom?" Sophie's voice was like a church hymn.

"Sophie, is it really you?" Frankie fought back tears.

"Yes. I can't talk more than two minutes though. So let me go first. I'm fine. No symptoms. We're past thinking this is contagious. I don't know when we'll be released from quarantine. The State Board of Health runs a tight ship. How are you doing?" Sophie barely got the question out as emotion took over.

"I'm fine, Honey. No need to worry about me. I feel better just hearing your voice. Okay, my turn. I've been investigating. If there's someone in charge there, tell them to look at pesticides. The Amish Yoder Brothers are using some kind of chemicals all over the county, and there's something off. They recently started using chemicals that came from Ray Pate. The pesticide use coincides with people getting sick." She paused to think.

"Okay. I'll tell the scientists. They're looking at mosquitoes as the culprits though. We're working with the necropsy lab. The dead animals had hundreds of mosquito bites. Now for the scary part: We can't identify this disease as anything known."

"Are your patients still just Whitman County people?" Frankie needed to know if the problem extended beyond their borders.

"Yes. And get this: Every patient and victim has B positive blood type. Except one of the dead. He's not from Whitman County though, so he's an outlier."

"John Van Cleef?"

"Mom, how did you know? Never mind. I shouldn't doubt my mother, the best sleuth in Whitman County." Sophie laughed, which was music to Frankie's ears.

"Not sure it matters, but what is John Van Cleef's type?"

"A positive. We're only focused on the B positive blood components, studying the sugars, proteins, and antigens for some clues and connections. Mom, I need to go. Dre took a huge risk letting me use his phone. I'm in the radiology darkroom where the signal won't track." She laughed mysteriously. "See, I can be stealthy, too. As soon as this is over, I'm coming straight to Deep Lakes. Love you."

The phone call dropped before Frankie could return the sentiment.

~

Garrett stared out the picture window overlooking the city lights and docks below his hotel suite. It was just after midnight and sleep had become his enemy, an untraceable one. Tonight was different. The ordinary stuffy air seemed fresh and the lights outside his window were warm and hopeful instead of menacing.

Garrett's oversized work area was clean—the copied case files were stacked in a neat pile occupying one corner. Over and over, he resisted the urge to call Frankie. He wanted to surprise her in person. The day was coming.

The coroner couldn't wait to share the news that, because of her, the case was cracked. Everything went down in less than thirty-six hours after Frankie sent him the photos from her bucket-trip balloon ride.

Something Frankie had said about rock climbing pinged in his brain like a weak GPS signal. Once she sent the photos, he stared at them again and again. First, his heart swelled at her happy face flying above the bluffs, the face belonging to the person he loved most in the world. He barely noticed the photos without her in them, but something struck a chord of another sort, and he began to study the others more closely as he wondered what drew him to the images.

His trusty magnifying glass revealed what he needed to know. Photos showed the rock climbers following the lead guide, held in place by nylon webbing and carabiners. Frankie made the analogy about the climbers' trust alongside her trust in him. She'd want him to be holding the rope that held her in place, she'd said. He went back to the autopsy photos, although he was certain he knew every mark on the victims by heart. He looked and found figure eight carabiner marks on four of the six. The figure eight carabiner, he discovered, was commonly used for rock climbing rescues.

Garrett called the ME team and detectives minutes later and they assembled at the downtown office on Sunday. Jaws dropped when Garrett suggested the marks on the victims' necks were a likely match for webbing used for rock climbing, while the imprints left on four of the victims were from figure eight carabiners.

"Finally, a new lead.," Detective Simms was beaming.

Olaf was already scrolling on his phone screen. "Great news. There are only four rock climbing gyms in Duluth. If our killer worked or climbed at any of them, it shouldn't take long to find out."

"Those gyms must keep a list of climbers for insurance purposes. Let's hope they have to keep them around a few months," Simms said.

The detectives didn't waste a minute and began tracking down the managers of each gym.

Kara and Leo applauded Garrett's efforts and even Dani

radiated approval. "Shall we go out for dinner and drinks?" Dani suggested.

Garrett held up a hand. "Let's wait until we have something to celebrate. This might be another rabbit hole." The possibility was like a gut punch.

But this time the good guys lucked out. The detectives found a matching photograph on file at all four gyms, although the photo came with four different names. A thirty-five-year-old expert climber volunteered to help all the female newbies. Once he gained their trust, the rest was easy. The four names led to four different Duluth addresses, which almost immediately became crime scenes thanks to a judge willing to issue search warrants on the fly.

While investigators from far and wide took control of each scene, the police caught a lucky break when the local hospital recognized the suspect. The killer was suffering from a serious case of pneumonia, which stymied his murder spree for a time. He was still a patient at St. Luke's, making it easy to arrest him and assign full-time guards to keep track of him until he could be released into custody.

Monday night, Garrett, the rest of the ME team, and most of the Duluth police department celebrated with drinks at The Ripple. Toasts to Garrett were led by Simms and Olaf, who presented him with a gallon jug of orange juice. "You deserve the title, Juice," Simms said, cuffing Garrett on the shoulder, while Olaf clapped.

Garrett stayed for one drink with many toasts, then excused himself to pack. "I'll stop by tomorrow morning to return my copies of the files." To her credit, Dani didn't coax him to stay longer.

After rewinding Sophie's phone call many times throughout the night and reviewing the map and plan for Callahan Acres posted beside her bed, Frankie had established a course of action for Tuesday. Another visit to Ray Pate's house and a surprise stopover at Bishop Yoder's would follow the morning baking. The hard part would be talking Carmen into going along.

Tuesday was typically cookie day during the summer months when people preferred fewer heavy treats or wanted portable snacks. Frankie iced kringles to complete shop orders, while Carmen, Tess, and Jovie batched cookies. Tia Pepita had the whole kitchen's attention with her mouthwatering pineapple upside-down cakes.

"We need to open the front door and windows, and the whole town will be under the spell of those cakes, Tia," Carmen giggled.

Tia jigged a happy dance around her station, making her hips sway to the salsa tunes playing on the music system.

When Jovie and Tia left the kitchen to open the shop, Frankie snagged the chance to butter up Carmen about her plans.

"Mexican Wedding cookies, yum," Frankie exclaimed, wetting one finger and dipping it into stray powdered sugar for a taste. "You haven't made these since Christmas."

Carmen playfully slapped Frankie's hand. "Gross. No licking your fingers in the shop."

Frankie swiped another finger full of sugar from the countertop in response.

"Ew, where's the health inspector when we need one?" Carmen made a face.

Frankie headed to the sink and ran hot water to wash her

hands. "Are you busy after the shop closes today?" Her tone was casual.

"What's brewing? If I know you, you're hot on the trail and there's no stopping you now. Whatever you're doing, I'm coming with you." Until Garrett returned, Carmen planned to keep tabs on her best friend.

At eleven a.m., Carmen drove to the seedy end of Kilbourn Avenue in her old VW Beetle, hoping to fool any prying eyes around the neighborhood.

"Thanks for driving, Carmie. I don't want us to get pegged for stalkers." Deep Lakes was small enough that nosy people kept track of familiar vehicles and faces that might be scoping out unusual places.

"No problem. Let's hope our buddy Ray isn't at home," Carmen replied.

The crumbling driveway was empty except for the old rust bucket pickup. Carmen parked up the street against the curb a few houses away from Ray's. Both women wore baseball caps pulled low over their foreheads.

The neighborhood was blessedly quiet as they approached Ray's unkempt yard and house. While Carmen stood watch near the front, Frankie steered toward the truck and peeked inside the interior and truck bed. A gas can, bungee cords, rusty wrenches, and a sack of garden soil made up its contents.

She ducked around the truck where a metal shed came into view behind the house. It was padlocked, so she looked through the grimy window, wiped it off with one sleeve, and looked again. She didn't see any metal canisters, but she could just make out a couple large bags with labels on them. She held up her phone, set the flash, and snapped two pictures. Then she took another two without the flash.

Carmen's whistle alerted Frankie. She skirted the other side of the house, looking under the bushes, as she made her way to Carmen's side. Carmen was chatting with a sixtyish woman in a housecoat and slippers who was walking a toy dog of some sort.

"No luck. I didn't see any sign of Skippy." A sorrowful Frankie looked from Carmen to the neighbor lady. "I've lost my cat."

The woman scooped up her little dog as if Frankie's make-believe cat might be a threat. "What does he look like? I'll keep an eye out," the woman said.

"Oh, just a tabby. He has white paws and white tipped tail." Frankie began embellishing until Carmen kicked her foot and shot her a warning look.

"Thank you for your help. We're going to search on the next street over now," Carmen closed the conversation.

The woman watched them walk to the VW and drive away. "I hope she didn't take down your license plate, Carmen."

"Geez Frankie. You don't have to make up such elaborate details about a phony cat, you know. Anyway, did you find anything?"

Frankie pulled out her phone and pressed on the photos icon. It turned out the combination of the flash photo and natural light photo allowed the women to read the bags. One was labeled "hydrated lime," and the other was labeled "rock salt." While Carmen drove, Frankie searched online for the products.

"This says hydrated lime is used for construction of dams, roads, and foundations. It's not a substitute for barn or garden lime because it's toxic and kills plants. Interesting. Rock salt is toxic to garden soil because it dehydrates the ground and anything rooted there. The sodium content can kill the soil for several years. Hmm." Frankie sorted the information into possible file folders in her head.

"What are you thinking, Sherlock?" Carmen drove down County HH, the breeze from the rolled down windows smelled of plowed earth and mowed grass.

"I definitely see why city people want to buy land around here. It smells so good and there's very little noise from planes, trains, and traffic." Frankie lifted her face toward the breeze.

"Indeed. But let's get back to hydrated lime and rock salt. I've never seen that around our farm. Do you think Ray might have used it as a pesticide?"

"I'm not sure. I want to see if the Amish bishop has any sacks of the same stuff. I guess it might be a cheap way to kill pests, and a shortcut for Ray to make more profits," Frankie speculated.

"Where is the bishop's farm?" Carmen asked.

Frankie suspected the property where they'd seen Bram Callahan talking with two Amish elders might belong to the bishop. They would try that address first. She pointed to a small white house that came into view as they rounded a bend in the road.

Carmen pulled in, careful to stay near the end of the driveway in case they needed a fast getaway. They closed the VW doors quietly and walked toward the barn, avoiding the house on purpose. The barn seemed to be void of life except for some straw bales and dust motes floating around the sunbeams. The women explored in two different directions, looking for canisters and sacks.

Carmen rounded a corner and saw two sacks of hydrated lime leaning against the back wall. She almost dropped her phone in her panic to take a photo but captured the image and backtracked to find Frankie. Careful not to speak, Carmen waved her phone and pointed at the screen. Frankie nodded and did the same.

They left the barn and walked to the next outbuilding, which appeared to be a stable.

"I found hydrated lime," Carmen whispered and indicated her phone.

Frankie pointed to her phone, too. "I found several canisters with skulls and crossbones. We can compare them to Joanna's photos later."

Light poured into the stable from both ends where the doors were opened for ventilation. Three stalls revealed stately, well-groomed horses. Carmen's deep frown registered trouble.

"What is it, Carmen?" Frankie asked.

"These are quarter horses. I would expect to see draft horses of some kind, like the Amish typically use. These are much finer than work horses, probably used for riding. I guess the bishop is too hoity-toity for farm work."

On cue, the bishop rode up to the stable on a glamorous palomino with a white blaze face marking. He deftly dismounted, scowling at Carmen and Frankie.

"What do you want here? Why are you in my stable, bothering my horses?"

Carmen looked down at the dirt, silent. Frankie's sheepish reply was apologetic. "We're so sorry for intruding. We're here to buy eggs. When nobody answered the door, we started looking for someone."

The bishop snorted but backed up a step. "Eggs? I don't sell eggs. What farm are you looking for?" The bishop led the palomino into an empty stall, gently patted its neck, and scooped some feed from a burlap sack for the horse.

"Gabriel Shumaker," Frankie faltered.

"Why, you passed that farm. It's back about a half-mile." Impatience returned to his voice.

"We're very sorry, sir," Carmen managed to speak but wouldn't raise her face to the bishop's. "Your horses are beautiful and well cared for. They don't resemble most of the work horses around the county." Carmen risked a pointed comment.

The vain bishop puffed up taller and gazed at his fine fleet of animals like they were prized muscle cars. "I am not a farmer, young woman. I don't use my animals to eke out a living from the land. My horses are purely for pleasure." The moment passed and the bishop once again looked cross.

"I like my privacy, so please take your business off my property," he snapped.

Frankie and Carmen departed without fanfare, raced to the Beetle, and headed back the way they'd come. At least it was in the direction of Gabriel Shumaker's farm, even though they didn't intend to stop there.

"What do you think?" Carmen asked.

"Hydrated lime and canisters of poisons. I think the bishop is in cahoots with his nephew, Ian. Did you see the horse trailer parked behind the barn? You can't pull that with an Amish wagon. I just wish I could figure out how Bram Callahan is involved."

Carmen stepped hard on the brakes. "Bram Callahan. What are you talking about?"

"Turn right at the next road, the one that leads to Lake Nochber and the Amish park. I'll fill you in while we look around."

A couple miles down Wagon Trail, the road narrowed,

changed from pavement to gravel and dead-ended in a wide parking area above Lake Nochber. The picnic grounds were pristine with mowed grass, many pine tables, and two covered shelters. The pebbly path led to the lake where fishing piers lined the south side, and a sandy beach sat adjacent to the piers where the water was roped off for swimming.

"What a beautiful lake and park," Carmen exclaimed. "I've never been down here before."

Frankie agreed, took a few photos, then opened her saved documents to show Carmen the plan for Callahan Acres. "You can see the development includes annexing part of this lake and changing its name. I think Bram intends to control the whole lake by buying off the surrounding properties."

"And you think the bishop's involved? Is that what your questions for Emma Dunkel were about yesterday?" Carmen gazed at the sunlight dancing on the lake's surface. Despite the warm weather, she shivered.

"You can't mean to take on Bram Callahan, Frankie? That's a no-win situation," Carmen warned. She barely breathed. "He's unstoppable."

"There's the problem, Carmen. Everyone's afraid of Bram Callahan and his power. Someone needs to challenge him, knock him off his throne." Frankie spoke with bravado.

Carmen turned to face Frankie and held on to both of her shoulders. "Not you, though. Promise me."

"Who's going to do it, Carmen?" Frankie's question was lost in the breeze.

Frankie stopped at the O'Connor farm to take her favorite canine, Sonny the Sheltie, for a walk. Two days in a row of walking made the sheltie a happy dog and proved even an elder dog can have a spring in his step.

Carmen walked to the barn to see Ryan and acquire any news of the day. Frankie waved at Carlos as she strolled along the fence line where he was working with the border collies.

She wondered if it was time to call Alonzo to show him the photos she'd collected recently along with other tidbits. He might laugh, but he might be able to use the information for leverage. Maybe that was enough.

The day was growing warmer with the sun shining directly overhead, so Frankie cut the walk short and found Carmen. "I'm ready to go back into town whenever you are."

"Sounds good. I'm sure Tia Pepita will be ready to come home for a siesta. She doesn't like the summer afternoon sun."

Frankie thanked Carmen for being her getaway driver, said her farewells to Tia after marveling about their bakery sales, then climbed the stairs to her apartment. She made a beeline for the map in the bedroom and wrote down the names of the afflicted and dead on a notepad.

Her first call went to Julia Karlsen, who had Frankie listed as a contact on her phone.

"Hello Frankie. What can I do for you?"

"I'm on a fact-finding mission, Julia, and it's important. Did Elsa hire an Amish pest control business sometime before she passed away?"

Julia paused, then began rifling through her mother-in-law's papers. "Lew and I spent a couple of weeks going through her bills to see what needed to be paid. Ah, here it is. The Yoder Brothers sprayed her basement for mice, spiders, and centipedes on May fourteenth. What's this about?"

"I'm not sure, but I will update you as soon as I know more.

Thank you. Is everything in place for Elsa's funeral tomorrow?" Frankie remembered the upcoming funeral in the middle of the call.

"All set, Frankie. You know it's going to be at St. Mary's in Portage, right?"

"Yes. Thanks for reminding me."

She looked up Ann Malson's number in the St. Anthony's directory.

"Hello."

"Is this Ann?" Frankie was surprised to hear the familiar voice.

"Yes. Who's this?"

"Frankie Champagne. I'm relieved to hear your voice. I thought you might still be hospitalized from the day you worked in the church kitchen. How are you?"

"Oh Frankie. It's nice to hear a friendly voice. I've just been home a couple days now, but I'm still recovering. The hospital gave me an inhaler and some medicine to help my lungs heal. I'm lucky, though. Father and June are still there. I know others have died." Ann's voice broke off. She sounded weak and weary.

"This illness has knocked us all for a loop. I need to ask you a question if I may. Did you hire any Amish men to do pest control at your home this spring?"

"Why yes, I did. I think their name was Yoder. They treated my basement. I heard about them from June at church. She was happy with their work. I think June said they sprayed the church grounds, too."

Frankie remembered Ian Yoder in the church office picking up his payment for services rendered and making a case to get rid of the bats in the bell tower next.

"Thanks, Ann. Can I bring you something?" Frankie recalled she still had some leftover wedding food in the freezer. "How about a dinner?"

Ann was grateful.

Calling Ann allowed her to place a check mark next to June's name too. Frankie turned to Ruth Brandt's name in the directory. Ruth's husband answered, said Ruth was still hospitalized but was improving. Like the others, he confirmed the Yoder brothers sprayed around the foundation of their house and got rid of the bats living in their attic. Since the Brandts were friends and neighbors of Ken Pearse, Frankie chanced asking about Ken.

"Yeah, I heard Ken might be released sometime this week. He's a strong man and much younger than me and Ruth."

"Did he use the Yoders' services on his farm?" Frankie asked.

"Yeah, he sure did. That's why we hired the Amish. Ken used them in his barn."

"One more question, Mr. Brandt. What is your blood type, please?"

"Ha, funny you should ask that. The hospital asked me, too. It's O positive."

"Thank you for talking to me. Please give Ruth my best when you're able to."

Mr. Brandt's voice became unsteady. "I just want my wife back home."

Frankie hoped her call to Jovie would reveal that Helen Thurston, who was her neighbor, had used the Yoders, too. As a matter of fact, Jovie saw the Amish wagon there and asked Helen about it. Helen said she was tired of battling an overgrown patch of weeds, vines, and brambles by her woods, so the Yoders sprayed it, killing everything growing. A few days later, Helen was out raking up the dead brown mess.

Frankie stopped a moment to collect herself. This was both the easiest and hardest task she'd undertaken as an investigator, but she chastised herself for not thinking of making the calls weeks ago. Her final call was to Biddle's Blooms in Gibson. Dusty Biddle answered.

"Hello Mr. Biddle. This is Frankie Champagne in Deep Lakes. How is your wife doing?"

"We don't need an insurance supplement, and I'm getting sick of answering these calls." His voice rose throughout the delivery.

"No, no. I'm not with any insurance company. I'm friends with the Healys, and Meredith told me about Becky's unfortunate illness. I called to see how she's doing, and I have a quick question."

"Becky is still in the hospital, Ms. Champagne. I wish I could say she wasn't, but they seem to have stabilized her. What's your question?"

"Did you hire the Yoder Brothers to do any pest control at the greenhouse?"

"We've used them every year for the past three. We like it that they don't use chemicals. Why? Are they involved some way?"

"Honestly, Mr. Biddle, I'm investigating the illnesses and looking for commonalities. Can you tell me your blood type, please."

Dusty Biddle confirmed he was A positive and noted that the hospital had asked his blood type, too. Frankie signed off with good wishes for Becky.

There it was. Everyone who wasn't Amish on the map were Yoder customers. The ones who didn't succumb to the illness had different blood types. It was time to share her findings with

Alonzo.

She called Lon in his office saying the information she had was best seen in person. They met in his office, shades pulled over the window. It was his job to decide if Frankie had anything real.

When she was finished, Lon leaned back in his oversized office chair and closed his eyes. He began humming as his brain computed the data.

"Thanks for telling me how you attained the blood type information. I sure don't want Sophie facing charges or losing her nursing license over this." He cleared his throat, letting the details sink in.

Frankie puffed out her lips, ready to defend Sophie's underground facts. Before she could, Alonzo continued.

"Now these photos of Yoder and Pate are worth some questions. And the photos you took at the bishop's and in Pate's shed. I'm asking myself; how do I get the bishop or the Yoders to surrender one of the canisters to evaluate at the lab?"

Frankie grinned. "Your best bet is to ask Ethan Yoder. He's been against the deal between Ian and Pate from the beginning. I think he'll cooperate with you."

"It's going to take a search and seizure warrant for us to take those canisters. I'm on the good side of Judge Wheaton, so I suspect I can get the warrant, maybe even tomorrow. On to the next problem: how did you get a copy of these Callahan plans?" Alonzo's face reddened as he prepared himself for the worst.

"I took it from their office copier. Before you say anything, the realty is a public place and the copy room is an open space without doors, so technically, I could have accidentally grabbed the copies." Lon saw through her fake recitation.

"But that's not how it happened, I'm sure. The problem is that this is considered a work product and if it hasn't been filed with the state, it's not for public consumption, Frankie. Don't tell me you think you're going to the big league and try to take down the Callahans." Lon lowered his voice. Anyone might be listening.

"It's worth investigating. Make a couple phone calls. You must have favors to call in."

Alonzo rose and stood over Frankie, making her shrink into the chair. "What I insist you do is not tell anyone about this Callahan deal or about your theories regarding the bishop, Pate, or the Yoders. The element of surprise is on our side, so we need to flush out these characters and hope they turn on each other. I'm keeping the plans and your checklist. Send the photos to me."

"I already did before I drove here, Lon. I want justice for the victims. You have my word I won't talk about this." She hesitated. Lon waited. "If you tell me how things transpire."

"Frankie Champagne, I'll tell you exactly what I'll share with the rest of the public, and not a smidge more. Thank you for your work. Now let me do my job."

CHAPTER TWENTY-TWO

I can't change the direction of the wind,
but I can adjust my sails to always reach my destination.

⤞

Jimmy Buffett

Garrett paced the hotel suite, itching for time to pass faster. He'd packed the night before, settled himself onto the living room sofa, and began browsing TV channels. He landed half-heartedly on an espionage film after skipping over a gory thriller. He'd had his fill of gore in real life lately, thanks just the same. When the spy movie ended, it looped back to the beginning, so Garrett picked up the remote to channel surf once more. He fell asleep after watching several episodes of a cooking competition program, then was startled awake from a dream where chefs chased each other with fire extinguishers riding on unicycles.

By four a.m., he'd had enough. He went for a brisk walk along the lakeshore followed by a cool swim in the hotel pool. He wondered how much it would set him back to put a pool on his property and decided he'd at least check it out. He pictured

Frankie there, cooling off after a long day in the hot bakery, and smiled. With a prolonged Wisconsin winter, a hot tub might be another enjoyable addition.

He continued to resist the urge to call Frankie or text her, saying she should be ready for a surprise. The truth was he felt nervous about their reunion, how it would go, if there would be residual tension. He thought about bringing her a gift, maybe an ostentatious floral bouquet. But his memory alerted him that Frankie was literally buried in flowers from a postponed wedding. He didn't have the time or rationality right now to buy her a piece of jewelry, which left him with perfume and chocolates.

As much as he knew Frankie would dive into a vat of chocolates naked, it didn't seem the wisest of options. When Garrett closed his eyes, he could smell Frankie's aroma, the scent of sugar, vanilla, spices, and some underlying fragrance that made him heady. He smiled at the memory of her. No, that fine woman didn't need the cover of perfume.

Finally, his phone alarm sounded, meaning his confinement was over. He rode the elevator downstairs, tossed his room key card into the checkout slot, and flew out the double doors to his waiting vehicle. He tipped the valet and drove the eight miles to the city building downtown.

Garrett opened the ME office door where Dani was waiting for his arrival. To his surprise, she was dressed formally in a skirt, jacket, and high heels. She surveyed his appearance and handed him a mug of coffee.

"This is the most relaxed I've seen you since, well, since you arrived here," she said, reluctance in her voice. "I'll have you know I got up extra early to come in this morning."

Garrett's smile was disarming. "I suppose going home agrees with me." He peered over the coffee mug. "You didn't have to dress up on my account."

Dani's eyes swept right to left and back again, in a teasing fashion. "I'm making a presentation to the top brass in a couple of hours if you care to stick around. I'd love to introduce you as the hero of the day." She doubted she could entice him to stay for the presentation, nor any other reason.

Garrett shook his head. "No thanks. But you should introduce your crack ME team. Leo and Kara worked tirelessly on autopsy reviews. You're lucky to have them, Dani."

Dani's gaze slipped sideways toward her team's work area. "Don't worry. I wasn't planning to bask in the glory alone." She balanced against the edge of the reception desk, arms folded.

"So, it's back to the white-bread town with the rest of the village people for you?" Dani blinked a few times.

Garrett brushed off the comment, smiling even wider. "Exactly. But I want to thank you for reminding me of all the reasons I left in the first place."

Dani smirked. "Say hello to the little baker from me."

Garrett resisted the urge to tell her they had Frankie to thank for the break in the case. Instead, he raised his hand in farewell and left. In about five hours, he would be home.

~

Judge J.J. Wheaton only hesitated briefly when Alonzo requested the search and seizure warrant.

"You know I don't make it my practice to mess with the Amish, Sheriff, so tell me what's got you all hot under the collar." The judge was part of the old guard. He preferred to let sleeping dogs lie, but he trusted Alonzo because it was the rare occasion when the sheriff brought trouble to his door.

"These chemicals we're looking for are likely related to the outbreak that's been plaguing the county. It's a solid lead. We seize the chemicals and send them straight to Madison for evaluation. Maybe nobody else has to die, Judge." Alonzo stood straight and tall, hat in hand.

The judge squinted to read the warrant a second time. "Well, I guess it's been a while since we riled up the Amish. I imagine they'll get over it." He scrawled his signature and sent Alonzo on his way with a piece of advice.

"Sheriff, if I were you, I'd leave that snarly Pflug behind on this expedition. He's like inviting a grizzly bear to a beehive if you get my meaning."

Alonzo, accompanied by Officer Green, drove down County HH in the sheriff's black Jeep, towing a trailer. Shirley Lazaar followed in the sheriff's other vehicle, an unmarked pickup. Based on Frankie's information, including Joanna Yoder's photos, they decided to go to Ian Yoder's farm first as the most likely place to locate contraband chemicals.

They encountered Caroline at the door, who was a force to be reckoned with. First, she insisted her husband was gone for the day, and when Alonzo said they didn't need him to be present for their search, she threw a fit and charged at Officer Green with a rolling pin. Shirley intervened.

"Now Mrs. Yoder, you don't want to do that. Who would take care of your children while you sat cooling off in a jail cell?" Shirley calmly stood between the rolling pin and Green. "Let's sit at the table and have some tea while the men do their work, yes?"

Caroline took a few backward steps to the kitchen counter and retired her weapon. Two small children stood wide-eyed by the table after hearing their mother shouting. She walked over and patted their heads, then gave each of them a piece of bread and shooed them out the door to play.

The Amish woman, calmer now, set the teakettle on the woodstove and took cups from the dish board. Once Alonzo and Green were assured Shirley was out of danger, they turned toward the door.

"You'll find my husband in the field behind the big barn, directly to the right," Caroline spoke softly but there was steel in her voice.

To say Ian Yoder was astonished would be an understatement, and he immediately began to weave a tale of abject denial about any wrongdoing. Alonzo won the Amish man's cooperation by placing all the blame on Ray Pate.

"If the chemicals contain illegal substances, I'm going to assume you don't know anything about that, and Ray Pate is going to be prosecuted. Your cooperation with law enforcement would sure go a long way, Mr. Yoder."

Ian understood. He led Alonzo and Green to a storage shed far away from his house and other outbuildings. Pest control equipment, including sprayers, hoses, masks, and generators were organized inside. Several metal canisters were lined up against two walls, and freestanding metal shelves held containers of labeled powders and plastic jugs of liquid. Ian said the canisters were all the same, having been purchased in bulk from Ray Pate.

"I'm going to need to see your permit to use these pesticides." Alonzo instructed Green to get the Jeep and drive it to the shed while Yoder opened a drawer to retrieve the permit.

He handed a thin file folder to Alonzo, who walked outside to read the contents in better light. Just as he thought, the Yoders had permits for their powders and natural sprays, but not for the chemicals in the metal canisters. Pate had given Ian a pamphlet with the name and ingredient list for the canisters, which Alonzo took.

He turned, grim-faced, back to Ian. "We're going to be confiscating all the canisters. You don't have a permit to use them, which is a violation of state law. I'd like you to come in with me so I can take your statement."

Green was back with the Jeep and Alonzo instructed him to load the canisters into the trailer.

"Are you arresting me, Sheriff?" Ian asked, shame faced. It appeared, at least for now, that he would cooperate.

"I'm not arresting you, Mr. Yoder. I hope you will come to the station willingly to offer your statement. You know about the outbreak of illnesses and deaths around the county. I can tie them to you. They're all your customers, Mr. Yoder." Alonzo indicated the list in his hand.

Ian peered at the ground and walked to the back of the Jeep where he took a seat. When Alonzo and Green buckled up, Ian mumbled, "Maybe we should have our bishop come along. That's how we do things here."

"I'm afraid we can't do that, Mr. Yoder. You see, the bishop is already in police custody." Alonzo couldn't be sure if what he said was true, but he'd sent the grizzly, Donovan Pflug, to pick up the bishop and the canisters from his barn. A thunderstruck Ian Yoder was looking green around the gills. Alonzo saw that as a good sign.

When the Jeep and trailer rolled past the Yoder's kitchen window, it was Shirley's cue to depart. She continued down HH to Joanna's and Ethan's farm, Yoders who were more willing to be helpful.

After Shirley spoke with Joanna about the photos she'd taken of Ian and Ray Pate, she picked her brain, woman to woman, and found a fountain of information, facts mixed with theories. Joanna believed the bishop was stealing money meant for the whole community, and she saw red. Her ideas coincided with the intel Frankie had passed to them from Emma Dunkel. The exchange between Shirley and Joanna involved Amish friendship bread and molasses cookies, after which Shirley went to the barn to ask Ethan to give a voluntary statement at the sheriff's office.

Traversing between Ian and Ethan; Alonzo, Green and Pflug gathered details, while Shirley sat like a guard dog outside the conference room containing the nervous bishop. The department knew better than to use Shirley for questioning as the Amish men might view her with disdain. Sad, since Shirley had questioning skills that generated thumb-sucking in the most callous of suspects.

The department confirmed the Yoder brothers' customer list and dates, both the Amish and non-Amish clients. All the sicknesses or deaths transpired after Pate's sale of the chemicals, and Ian stated the canisters were used at every job where someone had become afflicted.

Ethan was heartsick about the situation, insisted that his statement include his objection to buying Pate's chemicals and his desire to only use natural products. Ethan was present at the first few jobs where Pate's products were used, but after a couple of customers died, he refused to even be in the presence of the chemicals.

Ian, on the other hand, seemed more upset about the possibility of being tricked by Pate than by using chemicals that hurt people. He proudly mentioned how lucrative it was to have the only pest control operation in the county.

"About that," Alonzo said. "How were you able to gain so much business so quickly around the county?" The sheriff hoped to catch Ian in a bragging mood. He sat down across from Ian in a friendly pose.

"Word of mouth doesn't hurt." Ian grinned.

"You're right about that. Still, it doesn't hurt to have friends in high places either."

"Ah, you mean my uncle, the bishop?" Ian smiled.

Alonzo meant the bishop and maybe Bram Callahan. "Sure. But he's traveling the same circles as you, knows the same people. I was thinking of someone on the outside," Alonzo encouraged him.

"Aya. It's the bishop that knows people. He got us the big jobs." Ian brightened, recalling the money he was making because of it.

"What kind of big jobs do you mean?" The sheriff prodded.

"The English landlord, uh realtor…he buys huge properties and we're hired to get rid of everything."

"And what do you mean by everything?" Alonzo wanted specifics.

"The land is gutted, so it can be used for something besides farming." Ian didn't seem to comprehend what his actions meant for the lands in question.

"Is the realtor you mentioned named Callahan?" Alonzo asked.

Ian shrugged. "I never met the man. All the deals are made through the bishop. So, you're going to have to ask him."

~

In the spirit of decency, Donovan Pflug had hauled in Bishop Jacob Yoder without fanfare, lights, or sirens. They didn't know how long they could hold him before he went silent based on his religious rights, hopefully long enough to fill in some blanks. Hopefully long enough for him to incriminate Bram Callahan.

Pflug didn't relish going toe-to-toe with Callahan based on flimsy information from Frankie Champagne, the meddling baker. If Callahan was going to be taken down, Pflug wanted a treasure trove of evidence to crush the slimy real estate mogul.

With Ian and Ethan Yoder in custody, the bishop might sing a few bars in the name of protecting the family, but then again, Pflug had watched plenty of families eat their own. Alonzo rapped on the interrogation room door and motioned Pflug to come out for a chat.

The sheriff shared the pertinent details from his interviews with the brothers and the two strategized. Alonzo would counter Plfug's bad cop role. To the bishop's credit, his perspiration indicated anxiety, a possible sign he would cooperate.

"Good afternoon, Bishop. Can we get you some water before we start?" Alonzo asked.

Yoder shook his head and stared at the black hat he'd set on the conference table. "I'd like to get this over with so I can return to my community, if you please." He wore an earnest expression.

"Ethan and Ian Yoder told us you knew the chemicals they used were making people sick, yet you said nothing. Why?" Pflug's eyes bored into the bishop's.

"I didn't want them to get into trouble. I didn't want the community to have a black eye. It could ruin us." Yoder's defensive posture might be good news for the officers.

It was Alonzo's turn. "That makes sense. You're the leader of the community. Your job is to protect everyone, isn't it?"

The bishop nodded, caught off guard by Alonzo's carefully worded statement. He wasn't sure if his response was prudent, and he began to fidget.

"How were you protecting the community by allowing people to get sick and die when you knew the reason behind it all?" Alonzo continued, matter-of-factly.

"You don't understand our ways. The boys and their families would be shunned. Where would they go if that happened?" The bishop raised pleading eyes to the sheriff.

As Alonzo stepped back, Pflug leaned downward to stare into Yoder's eyes. "I think you were worried about saving your own skin, Bishop. You would surely be found out, and it would ruin you." Pflug's tone made the bishop flinch.

Pflug drove the knife deeper. "Your nephews' business wasn't just good for them; it was good for you. Why else would Bram Callahan be able to keep finding properties to buy in your neighborhood?"

The bishop's sweat came in rivulets now. He pulled a cotton handkerchief from his coat pocket and wiped his forehead. Pflug pushed a bottle of water toward him, and he gratefully gulped some.

"Callahan brings reliable business to our people, not just my nephews. He sees that our builders are hired to construct new houses when he sells the land. There's land to clear and wells to dig. Once those people become customers, they keep doing business with us. They buy our products, our groceries, furniture, crafts. You name it. The English are like a never-ending fountain of cash." Yoder's tone went from distressed to amused.

Pflug read Alonzo's angry tick in his jaw as a sign the bad cop should press on. All six foot six inches of Pflug towered over the bishop, and his steely eyes drilled into the Amish man's soul. "You have a nice little arrangement with Mr. Callahan, don't you? What's in it for you, Bishop? You are just a man, after all. Don't try to sell me on your act that this is all about the good of your community."

The bishop sneered at Pflug's accusations and began to sputter grunts and groans. He reached for the water again and swigged. In sync, Pflug stepped back while Alonzo stepped forward, bearing a sympathetic smile.

"I know Bram Callahan. He has quite a reputation around town. He won't make deals unless he has the most to gain, so what did you offer up in exchange for all the business Callahan promised to the Amish?"

The bishop looked from sheriff to officer and back again, then folded his hands as if in prayer, and looked downward, eyes shut. Alonzo and Pflug waited one minute, two minutes. The silence persisted. The officers exchanged shrugs, frowns, but waited patiently. Finally, Lon tagged Pflug to proceed.

"If you're through praying, Bishop, we're waiting for an answer. What did you give away to get all this free business?" Pflug smacked his hand on the table in front of Bishop Yoder.

But the momentum was gone. The bishop locked his lips and tossed away the key. The officers escorted each Yoder separately back home. Elders from other communities awaited all three men, thanks to Shirley contacting a quasi-hotline for the Amish justice system the day before. In any serious legal matters, elders from other communities were brought in as judges of the accused. The Yoders would meet their fate served up by other Amish.

Meanwhile, Alonzo paid a visit to Callahan Realty, while Pflug did research, and Officer Green drove the canisters to officials in Madison.

Kimberly Nichols, the receptionist, escorted Alonzo to Bram's office and closed the door.

Bram offered a disarming smile but sobered when he saw Alonzo's stone face. "Is this an official call, Sheriff?" He gestured for Alonzo to sit down.

"Let's say this is a courtesy call, Mr. Callahan." Alonzo ignored the invitation and remained standing.

"What's this about?" Bram asked.

"We brought the Yoder brothers in. We believe the pesticides they're using caused people to get sick or die. The Yoders don't have a permit to use them. The chemicals are on their way to the lab in Madison." Alonzo began to parcel out the story.

"I'm sorry. What does this have to do with me?" Bram's nonchalant tone didn't match his frown.

"Of course, you already know. You hired the Yoders to spray pesticides on all your recent land acquisitions."

Bram sat back attempting to look more relaxed. "So, what? I do business with the most affordable, yet reputable, pest control people. They do business all over the county."

"Did you check their permits before you hired them to do those substantial properties, Bram?"

"I'm certain someone from our office checked, Sheriff." There was that greasy grin.

"I'm surprised you continued to hire them after their other customers began getting sick and dying. Even your own customers, like the Grahams." Alonzo cast his net out deeper.

"The Grahams? I'm afraid I don't know what you're talking about."

"Sure, you do. You offered to purchase Harry Graham's farm with the contingency they gut the area clean of crops and any likely pests. You recommended the Yoder Brothers. Both Harry and Donna Graham died shortly after the chemical treatment."

Bram sat up straight, swallowed a couple of times, and narrowed his eyes. "You better have direct evidence against me, Sheriff, or you can be on your way."

"I told you this was a courtesy call, Mr. Callahan. You should know we brought Bishop Yoder in for questioning as well." Alonzo spoke lightly.

"The bishop? Whatever for?" The sheriff caught Callahan by surprise.

"He had canisters of chemicals in his barn, for starters." Lon's sly smile grew. "That bishop is the wheeler-dealer of the community. For a man of the cloth, he knows how to make money for the whole community. But I guess I don't have to tell you that, eh Bram?"

"Since when are business deals against the law, Sheriff?" Bram recovered too quickly and looked cucumber cool. "Capitalism is America's bread and butter, after all."

"You would know. You've got a lot more bread and butter than most of us." Alonzo wished he could shove the purloined Callahan Acres plan down Bram's throat and watch him stew. Instead, he whirled around and strode out the door, closing it with a bang.

Alonzo stopped at Bubble & Bake after leaving the realty office, happy to see Frankie standing alone behind the wine bar. The tinkling bell distracted her from the task of wiping wine tasting glasses and setting them back on shelves.

"Hey Alonzo. What brings you here?" Frankie wished the sheriff's tidings included an arrest of the notorious Bram Callahan.

"I was in the neighborhood, calling on your favorite realtor. Thought I'd let you know how my day went," he began. What followed was a summary that started at the Yoder farms and ended down the street in Callahan's office.

"Let's see. The Amish will be tried according to their own customs. You need to wait to see if the chemicals are tainted before you bring in Ray Pate. Oh, and the best part of all: Bram Callahan is off the hook." Frankie wiped one of the wine glasses hard enough to melt it.

"It's just the first step. Calm down, Frankie. It won't take the lab long to evaluate the chemicals. Hopefully, that will connect the dots to the mystery plague and end the quarantine. We can charge the Yoder brothers for not having a permit for the chemicals, but we confiscated them, and they know they're being watched by the police. That's enough for now."

Frankie moaned in disgust. "It sure doesn't sound like justice to me. I'm perturbed about the whole thing."

"Sometimes that's how things work, Frankie. We apply the laws and make the best of a bad situation." Alonzo frowned. He wasn't celebrating the outcome either. "At least we can hope nobody else will get sick."

"Tell that to Helen Thurston's and Elsa Karlsen's families. I'm sure that will make them feel better."

Alonzo shook his head. "I'm disappointed too. And hey, we're not done with Bishop Yoder and Bram Callahan. They're still under investigation." He hoped sharing that tidbit would brighten Frankie's mood.

It worked, but the tidbit only whetted a voracious appetite. "What kind of investigation? Did you find anything valuable at the bishop's in your search?"

Leave it to Frankie to sniff in the right direction. Alonzo leaned across the bar and motioned for Frankie to join him. "Accidentally. Pflug stumbled upon a deed to a property in Kentucky. It's being used as a horse ranch and there are no Amish in the area."

"Interesting indeed. I wonder if the bishop was getting a cut from Callahan's property deals. You know, like a finder's fee? I don't suppose you can look at the bishop's bank statements, huh?" Frankie was salivating.

Alonzo chortled. "You watch too many crime dramas. We'd have to go back to Judge Wheaton and request another search warrant for the whole property, and there must be cause to do so. I guess the Amish community will have to apply its own justice."

Frankie closed the wine lounge following a quiet day. It was too early in the summer for Tuesdays to have much business yet. She'd relieved Jovie and Tess and allowed herself time to decompress for the first time in weeks.

After Alonzo's visit, curiosity won the day, and Frankie trekked out County HH to Bishop Yoder's property. She parked the SUV in the farm driveway across the road in the hope nobody would notice. She didn't plan to spend much time at the bishop's, intent her stopover would be little more than a haunt.

Cloaked in camouflage pants and shirt reserved for duck hunting with Garrett, Frankie bobbed behind trees and shrubs as she made her way to the bishop's outbuildings. She noticed several buggies parked near the house and wondered if the inquisition had begun. "I hope so, and that it keeps everyone inside the house while I'm here," she whispered into the air.

Frankie crouched behind the stable where she'd seen the horse trailer a day ago. One of the horses, a beautiful chestnut, whinnied in her presence. She backtracked behind a stand of shrubs and waited, drops of sweat rolling down her neck. Nobody appeared from the house, and she decided they were too busy or out of earshot.

She proceeded with caution. The horse trailer wasn't where it had been, so she kept hunting. Another long driveway wound downward to a grassy field where a wide building sat, an open parking garage for buggies and horses. Next to the garage was a small chapel and gathering area with tables and chairs, covered by a roof and partial walls.

She let down her guard a little since a slope stood between her and the bishop's house. She scurried to the garage, which was empty. On a walk-through, she noticed tires and the glint of metal beyond. There it was—the horse trailer. She promptly snapped a photo with her camera as the trailer came into full view, then she hurried to the back and snapped a photo of the Kentucky license plate, labeled "trailer," with an unexpired tag.

Frankie balked. She got what she came for but wasn't satisfied. She could only imagine what else there was to discover, but she left the same way she came, under the cover of the land and its obstacles. Once free from prying eyes, she darted to the SUV, crept out of the driveway, and sped away.

Instead of going home, Frankie headed to Carmen's to apprise her of Alonzo's interviews and her reconnaissance mission out to Bishop Yoder's. Carmen invited Frankie to dinner—Tia Pepita's Ropa Vieja had been stewing all day in a Dutch oven, her own version of the famous Cuban dish.

After dinner, Frankie and Carmen walked Sunny the sheltie as the sky darkened with stars. "Please be careful. You never know if this Amish mafia is real or not, Frankie," Carmen warned.

"I'm just checking out the license plate with a phone call to Magda. She has access to databases of stuff. Is it too much to hope that the lab will process those chemicals and the quarantine can be lifted right away? I wonder how long it will all take." Frankie yawned. She was tired of drama.

CHAPTER TWENTY-THREE

The life you have led doesn't need to be the only life you have.

❦

Anna Quindlen

At least one of Frankie's wishes came true the next day. Thanks to her connection with Dre in security, Sophie called as soon as the preliminary determination came down from the head honchos.

"Mom, the quarantine is being lifted. I'm going to be released in twenty-four to forty-eight hours, however long it takes to run my bloodwork and go through debriefing by the powers that be. Then I'm coming home." Emotion caught in Sophie's voice, a small release after a long ordeal.

"You don't know how happy that makes me, Honey. Let me know when you're on the way."

Frankie called Alonzo on his personal cell. "Frankie Champagne! Looks like everything's coming up daisies, huh? I assume that's why you're calling."

Frankie snorted. "It's roses, Lon. Coming up roses and pushing daisies. Definitely different. What's the news? Chemicals? Ray Pate?"

"That nose of yours should be registered as a secret weapon. The lab treated the chemicals as top priority and they found…," shuffling noises ensued as Alonzo looked for the official findings. "Well, it's a long name I can't pronounce but it's a lethal poison. Not part of the original compounds in the pesticides Pate used. Anyway, we arrested him before daylight. Of course, there's more ground to cover there."

Frankie didn't set the record straight about her nose being tipped off by Sophie's phone call. Let the sheriff hold her in high esteem. "Anything else you can tell me regarding Callahan and the bishop?"

"Geesh. It's only been a day, Frankie. If the world ran on your schedule, there'd be no problems to solve."

Frankie's skeptic chortle rattled the line. "If only. I'm ticked off about Bram Callahan. It seems like sunshine and rainbows follow him everywhere. He's nothing but an oily sardine."

"Don't waste your time being bitter, Frankie. It gets you nothing and nowhere. Trust me, I know. At least Sophie can go on with her life now. That's something. And you helped us nail Ray Pate. He's the real culprit here." Alonzo, the voice of reason.

"We can thank the bravery of Joanna Yoder for that. Without the photos, we probably wouldn't have even given Pate a glance."

"I have you and Carmen to thank for making inroads with the Amish women. As for Callahan, that oily sardine knows he's being watched, so I think he's going to swim in safe waters for now. I'll update you when I can. I'm holding off on a press conference. This situation is being managed by the state, so we're waiting politely for the green light to share anything. I hope you know this conversation is off the record."

Frankie didn't have enough information to report anything logical yet. She needed the name of the chemical poison and its properties to understand how it caused people to get sick and die. Her immediate hope was for viable treatment for the sick, so they could heal and come home again.

She checked the time and called Magda. It was early, but Magda was a short sleeper who seemed to function well at all hours on the clock.

"Frankie. What's cooking?" Magda sounded caffeinated.

Frankie requested the owner's name and address for the Kentucky license plate. To her astonishment, Magda asked her to hold a minute.

"Okay, got it. Here you go." Magda read the name and a Kentucky address.

Frankie assumed this might be the address of a new property owned by the bishop.

"That was fast. Can you get information on the property? Like the selling price and the lender?"

"I'll call you back. This could take a minute." Magda was gone.

Frankie sat at her breakfast bar with a coffee refill, her brain picking at a loose end. Something didn't add up in the Amish world.

Her past conversation with Sophie played on repeat in her mind. Everyone afflicted with Robli24 had the same blood type in common, B positive. Everyone except John Van Cleef, who was A positive. The detestable mosquitoes carried a disease that latched on to the B positive types with little to no resistance, maybe. The verdict wasn't in yet. Who knew how the poisonous chemicals interacted with mosquitoes and humans?

She reminded herself that a good reporter always follows up. It wasn't enough to know that St. Anthony's used the Yoders' services for pest control, she wanted to confirm the Dutch Reformed church in Zeeland had, too.

When the office phone rang, Frankie hoped she could make a quick confirmation one way or the other. "Good morning. First Reformed Church. This is Beth."

"I'm glad I caught you. This is Mary at Smith Accounting. I'm looking at an invoice for services from Yoder Brothers Pest Control. It looks like your church is the customer, and the invoice hasn't been paid yet. Can you check on that please?" Frankie's nasal voice might have come from Brooklyn, but oh well.

"Just a minute, please. Let me check my files, but I don't think that's our invoice." Beth set down the phone and Frankie could hear a drawer open and close. Beth returned. "We haven't had any pest control done at the church this year. The men here trap mice the old-fashioned way. We don't like using pesticides. But there's another Reformed Church in Zeeland, so you might try calling there."

"Bingo." Frankie only needed the rest of Magda's information to be sure. She wanted to cheer, but she took no pleasure in solving the death of John Van Cleef.

Compared to the last few weeks, the wheels turned like a steamboat, churning up information in its wake. Minutes later, Magda called Frankie with more information than she'd asked for.

As she tapped on the computer keyboard, desperate to keep up with Magda, the regional editor chattered in her ear. "What's this mean, Frankie? Is this another crime you're covering?" Magda smacked her lips.

"No, I mean yes. I don't know, Magda. It's all connected to the mystery disease, which is coming to a close. I hope to have a full story next week. We're waiting on the state. Until they release their findings, mum's the word."

Magda moaned. "Yuck. That's the worst of it. By the time we get anything from the state, it'll be so sanitized, the ink won't stick to the page." She snorted and hung up before Frankie could thank her.

Frankie called Carmen and asked if she would ride to Sarah Van Cleef's house with her. "Frankie, I'm in the bakery kitchen. Why don't you come down here to talk?"

Frankie quickly briefed Carmen, who scolded her.

"You're going to call Alonzo with this, or I will." She hung up.

~

After sharing her discoveries with Alonzo, the sheriff collaborated with Vandenberg County law enforcement, namely Deputy Luke Boomsma, a Zeeland native.

"Explain to me why you want to use civilians wearing a wire for this situation, Goodman? Is this how you operate in Whitman County?" Boomsma scratched his head.

Alonzo sighed heavily. He couldn't believe he was suggesting this course of action either. "This woman trusts these two civilians. She may spill some useful information in an ongoing investigation. If they're in danger, we'll be on the scene in seconds, Luke."

Frankie and Carmen drove to Zeeland, up hilly Vermeer Drive, and parked near, but not right in front of Sarah Van Cleef's house as instructed. Like the last time Frankie visited, Sarah's garage door was open, and the truck bed was filled with boxes.

Frankie and Carmen greeted a smiling Sarah with a bakery box of pastries.

"Come in. Come in. Carmen, I'm glad you could join us this time." Sarah invited them to sit in her living room, while she walked the bakery box to the kitchen.

"I'm trying to get everything in place for John's funeral, but there's been a snag."

Frankie pretended surprise. "But I thought the funeral was set for tomorrow."

"There's a backlog in Madison. Between the autopsies and the paperwork, there's not enough staff to handle everything. So, it's postponed until next week. I'm told the paperwork should be finalized in a day or two." Sarah looked weary.

"It looks like you're doing a lot of cleaning. It's good to stay busy," Carmen commented.

"I'm in donating mode. We've accumulated more than we need over the years."

Frankie and Carmen gazed around the living room. The walls were empty, as were the bookshelves and curio cabinet. "It looks like you're moving out, Sarah. Did your dream of that horse ranch in Kentucky come true?" Frankie tried to make light of Sarah's past conversation, but the statement hit Sarah like a barb.

Sarah sat forward in her chair as a flush of anger rose upward. "What in the world are you talking about? I'm not thinking of anything but burying my poor husband." She spoke in fits and starts.

"But after that, you're free to leave. There's nothing keeping you here is there?" Frankie purred, like a cat on the prowl.

Sarah wore a mixture of confusion and dismay on her face.

"I don't understand where you're coming from, Frankie." She turned her gaze to Carmen.

"You'll have to excuse Frankie," Carmen began. "She's had very little sleep since her daughter's been quarantined. Oh, and she's been working undercover in the Amish community, too." Carmen giggled.

Frankie leaned toward Carmen in confidence. "Oh my. I forgot to tell you. Do you know what I found at Bishop Yoder's yesterday?"

Sarah's ears burned. She leaned toward both women.

"A horse trailer! And a stable full of expensive quarter horses. Can you believe that?" Frankie looked from Carmen to Sarah.

"Why would an Amish bishop have riding horses and a horse trailer? You can't pull that with an Amish buggy." Carmen pretended shock.

Sarah started to get up until she saw Frankie's grim expression. "What is this?"

"You tell me, Sarah. Because I'm all kinds of confused to find out the horse trailer is registered to you. And so is a large piece of ranch property in Kentucky. How long have you and Bishop Yoder been in the saddle together?"

Sarah knitted her fingers together and stared at the floor as she contemplated what to do next. After a few minutes, she raised her head, a contrite expression playing on her face.

"Believe it or not, Bishop Yoder offered consolation after John's death. He came to me and asked me to consider rejoining the community. He was kind, kinder than anyone has been to me in a long time," she paused to wipe away fake tears.

Frankie and Carmen exchanged knowing glances and waited, but Sarah appeared to be stuck.

"So, you're going back to the Amish community?" Carmen asked, a knot of confusion in her voice.

"Well no."

Frankie had no patience for the charade. "You bought the Kentucky property before John's death. The horse trailer, too. The bishop's been raising those horses for over a year, and you've been out there riding them for almost as long. Tell the truth, Sarah. You and the bishop are leaving together, aren't you?" Frankie jabbed the accusations like boxer punches.

Sarah glared at Frankie. "What I said was true. Jacob was kinder to me than anyone. He wanted to understand why I left the community because he questioned his reasons for staying, too. We had so much in common. A love for horses, for starters. We grew close." Sarah's faraway look was replaced with curiosity. "How did you find out about Kentucky?"

"It wasn't difficult, Sarah. The horse trailer is parked at the bishop's farm. You've been out of the Amish community long enough to understand that just about anything is an internet search away. I'll answer your questions if you answer mine." Frankie wondered how the police worked undercover when she could barely figure out what to say, much less how to say it.

"Where did you get all the money that's sitting in the bank in Kentucky?" Frankie wanted to land another strong blow. She succeeded in catching Sarah off guard again.

"How could you get access to my bank account? That's private. That's…argh," Sarah couldn't find the words, but she clenched her fists and held her breath.

Carmen shot Frankie a warning look, then moved further away from Sarah. "Bishop Yoder gave you the money he's been skimming from the Amish coffers, didn't he? It couldn't be traced back to him that way."

Sarah fumed. "Jacob didn't steal that money from anyone. He made that money from his own business." Sarah jutted out her bottom lip and lifted her chin in defiance.

"What business are you talking about? He's a bishop, Sarah. Do you know how ridiculous you sound?" Frankie cringed inside as she baited the woman. It wasn't her nature to be a bully.

"Ha, ridiculous. I'll have you know the bishop made real estate deals right under the nose of your stupid town. He's partners with Bram Callahan. Jacob finds the property and makes sure no Amish buy it, so Callahan can get it at or below market value. For every property Callahan buys, Jacob gets a kickback. Callahan agrees to hire Amish businesses to clear the land, build the houses, and so forth in exchange for a small cut that he shares with Jacob. It's all part of making hay." Sarah's winning smile held pride for playing her part in the racket.

"It's pretty shady if you ask me," Frankie said. "I guess John found out you were going to confession with Bishop Jacob, or did he discover your secret stash?"

Sarah laughed in scorn. "John was a smart man. I didn't give him enough credit. He accumulated information. He knew I rode horses at Jacob's. He found the bank account when I wasn't careful enough about hiding my online activity."

"Did John threaten you or threaten Jacob?" Frankie prodded.

"John said he was going to the Amish authorities to expose Jacob's business dealings and our affair if I didn't end it. I knew Jacob would be cast out, but I feared he might go to prison, too."

"Let me guess. You told Jacob about John's plan, and the good bishop offed your husband and made it look like he was just another sick person from the area. The bishop even helped you out by making sure John was exposed to the illness when you two took the Shumaker children to the hospital." Frankie's disgust for Yoder and Sarah couldn't be hidden.

"Not quite. Jacob gave me the powder to put in John's coffee. He said it might take a few doses, but it only took two. It was a convenient time for John to die. Just another number. I wasn't even worried when they did the autopsy." Sarah continued to raise her head in defiance.

"Hydrated lime, I read about it. You can find out a lot online," Frankie said. "There's a bag of it in the bishop's barn. It also kills soil so nothing will grow. He saw an easy way to make the land useless for farming, because the Amish don't want land where they can't raise crops. How perfect for Bram Callahan to buy the property and start from scratch to make his own country developments where he can make bank."

Carmen interceded. "You forgot to mention the good part, Frankie." She turned toward Sarah. "The Madison ME is taking another look at your husband's body. This time, they're looking for poisoning, hydrated lime to be exact."

Deputy Boomsma and Alonzo made their entrance and took Sarah into custody without a tussle. Boomsma stared at Frankie and Carmen with a furrowed brow.

"I don't get it. You two look like perfectly nice ladies. Don't you have other hobbies you can pursue?"

Frankie and Carmen broke out in raucous laughter as soon as Boomsma exited with Sarah in tow. Alonzo joined them. "He's right, you know. Maybe you should try baking," Alonzo said, unable to keep from snorting. "Thanks, you two. I'd say that went well."

Frankie removed the wire, handed it to Alonzo, and walked

beside Carmen to the SUV. "Way to get in there with that jab at the end. I'd say you scored the knockout punch, Carmie."

Carmen chortled. "I couldn't let you have all the fun."

~

Frankie dropped Carmen off at the sheep farm and returned home, consumed by an overwhelming sense of loss. The letdown from discovering a murderer left her shell-shocked, especially in this case where the solution arrived like lightning strikes. Besides, she was weary from the stress brought on by the mysterious plague and canceled wedding. What she yearned for now was closure.

Her bed beckoned and she imagined she closed her eyes for a mere few minutes when she felt herself gathered into someone's strong arms. She felt weightless in a dream world where a gentle breeze carried Garrett's scent to her and left it there, a lingering warm spicy fragrance, mixed with timber and citrus.

She opened her eyes when she heard her name, reluctant to let go of the dream where the world was in balance again. Then she saw Garrett sitting on her bed, holding her close to his heart. The real deal. She smiled.

"When did you get back?" Frankie asked.

"Yesterday, Miss Francine, and I've been trying to catch up with you ever since, but you're like trying to chase down the will-o'-the-wisp." Garrett smiled. "I know you've been busy. I stopped by last night, but you were out at Carmen's. I stopped at Bubble & Bake this morning and Carmen told me. She said you were cracking a murder case, so I went to the sheriff's office, and Alonzo said our reunion would have to wait until after you and Carmen went undercover. I felt like I stepped into a parallel universe."

He and Frankie gazed into each other's eyes and laughed about the situation. Then they kissed, hugged, and stayed that way a long time.

~

Frankie and Garrett barely had time to reconnect when Sophie appeared at Bubble & Bake and dashed to the walnut wine bar. She laid her hand lovingly over the polished wood, remembering her grandpa's connection to the giant tree that had provided shade, homes to birds and squirrels, a swing, and treehouse. It was only fitting that the old walnut lived on after a storm took it out.

Peggy saw Sophie first and scooped her up in a warm embrace, then called Frankie's name. It was Friday night, the wine lounge was hopping, and Frankie was pulling kitchen duty. She carried a tray with two flatbread pizzas in one hand and a charcuterie board in the other and turned away from the bar to take them to customers on the deck.

When she walked back through, Sophie caught her eye and Frankie thought the light was playing tricks on her. She inched closer, saw Peggy's wide grin, and skipped to Sophie's side, embracing her tightly with motherlove.

"Let me grab an apron and help you in the kitchen. We have lots to catch up on," Sophie beamed with happiness and something else Frankie recognized but couldn't define.

Alone in the kitchen, the two began sharing essential information first until only the fine points of great magnitude were left to discuss.

"I love Garrett and I trust him. He had to leave Deep Lakes for me to discover that truth," Frankie said.

"Max and I have grown apart since he decided to become a doctor. It's not just the miles, Mom, it's an emotional distance. He's passionate about being a doctor. I have greater respect for him now than ever before."

"No wedding then?" Frankie kept it short.

Sophie shook her head and allowed a single tear to fall. "It's mutual. Being quarantined changed my life, Mom. I spent every hour of every day working with the scientists who study diseases and their origins. I was caught up. I found a new passion for medicine."

"And you want to study something different, too?" Frankie asked.

"A group of scientists will be evaluating the chemicals, how they altered the mosquitoes, and how they affected humans, for a long time. It's a study that will take a year or two. I can join them and enter the epidemiology program at the same time." Sophie glowed with the passion of a new undertaking.

"I see. Where will you study?" Frankie was proud of Sophie for following her dreams.

"Loyola in Chicago. I'll be crazy busy but not on another planet, Mom." Sophie's concern for Frankie was evident.

Frankie laughed. "Hey, I'm not that fragile. If you were going to the Moon, I'd cheer for you from down here. There's no place you can go where my love can't travel." The two grabbed each other and held on tight.

When the wine lounge closed, Sophie left the kitchen to visit with her grandmother. Cherry took advantage of the situation to get Frankie's attention. "Hey, I've been meaning to talk to you, but with everything going on, there's never been a good time."

"How about now?" Frankie smiled in encouragement.

"I'm wondering how you'd feel…" Cherry faltered, then remembered what Shauna and Pom said about self-confidence. "The truth is, I want to move out of my parents' house. I applied for the office manager position at Champagne Builders and James wants to hire me."

Frankie bounded around the counter and hugged her. "That's wonderful news, Cherry. Tell me more. What are your plans?"

"James wants me to start in two weeks. I'd like to keep working here on weekends, though. I love Bubble & Bake, and I'm saving money to buy a place in the barn-style condos being built in the new subdivision near the quarry." Cherry radiated excitement.

"That sounds marvelous. I know you're going to be a great office manager. But don't you think it's a little much to work all week and weekends, too?"

"If I could work Friday night and a shift on either Saturday or Sunday, I'd have one day off. I think that would work just fine. And thanks for thinking I'll be good. I'm lucky I'll have Shauna training me."

Frankie was proud of Cherry. She and Carmen both wanted Cherry to find more independence and perhaps a better relationship than the safety blanket she shared with Frankie's charming brother, Nick. This new beginning was an important first step.

Now the Bubble & Bake family had two reasons to celebrate. Frankie broke out the last case of Golden Desire, the award-winning cinnamon apple mead Violet designed and crafted last autumn. She carried two chilled bottles out to the wine lounge and gathered her people into the large alcove to toast new beginnings.

CHAPTER TWENTY-FOUR

The greatest adventure is what lies ahead.

&

JRR Tolkien

Things returned to normal in Frankie's world almost as suddenly as they'd turned topsy-turvy. Somehow, the passage of time managed to bring perspective, like a healing balm. Much of Frankie's free time was spent catching up with Garrett, who shared the details of the murder case and its victims, along with Frankie's role in turning the tide to capture the killer.

"It wasn't me, Garrett. It was you. You just needed a fresh look, a new way of thinking about all the evidence. I'm glad the psycho was caught, and that you're back." Frankie smiled.

"So, you've taken up swimming." She giggled.

"It's a good outlet for me, Frankie. Just as baking and viticulture are therapy for you. In fact, I was thinking about putting in a backyard pool. Right about there." He pointed straight ahead from the patio where the two were sharing dinner. "What do you think about that? Nice moonlight swims.

We could host pool parties and barbecues."

Frankie rustled Garrett's wavy hair around his ears with her fingers. "You know G, we live in a town with three major lakes and a smattering of smaller ones. A pool seems like a lot of work and trouble to only enjoy it three months of the year."

"I understand, but I think you're missing the point about the moonlight swims." He brushed a kiss on her brow.

Garrett stowed away Frankie's comment for a few days until several serendipitous events converged on his behalf.

First, he received a substantial paycheck from the city of Duluth for his work on the Garden Killer victims. Two days later, two more checks arrived in the mail, each containing a thank-you letter. Family members of the victims had offered rewards for finding the killer and bringing him to justice. City employees couldn't accept reward money personally, but some city official tipped off the families about Garrett's role in breaking the case. The families thanked him personally and insisted he accept a portion of the reward for his tireless effort. Both bank-issued drafts came from anonymous donors.

The same day, Mayor Adele Lundgren stopped by Garrett's house for an unexpected visit. She explained that her daughter, husband, two children, and a menagerie of animals planned to relocate to Deep Lakes from Arizona.

"They want to raise their children in a small community near their grandparents." Adele paused to smile and point to herself, then continued her fast-paced cadence. "And since my son-in-law is from Green Bay, Deep Lakes is the optimum locale. Which brings me to your door, Garrett. They're looking for a house in the country with lots of room for animals and a garden. They have a penchant for antiques and Victorian-style architecture. Your house is the quintessential location. Would you be interested in selling?"

Garrett raised his hand hoping to locate Adele's pause button. "Let me take you on a tour of the house and property first."

Forty minutes later, Adele recommitted her daughter's family to the purchase. "They're coming here next week. Can we schedule a time for them to see it?"

In the days leading up to showing the house to Adele's daughter and son-in-law, Garrett focused all his energy on looking at lake properties and keeping it a secret from Frankie. He enlisted Ava Andersen to scout out homes on the condition she tell absolutely nobody within thirty miles that he was house hunting.

Once Adele's daughter and family toured Garrett's property, they were smitten and wanted to seal the deal with an offer he couldn't refuse. Garrett accepted but added a caveat. "None of you may breathe a word of this around Deep Lakes until I say so. Frankie doesn't know anything about it, and I plan to keep it that way." They promised, but inwardly, Garrett wondered if Adele would need sedation to keep it under wraps.

Fortune found favor with Garrett again, and he didn't have to be patient for long.

"Hello Garrett. Ava Andersen calling. I've just been contracted to handle the Lars Paulsen bungalow on Lake Joy. You may remember that Mr. Paulsen was in some trouble last year? Well, he's been liquidating properties while he's indisposed, and he's anxious to sell. I'd love to show this one to you. But it's going for a pretty price, considering. It is a year-round home though."

Garrett met Ava at the property, one of five charming mushroom-style homes designed by Rasmus Dane, a descendant of Hogar Dane, one of the town's founding families. Rasmus Dane was friends with Earl Young, the designer of ten mushroom houses made from stone, timber, and thatch in Charlevoix, Michigan. Like Young, Dane was influenced by Wisconsin's very own Frank Lloyd Wright.

To his credit, Lars Paulsen had taken meticulous care of the Lake Joy home made from large boulders. It's toadstool shape featured curved lines, a floor-to-ceiling fireplace in the main room, and rounded entrance doors. The roof, once made of thatch, was replaced by cedar shakes modeled to resemble thatch. A wall of lake rocks lined the front walkway, and a new deck was added to the 1924 house only a few years ago. For Garrett, the cozy lake bungalow was love at first sight, and he couldn't wait to show it off to Frankie.

After a romantic dinner at the Lake Joy Bistro, Garrett and Frankie walked along the lakeshore, chatting about family and life in Deep Lakes. Garrett surprised her by stopping at the wall in front of the mushroom house, grabbing her hand, and leading her through the front door.

"Wait a minute. How do you have a key to Lars Paulsen's cottage, Garrett?" Frankie's mouth fell open.

Garrett winked and held his index finger to his lips.

"Before I left Duluth, I agonized about bringing you a gift. I don't know if it was an apology, a lame attempt to make up for lost time, a symbol of a fresh start, or just a simple reminder of my love for you, Frankie."

"But you already know that I didn't bring you a gift. At the time, you didn't need flowers since you were up to your eyeballs in them from Sophie's wedding. Chocolates seemed too easy, like a no- brainer. Jewelry felt like a bribe. All I really wanted to do was spend time with you, get back to the life I left here—the life we were building together." Garrett's eyes twinkled in the low light reflected from the streetlamp through the windows.

"I never stopped thinking about that gift, and I knew if I was patient, something would come to me. And it has." Garrett spun Frankie around the bungalow's cozy living room, making her laugh in bewilderment.

"You know I'm not as patient as you are G, so could you get to it, please? What in the world are you talking about?"

Garrett's entire face lit up. "There's the Frankie I know and love. You challenge me, but always in a good way. You are a light-bearer, Frankie Champagne."

He pulled her out to the deck overlooking Lake Joy and turned her face up to the night sky. "Just like the stars, you carry your own light, shedding your sparkle wherever you go." He bent on one knee and held out a small velvet box toward Frankie. "This house would be the perfect home for us, here on Lake Joy. Will you marry me, Miss Francine?"

A wisp of air might have knocked Frankie over. She hadn't seen any of this coming, yet she knew the answer before the question was asked. "Oh Garrett," she whispered. "Let's make a life together."

~

The Festival of the Lakes was held in mid-August every year, ending with a cavalcade of fireworks that lit up Lake Joy and could be seen for miles, even at Bountiful Fruits vineyard, where Frankie and Garrett vowed to love one another for life.

Friends and family rallied to help the couple plan the celebration in a few weeks. Meredith Healy spruced up the

French border gardens with her magical green thumbs, while Hannah and Ashley Turner organized reception food with the Bubble & Bake crew. Sophie and Max insisted the pair use their Sun Velvet wedding cake, which Coral and Aunt CeCe decorated with camelias and tea roses.

Frankie's four brothers paraded down the grassy aisle first, in a choreographed strut, singing an acoustic version of "Stand by Me"; while Carmen, Sophie, Violet, and Garrett's daughter, Amanda, danced behind them, adding harmony here and there. In front of the gazebo, they split off, and the singing quieted in anticipation.

Frankie emerged from behind an old oak tree, her mother beside her. Peggy cherished the honor of assisting Frankie as she dressed for the wedding. Along with Carmen, the three women had hunted through dress shops in search of a perfect off-the-rack gown. Frankie donned the unanimous choice, an Edwardian style tea length dress in ivory tulle, with embroidered lace overlays. The dress was longer in the back than the front, creating a faux train. As a special adornment, Peggy made a traditional Danish head piece, a wreath of small star flowers intertwined with pearls, a waist-length piece of sheer gossamer attached at the back.

"What A Wonderful World" echoed around the vineyard in four-part harmony from the Champagne brothers: James, Julius, Nick, and Will. Peggy turned to Frankie. "I didn't ask you this when you married Rick, my dear, and I'm sorry. This time I'm asking: Are you ready to get married, Sweetheart?"

Frankie nodded. "Ready and willing. Thank you for being my companion today, Mom." "Thank you for being the reason all of my children are home. I love you, Frankie. Your father would be the proudest one here today, you know." Peggy gasped back a sob as tears welled in her eyes.

Frankie hugged her mother and let a tear fall in honor of Charlie Champagne, then the two floated between the waves of blue, yellow, and white flowers to the gazebo where Garrett waited with his bright smile and melted caramel eyes.

He held out his hand to Frankie and they shared their promises in front of the people who mattered most to them at one of Frankie's favorite places on earth. As they were declared husband and wife, a glorious painted sunset danced across the twilit sky.

In the Wisconsin tradition of celebrating, food was plentiful, drinks flowed freely, and people laughed and danced until midnight.

Garrett pulled Frankie behind a stand of willows to share a private wedding toast. They raised glasses of Spinning Dreams, the special vintage Frankie and Violet had crafted, pledged their love privately to each other, and sealed it with a lingering kiss.

"You had a chance to live on a bigger stage with a power job and grand opportunities. Why choose Deep Lakes?" Frankie asked Garrett.

"I don't know how I could ask for a bigger life than this. Look around us. This town, the people, your vineyard and shop, our friends and family. Life is full. This is our stage, Miss Francine, and we're the directors," Garrett whispered, kissing her ear.

Frankie melted into the moment. "All I have to say is lights, camera, action."

Trust Me Tarts

CRUST: Use phyllo dough sheet cut in squares to fit your tart pan

Frankie likes to use this crust recipe:

½ cup butter, softened

3 oz cream cheese, softened

1 cup all-purpose flour

Mix butter and cream cheese together until smooth.

Add in flour. Form into one inch balls and press each ball into the cup of the tart pan, smoothing the dough up the sides to make a shell.

FILLING:

20 oz can pineapple tidbits

(or chunks cut into three pieces each) – drain all liquid

⅓ cup brown sugar

1–2 tsp of cake or pie spice

(cinnamon, allspice, nutmeg, cloves, ginger)

½ tsp vanilla extract

2 TB butter, melted

⅓ cup dried cranberries

1 tsp cornstarch dissolved in 2–3 tsp pineapple juice from can

PROCEDURE:

Place pineapple in saucepan with brown sugar, butter, vanilla, spices. Cook over medium heat until thickened, golden brown in color. Mixture will look syrupy and fruit will be glazed *(about 15 minutes or so)*. Add cranberries and stir together for 2–4 minutes longer. Add the cornstarch mix and turn off the heat. Mixture will be thick.

Cool slightly before spooning into the tart shells. Don't overfill. Bake at 350^0 13-14 minutes. *(Oven temperatures vary so look for the tart shell to just begin to brown.)*

Sprinkle with sifted powdered sugar.

$\mathcal{O}$pen House Zucchini Quiche Muffins ✌

INGREDIENTS:

      Mozzarella and Parmesan cheese
      1 small zucchini quartered, sliced
      1 cup portabella mushrooms quartered and sliced
      1 small garden onion or green onions sliced
      Garlic powder or fresh diced garlic
      Basil, Tarragon, Dill, Black pepper
      Vegetable or olive oil, butter
      3 eggs
      1 cup milk *(of choice)*
      Pie crust *(of choice)*

VEGETABLE MIX:

Sauté zucchini, mushrooms, and onion in oil of choice with a little butter for flavor until glistening

Add seasoning: garlic powder or fresh diced garlic, basil, tarragon, dill, black pepper–combine to make 2 TB
(stir into veggie mix and remove from heat to cool)

In separate bowl, whisk together 3 eggs, 1 cup milk of choice

CRUST:

Cut pie crust into squares to insert in a muffin tin. Be sure the squares fill the muffin cup to the top with overlap. Use the tines of a fork to make an edging. Blind bake 10 minutes at 400° till firm and bottoms are done.

ASSEMBLE:

Cool slightly, fill ⅔ full with sautéed veggie mix. Pour egg mix over the veggies until almost full. Press shredded cheeses onto top so cheese is mostly submerged.

BAKE:

Bake at 350⁰ until golden brown on top, about 12–15 minutes. Test with a butter knife inserted into the tart. If there is little to no liquid, it's done.

Sun Velvet Cake (Frankie's knock-off) 🍋

SPONGE INGREDIENTS:

Grease and flour 2 nine-inch cake pans

2½ cups cake flour *(cake flour produces the finest texture)*

2 tsp baking powder	2 oz light olive oil
1 tsp salt	Zest of 3 lemons
1½ cups granulated sugar	4 TB fresh lemon juice
1 cup softened butter	1 tsp vanilla extract
4 large eggs	2 tsp lemon extract
1 cup buttermilk	Lemon curd

Optional: 4–6 TB fresh thyme leaves *(this adds another layer of flavor. You should be able to see the thyme in the cake batter. If you cannot see it, add more.)*

MAKE THE SPONGE:

Preheat oven to 340°. Combine flour, powder, salt, and sugar in a large mixing bowl and set aside. Combine ½ cup of the buttermilk with the olive oil and set aside. Combine the other ½ cup of buttermilk with the 4 eggs, both extracts and whisk to break up eggs. Add the buttermilk/olive oil mixture into the dry mix and stir. *It will look like sand.*

Add softened butter to the mixture until well combined. Add in lemon juice and zest, stir. Then beat in the egg mixture in three parts. This will aerate your batter and make the texture velvety. Beat well after adding each part of the egg mix. Fold in fresh thyme, if you decide to try it. Pour evenly into two pans. Smack the pans on the counter to eliminate bubbles. Bake at 340° for 23–26 minutes (depending upon your oven). Use toothpick test.

Hit the pans on the counter after taking them out so the cakes will release easily. Let cool about 10 minutes before turning the cakes out onto a rack to cool completely.

Use lemon curd between cake layers *(you can purchase in the jelly/jam section of the store). Use about ⅔ of the jar.*

Recipe continues on next page...

You can make a lemon buttercream icing if you want a sweeter cake. Frankie used Mascarpone Whipped Cream, which is lightly sweetened. The cake must be refrigerated if you use the whipped cream frosting.

1 pint of cold heavy whipping cream

½ cup powdered sugar, and ⅓ cup powdered sugar

12 oz softened Mascarpone

(find this by the cream cheese or brie cheese)

⅓ cup fresh lemon juice

Pinch of salt

1 tsp vanilla or lemon extract or both *(1 tsp of each)*

lemon slices and sprigs of thyme *(for garnish)*

MAKE THE TOPPING:

Combine the mascarpone, lemon juice, salt, ½ cup powdered sugar, and extract until smooth.

In a chilled bowl, beat heavy cream until soft peaks form. Add ⅓ cup powdered sugar. Beat until stiff peaks form. Fold in mascarpone mixture until blended. Ice the sides and top. Garnish with lemon slices and sprigs of thyme.

Brunette Blondies

INGREDIENTS:

½ cup butter
3 TB strong coffee
¾ cup brown sugar
½ cup maple sugar
*(if you can't find maple sugar,
use all brown sugar instead)*

2 eggs
1 tsp maple extract
½ tsp vanilla extract
1 cup flour
¾ tsp baking powder
¾ tsp salt
Chopped walnuts, optional

PROCEDURE:

Place 2 TB of finely ground coffee into a small bowl and pour about ¼ cup boiling water into the grounds, slowly. You want the coffee to bloom (crema should rise to the top). Stir a little to initiate the blooming process. Let the coffee sit.

Brown butter in saucepan over medium heat. Mixture will be caramel brown and smell nutty. This takes 10 minutes or so. Once browned, remove from heat and spoon 2–3 TB of the bloomed coffee liquid into the butter. It will bubble. Set aside to cool slightly.

In a large bowl, dump in the sugars. Pour the lightly cool butter mixture over the sugar and mix well for 2 minutes on medium speed.

Add 2 eggs and beat for 2 minutes. Add extracts. Stir in flour on low setting. Mixture will be caramel colored and smell fantastic! Add nuts last, if using.

Pour into sprayed 8 × 8" dish and bake at 350° about 30 minutes. Test with toothpick.

Eat these chewy decadent blondies as is or if you want to be fancy add Nutella drizzle.

OPTIONAL TOPPING:

Thin Nutella by placing half of it from the jar into a bowl. In a second, larger bowl, add boiling water, to make a water bath. Place the smaller bowl of Nutella into the larger bowl and stir until thinned. Do not get water into the Nutella. Then drizzle the thinned Nutella onto the blondies.

Because early readers asked...

Ramps: are a type of wild allium that are related to spring onions and leeks and boast a pungent garlicky onion flavor. They are widespread across eastern U.S. and Canada.

Mosquitos: The Centers for Disease Control and Prevention lists these tiny insects as "the world's deadliest animal." Mosquito-transmitted diseases are responsible for more than seven hundred thousand deaths annually around the world. Scientists continue to research methods for eliminating the diseases these insects carry, including a genetic engineering trial that results in the early death of females (the biters of the species), and a new pesticide trial. More information can be found online regarding the studies and the strides being made to prevent mosquito-borne illnesses. Although this book is fiction, real world science shows that mosquitos (among other insects) have developed resistance to pesticides, including genetic mutation. It's well known that pesticides are harmful to humans, but in the name of creativity, I made the jump to combine pesticide use with mosquito populations carrying pesticide toxins to produce a powerful superbug infection.

Yes! Frankie published an article in *Point Press*, but I'll let you imagine how it might go.

Yes! I'm grateful to all those who helped me complete this book in any fashion, especially my editor, Kay Rettenmund, and my cover/interior designer, Terry Rydberg of Fine Print Design.

No! This isn't the end of the series, but Frankie has plans that may take her away from Deep Lakes where other mysteries await. *Be patient. Let's allow her to enjoy her honeymoon.*

With love and gratitude,
JAR

You may contact the author at *joyribar.com*
Go to *https://joyribar.com/signup to* sign up for newsletters
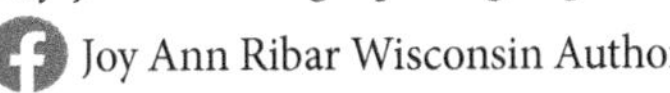 Joy Ann Ribar Wisconsin Author

Deep Dark Secrets
Book 1

Deep Bitter Roots
Book 2

Deep Green Envy
Book 3

Deep Dire Harvest
Book 4

Deep Flakes Christmas
A Nisse Visit • Prequel

Like the **Deep Lakes Cozy Mystery Series?** Give my new **Bay Browning mystery series a try**: a little edgy, a little less cozy. Get to know English Professor **Bay Browning**, her ex-con grifter sister, **Cassandra**, surly **Detective Downing**, and several supporting characters of interest.

Here's what others say about *The Medusa Murders*, BOOK 1:

Professor L.L. Browning is an empowered modern woman who doesn't take any crap. I like her! She is strong, sassy, smart, and comfortable in her own skin, which makes for a solid series debut and leaves the reader anticipating the next entry in the series. Joy Ann Ribar writes with abandon, fiercely describing scenes that pop off the page. Well done.

- It's All About the Book

Step into a world where the boundary between mythology and reality blurs in Joy Ann Ribar's gripping mystery, The Medusa Murders. As a fan of both mystery and mythology, I found Ribar's novel to be an interesting blend of these two worlds, creating a unique and compelling narrative.   - The Book Review Crew

The Medusa Murders is an intriguing and captivating story that will take you on a wild journey. Joy Ann Ribar beautifully combines mystery, mythology, and psychic elements to present a thrilling serial murder drama. In addition to the murder plot, there is also a family secret storyline and some romantic vibes between Bay and Detective Downing. Everything fits perfectly into the plot, making it entertaining and unique. The story is memorable because of its outstanding cast of characters. The dynamics between Bay and her family, colleagues, and Downing were interesting and built the core of the story. This is one of those murder mysteries that will have you on the edge of your seat because you can sense that the murderer is close by, but you have no clue who it is, making everyone seem suspicious. I enjoyed reading this book and recommend it to anyone who loves murder mysteries with a dose of mythology and family drama.   –Readers' Favorite

This cozy mystery adds to the genre with a main character, whose esoteric field of study offers a new aspect to sleuthing. If you enjoy an unusual mystery with an academic flare, this may be a good choice for your own bookshelf!   - Waterside Kennels Mysteries

There was so much to like about this mystery. The characters. The mix of archaeology and mythology. A truly bad, bad guy. A convoluted, not easily solved mystery. And did I mention the characters? It's exciting to find and try a new series and author. I had high hopes for The Medusa Murders and Author Joy Ann Ribar… delivered.   - fuonlyknew

This was a fun and well written mystery. The story is engaging and grabs you quick. I think I finished this one in a little over a day and that's quite a feat! … just plain fun.
                                                                                  - Must Read Faster

This was a very interesting murder mystery… highly entertaining and sufficiently gritty… the family drama mixed with gritty detective work AND amateur sleuthing was a perfect combination.   - booking.with.janelle

Mystery enthusiasts looking for more complexity and challenge than the cozy mystery genre offers will appreciate the tension and compulsion of a story that grows relationships, individuals, and careers during a careening course towards disaster and discovery. The Medusa Murders should be in any library collection strong in murder mysteries that reside a cut above the ordinary.   - D. Donovan, Senior Reviewer, Midwest Book Review

Shake-speared in the Park
A BAY BROWNING MYSTERY #2

Flourish College's summer production of a Shakespeare mash-up is cursed from the beginning. Rehearsals barely begin when one of the actors drops dead on stage right in front of professors Bay Browning and Jen Yoo, summer theater volunteers. As more accidents happen and the body count grows, the women are urged to investigate behind the scenes in this real-life Shakespearean tragedy. Detective Downing is sticking to his own script, while Bay and Jen are taking cues from college officials who want to control the drama. But the stage is set when Cassandra, Bay's ex-con sister, becomes part of the action in this puzzling crime spree. Can the players discover who the murdering director is before Flourish College becomes a ghost town?

About the Author

Joy Ann Ribar is an RV author, writing on the road wherever her husband and their Winnebago View wanders. Joy's cocktail of careers includes news reporter, paralegal, English educator, and aquaponics greenhouse technician, all of which prove useful in penning mysteries. She loves to bake, read, research wines, and explore nature. Joy's writing is inspired by Wisconsin's four distinct seasons, natural beauty, and kind-hearted, but sometimes quirky, people.

Joy holds a BA in Journalism from UW-Madison and an MS in Education from UW-Oshkosh. She is a member of Mystery Writers of America, Sisters in Crime, Blackbird Writers, Cozy Crime Collective, and Wisconsin Writers Association. Her essay, Bird Envy, won third place in the WWA 2021 Jade Ring Contest. Two of her Deep Lakes mysteries were recognized by Chanticleer Cozy and Not-So-Cozy mystery awards.

See more at JoyRibar.com

www.ingramcontent.com/pod-product-compliance
Lightning Source LLC
Chambersburg PA
CBHW071350300726
48976CB00006B/1832